THE
ATLANTIS
GENE

A.G. RIDDLE spent ten years starting and running internet companies before retiring to focus on his true passion: writing fiction. He grew up in a small town in North Carolina and attended UNC-Chapel Hill, where he founded his first company with one of his childhood friends. He currently lives in Parkland, Florida and would love to hear from you: agriddle.com

THE ATLANTIS TRILOGY

The Atlantis Gene
The Atlantis Plague
The Atlantis World

THE ATLANTIS GENE

A.G. RIDDLE

HEAD OF ZEUS

First published in the USA in 2013 by Modern Mythology.

First published as an ebook in the UK in 2014 by Head of Zeus Ltd.
This paperback edition first published in the UK in 2015
by Head of Zeus Ltd.

9 7 6 8

A catalogue record for this book is available from the British Library.

ISBN (PB) 9781784970093
ISBN (E) 9781784970086

Printed and bound by CPI Group (UK) Ltd,
Croydon, CR0 4YY

Head of Zeus Ltd
First Floor East
5-8 Hardwick Street
London EC1R 4RG
WWW.HEADOFZEUS.COM

For Anna

PROLOGUE

Research Vessel Icefall
Atlantic Ocean
88 Miles off the Coast of Antarctica

Karl Selig steadied himself on the ship's rail and peered through the binoculars at the massive iceberg. Another piece of ice crumbled and fell, revealing more of the long black object. It looked almost like... a submarine. But it couldn't be.

"Hey Steve, come check this out."

Steve Cooper, Karl's grad-school friend, tied off a buoy and joined Karl on the other side of the boat. He took the binoculars, scanned quickly, then stopped. "Whoa. What is it? A sub?"

"Maybe."

"What's under it?"

Karl grabbed the binoculars. "Under it..." He panned to the area under the sub. There was something else. The sub, if it was a sub, was sticking out of another metallic object, this one gray and much larger. Unlike the sub, the gray object didn't reflect light; it looked more like waves, the kind that shimmer just over the horizon of a warm highway or a long stretch of desert. It wasn't warm though, or at least it wasn't melting the ice around it. Just above the structure, Karl caught a glimpse of some writing on the sub: *U-977* and *Kriegsmarine*. A Nazi sub. Sticking out of... a structure of some sort.

Karl dropped the binoculars to his side. "Wake Naomi up and prepare to dock the boat. We're going to check it out."

Steve rushed below deck, and Karl heard him rousing Naomi

from one of the small boat's two cabins. Karl's corporate sponsor had insisted he take Naomi along. Karl had nodded in the meeting and hoped she wouldn't get in the way. He had not been disappointed. When they had put to sea five weeks ago in Cape Town, South Africa, Naomi had brought aboard two changes of clothes, three romance novels, and enough vodka to kill a Russian army. They had barely seen her since. *It must be so boring for her out here*, Karl thought. For him, it was the opportunity of a lifetime.

Karl raised the binoculars and looked again at the massive piece of ice that had broken off from Antarctica nearly a month ago. Almost ninety percent of the iceberg was underwater, but the surface area still covered forty-seven square miles—one and a half times the size of Manhattan.

Karl's doctoral thesis focused on how newly calved icebergs affected global sea currents as they dissolved. Over the last four weeks, he and Steve had deployed high-tech buoys around the iceberg that measured sea temp and salt-water/fresh-water balance as well as took periodic sonar readings of the iceberg's changing shape. The goal was to learn more about how icebergs disintegrated after leaving Antarctica. Antarctica held ninety percent of the world's ice, and when it melted in the next few centuries, it would dramatically change the world. He hoped his research would shed light on exactly how.

Karl had called Steve the minute he found out he was funded. "You've got to come with me—No, trust me." Steve had reluctantly agreed, and to Karl's delight, his old friend had come alive on the expedition as they took readings by day and discussed the preliminary findings each night. Before the voyage, Steve's academic career had been as listless as the iceberg they were following, as he floated from one thesis topic to another. Karl and their other friends had wondered if he would drop out of the doctoral program altogether.

The research readings had been intriguing, and now they had found something else, something remarkable. There would

2

be headlines. But what would they say? "Nazi Sub Found in Antarctica"? It wasn't inconceivable.

Karl knew the Nazis had been obsessed with Antarctica. They'd sent expeditions there in 1938 and 1939 and even claimed part of the continent as a new German province—Neuschwabenland. Several Nazi subs were never recovered during World War II and were not known to have been sunk. The conspiracy theorists claimed that a Nazi sub left Germany just before the fall of the Third Reich, carrying away the highest ranking Nazis and the entire treasury, including priceless artifacts that had been looted and top-secret technology.

At the back of Karl's mind, a new thought emerged: reward money. If there was Nazi treasure on the sub, it would be worth a huge amount of money. He would never have to worry about research funding again.

The immediate challenge was docking the boat to the iceberg. The seas were rough, and it took them three passes, but they finally managed to tie off a few miles from the sub and the strange structure under it.

Karl and Steve bundled up and donned their climbing gear. Karl gave Naomi some basic instructions, the long and short of which were "don't touch anything," and then he and Steve lowered themselves to the ice shelf below the boat and set off.

For the next forty-five minutes, neither man said anything as they trudged across the barren ice mountain. The ice was rougher toward the interior and their pace slowed, Steve's more than Karl's.

"We need to pick it up, Steve."

Steve made an effort to catch up. "Sorry. A month on the boat has got me out of shape."

Karl glanced up at the sun. When it set, the temperature would plummet and they would likely freeze to death. The days were long here. The sun rose at 2:30 P.M. and set after 10 P.M., but they only had a few more hours. Karl picked up his pace a little more.

Behind him, he heard Steve shuffling his snowshoes as fast as he could, trying desperately to catch up. Strange sounds echoed up from the ice: first a low drone, then a rapid hammering, like a thousand woodpeckers assaulting the ice. Karl stopped and listened. He turned to Steve, and their eyes met just as a spider web of tiny cracks shot out across the ice below Steve's feet. Steve looked down in horror, and then ran as hard as he could toward Karl and the untouched ice.

For Karl, the scene was surreal, unfolding almost in slow motion. He felt himself run toward his friend and throw a rope from his belt. Steve caught the rope a split second before a loud crack filled the air and the ice below him collapsed, forming a giant chasm.

The rope instantly pulled tight, jerking Karl off his feet and slamming him belly first into the ice. He was going to follow Steve into the ice canyon. Karl scrambled to get his feet under him, but the tug of the rope was too strong. He relaxed his hands, and the rope slid through them, slowing his forward motion. He planted his feet in front of him, and the crampons beneath his boots bit into the ice, sending shards of ice at his face as he came to a halt. He squeezed the rope, and it pulled tight against the ledge, making a strange vibrating sound almost like a low violin.

"Steve! Hang on! I'm going to pull you up—"

"Don't!" Steve yelled.

"What? Are you crazy—"

"There's something down here. Lower me, slowly."

Karl thought for a moment. "What is it?"

"Looks like a tunnel or a cave. It's got gray metal in it. It's blurry."

"Okay, hold on. I'm going to let some slack out." Karl let ten feet of rope out, and when he heard nothing from Steve, another ten feet.

"Stop," Steve called.

Karl felt the rope tugging. Was Steve swinging? The rope went slack.

"I'm in," Steve said.

"What is it?"

"Not sure." Steve's voice was muffled now.

Karl crawled to the edge of the ice and looked over.

Steve stuck his head out of the mouth of the cave. "I think it's some kind of cathedral. It's massive. There's writing on the walls. Symbols—like nothing I've ever seen. I'm going to check it out."

"Steve, don't—"

Steve disappeared again. A few minutes passed. Was there another slight vibration? Karl listened closely. He couldn't hear it, but he could feel it. The ice was pulsing faster now. He stood up and took a step away from the edge. The ice behind him cracked, and then there were cracks everywhere—and spreading quickly. He ran full speed toward the widening fissure. He jumped—and almost made it to the other side but came up short. His hands caught on the ice ledge, and he dangled there for a long second. The vibrations in the ice grew more violent with each passing second. Karl watched the ice around him crumble and fall, and then the shard that held him broke free, and he was plummeting down into the abyss.

On the boat, Naomi watched the sun set over the iceberg. She picked up the satellite phone and dialed the number the man had given her.

"You said to call if we found anything interesting."

"Don't say anything. Hold the line. We'll have your location within two minutes. We'll come to you."

She set the phone on the counter, walked back to the stove, and continued stirring the pot of beans.

The man on the other end of the satellite phone looked up

when the GPS coordinates flashed on his screen. He copied the location and searched the satellite surveillance database for live feeds. One result.

He opened the stream and panned the view to the center of the iceberg, where the dark spots were. He zoomed in several times, and when the image came into focus, he dropped his coffee to the floor, bolted out of his office, and ran down the hall to the director's office. He barged in, interrupting a gray-haired man who was standing and speaking with both hands held up.

"We've found it."

PART I
JAKARTA BURNING

1

Autism Research Center (ARC)
Jakarta, Indonesia
Present Day

Dr. Kate Warner awoke to a terrifying feeling: there was someone in the room. She tried to open her eyes but couldn't. She felt groggy, almost as though she had been drugged. The air was musty... subterranean. She twisted slightly and pain coursed through her. The bed below her was hard—a couch, maybe; definitely not the bed in her nineteenth-floor condo in downtown Jakarta. *Where am I?*

She heard another quiet footfall, like tennis shoes on carpet. "Kate," a man whispered, testing to see if she was awake.

Kate managed to open her eyes a little. Above her, faint rays of sunlight filtered in through metal blinds that covered short, wide windows. In the corner, a strobe light pierced the room every few seconds, like the flash of a camera snapping a photo incessantly.

She took a deep breath and sat up quickly, seeing the man for the first time. He reeled back, dropping something that clanged as brown liquid splashed on the floor.

It was Ben Adelson, her lab assistant. "Jesus, Kate. I'm sorry. I thought... if you were up, you might want coffee." He bent to pick up the remnants of a shattered coffee cup, and when he got a closer look at her, he said, "No offense, but you look horrible, Kate." He stared at her for a moment. "Please tell me what's going on."

Kate rubbed her eyes, and her head seemed to clear a bit as she realized where she was. She had been working at the lab day and night for the last five days, virtually nonstop since she had gotten the call from her research sponsor: produce results now, any results, or the funding goes away. No excuses this time. She hadn't told any of the staff on her autism study. There was no reason to worry them. Either she got some results and they went on, or she didn't and they went home. "Coffee sounds nice, Ben. Thanks."

The man exited the van and pulled his black face mask down. "Use your knife inside. Gunfire will draw attention."

His assistant, a woman, nodded and pulled her face mask down as well.

The man extended his gloved hand to the door, but then hesitated. "You're sure the alarm is off?"

"Yeah. Well, I cut the outside line, but it's probably going off inside."

"What?" He shook his head. "Jesus—they could be calling it in right now. Let's be quick." He threw the door open and charged inside.

Above the door, a sign read:
Autism Research Center
Staff Entrance

Ben returned with a fresh cup of coffee, and Kate thanked him. He plopped down in a chair opposite her desk. "You're going to work yourself to death. I know you've slept here for the past four nights. And the secrecy, banning everyone from the lab, hoarding your notes, not talking about ARC-247. I'm not the only one who's worried."

Kate sipped the coffee. Jakarta had been a difficult place to run a clinical trial, but working on the island of Java had some bright spots. The coffee was one of them.

She couldn't tell Ben what she was doing in the lab, at least not yet. It might amount to nothing, and more than likely, they were all out of a job anyway. Involving him would only make him an accomplice to a possible crime.

Kate nodded to the flashing fixture in the corner of the room. "What's that strobe light?"

Ben glanced over his shoulder at it. "Not sure. An alarm, I think—"

"Fire?"

"No. I made the rounds when I got here, it's not a fire. I was about to do a thorough inspection when I noticed that your door was cracked." Ben reached into one of the dozen cardboard boxes that crowded Kate's office. He flipped through a few framed diplomas. "Why don't you put these up?"

"I don't see the point." Hanging the diplomas wasn't Kate's style, and even if it were, who would she impress with them? Kate was the only investigator and physician on the study, and all the research staff knew her CV. They received no visitors, and the only other people who saw her office were the two dozen staff who cared for the children with autism in the study. The staff would think Stanford and Johns Hopkins were people, long deceased relatives maybe, the diplomas perhaps their birth certificates.

"*I'd* put it up, if I had an MD from Johns Hopkins." Ben carefully placed the diploma back in the box and rummaged around in it some more.

Kate drained the last of the coffee. "Yeah?" She held the cup out. "I'll trade you for another cup of coffee."

"Does this mean I can give you orders now?"

"Don't get carried away," Kate said as Ben left the room. She stood and twisted the hard plastic cylinder that controlled the blinds, revealing a view of the chain-link fence that circled their building, and beyond it, the crowded streets of Jakarta. The morning commute was in full swing. Buses and cars crept along as motorcycles darted in and out of the tight spaces between them.

Bicycles and pedestrians filled every square inch of the sidewalks. And she had thought the traffic in San Francisco was bad.

It wasn't just the traffic; Jakarta still felt so foreign to her. It wasn't home. Maybe it never would be. Four years ago, Kate would have moved anywhere in the world, any place that wasn't San Francisco. Martin Grey, her adoptive father, had said, "Jakarta would be a great place to continue your research... and... to start over." He had also said something about time healing all wounds. But now she was running out of time.

She turned back to the desk and began clearing away the photos Ben had taken out. She stopped at a faded picture of a large dancing room with a parquet floor. How had that gotten in with her work things? It was the only photo she had of her childhood home in West Berlin, just off Tiergartenstraße. Kate could barely picture the massive three-story residence. In her memory, it felt more like a foreign embassy or a grand estate from another time. A castle. An empty castle. Kate's mother had died during childbirth, and while her father had been loving, he had rarely been present. Kate tried to picture him in her mind's eye, but she couldn't. There was only a vague recollection of a cold day in December when he had taken her for a walk. She remembered how tiny her hand felt inside of his, how safe she felt. They had walked all the way down Tiergartenstraße, to the Berlin Wall. It was a somber scene: families placing wreaths and pictures, hoping and praying for the Wall to fall and their loved ones to return. The other memories were flashes of him leaving and returning, always with some trinket from a faraway place. The house staff had taken up the slack as best they could. They were attentive but perhaps a little cold. What was the housekeeper's name? Or the tutor who lived with her and the other staff on the top floor? She had taught Kate German. She could still speak German, but she couldn't remember the woman's name.

About the only clear memory of the first six years of her life was the night Martin came into her dance room, turned the music off, and told her that her father wasn't coming home—ever again—and that she would be coming to live with him.

She wished she could erase that memory, and she'd just as soon forget the thirteen years that followed. She had moved to America with Martin, but the cities ran together as he rushed off to one expedition after another, and she was shipped off to one boarding school after another. None of them ever felt like home either.

Her research lab was the closest thing she had ever had to a real home. She spent every waking moment here. She had thrown herself into her work after San Francisco, and what had started as a defense mechanism, a survival mechanism, had become her routine, her lifestyle. The research team had become her family, and the research participants her children.

And it was all about to go away.

She needed to focus. And she needed more coffee. She pushed the pile of photos off the desk and into the box below. Where was Ben?

Kate walked out into the hall and made her way to the staff kitchen. Empty. She checked the coffee pot. Empty. The strobe lights were going off here, too.

Something was wrong. "Ben?" Kate called out.

The other research staff wouldn't be in for hours. They kept a strange schedule, but they did good work. Kate cared more about the work.

She ventured out into the research wing, which consisted of a series of storage rooms and offices surrounding a large clean-room lab where Kate and her team engineered gene therapy retroviruses they hoped would cure autism. She peered through the glass. Ben wasn't in the lab.

The building was creepy at this time of morning. It was empty, quiet, and not quite dark, but not light either. Shafts of focused sunlight poured into the hallways from the windows in the rooms on each side, like searchlights probing for signs of life.

Kate's footfalls echoed loudly as she prowled the cavernous research wing, peeking into each room, squinting to see through the bright Jakartan sun. All empty. That left the residential section—the housing units, kitchens, and supporting facilities for the study's roughly one hundred children with autism.

In the distance, Kate could hear other footsteps, faster than hers—running. She began walking more quickly, in their direction, and just as she turned the corner, Ben reached out and grabbed her arm. "Kate! Follow me, hurry."

2

Manggarai Train Station
Jakarta, Indonesia

David Vale stepped back into the shadow of the train station's ticket counter. He studied the man buying a *New York Times* from the newsstand. The man paid the vendor, then walked past the trash can without throwing the paper away. Not the contact.

Behind the newsstand, a commuter train crept into the station. It was packed to the walls with Indonesian workers coming into the capital from the outlying cities for the day's work. Passengers hung out of every set of sliding double doors, middle-aged men mostly. On the roof of the train, teenagers and young adults sat, squatted, and stretched out, reading newspapers, fiddling with smart phones, and talking. The crowded commuter train was a symbol of Jakarta itself, a city bursting at the seams with a growing population struggling to modernize. Mass transit was only the most visible sign of the city's struggle to accommodate the twenty-eight million people in its metro area.

The commuters were fleeing the train now, swarming the station like shoppers on Black Friday in America. It was chaos. Workers pushed, shoved, and shouted as they ran out the station's doors, while others fought to get into the station. This happened here and in other commuter train stations throughout the city every day. It was the perfect place for a meet.

David kept his eyes focused on the newsstand. His earpiece crackled to life. "Collector, Watch Shop. Be advised, we're at zero-hour plus twenty."

The contact was late. The team was growing nervous. The unspoken question was: do we abort?

David raised his mobile phone to his face. "Copy, Watch Shop. Trader, Broker, report."

From his vantage point, David could see the two other operatives. One sat on a bench in the middle of the bustling crowd. The other man was working on a light near the restrooms. Both reported no sign of their anonymous informant, a man who claimed to have details of an imminent terrorist attack called Toba Protocol.

The operatives were good, two of Jakarta Station's best; David could barely pick them out of the crowd. As he surveyed the rest of the station, something unnerved him slightly.

The earpiece crackled again. It was Howard Keegan, the director of Clocktower, the counter-terrorism organization David worked for. "Collector, Appraiser, it seems the seller didn't like the market today."

David was the chief of Jakarta Station, and Keegan was his boss and mentor. The older man clearly didn't want to step on David's toes by shutting down the operation, but the message was clear. Keegan had come all the way from London, hoping for a break. It was a big risk given the other ongoing Clocktower operation.

"I agree," David said. "Let's shut it down."

The two operatives casually vacated their positions and melted into the throngs of scurrying Indonesians.

David took one last look at the newsstand. A tall man with a red windbreaker was paying for something. A newspaper. The *New York Times*.

"Stand by, Trader and Broker. We have a buyer looking at merchandise," David said.

The man stepped back, held the paper up, and paused for a few seconds to read the front page. Without looking around, he folded the newspaper, tossed it in the trash can, and walked quickly toward the loaded train moving away from the station.

"Contact. I'm engaging." David's mind raced as he bounded from the shadow and into the crowd. Why was the man late? And his appearance—it was... wrong. The overt red windbreaker, the posture (a soldier's posture, or an operative's), the way he walked.

The man pushed onto the train and began snaking through the thick crowd of standing men and sitting women. The man was taller than almost everyone on the train, and David could still see his head. David squeezed onto the train and stopped. Why was the contact running? Had he seen something? Been spooked? And then it happened. The man turned, glancing back at David, and the look in his eyes said it all.

David wheeled around and swept the four men standing in the doorway out onto the platform. He pushed them away from the train as more anxious commuters poured onto the train in the hole he had made. David was about to shout when the explosion tore through the train, spraying shards of glass and metal into the station. The blast threw David to the concrete floor of the platform, sandwiching him between bodies, some dead, others writhing in pain. Screams filled the air. Through the smoke, pieces of ash and debris drifted down like falling snow. David couldn't move his arms or legs. His head rolled back, and he almost lost consciousness.

For a moment he was back in New York, running away from the crumbling building, then he was under it, trapped, waiting. Hands from unseen arms grabbed him and pulled him out. "We got you, buddy," they said. The sirens from trucks labeled "FDNY" and "NYPD" rang out as the sunlight hit his face.

But it wasn't an ambulance this time. It was a black delivery van outside the train station. The men, not FDNY. The two operatives, Trader and Broker. They hoisted David into the van and sped away as Jakartan police and fire teams filled the streets.

3

Playroom Four buzzed with activity. The scene was typical: toys strewn everywhere, with about a dozen children scattered throughout the room, each playing alone. In the corner, an eight-year-old child named Adi rocked back and forth as he built a puzzle with ease. When he placed the last block, he looked up at Ben, a proud smile on his face.

Kate couldn't believe it.

The boy had just assembled a puzzle her team used to identify savants—individuals with autism and special cognitive abilities. The puzzle required an IQ in the 140 to 180 range. Kate couldn't do it, and only one child in the study could—Satya.

Kate watched the child quickly build the puzzle, tear it down, and build it again. Adi stood up and took a seat on a bench beside Surya, a seven-year-old in the study. The smaller boy moved to the puzzle and completed it with just as much ease.

Ben turned to Kate. "Can you believe it? You think they're doing it from memory? From watching Satya?"

"No. Or maybe. I doubt it," Kate said. Her mind raced. She needed time to think. She had to be sure.

"This is what you've been working on, isn't it?" Ben said.

"Yes," Kate said absently. It was impossible. It shouldn't have worked so quickly. Yesterday, these children displayed classic signs of autism—if there was such a thing. Increasingly, researchers and physicians had begun recognizing autism as a spectrum of disorders with a wide range of symptoms. At

18

the core of autism was a dysfunction in communication and social interaction. Most affected children avoided eye contact and socializing, others wouldn't respond to their names, and in severe cases, children couldn't stand any contact. Yesterday neither Adi nor Surya could have completed the puzzle, made eye contact, or even taken turns.

She had to tell Martin. He would make sure that their funding wasn't cut off.

"What do you want to do?" Ben said, excitement in his voice.

"Take them to Observation Two. I need to make a call." Disbelief, exhaustion, and joy fought a battle in Kate's mind. "And, uh, we should administer a diagnostic. ADI-R. No, ADOS 2, it will take less time. And let's film it." Kate smiled and gripped Ben's shoulder. She wanted to say something profound, something that would mark the moment, words like she imagined brilliant and soon-to-be-famous scientists say at the breakthrough moment, but no words came, just a weary smile. Ben nodded and then took the children by the hands. Kate opened the door, and the four of them walked out into the corridor where two people were waiting. No, not people—monsters, dressed head to toe in black military gear: a helmet that covered a cloth mask, dark ski-like goggles, body armor, and black rubber gloves.

Kate and Ben stopped, glanced at each other in disbelief, and corralled the children behind them. Kate cleared her throat and said, "This is a research lab, we don't have any cash here, but take the equipment, take whatever you want. We won't—"

"Shut up." The man's voice was rough, like someone who had spent a lifetime smoking and drinking. He turned to his smaller black-clad accomplice, who was clearly a woman, and said, "Take them."

The woman took a step toward the children. Without thinking, Kate moved into her path. "Don't. Take anything. Take me instead—"

The man took out a handgun and pointed it at her. "Step aside, Dr. Warner. I don't want to hurt you, but I will."

He knows my name.

Out of the corner of her eye, Kate saw Ben move closer, making for the gap between her and the monster with the gun.

Adi tried to run, but the woman grabbed him by his shirt.

Ben moved beside Kate, then in front of her, and they both rushed the man with the gun. They tackled him as the gun went off. Kate saw Ben roll off the black-clad man. Blood was everywhere.

She tried to get up, but the man had her. He was too strong. He pinned her to the ground, and she heard a loud crack—

4

Thirty minutes after the train blast, David sat at a cheap foldout table in the safe house, enduring the medical tech's treatment and trying to make sense of the attack.

"Ow." David winced and reeled back from the alcohol swab the tech had dabbed on his face. "Thank you, really, but let's do this after. I'm fine. Flesh wounds."

Across the room, Howard Keegan stood up from the bank of computer screens and walked over to David. "It was a setup, David."

"Why? It makes no sense—"

"It does. You need to see this. I received it right before the blast." Keegan handed him a sheet of paper.

```
<<< EYES ONLY >>>
<<< CLOCKTOWER >>>
<<< CENTCOMM >>>
Clocktower under attack.
Cape Town and Mar del Plata Stations destroyed.
Karachi, Delhi, Dakha, and Lahore breached.
Recommend initiate Firewall.
Please advise.
<<< END BULLETIN >>>
```

Keegan tucked the page back in his coat pocket. "He lied about our security problem."

David rubbed his temples. It was a nightmare scenario. His head was still throbbing from the bomb blast. He had to think. "He didn't lie—"

"Underestimated at the very least, or more likely a lie of omission to cripple and distract us for this larger attack on Clocktower."

"The attack on Clocktower doesn't mean the terrorist threat isn't real. It could be a prelude—"

"Maybe. But the only thing we know is that Clocktower's back is against the wall. Your first duty is to secure your station. You're the largest operation in Southeast Asia. Your HQ could be under attack right now." Keegan picked up his bag. "I'm going back to London to try to manage things from there. Good luck, David."

They shook hands, and David saw Keegan out of the safe house.

On the street, a kid carrying a stack of newspapers ran up to David, waving them in the air and screaming, "Have you heard? Jakarta is under attack."

David pushed him away, but the kid shoved a rolled up newspaper into his hand and darted off around the corner.

David started to toss the newspaper aside, but... it was too heavy. And there was something wrapped inside. He unrolled the paper, and a round black pipe about a foot long fell out. A pipe bomb.

5

Autism Research Center (ARC)
Jakarta, Indonesia

West Jakarta Police Chief Eddi Kusnadi mopped sweat from his brow as he walked into the crime scene—some science lab on the west end of town. A neighbor had reported a gunshot. It was a nicer neighborhood, the type where neighbors had political connections, so he had to check it out. The place was obviously some kind of medical facility, but some of the rooms looked almost like a daycare.

Paku, one of his best plainclothes officers, waved him to a room in the back where he found an unconscious woman on the floor, a dead man in a pool of his own blood near her, and several cops standing around.

"Lover's quarrel?"

"We don't think so," Paku said.

In the background the chief could hear several kids crying. A native Indonesian woman entered the room, and upon seeing the bodies, instantly began screaming.

"Get this lady out of here," the chief said. Two officers corralled her out of the room. He said to Paku, the only remaining policeman, "Who are they?"

"The woman is Dr. Katherine Warner."

"Doctor? This is a medical clinic?"

"No. A research facility. Warner is the head of it. The woman you just saw is one of the nannies for the children—they're doing research on disabled kids."

"Doesn't sound very profitable. Who's the guy?" the chief said.

23

"One of the lab technicians. The nanny says another technician offered to watch the kids, so she went home. The nanny claims that two kids are missing."

"Runaways?"

"She thinks not, says the building has safeguards," Paku said.

"Security cameras on the building?"

"No. Some observation cameras in the rooms with the kids. We're checking footage."

The chief bent down and looked the woman over. She was skinny, but not too skinny. He liked that. He felt for a pulse, then turned her head side to side to see if she had any head trauma. He noticed minor bruises on her wrists, but she seemed otherwise unharmed. "What a mess. Find out if she has any money. If so, bring her to the station. If not, dump her at the hospital."

6

Immari Corp. Research Complex
Outside Burang, China
Tibet Autonomous Region

The project director strolled into Dr. Shen Chang's office and tossed a file onto his desk. "We have a new therapy."

Dr. Chang grabbed the file and began riffling through the pages.

The director paced the length of the room. "It's very promising. We're fast-tracking it. I want the machine ready and subjects treated with the new therapy within four hours."

Chang dropped the file and looked up.

The scientist opened his mouth, but the director waved him off. "I don't want to hear it. The singularity could happen at any time—today, tomorrow, it could have already happened for all we know. We don't have time for caution."

Chang began to speak, but the director cut him off again. "And don't tell me you need more time. You've had time. We need results. Now tell me what it's going to take."

Chang slumped in his chair. "The last test was a strain on the local power grid; we exceeded our capacity onsite. We think we fixed the problem, but the regional power authority has to be suspicious about what we're doing. The bigger issue is that we're low on primates—"

"We're not testing it on primates. I want a human cohort of fifty ready to test."

Chang straightened himself and said with more force, "Setting the morality aside, which I urge you not to do, we would simply need a lot more data to begin a human trial, we would need—"

"You have it, doctor. It's all in the file. And we're retrieving more data now. That's not all. We have two subjects with sustained Atlantis Gene activation."

Chang's eyes widened. "You... two... how—"

The man pointed to the file in a quick, cobra-like motion. "The file, doctor; it's all there. And they'll be here, soon. You'd better be ready. All you have to do is replicate the gene therapy."

Chang was flipping through the pages, reading, and murmuring to himself. He looked up. "The subjects are children?"

"Yes. Is that a problem?"

"Uh, no. Well, maybe. Or maybe not."

"*Maybe not* is the right answer. Call me if you need me, doctor. Four hours. I don't have to tell you what's at stake."

But Dr. Chang couldn't hear him. He was lost in the notes of Dr. Katherine Warner.

7

David peered at the black pipe through the narrow window of the blast shield. Turning the cap on the pipe had taken forever with the manually operated arm. But he had to look inside. It was the weight—the pipe was too light to be a bomb. Nails, buckshot, and BBs would weigh a lot more.

Finally, the end fell off, and David tipped the pipe to one side. A rolled-up paper slid out. A thick, glossy page. A photo.

David unrolled it. It was a satellite image of an iceberg floating in a deep blue sea. In the center of the iceberg, there was an oblong black object. A submarine, sticking out of the ice. On the back, a message read:

```
Toba Protocol is real.

4+12+47 = 4/5; Jones
7+22+47 = 3/8; Anderson
10+4+47 = 5/4; Ames
```

David slipped the photo into a thick manila folder and walked over to the surveillance room. One of the two techs turned from the bank of screens. "No sign of him yet."

"Anything from the airports?" David asked.

The man worked the keyboard, then looked up. "Yes, he landed a few minutes ago at Soekarno-Hatta. You want us to have him detained there?"

"No. I need him here. Just make sure they can't see him on surveillance upstairs. I'll take it from there."

8

BBC World Report – Wire Release

Potential terror attacks in residential neighborhoods in Mar del Plata, Argentina and Cape Town, South Africa

*** Breaking News Update: Additional blasts reported in Karachi, Pakistan and Jakarta, Indonesia. We will update this report as details emerge. ***

Cape Town, South Africa // The sound of automatic gun fire and grenade explosions shattered the early morning calm in Cape Town today, as a group estimated at twenty armed assailants entered an apartment building and killed fourteen people.

Police have released no official information about the attack.

Eyewitnesses at the scene described it as a special-operations-style attack. A BBC reporter onsite took this eyewitness statement: "Yeah I seen it, looked like a tank or something, you know, one of them armored troop carriers, rolling up on the curb and then dudes was pouring out it like ninjas or robot soldiers or something, moving all mechanical-like, and then it's like the whole building exploded, glass falling all over the place, and I ran up on out of there. I mean, it's a rough neighborhood, but man, I ain't never seen nothing like that. I figured, at first, it was, you know, a drug raid. Whatever it was, it done gone real wrong."

Another witness, also speaking on the condition of anonymity, confirmed that the group had no official insignia on their vehicle or uniforms.

A reporter with Reuters, who briefly gained access to the scene before police removed him, described it this way: "It looked to me like a safe house, maybe CIA or MI6. It would have to be somebody very well funded to have that kind of technology: a situation-room with wall-to-wall computer screens and a massive server room. There were bodies everywhere. About half wore plainclothes; the rest were dressed in black body armor similar to what witnesses say the attackers wore."

It remains unclear if the attackers incurred any casualties and were forced to leave anyone behind or if the bodies were those of individuals defending the location.

The BBC sought a comment from both the CIA and MI6 for this report. Both declined.

It's unknown whether this incident is in any way related to a similar incident earlier today in Mar del Plata, Argentina, where a massive explosion in a low-income neighborhood killed twelve people at approximately two A.M. local time. Bystanders say the explosion followed a raid by a heavily armed group that no one could identify.

As with the attack in Cape Town, no one has claimed responsibility for the attack in Mar del Plata.

"It's very concerning that we have no idea who's involved," said Richard Bookmeyer, a Professor at American University. "Based on the initial reports, if either the victims or the perpetrators of the attacks are part of a terrorist network... it would indicate a level of sophistication not currently thought possible by any known terror entity. It's either a new actor or a significant evolution of an existing group. Both scenarios would require re-examining what we think we know about the global terrorism landscape."

We will update this story as details unfold.

9

Clocktower Station HQ
Jakarta, Indonesia

David was studying a map of Jakarta and Clocktower's safe houses around the city when the surveillance tech walked in. "He's here."

David folded the map up. "Good."

Josh Cohen walked toward the nondescript apartment building that housed Clocktower's Jakarta Station Headquarters. The buildings around it were mostly abandoned—a mix of failed housing projects and dilapidated warehouses.

The sign on the building read "Clocktower Security, Inc.," and to the outside world, Clocktower Security was just one of a growing number of private security firms. Officially, Clocktower Security offered personal protection and bodyguard services to corporate executives and high-value foreign nationals visiting Jakarta, as well as private investigation services when local law enforcement was "less than cooperative." It was the perfect cover.

Josh entered the building, walked down a long hallway, opened a heavy steel door, and approached the shiny silver elevator doors. A panel beside the doors slid back, and he placed his hand on the reflective surface and said, "Josh Cohen. Verify my voice."

A second panel opened, this one level with his face, and a red beam scanned up and down while he held his eyes open and head still.

The elevator dinged, opened, and began carrying Josh to the building's middle floor. The elevator ascended silently, but Josh knew that elsewhere in the building a surveillance tech was reviewing a full body scan of him, verifying he had no bugs, bombs, or otherwise problematic items. If he was carrying anything, the elevator would fill with a colorless, odorless gas and he'd wake up in a holding cell. It would be the last room he'd ever see. If he passed, the elevator would take him to the fourth floor—his home for the last three years and the Jakarta headquarters of Clocktower.

Clocktower was the world's secret answer to state-less terror: a state-less counterterrorism agency. No red tape. No bureaucracy. Just good guys killing bad guys. It wasn't quite that simple, but Clocktower was as close as the world would ever get.

Clocktower was independent, apolitical, anti-dogmatic, and most importantly, extremely effective. And for those reasons, the intelligence services of nations around the world supported Clocktower, despite knowing almost nothing about it. No one knew when it had started, who directed it, how it was funded, or where it was headquartered. When Josh had joined Clocktower three years ago, he had assumed he would get answers to those questions as a Clocktower insider. He had been wrong. He had risen through the ranks quickly, becoming Chief of Intelligence Analysis for Jakarta Station, but he still knew no more about Clocktower than the day he'd been recruited from the CIA's Office of Terrorism Analysis. And they seemed to want it that way.

Within Clocktower, information was strictly compartmentalized among the independent cells. Everyone shared intel with Central, everyone got intel from Central, but no cell had the big picture or insight into the larger operation. And for that reason, Josh had been shocked to receive an invitation six days ago to a sort of "summit meeting" for the chief analysts of every Clocktower cell. He had confronted David Vale, the Jakarta station chief, asking him if this was a joke. He'd said that it wasn't and that all the directors had been made aware of the meeting.

Josh's shock at the invitation was quickly trumped by the revelations at the conference. The first surprise was the number of attendees: two hundred and thirty-eight. Josh had assumed Clocktower was relatively small, with maybe fifty or so cells in the world's hot spots, but instead, the entire globe was represented. Assuming each cell was the size of Jakarta Station—about fifty agents—there could be over ten thousand people working in the cells, plus the central organization, which had to be at least a thousand people just to correlate and analyze the intel, not to mention coordinate the cells.

The organization's scale was shocking—it could be almost the size of the CIA, which had around twenty thousand total employees when Josh worked there. And many of those twenty thousand worked in analysis in Langley, Virginia, not in the field. Clocktower was lean—it had none of the CIA's bureaucracies and organizational fat.

Clocktower's special ops capabilities likely dwarfed that of any government on Earth. Each Clocktower cell had three groups. One third of the staff was case officers, similar to the CIA's National Clandestine service; they worked undercover in actual terror organizations, cartels, and other bad-guy-run groups, or in places where they could develop sources: local governments, banks, and police departments. Their goal was Human Intelligence (HUMINT)—first-hand intel.

Another third of each cell worked as analysts. The analysts spent the vast majority of their time on two activities: hacking and guessing. They hacked everyone and everything: phone calls, emails, texts. They combined that Signals Intelligence, or SIGINT, with the HUMINT and any other local intel, and transmitted it to Central. Josh's chief responsibilities were to make sure Jakarta Station maximized its intelligence gathering and to draw conclusions about the intel. Drawing conclusions sounded better than guessing, but his job essentially came down to guessing and making recommendations to the station chief. The station chief, with counsel from Central, then authorized local operations, which were conducted by the cell's covert operations group—the last third of the staff.

Jakarta's covert ops group had developed a reputation as one of Clocktower's leading strike teams. That status had afforded Josh something of a celebrity status at the conference. Josh's cell was the de facto leader of the Asia-Pacific region and everyone wanted to know what their tricks of the trade were.

But not everyone was star-struck with Josh—he was glad to see many of his old friends at the conference. People he had worked with at the CIA or liaised with from other governments. It was incredible; he had been communicating with people he had known for years. Clocktower had a strict policy: every new member got a new name, your past was destroyed, and you couldn't reveal your identity outside the cell. Outbound phone calls were voice-altered by computer. In-person contact was strictly forbidden.

A face-to-face meeting—with every chief analyst of every cell—shattered that veil of secrecy. It went against every Clocktower operating protocol. Josh knew there must be a reason—something extremely compelling, and extremely urgent—to take the risk, but he never would have guessed the secret Central revealed at the conference. He still couldn't believe it. And he had to tell David Vale, immediately.

Josh walked to the front of the elevator and stood close to the doors, ready to make a beeline for the station chief's office.

It was nine A.M., and Jakarta Station would be in full swing. The analysts' pit would be lit up like the floor of the New York Stock Exchange, with analysts crowded around banks of monitors pointing and arguing. Across the floor, the door to the field ops prep room would be wide open and likely full of operatives getting ready for the day. The late arrivals would be standing in front of their lockers, donning their body armor quickly and stuffing extra magazines in every pocket on their person. The early risers usually sat around on the wood benches and talked about sports and weapons before the morning briefings, their camaraderie interrupted only by the occasional locker-room prank.

It was home, and Josh had to admit that he had missed it, although the conference was rewarding in ways he hadn't anticipated. Knowing he was part of a larger community of chief analysts, people who shared the same life experiences as him, people who had the same problems and fears as he did, was surprisingly comforting. In Jakarta, he was head of analysis, he had a team that worked for him, and he answered only to the station chief; but he had no real peers, no one to really talk to. Intelligence work was a lonely profession, especially for the people in charge. It had certainly taken its toll on some of his old friends. Many had aged well beyond their years. Others had become hardened and distant. After seeing them, Josh had wondered if he would end up that way. Everything had a price, but he believed in the work they were doing. No job was perfect.

As his thoughts drifted back from the conference, he realized the elevator should have opened by now. When he turned his head to look around, the elevator lights blurred, like a video in slow motion. His body felt heavy. He could hardly breathe. He reached out to grab the elevator rail, but his hand wouldn't close; it slipped off, and the steel floor rushed up.

10

Kate's head was killing her. Her body ached. And the police had been no help at all. She had woken up in the back of a police car, and the driver had refused to tell her anything. Things had only gotten worse once she reached the police station.

"Why won't you listen to me? Why aren't you out there looking for those two boys?" Kate Warner stood, leaned over the metal table and stared at the smug little interrogator who had already wasted twenty minutes of her time.

"We are trying to find them. That is why we are asking you these questions, Miss Warner."

"I already told you, I don't know anything."

"Maybe, maybe not." The little man tilted his head from side to side as he said the words.

"Maybe, my ass. I'll find them myself." She stepped toward the steel door.

"That door is locked, Miss Warner."

"So unlock it."

"Not possible. It must be locked while a suspect is questioned."

"Suspect? I want a lawyer, right now."

"You are in Jakarta, Miss Warner. No lawyer, no call to the American Embassy." The man continued looking down, picking dirt off his boots. "We have many foreigners here, many visitors, many people who come here, who do not respect our country, our people. Before, we fear American Consulate, we give them

35

lawyer, they always get away. We learn. Indonesians are not as stupid as you think, Miss Warner. That is why you do your work here, is it not? You think we are too stupid to figure out what you are up to?"

"I'm not *up* to anything. I'm trying to cure autism."

"Why not do that in your own country, Miss Warner?"

Kate would never, in a million years, tell this man why she had left America. Instead she said, "America is the most expensive place in the world to conduct a clinical trial."

"Ah, then it is about the cost, yes? Here in Indonesia, you can buy babies to experiment on?"

"I haven't bought any babies!"

"But your trial owns these children, does it not?" He turned the file around and pointed at it.

Kate followed his finger.

"Miss Warner, your trial is the legal guardian of both of these children—of all one hundred three—is it not?"

"Legal guardianship is not ownership."

"You use different words. So did the Dutch East India Corporation. Do you know of it? I am sure you do. They used the word *colony*, but they owned Indonesia for over two hundred years. A corporation owned my country and its people, and they treated us as their property, taking what they wanted. In 1947, we finally got our independence. But the memory is still raw for my people. A jury will see this as just the same. You did take these children, did you not? You said it yourself, you did not pay for them. And I see no record of the parents. They gave no consent to the adoption. Do they even know you have their children?"

Kate stared hard at him.

"I thought so. We are getting somewhere now. It is best to be honest. One last thing, Miss Warner. I see that your research is funded by Immari Jakarta—Research Division. It is probably only coincidence… but very unfortunate… Immari Holdings purchased many of the assets of the Dutch when they were driven out sixty-five years ago… so the money for your work came from…"

The man stuffed the pages in the folder and stood, as if he were an Indonesian Perry Mason making his closing argument. "You can see how a jury might see this, Miss Warner. Your people leave, but return with a new name and continue to exploit us. Instead of sugarcane and coffee beans in the 1900s, now you want new drugs, you need new guinea pigs to experiment on. You take our children, run experiments you could not run in your own country, because you will not do this to your own children, and when something goes wrong—maybe a child gets sick or you think the authorities will find out—you get rid of these children. But something goes wrong. Maybe one of your technicians cannot kill these children. He knows it is wrong. He fights back, and he is killed in the struggle. You know the police will come, so you make up this story about the kidnapping? Yes. You can admit this; it will be better. Indonesia is a merciful place."

"It's not true."

"It is the most logical story, Miss Warner. You give us no alternative. You ask for your lawyer. You insist we release you. Think about how this looks."

Kate stared at him.

The man stood and made for the door. "Very well, Miss Warner. I must warn you, what follows will not be pleasant. It is best to cooperate, but of course, you clever Americans always know best."

11

Immari Corp. Research Complex
Outside Burang, China
Tibet Autonomous Region

"Wake up, Jin, they're calling your number."

Jin tried to open his eyes, but the light was blinding. His roommate huddled over him, whispering something in his ear, but he couldn't make it out. In the background, a booming voice called over the loudspeaker, "204394, report immediately. 204394, report immediately. 204394. 204394. Report."

Jin leaped out of the small bed. How long had they been calling him? His eyes darted left and right, searching the three-meter-by-three-meter cell he shared with Wei. Where were his pants and shirt? Please, no—if he was late and forgot his outfit, they would kick him out for sure. Where were they? Where—? His roommate, sitting on his bunk, held up the white cloth pants and shirt. Jin snatched them and pulled them on, almost ripping the pants.

Wei stared at the floor. "Sorry, Jin, I was asleep too. I didn't hear."

Jin wanted to say something, but there wasn't time. He ran out of the room and down the hall. Several of the cells were empty and most had only one occupant. At the door to the wing, the orderly said, "Arm."

Jin held out his arm. "204394."

"Quiet," the man said. He waved a handheld device with a small screen over Jin's arm. It beeped and the man turned his head and yelled, "That's it." He opened the door for Jin. "Go ahead."

Jin joined about fifty other "residents." Three orderlies

escorted them to a large room with several long rows of chairs. The rows were separated by tall, cubicle-like walls. The chairs looked almost like reclining beach chairs. Beside each chair, a tall silver pole held three bags of clear liquid, each with a tube hanging down. On the other side of each chair stood a machine with more readouts than a car dashboard. A bundle of wires hung from the bottom and was tied off on the right chair rail.

Jin had never seen anything like it. It never happened like this. Since he had arrived at the facility six months ago, the daily routine had rarely changed: breakfast, lunch, and dinner at the exact same times, always the same meals; after each meal, blood draws from the valve-like device they had implanted in his right arm; and sometimes, exercise in the afternoon, monitored by electrodes on his chest. The rest of the time, they were confined to the three-meter-by-three-meter cells, with two beds and a toilet. Every few days or so they took a picture of him with a big machine that made a low droning sound. They were always telling him to lie still.

They showered once per week, in a large, coed group shower. That was by far the worst part—trying to control the urges in the shower. During his first month, a couple was caught fooling around. No one ever saw them again.

Last month, Jin had tried to stay in his cell during shower time, but they had caught him. The supervisor had stormed into his cell. "We'll kick you out if you disobey again," he had said. Jin was scared to death. They were paying him a fortune, an absolute fortune. And he had no other options.

His family had lost their farm last year. No one could afford the taxes on a small farm anymore; a larger farm, maybe. Land values were skyrocketing, and the population was swelling throughout China. So his family did what many other farm families had done: sent their oldest for work in the city while the parents and younger children held on.

His older brother found work in a factory making electronics. Jin and his parents visited him a month after he started. The conditions were much worse than here, and the work was already taking its toll—the strong, vibrant, twenty-one-year-old man who had left his family's farm looked to have aged twenty years. He was pale, his hair was thinning, and he walked with a slight stoop. He coughed constantly. He said there had been a bug at the factory and everyone in his barracks had gotten it, but Jin didn't believe him. His brother gave his parents the little money he had saved from his salary. "Just think, in five to ten years, I'll have enough to buy us another farm. I'll come home and we'll start again." They had all acted very excited. His parents had said they were so proud of him.

On their way home, Jin's father told them that tomorrow, he would go and find better work. That with his skills, he could surely make supervisor somewhere. He'd make good money. Jin and his mother simply nodded.

That night, Jin heard his mother crying, and shortly after, his father shouting. They never fought.

The following night, Jin slipped out of his room, wrote them a note, and left for Chongqing, the nearest major city. The city was filled with people looking for work.

Jin was turned down at the first seven places he applied. The eighth place was different. They didn't ask any questions. They put a cotton stick in his mouth and made him wait in a large holding room for an hour. Most of the people were dismissed. After another hour, they called his number—204394—and told him they could hire him at a medical research facility. Then they told him the pay. He signed the forms so fast his hand hurt.

He couldn't believe his luck. He assumed the conditions would be dire, but he couldn't have been more wrong—it was practically a resort. And now he had screwed it all up. Surely they were kicking him out. They had called his number.

Maybe he had enough for a new farm. Or maybe he could find another research place. He'd heard that the big factories in China exchanged lists of bad workers. Those people couldn't find work anywhere. That would be the kiss of death.

"What are you waiting for!" the man shouted. "Find a seat."

Jin and the other fifty or so white-clad, barefooted "workers" scrambled for chairs. Elbows flew, people pushed, and several people tripped. Everyone seemed to find a chair but Jin. Every time he reached a chair, someone would sink into it at the last second. What if he didn't find a chair? Maybe it was a test. Maybe he should—

"People. Relax, relax. Mind the equipment," the man said. "Just find the closest chair."

Jin exhaled and walked to the next row. Full. In the last row, he found a seat.

Another group of orderlies entered. They wore long white coats and carried tablet computers. A young-looking woman came over to him, hooked the bags to his arm valve, and attached the round sensors to his body. She tapped a few times on her screen and moved to the chair beside him.

Maybe it's just a new test, he thought.

He suddenly felt sleepy. He leaned his head back and...

Jin woke in the same chair. The bags were detached, but the sensors were still connected. He felt groggy and stiff, like he had the flu. He tried to lift his head up. It was so heavy. A white coat came over, ran a flashlight across his eyes, then unhooked the sensors and told him to go and stand with the others by the door.

When he stood, his legs almost buckled. He steadied himself on the arm of his chair, then hobbled over to the group. They all looked half-asleep. There were maybe twenty-five of them, about half of the group that had entered. Where were the rest? Had he slept too long—again? Is this punishment? Would they tell him why? After a few minutes, another man joined them; he seemed in even worse shape than Jin and the rest.

The orderlies ushered them through another long passageway and into an enormous room he'd never seen before. The room was completely empty and the walls were very smooth. He got the impression that it was like a vault or something.

Several minutes passed. He fought the urge to sit down on the floor. He hadn't been told he could sit. He stood there, his heavy head hanging.

The door opened, and two children were escorted in. They couldn't have been more than seven or eight years old. The guards left them with the group, the door closing behind them with a loud boom.

The children weren't drugged, or at least Jin didn't think so. They looked alert. They moved quickly into the crowd of people. They were brown. Not Chinese. They both wandered from person to person, trying to find a familiar face. Jin thought they were about to begin crying.

At the far end of the room, he heard a mechanical sound, like a winch. After a few seconds, he realized something was being lowered. His head was so heavy. He strained to lift it. He could barely see the device. It looked like a massive iron chess pawn with a flat head, or maybe a bell with smooth, straight sides. It must have been four meters tall and heavy, because the four cables that lowered it were huge, maybe a quarter of a meter around. When it was about six meters off the ground, it stopped, and two of the cables moved down the wall along a track Jin hadn't noticed before. They stopped about level with the huge machine and seemed to tighten, anchoring it at each side. Jin strained to look up. There was another cable running from the top of the machine. It was even fatter than the ones at the sides. Unlike the others, it wasn't metal, or even solid. It seemed to hold a bundle of wires or computer cables, like some sort of electronic umbilical cord.

The children had stopped in the middle of the crowd. All the adults tried to look up.

His eyes adjusted, and Jin could just make out a marking etched into the side of the machine. It looked like the Nazi symbol, the... he couldn't remember the name. He felt so sleepy.

The machine was dark, but Jin thought he could hear a faint throbbing sound, like someone rhythmically beating on a solid door—boom-boom-boom. Or maybe the sound of the picture machine. Was it a different picture machine? A group picture? The boom-boom-boom grew louder with each passing second, and a light emerged from the top of the giant pawn—its head apparently had short windows. The yellow-orange light flickered with each pulse of the boom, giving it almost the effect of a lighthouse.

Jin was so entranced by the machine's sound and light pulses, he didn't notice the people falling around him. Something was happening. And it was happening to him too. His legs felt heavier. He heard a sound like bending metal—the machine was pulling against the cables at each side; it was trying to lift.

The pull of the floor got stronger with each passing second. Jin looked around but couldn't see the children. Jin felt someone grab his shoulder. He turned to find a man holding on to him. His face had deep wrinkles, and blood ran from his nose. Jin realized that the skin from the man's hands was coming off on Jin's clothes. It wasn't just skin. The man's blood began to spread over Jin's shirt. The man fell forward onto him, and they both collapsed to the ground. Jin heard the boom-boom-boom of the machine blend into one constant drone of sound and solid light as he felt the blood from his nose run down his face. Then the light and sound suddenly stopped.

In the control room, Dr. Chang and his team stood and watched as the test subjects collapsed into a pile of wrinkled, bloody bodies.

Chang slumped into his chair. "Okay, that's it, shut it off." He took his glasses off and tossed them on the table. He pinched the bridge of his nose and exhaled. "I have to report this to the director." The man would not be happy.

Chang rose and walked toward the door. "And start the cleanup; don't bother with autopsies." The result had been the same as the last twenty-five tests.

The two-man cleanup crew swung back-forth-back-forth and released the body, hurling it into the rolling plastic bin. The bin held around ten bodies, give or take. Today would probably mean three trips to the incinerator, maybe two if they could stack them on top.

They had cleaned up a lot worse; at least these bodies were intact. It took forever when they were in pieces.

It was hard to work in the hazmat suits, but it was better than the alternative.

They lifted another body and swung forward, then—

Something was moving in the pile.

Two children were struggling under the bodies, fighting to crawl out. They were covered in blood.

One man began clearing bodies. The other turned to the cameras and waved his arms. "Hey! We've got two live ones!"

12

"Josh, can you hear me?"

Josh Cohen tried to open his eyes, but the light was too bright. His head was throbbing.

"Here, give me another one."

Josh could barely make out a blurry figure sitting by him on a hard bed. Where was he? It looked like one of the station's holding cells. The man brought a pellet to Josh's nose and cracked it open with a loud pop. Josh inhaled the worst smell of his entire life—a sharp, overwhelming ammonia smell that coursed through his airways, inflated his lungs, and sent him reeling backward, hitting his head against the wall. The constant throbbing turned into a sharp pain. He closed his eyes tight and rubbed his head.

"Okay, okay, take it easy." It was the station chief, David Vale.

"What's going on?" Josh asked.

He could open his eyes now, and he realized that David was in full body armor and there were two other field operatives with him, standing by the door to the cell.

Josh sat up. "Someone must have planted a bug—"

"Relax, this isn't about a bug. Can you stand up?" David said.

"I think so." Josh struggled to his feet. He was still groggy from the gas that had knocked him out in the elevator.

"Good, follow me."

Josh followed David and the two operatives out of the room with the holding cells and down a long hallway that led to the server room. At the server room door, David turned to the other two soldiers. "Wait here. Radio me if anyone enters the corridor."

Inside the server room, David resumed his brisk pace, and Josh had to almost jog to keep up. The station chief was just over six feet tall and muscular, not quite as beefy as some of the linebacker-esque ops guys, but big enough to give any drunken bar-brawler pause.

They snaked their way through the crowded server room, dodging tower after tower of metal cabinets with green, yellow, and red blinking lights. The room was cool, and the constant hum of the machines was slightly disorienting. The three-person IT group was constantly working on the servers—adding, removing, and replacing hardware. The place was a pigsty. Josh tripped over a cord, but before he hit the ground, David turned, caught him, and pushed him back to his feet.

"You all right?"

Josh nodded. "Yeah. This place is a mess."

David said nothing, but walked a bit more slowly the rest of the way to a standing metal storage cabinet at the back of the server room. David pushed the cabinet aside, revealing a silver door and a panel beside it. The red light of a palm scan flashed over his hand, and another panel opened and performed a facial and retinal scan. When it finished, the wall parted, revealing a dark metallic door that looked like something from a battleship.

David opened the door with a second palm scan and led Josh into a room probably half the size of a high school gymnasium. The cavern had concrete walls and their footsteps echoed loudly as they approached the center of the room, where a small glass box, about twelve feet by twelve feet, hung from thick twisted metal cords. The glass box was softly lit, and Josh couldn't see inside it, but he already knew what it was.

Josh had suspected the cell had such a room, but he'd never seen it in person. It was a quiet room. The entire Jakarta station headquarters was a kind of quiet room—it was shielded from every manner of listening device. There was no need for further precautions within the station—unless you didn't want another member of the cell to hear you.

There were certainly protocols that required it. He suspected the chief talked with other station chiefs via phone and video in this room. Maybe even with Central.

As they approached the room, a short flight of glass stairs descended and quickly retracted after they climbed into the room. A glass door closed behind them. A bank of computer screens hung on the far wall of the room, but other than that, Josh thought the room was surprisingly sparse: a simple fold-out table with four chairs, two phones and a conference speaker, and an old steel filing cabinet. The furniture was cheap and a bit out of place, like something you might see in the on-site trailer at a construction site.

"Take a seat," David said. He walked to the file cabinet and withdrew several folders.

"I have a report to make. It's significant—"

"I think you better let me start." David joined Josh at the table and placed the files between them.

"With due respect, what I have to report may change your entire perspective. It may cause a major reassessment. A reassessment of every active operation at Jakarta station and even how we analyze every—"

David held a hand up. "I already know what you're going to tell me."

"You do?"

"I do. You're going to tell me that the vast majority of the terror threats we're tracking, including operations in developed nations that we don't yet understand—aren't the work of a dozen *separate* terrorist and fundamentalist groups as we'd suspected."

When Josh said nothing, David continued, "You're going to tell me that Clocktower now believes that these groups are all simply different faces of one global super-group, an organization with a scale exceeding anyone's wildest projections."

"They already told you?"

"Yes. But not recently. I began putting the pieces together before I joined Clocktower. I was officially told when I made station chief."

Josh looked away. It wasn't exactly a betrayal, but realizing something this big had been kept from him—the head of analysis—was a punch in the gut. At the same time, he wondered if he should have put it all together, if David was disappointed that he hadn't figured it out on his own.

David seemed to sense Josh's disappointment. "For what it's worth, I've wanted to tell you for a while now, but it was need-to-know only. And there's something else you should know. Of the 240-or-so attendees at the analysts conference, 142 never made it home."

"What? I don't understand. They—"

"They didn't pass the test."

"The test..."

"The conference was the test. From the minute you arrived until you walked out, you were under video and audio surveillance. Like the suspects we interrogate here, the conference organizers were measuring voice stress, pupil dilation, eye movement, and a dozen other markers. In short—watching the analysts' reactions throughout the conference."

"To see if we would withhold information?"

"Yes, but more importantly, to see who already knew what was being presented; specifically, which analysts already knew there was a super-terror group behind the scenes. The conference was a Clocktower-wide mole hunt."

At that moment, the glass room around Josh seemed to disappear. He could hear David talking in the background, but he was lost in his thoughts. The conference was a perfect cover for a sting. All Clocktower agents, even analysts, were trained in standard counter-espionage methods. Beating a lie detector

48

was standard training. But telling a lie, as if it were true, was much easier than faking an emotional response to a surprise, and sustaining the reaction, with credible body metrics, for three days—it was impossible. But to test *every* chief analyst. The implication was...

"Josh, did you hear me?"

Josh looked up. "No, I'm sorry, it's a lot to take in... Clocktower has been compromised."

"Yes, and I need you to focus now. Things are happening quickly, and I need your help. The analyst test was the first step in Clocktower's firewall protocol. Around the world, right now, the chief analysts who returned from the conference are meeting with their station chiefs in quiet rooms just like this one, trying to figure out how to secure their cells."

"You think Jakarta Station has been compromised?"

"I'd be shocked if it wasn't. There's more. The analyst purge has set events in motion. The plan, Firewall Protocol, was to screen the analysts for moles and for the remaining chief analysts and station chiefs to work together to identify anyone who could be a double."

"Makes sense."

"It would have, but we've underestimated the scope of the breach. I need to tell you a little about how Clocktower is organized. You know about how many cells there are: 200 to 250 at any given time. You should know that we had already identified some of the chief analysts as moles—about sixty. They never made it to the conference."

"Then who were—"

"Actors. Mostly field agents who had worked as analysts before, anyone who could fake it. We had to. Some of the analysts already knew the approximate number of Clocktower cells, and the actors provided an operational benefit: they could facilitate the three-day lie-detection, ask pointed questions, elicit responses, get reactions."

"Unbelievable... How could we be so deeply compromised?"

"That's one of the questions we have to answer. There's more. Not all the cells are like Jakarta Station. The vast majority are little more than listening posts; they manage a small group of case officers and send Central the HUMINT and SIGINT they collect. A compromised listening post is bad—it means whoever this global enemy is, they have been using those cells to collect intel and maybe even send us bogus data."

"We could be essentially blind," Josh said.

"That's right. Our best-case scenario was that this enemy had co-opted our intelligence gathering in preparation for a massive attack. We now know that that's only half of it. Several of the major cells are also compromised. These are cells similar to Jakarta station, with intelligence gathering *and* significant covert ops forces. We are one of twenty major cells. These cells are the last line of defense, the thin red line that separates the world from whatever this enemy is planning."

"How many are compromised?"

"We don't know. But three major cells have already fallen—Karachi, Cape Town, and Mar del Plata have all reported that the cell's own special forces swept through their HQ, killing most of the analysts and the station chiefs. There have been no communications from them for hours. Satellite surveillance over Argentina confirms the destruction of the Mar del Plata HQ. The Cape Town insurgents were assisted by outside forces. As we speak, firefights are ongoing in Seoul, Delhi, Dhaka, and Lahore. Those stations may hold, but we should assume they will be lost as well. Right now our own special ops forces could be preparing to take over Jakarta Station, or it could be happening this second, outside this room, but I doubt that."

"Why?"

"I believe they'll wait for you to return. Given what you know, you're a liability. Whenever they attack, you'll be at the top of the target list. The morning briefing would be the ideal time for a strike; they're probably waiting for that."

Josh felt his mouth go dry. "That's why you grabbed me off

the elevator." He thought for a moment. "So what now, you want me to identify the threats on the staff before the briefing? We initiate a preemptive attack?"

"No," David said, shaking his head. "That was the original plan, but we're past that now. We have to assume Jakarta Station will fall. If we're compromised as badly as the other major cells, it's only a matter of time. We have to look at the big picture and try to figure out our adversary's endgame. We have to assume that one or more cells will survive and that they will be able to use anything we learn. If not, maybe one of the national agencies. But there's still one question you haven't asked, a very important one."

Josh thought for a second. "Why now? And why start with the analysts? Why didn't you clean the field operatives first?"

"Very good." David flipped open a folder. "Twelve days ago, I was contacted by an anonymous source who said two things. One, there was an imminent terrorist attack—on a scale we've never seen before. And two, Clocktower had been compromised." David arranged a few pages. "He included a list of sixty analysts that he claimed were compromised. We shadowed them for a few days and confirmed them making dead-drops and unauthorized communications. It checked out. The source said there might be more. The rest you know: the other station chiefs and I organized the analyst conference. We interrogated and quarantined the compromised analysts, replacing them with actors at the conference. Whoever the source is, he either didn't know about the field agents or didn't disclose it for his own reasons. The source refused to meet, and I received no other communications from him. We proceeded with the conference and after... the purge. The source was radio-silent. Then, late last night, he contacted me again. He said he wanted to deliver the other half of the intel he promised, details of a massive attack code-named Toba Protocol. We were supposed to meet this morning at Manggarai Station, but he didn't show. Someone with a bomb did. But I think he wanted to be there. A kid gave me a newspaper with this message right after the attack." David pushed a page across the table.

```
Toba Protocol is real.
4+12+47 = 4/5; Jones
7+22+47 = 3/8; Anderson
10+4+47 = 5/4; Ames
```

"Some kind of code," Josh said.

"Yes, it's surprising. The other messages were straightforward. But now it makes sense."

"I don't understand."

"Whatever the code is, it's the real message—it's what the entire setup has been about. The source wanted the analyst purge to happen so he could send his coded message at the right time—and know it would be decoded by someone who wasn't a double agent—namely you. He wanted us focused on cleaning up the analysts and delaying the fireworks until he could send this message. Had we known how thoroughly we had been compromised, we would have quarantined the field operatives first and sent Clocktower into total lockdown. We wouldn't be having this conversation."

"Yeah, but why even bother with a code? Why not send the message in the open like the previous communications?"

"It's a good question. He must be under surveillance as well. Communicating whatever he's trying to tell us in the open must have repercussions; maybe it would cause his death or speed up this terrorist attack. So whoever is watching him assumes we don't know what the message says yet. That may be why they haven't taken more of the cells down—they still think they can contain Clocktower."

"Makes sense."

"It does, but one question still bothered me: why me?"

Josh thought for a moment. "Right, why not the director of Clocktower, all the other Clocktower station chiefs, or simply alert all the world's intelligence agencies? They would have more far-reaching power to stop an attack. Maybe tipping them would start the attack early—just like sending the message in the open. Or... you could be in a unique position to stop the attack..." Josh looked up. "Or you know something."

"Very good. I mentioned earlier that I began investigating this super-terrorist group before I joined Clocktower." David stood, walked to the filing cabinet and withdrew two more folders. "I'm going to show you something I've been working on for over ten years, something I've never shown anyone else; not even Clocktower."

13

Kate leaned back in the chair and thought about her options. She would have to tell the investigator how the trial had begun. Even if he didn't believe it, she had to get it on the record in case they tried her. "Stop," she said.

The man paused at the door.

Kate set her chair legs down and put her arms on the table. "There's a very good reason why my trial adopted those children. There's something you should understand. When I came to Jakarta, I expected to run this trial like any other trial in America. That was my first mistake. We failed... and we... changed our approach."

The little man turned from the door, sat down, and listened as Kate described how she had spent weeks preparing for patient recruitment.

Kate's organization had hired a Contract Research Organization (CRO) to run their trial, just as they would have in the US. In the US, pharmaceutical companies focus on developing a new drug or therapy, and when they have something promising, they often outsource the management of the trial to CROs. CROs find medical clinics with doctors interested in the trial. The clinics, or sites, then enroll willing patients into the trial, administer the new drug/therapy, then test them periodically for any health problems—adverse events. The CRO keeps close tabs on every site in the trial, reporting results to the sponsor/ research organization, who makes their own reports to the FDA or governing body in countries around the world. The endgame was a trial with the desired therapeutic effect without any negative or adverse effects. It was a long road, and less than 1% of drugs that worked in the lab ever made it to pharmacy shelves.

There was only one problem: Jakarta, and Indonesia at large, had no autism clinics and only a handful of specialty practices focusing on developmental disorders. Those clinics weren't experienced in clinical research—a dangerous situation for patients. The pharmaceutical industry was tiny in Indonesia, mostly because the market was small (Indonesia imported mostly generic drugs), so very few doctors were ever contacted about research.

The CRO came up with a novel concept: engage parents directly and run a clinic to administer the therapy. Kate and the trial's lead investigator, Dr. John Helms, met with the CRO at length, searching for any alternatives. There were none. Kate urged Dr. Helms to move forward with the plan, and finally, he agreed.

They built a list of families within one hundred miles of Jakarta that had a child on the autism spectrum. Kate booked an auditorium at one of the nicest hotels in town and invited the families to a presentation.

She wrote, re-wrote, and revised the trial booklet for days on end. Finally, Ben had barged into her office and said he would leave the trial if she didn't just let it go. Kate relented, the trial booklet went to an ethics committee, then the printer, and they prepared for the event.

When the day came, she stood by the door, ready to greet each family as they arrived. She wished her hands would stop sweating. She wiped them on her pants every few minutes. First impressions are everything. Confidence, trust, expertise.

She waited. Would they have enough booklets? They had one thousand on hand, and although they had sent only six hundred invitations, both parents could show up. Other families could show up—there was no reliable database or registry of affected families in Indonesia. What would they do? She told Ben to be ready to use the hotel copier just in case; he could prepare copies of the highlights while she talked.

Fifteen minutes past the hour. The first two mothers appeared. Kate dried her hands again before shaking vigorously and talking just a little too loud. "Great to have you here—thank you for coming—no, this is the place—take a seat, we'll get started any moment—"

Thirty minutes past the hour.

An hour past the start time.

She circled the six mothers, making small talk. "I don't know what happened—what day did you get the invitation?—No, we invited others—I think it must be a problem with the post..."

Finally, Kate led the six attendees to a small conference room in the hotel to make it less awkward for everyone. She gave a short presentation as, one by one, each of the mothers excused themselves, saying they had children to pick up, jobs to get back to, and the like.

Downstairs at the hotel bar, Dr. Helms got drunk as a skunk. When Kate joined him, the gray-haired man leaned close and said, "I *told* you it wouldn't work. We'll never recruit in this town, Kate. Why the—hey-ho, barkeep, yeah, over here, I'll have another, uh-huh same thing, good man—What was I saying? Oh yes, we need to wrap it up, quickly. I've got an offer in Oxford. God, I miss Oxford, it's too blasted humid here, feels like a sauna all the time. And I must admit, I did my best work there. Speaking of..." He leaned even closer. "I don't want to jinx it by saying the words No. Bel. Prize. But... I've *heard* my name's been submitted—this could be my year, Kate. Can't wait to forget about this debacle. When will I learn? I guess I've got a soft heart when it comes to a good cause."

Kate wanted to point out that his soft heart had certainly driven a hard bargain—three times her salary and his name first on any publication or patents, despite the fact that the entire study was based on her post-doctoral research—but she held her tongue and swallowed the last of her Chardonnay.

That night she called Martin. "I can't—"

"Stop right there, Kate. You can do anything you set your mind to. You always have. There are two hundred million people in Indonesia and almost seven billion people on this little world. And as many as half of one percent could be somewhere on the autism spectrum—that's thirty-five million people—the population of Texas. You've sent letters to six hundred families. Don't give up. I won't let you. I'll make a call tomorrow morning to Immari Research's head of funding; they'll continue funding you—whether that hack John Helms is on the study or not."

The call reminded Kate of the night she had called him from San Francisco, when Martin had promised her Jakarta would be a great place to start over and to continue her research. Maybe he would be right after all.

The next morning, she walked into the lab and told Ben to order a lot more study booklets. And to find translators. They were going out to the villages. They would widen the net—and they wouldn't wait for families to come to them. She fired the CRO. She ignored Dr. Helms's protests.

Two weeks later, they loaded up three vans with four researchers, eight translators, and crate after crate of the trial books printed in five languages: Indonesian/Malay, Javanese, Sundanese, Madurese, and Betawi. Kate had agonized over the language choices as well: over seven hundred distinct languages were spoken throughout Indonesia, but in the end, she had chosen the five most commonly spoken in Jakarta and throughout the island of Java. Irony aside, she wasn't going to let her autism trial fail due to communication problems.

As with the hotel in downtown Jakarta, her preparations were an entirely wasted effort. Upon entering the first village, Kate and her team were amazed: there were no children with autism. The villagers weren't interested in the booklets.

The translators told her that no one had ever seen a child with these problems.

It didn't make any sense. There should have been at least two, maybe three potential participants in every village, possibly more.

At the next village, Kate noticed one of the translators, an older man, leaning against the van while the team and remaining translators went door to door.

"Hey, why aren't you working?" Kate had asked.

The man shrugged. "Because it won't make any difference."

"The hell it won't. Now you better—"

The man held up his hands. "I mean no offense, ma'am. I only mean you ask the wrong questions. And you ask the wrong people."

Kate scrutinized the man. "Okay. Who would you ask? And what would you ask them?"

The man pushed off from the van, gestured for Kate to follow, and walked deeper into the village, past the nicer homes. On the outskirts, he knocked on the first door, and when a short woman answered, he spoke quickly, in a harsh tone, occasionally pointing at Kate. The scene made her cringe. She self-consciously pulled the lapels of her white coat together. She had agonized over her wardrobe as well, ultimately deciding that projecting a credible, clinical appearance was the order of the day. She could only imagine how she looked to the villagers, who were mostly dressed in clothes they had made themselves from scraps taken home from the sweatshops or the remains of partially disintegrated hand-me-downs.

She realized the woman was gone, and Kate stepped forward to question the translator, but he held up a hand as the woman returned to the door, pushing three children out to stand before them. They stared at their feet and stood still as statues. The translator walked from child to child, looking them up and down. Kate shifted her weight a bit, contemplating what to do. The children were healthy; none showed even the slightest signs of autism. At the last child, the man bent down and shouted again. The mother quickly said something, but he yelled at her, and she fell silent. The child nervously said three words. The translator said something, and the child repeated the words. Kate wondered if they were names. Possibly places?

The translator stood and began pointing and yelling at the woman again. She shook her head furiously, repeating a phrase over and over. After several minutes of the translator's badgering, she looked down and began speaking in low tones. She pointed to another shack. The translator's voice was soft for the first time, and the woman seemed relieved by his words. She herded the children back inside, almost cutting the last one in half as she quickly closed the door.

The scene at the second shack unfolded much like the first: the translator shouted and pointed, Kate stood awkwardly, and the nervous villager presented her four children, then waited with worry in her eyes. This time, when the translator asked one of the children his questions, the child said five words, names Kate believed. The mother protested, but the translator ignored her, pressing the child. When he answered, the large man sprang up, pushed the children and their mother aside, and burst through the door. Kate was caught off guard, but when the mother and children followed into the home, she did as well.

The shack was a crowded, three-room hovel. She almost tripped walking through it. At the rear of the home, she found the translator and woman arguing more vehemently than before. At their feet, a small child, a gaunt child, was tied to a wooden beam that held the roof up. He was gagged, but she could hear low rhythmic noises coming from his mouth as he rocked back and forth, hitting his head on the beam.

Kate grabbed the translator's arm. "What is this? Tell me what's going on here."

The man looked from Kate back to the mother, seemingly caught between his master and a caged animal whose volume and hysterics grew by the second. Kate squeezed the man's arm and jerked him toward her, and he began explaining. "She says it is not her fault. He is a disobedient child. He will not eat her food. He will not do as she says. He does not play with the children. She says he does not even answer to his own name."

They were all classic signs of autism; a severe case. Kate looked down at the child.

The man added, "She insists it is not her fault. She says she has kept him longer than the others, but she cannot—"

"What others?"

The translator conversed with the woman in a normal tone, then turned to Kate. "Beyond the village. There's a place where they take the children who won't respect their parents, the ones that disobey constantly, that won't be a part of their family."

"Take me there."

The translator coaxed more information out of the woman, then pointed toward the door for them to leave. The woman called after them. The man turned to Kate. "She wants to know if we will take him."

"Tell her yes, and to untie him and that we will return."

The translator led Kate to a patch of deserted forest just south of the village. After an hour of looking they had still found nothing, but they continued searching. Occasionally, Kate heard the leaves and trees rustle as game moved about. The sun would set soon, and she wondered what this forest would be like then. Indonesia was entirely tropical; the temperature was nearly constant from day to day and season to season. The Javanese jungles were dangerous, untamed areas, home to all sorts of snakes, large cats, and insects. No place for a child.

In the distance, she heard screaming and the translator call to her, "Dr. Warner, come quickly!"

She dashed across the dense forest, tripping once and fighting her way through the overgrowth. She found the translator holding a child, even more gaunt than the boy at the shack. Even with his dark brown skin, she could see the dirt and grime caked on his face. He fought the translator's hold like a caged banshee.

"Are there any others?" Kate asked. She saw a lean-to, a ragged shelter about fifty yards away. Was there a child lying there? She started for it.

"Do not go there, Dr. Warner." He tightened his grip on the child. "There are no others... to take back. Please help me."

She took the child's other arm, and they escorted him back to the vans. They gathered the research team, then retrieved the child that had been tied to the beam, who they learned was named Adi. The child from the forest had no name, and they knew they would never find his parents or anyone who would ever own up to what had been done to him. Kate named him Surya.

When the research team assembled at the van, Kate cornered her translator. "Now I want you to tell me what you did back there—exactly what you said."

"I think maybe you do not want to be knowing, Doctor."

"I think I do definitely want to be knowing. Now start talking."

The man sighed. "I told them you are a humanitarian organization who is doing child welfare—"

"What?"

The man straightened. "That is what they are thinking you are anyway, so it makes no difference. They do not know what this clinical trial is. They have never heard of such a thing. Look around you; these people live just as they did a thousand years ago. I tell them you have to see their children and that you will help any that need help. Still they do not trust us. Some believe they will get in trouble, but many simply worry word will get around. Here, it is a dangerous thing to have a child with problems; people keep them out of sight. If word gets around, the other children will have problems finding a mate—they will say, 'maybe you have his child and he is a problem like his father's brother.' They will say, 'it is in his blood.' But the children tell the truth when I ask them to name their brothers and sisters. Children do not yet know to lie about this."

Kate considered the man's story. It had certainly worked. She turned to the team: "Okay. This is our new approach."

Dr. Helms stepped toward Kate and the translator. "I won't do it. Lying to a parent to enroll a child in a clinical trial violates basic medical ethics and is, simply, morally wrong." He paused for effect. "Regardless of their circumstances or the community's social norms." He stared at Kate and then the other staff.

Kate interrupted his revelry. "Suit yourself. You can wait in the van, and so can anyone else who wants to leave these kids here to die."

The doctor turned to her to fire another volley, but Ben cut him off. "Well, I'm in. I hate waiting in the van. And killing kids, for that matter." He turned and started packing up the gear, only pausing to ask the other staff for help.

The remaining three assistants reluctantly began to help, and only then did Kate realize how on the fence they had been. She made a mental note to thank Ben, but the pace of the day soon picked up, and she forgot.

At the next village, the team tossed out the trial booklets, but when the villagers began collecting them, the team shifted to handing the booklets out—as insulation for the villagers' homes. The act of goodwill helped to corroborate their story as aid workers, and it was nice for Kate to see the booklets she'd spent so much time on go to good use.

Dr. Helms continued protesting, but the rest of the staff ignored him. As the vans filled up with children, his protests tapered off, and by the end of the day, it was clear to everyone that he regretted his actions.

Back in Jakarta, he approached Kate in her office after the other staff had left. "Listen, Kate, I've been meaning to speak with you. After, um, some consideration... and to be frank, after seeing some of the effects of this work, on, uh, the children... I have to say I've decided that we are well within the norms of medical ethics and my personal comfort zone and thus, I am, well, quite comfortable leading this trial." He moved to sit down.

Kate didn't look up from her document. "Don't sit down, John. There's something I've been meaning to tell you as well.

Out there in the field, you put your safety—your personal reputation—ahead of those children's lives. That's unacceptable. We both know I can't fire you. But I simply can't work with you on a trial where children's lives are at stake. If something happened to one of them, if you put them in danger, I couldn't live with it. I informed the trial sponsor, Immari Research, that I would be leaving, and the funniest thing happened." She looked up from the paper. "They told me they wouldn't fund the trial without me. So you can either resign or I will, in which case you'll lose your funding, and I'll simply start the same trial with a different name. Oh, and by the way, the movers are coming to pack up your office tomorrow—so whatever you decide, you'll have to find a new lease."

She walked out of the office and left for the night. The next day, Helms left Jakarta for good, and Kate became the project's sole investigator. Kate asked Martin to make a few phone calls, some favors were exchanged, and the study became the legal guardian of every child enrolled.

When Kate finished her story, the interrogator stood and said, "You expect me to believe that? We're not savages, Miss Warner. Good luck telling that story to a jury in Jakarta." He left the tiny room before Kate could respond.

Outside the interrogation room, the small man walked up to the rotund police chief, who put his sweaty arm around him and said, "How did it go, Paku?"

"I think she's ready, boss."

14

Josh looked out of the glass room at the concrete walls beyond as he tried to digest what David had told him. Clocktower was compromised. Several major cells were already fighting for their survival. Jakarta Station would soon be under attack, and on top of that, there was an imminent terrorist attack on a global scale.

And David needed Josh to unravel a code to stop it.

No pressure.

David returned from the filing cabinet, and sat down at the table again. "I've been working on a theory I formed ten years ago, just after 9/11."

"You think this attack is connected to 9/11?" Josh asked.

"I do."

"You think this is an Al Qaeda operation?"

"Not necessarily. I believe Al Qaeda only carried out the 9/11 attacks. I believe another group, a global corporation called Immari International, actually planned, funded, and benefited from the attack. I think it was a cover for various archaeological digs Immari conducted in Afghanistan and Iraq, and a very sophisticated heist. A robbery."

Josh looked at the table. Had David lost it? This sort of 9/11 conspiracy-theory stuff was fodder for internet forums, not serious counterterrorism work.

David seemed to recognize Josh's reluctance. "Look, I know it sounds farfetched, but hear me out. After 9/11, I spent almost a year in a hospital and then rehab. That's a lot of time to think. A lot of things about the attacks made no sense to me. Why attack New York first? Why not hit the White House, Congress, the CIA, and the NSA simultaneously? Those four plane crashes would have crippled the country, especially our defensive capabilities. It would have thrown us into utter chaos. And why use only four planes? Surely they could have trained more pilots. They could have hijacked thirty planes that morning if they simply took planes from Dulles and National Airports in DC, from Baltimore, maybe Richmond. You've got Atlanta pretty close; Hartsfield-Jackson is the busiest airport in the world. Who knows, they could have probably crashed a hundred planes that day before passengers started fighting back. And they had to have known that crashing planes was a one-time-only tactic, so they would have maximized the impact."

Josh nodded, still skeptical. "It's an interesting question."

"And there were others. Why strike on a day when you know the President is out of town, in an elementary school in Florida? Clearly the goal wasn't to remove our fighting capabilities— sure the Pentagon was hit and many brave Americans died, but the overall effect was to really, really piss the Pentagon and the armed forces off—the whole country for that matter. After 9/11, America had an appetite for war the likes of which it had never seen before. There was one other striking effect: the stock market crashed, a historical crash. New York is the financial capital of the world; hitting it makes sense if you want to do one thing: crash the stock market. The attacks did two things really well: ensured there was a war, a big one—*and* crashed the stock market."

"I never looked at it that way," Josh said.

"Things look a lot different when you spend almost a year in a hospital, learning to walk by day and asking why by night. I couldn't do much research on terrorists from a hospital bed, so I focused on the financial angle. I started looking at who the big winners were from the financial collapse. Who was betting against American stocks. What companies were shorting the market, who owned put options, who made a fortune. It was a long list. Then I started looking at who benefited from the wars, especially private security contractors and oil and gas interests. The list got shorter. And something else intrigued me: the attacks nearly guaranteed a war in Afghanistan. Maybe whatever this group wanted was there and they needed a cover to go in and search for it. Or maybe it was in Iraq. Maybe both. I knew I needed to get out in the field to find some real answers."

David took a breath and continued. "By 2004, I was back on my feet. I applied to the CIA that year but was turned down. I trained for another year, got turned down again in 2005, and trained some more. I thought about joining the Army, but I knew I would need to be part of covert ops to get real answers."

Josh looked down, taking it in, seeing David in a completely different light now. He had always thought of the station chief as this invincible super-soldier, had always assumed that was all David had ever been. The idea of him lying broken in a hospital bed for a year, of him being *turned down* as a field operative—twice—was slightly jarring.

"What?" David said.

"It's nothing... I just... assumed you were a career operative. That you were with the agency on 9/11."

An amused smiled crossed David's lips. "No, not even close. I was a grad student, actually. At Columbia, if you can believe that. Might be why the CIA kept rejecting me—didn't want anyone overthinking things in the field units. But apparently the third time's the charm—they took me in 2006. Maybe they had lost enough operatives or enough had joined the private contractors; whatever the reason, I was glad to be in Afghanistan. I found my answers. The short list I had, the three companies, were all subsidiaries of one company: Immari International. Their security division, Immari Security, coordinated their operations, but the funds from 9/11 went into several of their front companies. And I found something else. A plan for a new

66

attack, code-named Toba Protocol." David pointed at the file. "That file is all I have on that attack. It's not much."

Josh opened the file. "This is why you joined Clocktower, to investigate Immari and Toba Protocol?"

"Partly. Clocktower was the perfect platform for me. I knew back then that Immari was behind 9/11, that they had made a fortune from the attacks, and that they were actively looking for something in the mountains of eastern Afghanistan and Pakistan. But they got to me before I could figure out the big picture. They almost killed me in northern Pakistan. I was officially listed as killed in action. It was the perfect opportunity to exit. I needed a new identity and somewhere to continue my work. I had never heard of Clocktower before I was in-theater in Afghanistan, but I took refuge here. It was perfect. We all come to Clocktower for our own reasons; it was the key to my survival at the time and the tool I needed to finally learn the truth about Immari and Toba. I never told anyone my real motivation, except the director. He took me in and helped me start Jakarta Station four years ago. I hadn't made much substantial progress on the Immari question until a week ago when the source contacted me."

"That's why the source picked you."

"Apparently. He knows about my investigation. He knew I would have this file. It may hold the key to decrypting the code. What I know is that Immari Corporation is somehow involved in 9/11, maybe in other terrorist plots before and after, and that they're working on something much, much bigger: Toba Protocol. It's why I chose Jakarta—the closest major city to Mount Toba. I think it's a reference to where the attack will start."

"A logical assumption. What do we know about Toba Protocol?" Josh said.

"Not a lot. Apart from a few references, there's one memo about it. It's a report about urbanization, transportation infrastructure, and the potential to reduce the total human population. Whatever Toba is, I believe that's the goal: to drastically reduce the total human population."

"That limits the possibilities somewhat. A terrorist attack that could reduce the global population would have to be biological; maybe a drastic change in the environment, or inciting a new world war. We're not talking about suicide bombers; it's something bigger."

David nodded. "Much bigger, and probably something we would never expect. Jakarta is the perfect place to start an attack—the population density is high and there are tons of expatriates here. The start of an attack would send wealthy foreigners in Jakarta to the airport and from there to almost every country in the world."

David motioned to the bank of computer screens behind Josh. "The computers behind you are connected to Central, to our own servers, and to the remaining cells. They have everything we know about what's going on around the world, the various terrorist groups and organizations we now know are fronts for Immari International. It's not much. Start there, get up to speed, then move on quickly to the latest local intel. If there's anything going on here in Jakarta, we have a responsibility to investigate it first. We will need to hand off what we know in case Jakarta Station falls. Think outside the box. Whatever is going on, it may not fit any normal patterns. Look for something we wouldn't suspect—like Saudi nationals taking flying lessons in Germany, then moving to the US; like someone in Oklahoma buying tons of fertilizer, someone who isn't a farmer."

"What's in the rest of the folders?" Josh said.

David pushed a folder across the desk. "This folder contains the rest of the information on Immari that I collected before I joined Clocktower."

"It's not in the computer?"

"No. I never turned it over to Clocktower either. You'll see why. The other envelope contains a letter, from me to you. You should open it when I die. It will provide you with instructions."

Josh started to say something, but David interrupted. "There's one last thing."

David stood and retrieved a small case from the corner of the room. He set the case on the table. "This room and the outer chamber will give you some protection, and, I hope, enough time to find something and decode the message. Clocktower HQ is the last place they'll be looking for you. Nevertheless, I doubt we have a lot of time. Send whatever you find to my mobile. The top right monitor shows a camera feed. That camera is over the door, looking out into the server room, so you'll know if someone is trying to get in here. As you know, there are no cameras in the main HQ, for security reasons, so you may not have much notice." He opened the case and took out a handgun. He slid the magazine into the handle of the gun and placed it on the table in front of Josh. "You know how to use this?"

Josh eyed the gun and leaned back in the chair. "Uh, yes. Well, I had basic training when I joined the Agency twelve years ago, but I haven't used one since. So… no, not really." He wanted to say, "If covert ops forces get in this room, what kind of chance do I really have?", but he didn't; he knew David was showing him the gun to make him feel safer. Not being scared to death would clear his mind and help him do his job, but Josh felt that was only half of the chief's motivation.

"If you need to use it, you pull the slide back. That chambers a round. When you're empty, you click here, the magazine slides out. You put another one in and press this button, the slide returns and chambers the first round from the new magazine. But if that door is breached, there's something you have to do before you use the gun."

"Wipe the computers?"

"Exactly. And burn this folder as well as the letter." David pointed to a small metal wastebasket and handed him a small butane torch from the gun box.

"What else is in the box?" Josh thought he knew, but he asked anyway.

The Jakarta Station chief paused for a seconds, then reached into the box and took out a small capsule.

"Do I swallow it?"

"No. If the time comes, you bite into it. The cyanide works pretty quick, maybe three or four seconds." David handed Josh the capsule. "Keep it with you. I hope you won't need it. This is a very hard room to get into."

David put the gun back in the box and returned it to the corner of the room. "Let me know as soon as you have something." He turned and walked toward the door.

Josh stood and said, "What are you going to do?"

"Buy us some time."

15

Kate looked up as the interrogation room door opened, revealing a fat, sweaty man. He carried a folder in one hand and extended his other hand to her. "Dr. Warner, I am Police Chief Eddi Kusnadi. I ho—"

"I've been waiting here for hours. Your men have interrogated me about useless details of my study, threatened to imprison me. I want to know what you're doing to find those kidnapped children."

"Doctor, you don't understand the situation here. We are a small department."

"Then call the national police. Or—"

"The national police have problems of their own, Doctor, and they don't include finding retarded children."

"Don't call them retarded."

"They're not retarded?" He flipped the file open. "Our notes say your clinic is testing a new drug for retarded—"

"They're not retarded. Their brains work differently than other people's. Just like my metabolism works differently than yours."

The corpulent chief looked down at his body, as if trying to find his metabolism to examine and compare it with Kate's.

"You either begin searching for those children, or release me so I can."

"We can't release you," Kusnadi said.

"Why not?"

"We haven't ruled you out as a suspect."

"That's absurd—"

"I know, Doctor, I know, trust me. But what would you have me do? I can't tell my investigators who is and is not a suspect. That would be improper. I have, however, convinced them to keep you in this holding cell. They insisted I move you to the common holding area. Those are coed and, I'm afraid, not well-monitored." He paused a moment, then opened the file again. "But I think I can at least delay that for a while. In the meantime, I have some questions of my own. Our records say you bought a condo here in Jakarta. Paid cash, the equivalent of seven hundred thousand US dollars." He looked up at her, and when she said nothing, he continued. "Our bank contact says you keep a checking account with an average balance of three hundred thousand, US-equivalent, dollars. That account receives periodic transfers from a bank in the Cayman Islands."

"My bank balance has nothing to do with this."

"I'm sure it doesn't. But you can see how it looks to my investigators. How did you get so much money, if I may ask?"

"I inherited it."

The chief raised his eyebrows and seemed to brighten. "Ah, from your grandparents?"

"No, from my father. Look, we're wasting time here."

"What did he do?"

"Who?"

"Your father."

"Banking, I think, or he was an investor. I don't know, I was very young."

"I see." The chief nodded. "I believe we can help each other, Doctor. We can convince my investigators that you are not involved in the kidnapping and give my department the resources it desperately needs to find these re—these, ah… helpless children."

Kate stared at him. It all made sense now. "I'm listening."

"I believe you, Dr. Warner. But as I say, my investigators, they look at the evidence, and they know what a jury will think, and between me and you, Dr. Warner, I think maybe, a little bit, they dislike foreigners, maybe especially Americans. I believe the only way to really ensure your safety and to get what we both want is to find these children. That will clear your name."

"So what are you waiting for?"

"As I said before, Dr. Warner, we are a small department. Finding these children... I would need more resources, people outside my department. But, I am sorry to say, an investigation like this would cost a lot, probably two million dollars. Ah, US dollars. But if I call in some favors, I think we can do it for one point five million. But time is of the essence, my dear Doctor. The children could be anywhere by now. I can only hope they are still alive."

"One point five million dollars."

The chief nodded.

"You'll have it. But you release me first."

"I would like nothing more, Doctor, believe me. But promises made by suspects in interrogation rooms..." He lifted his hands.

"Fine, get me a phone and the details of your—the bank account. And get me a car."

"Right away, Doctor." He smiled, stood, and left.

He left Kate in the interrogation room alone. She sat at the table again, put a knee up in the chair, and ran her hand through her blond hair. The woman in the mirrored wall looked nothing like the hopeful scientist who had moved to Jakarta four years ago.

The chief shut the door to the interrogation room. One point five million! He could retire. His whole family could retire. One point five million... Could he have gotten more, maybe two, or two point five? Three million? She could have more. Much more. She agreed to one point five instantly. Maybe he could go back and say he'd have to hire more people. It will cost four million. He would have taken two hundred fifty thousand; he had expected to get less. He stood in front of the interrogation room and pondered what to do.

He wouldn't go back immediately. He could soften her up even more. A few hours in the drunk tank, with the cameras off. He'd have to be careful—he didn't want her running to the US Embassy afterward—but if he was careful, he could make some real money today.

16

Josh glanced at the red dots on the positioning screen. In the hour since David had left, the twenty-four red dots—representing all of Jakarta Station's field operatives—had moved from Station HQ to locations across the city. Now the map showed four groups of six dots each.

Josh knew three of the locations well: they were Jakarta Station's safe houses. The eighteen agents at these locations must be on David's suspect list. The dots at the safe houses moved about slowly, turning back when they reached the walls that held them, like an accused man pacing a holding cell, waiting to hear his fate.

The strategy was sound: David had divided the possible enemy forces and given himself time to see them coming, if they did attack. When they attacked. Seeing the dots on the map had given Josh a sense of dread, had made the threat real. It was happening. The battle for Jakarta Station was only a matter of time. At some point, the dots would break free from the safe houses, descend on David's group of six soldiers, then come back to HQ to take care of Josh.

David had simply bought them time. Time for Josh to sift the day's local intel and work on the code—to find something. And he wasn't sure if he had.

He watched the sat video again. It was all he had. What if he was wrong?

He ran his hand through his hair. It was certainly outside the box. But if it was nothing…

Intelligence work often came down to instinct. The van, the operation, it didn't feel right to Josh.

He dialed David and said, "I think I have something."

"Go ahead," David said.

"A kidnapping—two kids from a medical clinic. Reported to Jakarta PD several hours ago. Clocktower flagged it as a low-priority local incident. But the van is a commercial vehicle registered to a Hong-Kong-based dummy corporation that is a known Immari front. And frankly, it doesn't look like locals; this was a professional kidnapping. Usually we'd file it under standard kidnapping and ransom, but Immari wouldn't bother with a K&R. I'm still digging, but I'm ninety-nine percent sure this is an Immari operation, and a high-priority one given how overt it was—grabbing the kids during the day, and with a van they knew we would trace. It means they couldn't wait."

"So what does it mean?"

"I'm not sure yet. The strange thing is that it looks like another Immari company, Immari Research, funds the clinic. The money for the building and its monthly expenses is paid from a Jakarta-based holding corporation: Immari Jakarta. There are several references to it in your files. The company's history dates back almost two hundred years. It was a subsidiary of the Dutch East India Company during the colonial era. It could be Immari's major operating center here in Southeast Asia."

"Doesn't make sense. Why would one Immari unit take kids from another? Maybe an internal feud? What do we know about the staff at the clinic?"

"Not much. There aren't many of them. A few lab techs, one of them killed during the incident. A rotating staff of nannies for the kids. Mostly locals, not connected. And the lead scientist," he pulled up a file of Dr. Katherine Warner, "she was there during the breach, possibly incapacitated. No one left for over an hour. Local police have her now at a Jakarta substation."

"Have they put out any interagency alerts on the kids?"

"No."

"Public APBs?"

"Nope. But I have a theory. We have a source in the West Jakarta Police. He filed a report fifteen minutes ago, says the police chief is extorting an American national—female. I assume it's Dr. Warner."

"Hmm. What does the clinic do?"

"It's a research facility, actually. Genetic research. They're studying new therapies for children with autism, basically anyone with a developmental disorder."

"Doesn't exactly scream international terrorism."

"Agree."

"So what's the working theory here? What are we looking at?"

"Honestly, I have no idea. I haven't gotten too deep into the weeds on this one, but one thing jumps out: the study hasn't filed any patents."

"Why is that significant? You think they're not doing research?"

"No, I'm pretty sure they are, just based on the equipment they've imported and the setup. But it's not for the money. If they wanted to commercialize what they're studying, they would patent it first. That's standard procedure for clinical trials. You find a compound in a lab, patent it, then test it. The patent prevents the competition from stealing a sample from a trial and patenting it first, cutting you off from the market. You would only test something without a patent if you didn't want the world to know about it. And Jakarta makes sense to do that. A US-based trial with any patients would legally require an application to the FDA and disclosure of the trial therapy."

"So they're developing a bio weapon?"

"Maybe. But before today, the clinic hasn't had any incidents. They've registered no fatalities, so if they are testing it on the kids, it would make it the least effective bio weapon of all time. Based on what I can see, the research is legit. And well-intentioned. In fact, if they did achieve their research goal, it would be a huge medical breakthrough."

"Which would also make it a great cover. But one question: why steal from yourself? If Immari funds the clinic and runs the clinic, why would they need to use their own people to steal the kids? Maybe the researcher got cold feet about the weapon, about what they're doing?" David said.

"Could be."

"Does the source at Jakarta PD have the authority to release the doctor?"

"No, apparently he's a little lower on the totem pole."

"Do we have a file on the chief?"

"Stand by." Josh searched Clocktower's database, and when the chief's file appeared, he leaned back in his chair. "Yeah, we've got a file. Wow."

"Send it to my mobile command center. Have you gone through all of the local intel yet?"

"Yeah, this was the only thing that really jumped out. But there is something else." Josh had debated whether to mention it, but like the video of the kidnapping, it didn't feel right. "None of the other cells have reported being attacked, and Central hasn't released any advisories. There's been nothing in the news either—nothing since the fighting in Karachi, Cape Town, and Mar del Plata. All the cells are quiet, releasing routine reports as if nothing is going on."

"Speculation?" David said.

"Two possibilities: either they're waiting for something, maybe our next move, or..."

"The rest of the cells fell without a fight."

"Yeah. We may be the last major cell," Josh said.

"I want you to work on the code—as quickly as you can."

17

Immari Corp. Research Complex
Outside Burang, China
Tibet Autonomous Region

Dr. Shen Chang tried to relax as the videoconference connected.

When the man appeared, Chang swallowed hard and said, "The project director ordered me to contact you, Dr. Grey. We followed the protocol and research provided—to the letter—I don't know what—"

"I'm sure you did, Dr. Chang. But the result was very surprising. Why did the children survive and not the adults?"

"We're not sure. We've run tests on the children. They do show sustained Atlantis Gene activation."

"Is it possible the therapy won't work on adults?"

"Yes, perhaps. The therapy is a retrovirus that inserts a gene into the subject's genetic code. It's not a significant genetic change, but it does have a cascade effect at the epigenetic level, turning on and off a series of other, preexisting genes in the host. There are no physiological effects—not that we've been able to observe—but there is a massive change in the brain. The gene essentially re-wires the subject's brain. Neuroplasticity, the ability for the brain to re-wire or adapt, decreases with age—that's why it's harder to learn new things as we grow older. We've explored the idea that adults won't respond to the therapy because the gene activation can't trigger the changes in the brain—essentially, the genetic therapy virus tries to re-wire the brain, but the circuit boards are already hardwired. Have been since shortly after childhood."

"Is it possible that the adult subjects didn't have the precursor genes to affect the brain changes?"

"No, all the adult subjects had the cascade genes. As you know, we have known about these genes for some time, and we test every subject at our hiring facility in China. The adults should have survived the test."

"Is it possible the therapy only works on brains affected by autism?"

Chang hadn't considered this possibility. Dr. Grey was an evolutionary biologist with an interest in paleobiology, and he was Chang's boss's boss, all the way at the top of the Immari food chain. Chang had assumed this call wouldn't focus on the science. He had expected a tongue-lashing from this über-boss for his failed efforts.

He focused on Grey's hypothesis. "Yes, it certainly could be. Autism is fundamentally a disorder of brain wiring, especially in the areas that control communication and social understanding. And other areas are affected. Some affected individuals are highly intelligent with special abilities; others are on the complete opposite end of the spectrum: they can't even live independently. Autism is really a catch-all category for a variety of differences in brain wiring. We would have to look into this, and it could take some time. We would likely need more test subjects."

"Time we don't have, but we might be able to get more children. Although these are the only subjects we know of with Atlantis Gene activation. Let me look into that. Is there anything you haven't told me? Any other theories? There are no bad ideas at this point, Dr. Chang."

Chang did have another idea. Something he hadn't voiced to the rest of the team. "I've personally wondered whether the adults and the children were treated with the same therapy."

"A problem with replicating Dr. Warner's research?"

"No. As I say, we followed her protocol to the letter—I stand by that. I'm wondering if Dr. Warner... treated these children with something different, something not in her official notes or the trial protocol."

Grey seemed to consider Chang's idea. "That's very interesting."

"Would it be possible to speak with Dr. Warner?"

"I'm not sure… let me get back to you on that. Have any of the other team members voiced this concern?"

"No, not that I know of."

"For now, I'd like for you to keep your suspicions about Dr. Warner to yourself and to contact me directly with updates. We need to keep a tight lid on this. I'll inform the project director that you and I are working together. He'll support your efforts— no questions asked."

"I understand," Dr. Chang said, but he really didn't. The call had raised more questions, and he was now convinced of one thing: they had used the wrong therapy.

18

Chief Kusnadi was about to reach for the interrogation room door when a man blocked his path. He was an American, or maybe European, definitely a soldier of some sort. He had the build... and the eyes.

"Who are you?" Kusnadi asked the man.

"That's not important. I'm here to pick up Dr. Katherine Warner."

"Ah, funny man. Tell me who you are before I throw you in a cell."

The man handed him a manila envelope and said, "Take a look. It's nothing you haven't seen before."

The police chief opened the envelope and looked at the first few pictures. He couldn't believe his eyes. How? How could they have—?

"If you don't release her right now, you won't be the last to see those."

"I want the originals."

"Does this sound like a negotiation to you? Release her or my organization will release the contents of that envelope."

Kusnadi's eyes looked down, then darted side to side, like a cornered animal deciding which way to run.

"And just in case you're considering throwing me in a cell, if my people don't get my call within three minutes, they'll release this file anyway. You work for me now. You want to be Chief of Police or not?"

Kusnadi had to think. He looked around at the department. Who could do this?

"Time's up." The man turned to leave.

"Wait." The police chief opened the door to the interrogation room and motioned for the woman to come out. "This man will escort you out."

The woman paused at the door and looked at Kusnadi before looking the soldier up and down.

"It's okay, this man will take you now."

The man put his arm around her back and said, "Follow me, Dr. Warner. We're getting out of here."

Kusnadi watched them walk out of the station.

Outside the police station, Kate stopped and turned to the man who had rescued her. He was dressed in black body armor—eerily similar to the man who had taken her children. And so were his men—she saw them now—five of them, standing in front of a large black truck, like an oversized UPS delivery truck, and a black SUV with tinted windows.

"Who are you? I want to know—"

"Hang on just a second," he said.

The man walked over to the short interrogator who had accused Kate of buying the children. The soldier handed the little man a folder and said, "I hear you're in line for a promotion."

The little man shrugged. "I just do what I'm told," he said sheepishly.

"Your case officer says you're a good source. If you're smart enough to know what to do with this, maybe you'll be a better police chief."

The interrogator nodded. "Anything you want, boss."

The soldier walked back to Kate and motioned toward the large black delivery truck. "I need you to get in the truck."

"I'm not going anywhere until you tell me who you are and what's going on."

"I'll explain, but right now we have to get you to a safe location."

"No, you—"

"Here's a tip. The good guys ask you to get in the truck. The bad guys put a black bag over your head and throw you in the truck. I'm asking. Look, you can stay here or go with me. It's up to you."

He walked toward the truck and opened the double doors at the rear.

"Hold on. I'm coming."

19

Vincent Tarea, the head of field operations for Clocktower Jakarta, massaged his arm muscles as the station's staff filed into the primary conference room. His arms and legs still ached from the attack from those two fools at the clinic and those feral children. And the day had gotten worse from there. But he could put it back on track. He only needed to convince a few of the Jakarta staff to go along with the attack; the rest were already on the Immari payroll.

Tarea held his hands up to quiet the crowd. Everyone at Clocktower HQ was there: all the analysts, all the case officers, and all the field operatives—everyone except David Vale and the five operatives with him. Josh Cohen, the head of analysis, was also missing, but they would find him soon enough. The large screens on the conference room wall showed three crowded rooms, full of field operatives confined to safe houses across the city.

"Okay, listen up, everyone. Can you all hear me on the video links?"

Heads nodded, followed by a series of "yeah" and "we've got you."

"There's no easy way to say this, so I'll just say it: Clocktower has been compromised."

You could hear a pin drop in the room.

"And we're under attack. I received reports earlier today that several cells, including Cape Town, Mar del Plata, and

Karachi, have been completely destroyed. Several other stations are fighting for their lives as we speak."

People began talking in low tones. Some shouted questions.

"Hold on, everybody. It gets worse. I'm afraid the enemy we're fighting is one of our own. Here's what we know at this point: several days ago, David Vale, along with several other station chiefs, organized a meeting of all the chief analysts. Obviously this is strictly against protocol. We believe they told the analysts there was some new threat. We now know that over half the analysts never returned from the conference. The entire charade was a mass execution, we believe, to cripple our intelligence analysis before this larger attack. The analysts who returned to their cells are now actively working against Clocktower."

Tarea surveyed the doubtful looks around the room. "Look, I know this is hard to believe; and like you, I don't want to believe it. In fact I didn't believe, not until this morning, when David spread our field operatives out throughout the city. Think about it—he's spreading us out so we can't defend against an attack. He's preparing to take down Jakarta Station. It's only a matter of time."

"Why?" someone said. "He wouldn't do that," another person added.

"I asked the same question. I said the same thing," Tarea said. "He recruited me, I served with him, I know him. But there's a lot about David Vale we still don't understand. We all come to Clocktower for our own reasons. From what we can gather, David was seriously injured during the attacks on 9/11. I didn't know that until today. Since then, he's harbored a conspiracy theory about 9/11, some wild ideas about military contractors instigating the attack for their own gain. He may even be the victim of a lie himself. Someone could be using him. Either way, he's sick, turned around. And he's brought a lot of other people into the conspiracy. We think Josh Cohen has returned from the analyst conference and is working with the chief."

Everyone was silent, seeming to take the news in. A soldier

at one of the safe houses on the video screen said, "What's the operation? Bring him in?"

"That may not be possible. He'll fight to the end. The priority is to minimize the collateral damage. And we're going to have some help. Immari Security has offered to lend us some men. They're aware of the situation and they want to see this contained as much as we do. It seems Immari is the target of David's vendetta. We know that David has captured a scientist who works on an Immari-funded project. She could be a co-conspirator or just a victim in his plans; we're not sure yet. The plan is to recover the woman, a Dr. Katherine Warner, and neutralize the chief."

20

Josh waited nervously to find out whether his theory about the coded message David had given him was correct. It was Josh's best idea. Really his only idea.

He tried not to stare at the main computer screen on the long wall of the glass room. For the last thirty minutes, the screen had said the same thing:

Searching...

He glanced at the two screens beside it: a video feed of the door outside, and the city map with twenty-four red dots representing Clocktower Jakarta's field operatives. He didn't know which display made him more nervous. They might as well be giant countdown screens, ticking away the seconds to his death and some terrible, unknown catastrophe... The other screen still simply said, *Searching...*

Should the search have taken this long? What if he was wasting time?

Something else made him nervous. He glanced at the field box David had left on the table. He stood and grabbed the box, but as he lifted it, the bottom fell open. The gun and cyanide capsules tumbled onto the table, the clanging noise shattering the silence. The sound seemed to echo for hours. Finally, Josh reached for the gun and two pills. His hands were shaking.

On the wall, a beep snapped him out of the moment. The larger screen read:

5 results.

Five results!

Josh sat down at the table and worked the wireless keyboard and mouse. Three results from the *New York Times*, one from the *Daily Mail* in London, and one from the *Boston Globe*.

Maybe he was right. From the moment he had seen the names and dates, his first thought was: they're obituaries. Obituaries and classifieds were classic spycraft: operatives after World War II routinely used them to send messages across spy networks spread across the globe. It was old school, but if the message had been passed in 1947, it could have been a viable method. If it was true, this terrorist network was over sixty-five years old. He pushed the implications of that to the back of his mind.

He looked at the coded message David had given him:

```
Toba Protocol is real.
4+12+47  = 4/5; Jones
7+22+47  = 3/8; Anderson
10+4+47  = 5/4; Ames
```

Then he turned to the results. It was more likely the terrorists had used one paper—one paper that was available in cities around the world. The *New York Times* was the mostly likely candidate. Even in 1947, you could walk up to a newsstand in Paris, London, Shanghai, Barcelona, or Boston and get the day's copy of the *New York Times*, paid obituaries included.

If the obituaries were coded messages, they would have been flagged in some way. Josh saw it immediately: each of the *Times* obituaries had the words "clock" and "tower." He leaned back in his chair. Was it possible that Clocktower was that old? The CIA wasn't formally established until the National Security Act of 1947, although its precursor organization, the Office of Strategic Services (OSS), was created during World War II, in June of 1942.

Why would the terrorists mention Clocktower? Maybe they were fighting Clocktower back then—in 1947—sixty-six years ago?

He needed to focus on the obituaries. There must be a way to decode them. The ideal encryption system would feature a variable cipher: there would be no one key that could decrypt a message. Each message would include its own key—something simple.

He opened the first obituary, dated 4/12/1947:

Adam Jones, Pioneering Clockmaker, Dies at 77 Working on his Tower Masterpiece
Adam Jones, leading Gibraltar clockmaker, died Saturday in British Honduras. He was found by his valet. His bones will be interred near his late wife's—a site they selected together. Please send a card or advise family if visiting.

The message was here somewhere. What was the key? Josh opened the other obituaries and scanned them, hoping for some sort of clue. Each obituary contained a location, and each one was early in the text. Josh ran through several possibilities, rearranged several words, then sat back and thought. The obituaries were written awkwardly, like certain words were out of order. Or forced, like they *had* to use those words. The order, the intervals. He saw it. The names were the cipher—the lengths of the names. It was the second part of the code.

```
4+12+47 = 4/5;  Jones
```

The 4/12/1947 obituary was for Adam Jones. 4/5. The first name was four letters; the last name was five. If he took the fourth word of the obituary, then counted five words after that, and repeated, it yielded a sentence.

He re-examined the obituary:

Adam Jones, Pioneering Clockmaker, Dies at 77 Working on his Tower Masterpiece
Adam Jones, leading *Gibraltar* clockmaker, died Saturday in *British* Honduras. He was *found* by his valet. His *bones* will

be interred *near* his late wife's—a *site* they selected together. *Please* send a card or *advise* family if visiting.

Together, the message read:

Gibraltar, British found bones near site. Please advise.

Josh studied the message for a moment. He didn't see that coming. And he had no idea what it meant. He searched the internet and came up with a few results. Apparently the British had found bones in Gibraltar in the 1940s, in a natural sea cave called Gorham's Cave. But they weren't human bones. They were Neanderthal bones—and they had radically changed what the world knew about Neanderthals. Our prehistoric cousins were actually much more than archaic cavemen. They built homes. And they built huge fires on stone hearths, cooked vegetables, spoke a language, created cave art, buried their dead with flowers, and made advanced stone tools and pottery. The bones at Gibraltar also changed the Neanderthal time line. Before the Gibraltar find, Neanderthals were thought to have died out around forty thousand years ago. The Neanderthals at Gibraltar had lived roughly twenty-three thousand years ago—far later than previously thought. Gibraltar was likely the Neanderthals' last stand.

What could an ancient Neanderthal fortress have to do with a global terrorist attack? Maybe the other messages would shed some light. Josh opened the second obituary and decoded it.

Antarctica, U-boat not found, advise if further search authorized

Interesting. Josh ran a few searches. 1947 had been a busy year in Antarctica. On December 12th, 1946, the US Navy sent a huge armada, including thirteen ships with almost five thousand men, to Antarctica. The mission, code-named Operation Highjump, was to establish the Antarctic research base Little America IV.

There had long been conspiracy theories and speculation that the US was looking for secret Nazi bases and technology in Antarctica. Did the message mean they hadn't found it?

Josh turned the thick glossy page with the message over and examined the photo. A massive chunk of ice floated in a blue sea, and at its center, a black sub stuck out of the ice. The writing on the sub was too small to read, but it had to be the Nazi sub. Based on the likely size of the sub, the iceberg was maybe ten square miles. Big enough to be from Antarctica. Did this mean they had found the sub recently? Had the discovery set events in motion?

Josh turned to the last message, hoping it would provide a clue. Decoded, it read:

Roswell, weather balloon matches Gibraltar technology, we must meet

Together, all three messages were:

Gibraltar, British found bones near site, please advise
Antarctica, U-boat not found, advise if further search authorized
Roswell, weather balloon matches Gibraltar technology, we must meet

What did it mean? A site in Gibraltar, a U-boat in Antarctica, and the last one—a weather balloon in Roswell that matched technology in Gibraltar?

There was a larger question: Why? Why reveal these messages? They were sixty-five years old. How could it be connected to what's happening now—to the battle for Clocktower and an imminent terrorist attack?

Josh paced; he had to think. *If I were a mole inside a terrorist organization, trying to call for help, what would I do?* Trying to call for help... the source would have left a way to contact him. Another code? No, maybe he was revealing the method—how to contact him. The obituaries. But that would be inefficient, newspaper obituaries would take at least a day to appear, even online. Online. What would be the modern equivalent? Where would you post?

Josh ran through several ideas. The newspaper obituaries had been easy: there were only a few papers to check. Aggregating all the past obituaries had taken some time, but he had one key advantage: he knew where to look. The message could be anywhere online. There had to be another clue.

What did the three messages have in common? A location. What was different about them? There were no people in Antarctica, no classifieds, no... what? What was different about Roswell and Gibraltar? Both had newspapers. What could you do in one and not the other? To post something... the source was pointing him to a posting system as ubiquitous today as the *New York Times* was in 1947.

Craigslist. It had to be. Josh checked. No Craigslist in Gibraltar, but yes—there was a Craigslist board for Roswell / Carlsbad, New Mexico. Josh opened it and began reading through the messages. There were thousands of them, in dozens of categories: for sale, housing, community, jobs, résumés. There would be hundreds of new postings each day.

How could he find the source's message—if it was even there? He could use a web aggregation technology to gather the site's content—a Clocktower server would "crawl" the site, similar to the way Google and Bing indexed web sites, extracting content and making it searchable. Then he could run the cipher program, see if any of the postings translated. It would only take a few hours.

He didn't have a few hours.

He needed a place to start. Obituaries was the logical choice, but Craigslist didn't have obituaries. What would be the closest category? Maybe... personals? He scanned the headings:

strictly platonic
women seek women
women seeking men

93

```
men seeking women
men seeking men
misc romance
casual encounters
missed connections
rants and raves
```

Where to begin? Was he on a wild goose chase? He didn't have time to waste. Maybe a few more minutes, one more group of messages.

"Missed connections" was an interesting category. The idea was that if you saw someone you were interested in, but didn't get a chance to "make a connection"—ask them out—you posted here. It was popular with guys who, in the moment, couldn't find the courage to ask a cute waitress out. Josh had actually posted to it several times. If the person saw the message and replied, then there you were, no pressure. If not... it wasn't meant to be.

He opened it and read a few entries.

Subject> Green Dress at CVS
Message: My god you were stunning! You're perfect and I was totally speechless. Would love to talk to you. Email me.

Subject> Hampton Hotel
Message: We were getting water together at the desk and got on the elevator together. Didn't know if you wanted to get together for a little extra exercise. Tell what floor I got off on. I saw your wedding ring. We can be discreet too.

He read a few more. The message would be longer, if it followed the same pattern: a message within a message, decoded by the name length as a cipher. Craigslist was anonymous. The name would be the email address.

On the next page, the first entry was:

Subject> Saw you in the old Tower Records building talking about the new Clock Opera single

Promising... *Clock* and *Tower* in the subject line. Josh clicked the posting and read it quickly. It was longer than the others. The email address was andy@gmail.com. Josh scribbled down every fourth word then every fifth word from the posting. The decoded posting produced:

Situation changed. Clock tower will fall. Reply if still alive. Trust no one.

Josh froze. *Reply if still alive.* He had to reply. David had to reply.

Josh picked up the sat phone and dialed David, but it wouldn't connect. He had called him earlier. It wasn't the room or the phone. What could—

He saw it. The video feed from the door outside. It wasn't changing. He watched closely. The lights on the servers were staying on. But it never happened that way; they always blinked occasionally as the hard drives were accessed, as network cards sent and received packets. It wasn't a video feed, it was a picture—a picture put there by whoever was trying to get into the room.

21

Main Situation Room
Clocktower Station HQ
Jakarta, Indonesia

The situation room was busy. Operations technicians typed at keyboards, analysts filtered in and out with reports, and Vincent Tarea paced back and forth, watching the wall of screens. "Are we sure Vale is getting a false location map?"

"Yes, sir," one of the techs said.

"Tell the safe houses to move out."

Tarea watched the safe house video feeds as the soldiers marched to the doors and pulled them open.

The sound of the explosions turned every head in the large situation room to the monitors, which now showed fuzzy black and white static.

One of the techs punched a keyboard. "Switching to outside video. Sir, we have a massive detonation at—"

"I know! Safe houses, hold your positions," Tarea yelled.

No sound came over the speakers. The location map was completely black where the red dots had paced around the safe houses. The only dots left were David's convoy and the small group left at HQ.

The tech swiveled around. "He rigged the safe houses to blow."

Tarea rubbed the bridge of his nose. "Thank you, Captain Obvious. Are we in that quiet room yet? Did they find Josh?"

"No, they're about to start."

Tarea walked out of the situation room, into his private office, and picked up the phone. He dialed his counterpart at Immari Security. "We have a problem. He took out my men here."

He listened a moment.

"No, look, I convinced them, but he—it doesn't matter, they're all dead. That's the bottom line."

Another pause.

"No, well, if I were you, I would make sure you kill him with the first strike, no matter how many men you've got. He'll be incredibly hard to contain in the field."

He started to set the phone down, but jerked it back impatiently at the last minute.

"What? No, we're looking. We think he's here. I'll keep you posted. What? Fine, I'll come, but I only have two men I can bring, and we're staying in the rear in case it goes south."

22

Clocktower Mobile Operations Center
Jakarta, Indonesia

Kate followed the soldier into the large black truck. Inside, it looked nothing like the delivery truck it had appeared to be. It was part locker room, with weapons and gear she didn't recognize; part office with screens and computers; and part bus, with rows of sunken seats along each side.

There were three large screens. One showed dots on a map that she assumed was Jakarta. The other displayed a video feed of the front, rear, and both sides of the truck. On the top right picture, the black SUV could be seen leading the truck through Jakarta's crowded streets. The final screen was blank except for one word: **Connecting...**

"I'm David Vale."

"I want to know where you're taking me," Kate demanded.

"A safe house." David was fiddling with a tablet computer of some sort. It seemed to manipulate one of the screens on the wall. He glanced up at it, as if waiting for something to appear. When it didn't, he hit a few more buttons.

"So you're with the American government?" Kate said, trying to get his attention.

"Not exactly." He looked down, still working the tablet.

"But you *are* an American?"

"Sort of."

"Can you focus and talk to me?"

"I'm trying to conference in a colleague." The man looked worried now. He glanced around, as if thinking.

"Is there a problem?"

"Yeah. Maybe." He put the tablet aside. "I need to ask you some questions about the kidnapping."

"Are you looking for the children?"

"We're still trying to figure out what's going on."

"Who's we?"

"No one you've heard of."

Kate ran a hand through her hair. "Look, I've had a very bad day. I actually don't care who you are or where you're from. Someone took two children from my clinic today, and so far no one seems to want to find them. Including you."

"I never said I wouldn't help you."

"You never said you would, either."

"That's true," David said, "but right now, I've got problems of my own, big ones. Problems that could result in a lot of innocent people getting killed. A lot already have, and I think your research is somehow connected to it. I'm not quite sure how. Listen, if you answer some questions for me, I promise you I'll do what I can to help you."

"All right, that's fair." Kate leaned forward in the chair.

"How much do you know about Immari Jakarta?"

"Nothing really. They fund some of my research. My adoptive father, Martin Grey, is the Head of Immari Research. They invest in a broad range of science and technology research."

"Are you building a biological weapon for them?"

The question hit Kate like a slap in the face. She reeled back in her chair. "What? God no! Are you out of your mind? I'm trying to cure autism."

"Why were those two children taken?"

"I have no idea."

"I don't believe you. What's different about those two? There were over a hundred kids in the clinic. If the kidnappers were human traffickers, they would have taken them all. They took those two children for a reason. And they risked a lot of exposure to do it. So, I'll ask you again: why those two?"

Kate looked at the ground and thought. She said the first question that popped into her head. "Immari Research took my children?"

The question seemed to throw him. "Uh, no, Immari Security did. They're another division, but same general team of bad guys."

"That's impossible."

"See for yourself." He handed her a folder, and she flipped through, browsing satellite photos of the van at the clinic, the two black-clad assailants hauling kids into the van, and the van's registration records that traced back to Immari International, Hong Kong Security Division.

Kate considered the man's evidence. Why would Immari take the children? They could have asked her. Something else had been bothering her. "Why do you think I'm building a biological weapon?"

"It's the only thing that makes sense, based on the evidence."

"What evidence?"

"Have you ever heard of The Toba Protocol?"

"No."

He handed her another file. "This is about all we have on it. It's not much, but the bottom line is that Immari International is working on a plan to drastically reduce the human population."

She read through the file. "Like the Toba Catastrophe."

"What? I'm not familiar."

She closed the file. "Not surprising. It's not widely accepted, but it's a popular theory among evolutionary biologists."

"Popular theory for what?"

"The Great Leap Forward." Kate recognized David's confusion and continued before he could speak. "The Great Leap Forward is probably one of the most hotly contested aspects of evolutionary genetics. It's a mystery, really. We know that around fifty to sixty thousand years ago, there was a sort of 'Big Bang' in human intelligence. We got a lot smarter, very quickly. We just don't know exactly how. We believe it was some kind of change in brain wiring. For the first time, humans began using complex language, creating art, making more advanced tools, solving problems—"

David stared at the wall, processing the information. "I don't see—"

Kate brushed her hair back. "Okay, let me start over. The human race is about two hundred thousand years old, but we've only been so-called *behaviorally modern* humans—the really, really smart type that took over the globe—for around fifty thousand years. So fifty thousand years ago, we know there were at least three other hominids: Neanderthals, Homo Floresiensis—"

"Homo flor—"

"They're not widely known. We only recently found them. They were smaller, sort of hobbit-like humans. We'll just say Hobbits, it's easier. So fifty thousand years ago, there's us, the Neanderthals, Hobbits, and Denisovans. Actually, there were probably a couple more hominids, but the point is there were five or six subspecies of humans. And then our branch of the human tree explodes while the others die out. We go from a few thousand to seven billion people in the span of fifty thousand years, and the other human subspecies go extinct. We conquer the globe while they die in caves. It's the greatest mystery of all time, and scientists have been working on it since time began. Religion, too. At the heart of the question is how we survived. What gave us such a huge evolutionary advantage? We call this transformation the Great Leap Forward, and the Toba Catastrophe Theory proposes how this great leap forward could have happened—how we became so smart while our cousins, other hominids—Neanderthals, Hobbits, et cetera—they all remained basically cavemen. About seventy thousand years ago, the theory goes, a supervolcano erupted at Mount Toba, here in Indonesia. The ash from the eruption blotted out the sun over large parts of the Earth, causing a volcanic winter that lasted for years. That rapid climate change reduced the total human population drastically, maybe to as low as ten thousand or even less."

"Wait, the human race was down to ten thousand people?"

"We think so. Well, the estimates aren't exact, but we know there was a huge population reduction, and that it was marked in our subspecies. We think Neanderthals and some other hominids alive at the time might have fared better. The Hobbits were downwind of Toba and the Neanderthals were concentrated in Europe. Africa, the Middle East, and South Asia took the brunt of the effects of the Toba eruption, and that's where we were concentrated at the time. Neanderthals were also stronger than we were, and they had bigger brains; that could have given them an additional survival advantage, but we're still sorting that out. We do know that humans got hit hard by the Toba supervolcano. We were on the brink of extinction. That caused what population geneticists call a 'population bottleneck.' Some researchers believe that this bottleneck caused a small group of humans to evolve, to survive through mutation. These mutations could have led to humanity's exponential explosion in intelligence. There's genetic evidence for it. We know that every human being on the planet is directly descended from one man who lived in Africa around sixty thousand years ago—a person we geneticists call Y-Chromosomal Adam. In fact, everyone outside of Africa is descended from a small band of humans, maybe as few as one hundred, that left Africa about fifty thousand years ago. Essentially, we're all members of a small tribe that walked out of Africa after Toba and took over the planet. That tribe was significantly more intelligent than any other hominids in history. That's *what* happened, but we don't know *how* it happened. The truth is, we don't actually know how our subspecies survived Toba, or how they became so much more intelligent than the other human subspecies alive at the time. It had to be some sort of change in brain wiring, but no one knows how this Great Leap Forward occurred. It could have been due to a change in diet or a spontaneous mutation. Or it could have happened gradually. The Toba Catastrophe Theory and the subsequent population bottleneck is just one possibility, but it's gaining followers."

He looked down, seeming to consider this.

"I'm surprised this didn't come up in your research." When he said nothing, she added, "So... what do *you* think 'Toba' stands for? I mean, I could be wrong here—"

"No, you're right. I know it. But it's just a reference to the effect of the Toba Catastrophe in the past—how it changed humanity. That's their goal: to create another population bottleneck and force a Second Great Leap Forward. They want to bring about the next stage of human evolution. It tells me the why, which we didn't know before. We thought Toba was a reference to where the operation would start. Southeast Asia, especially Indonesia, makes sense. It's one of the reasons I established operations in Jakarta, sixty miles from Mount Toba."

"Right. Well, history can be pretty handy. And so can books. Maybe even as much as guns."

"For the record, I read a lot. And I like history. But you're talking about seventy thousand years ago. That's not history, it's prehistoric. Also, guns have their place; the world isn't as civilized as it looks."

She held up her hands and sat back in the seat. "Hey, just trying to help here. Speaking of, you said you would help me find those kids."

"And you said you would answer my questions."

"I have."

"You haven't. You know why those two kids were taken, or you at least have a theory. Tell me."

Kate thought for a moment. Could she trust him?

"I need some assurances." She waited, but the man just stared at the other screen, the one with all the dots on it. "Hey, are you listening to me?" He looked concerned now, glancing about. "What's wrong?"

"The dots aren't moving."

"Should they be?"

"Yeah. We're definitely moving." He pointed to the seat belts. "Strap yourself in."

The way he said it scared her. He reminded her of a father who had just realized his child was in danger. He was hyper-focused. His eyes didn't blink as he moved quickly, securing loose articles around the truck and grabbing a radio.

"Mobile One, Clocktower Commander. Alter course, new destination is Clocktower HQ, do you copy?"

"Copy Clocktower Commander, Mobile One altering course."

Kate felt the truck turning.

The man lowered the radio to his side.

She saw the flash on the screen a second before she heard—and felt—the blast.

On the screen, the large SUV in front of them exploded, lifting off the ground and falling in a heap of flames and burning metal.

There was gunfire and then their truck veered off the road—as if no one was driving it.

Another rocket struck the street beside the truck, barely missing it. The force of the blast almost rolled the van over and seemed to pull the air completely out of the room. Kate's ears rang. Her stomach throbbed where the seatbelt had cut into it. It was like sensory deprivation. Everything seemed to move in slow motion. She felt the truck fall back to the ground and bounce on its shocks.

Through the ringing, she looked over. The soldier was lying on the floor of the truck, not moving.

23

Josh had to think. Whoever had replaced the live feed of the door to the quiet room was no doubt outside, trying to get in. The glass room in the giant concrete tomb seemed so fragile now. It hung there, just waiting to explode, like a glass piñata. He was the prize inside.

Was there something on the door? A speck of orange? Josh walked to the edge of the glass room and looked closer. It *was* a tiny speck, growing brighter, like a heating element. It made the metal look wet... yes, the metal was flowing down the door. At that instant, sparks flew out of the top right corner of the door. The sparks slowly crept downward, leaving a narrow, dark rut behind.

They were coming in—with a torch. Of course. Blowing the door—using explosives—would obliterate the server room. It was just one more safety measure, meant to give whoever was inside more time.

Josh raced back to the table. What to do first? The source, the message on Craigslist. He had to respond. His email address, andy@gmail.com, was clearly fake: that address had probably been available for all of two seconds after Gmail launched. The source knew Josh would know that, knew he would see it for what it was: just another name with the proper length to decrypt the message using the code. The code... he would have to make up a message and name that followed the code.

He glanced over. The cutting torch was now halfway down the right side of the door. The sparks burned toward the ground like a fuse eating its way to a bomb.

Screw it, he didn't have time. He clicked the post button and wrote a message:

Subject> To the man at Tower Records.
Message: I wish we could have connected, but there wasn't time. I'm afraid I may be out of time again. My friend sent me your messages. I still don't understand. I'm sorry for being so direct. I really don't have time to play games with mixed messages. I couldn't reach my friend on the phone, but maybe you can contact him on this board. Please reply with any information that could help him. Thanks and good luck.

Josh hit send. Why couldn't he reach David? He still had internet access. It must be on a completely different connection, a connection the Clocktower operatives didn't know about. That made sense for the secure phone calls and videoconferences. The door camera was easy: they could have cut the cord and connected it to another video source, or simply placed a picture of the hall in front of the camera and let it run.

Out of the corner of his eye, Josh saw the display with the red dots change quickly: the dots in the safe houses were massing at the doors. They were making a move.

Then they disappeared. Dead.

Josh's eyes returned to the door. The torch was picking up speed. He refreshed the Craigslist page, hoping the contact would respond.

24

David looked up to see the woman—Dr. Warner—standing over him.

"Are you hurt?" she said.

He pushed her aside and got to his feet. The monitors revealed the scene outside: the Suburban with three of his field operatives lay in burnt pieces scattered about the deserted street. He didn't see the two men who had been driving the truck. The second blast must have gotten them. Or a sniper.

David shook his head to try to clear it, then stumbled over to the weapons lockers. He pulled out two smoke canisters, ripped the pin out of each one, and walked to the double doors at the rear of the truck.

Slowly, he pushed one of the doors open, then quickly dropped one canister and rolled the other a little farther out. He heard the soft hiss of smoke escape the cylinders as they spun around on the street. A small wisp of the gray-white smoke wafted into the truck as he carefully closed the door.

He had expected at least one potshot when he opened the door. They must want the girl alive.

He returned to the weapons locker and began arming himself. He slung an automatic assault rifle over his shoulder and stuffed magazines for the massive gun and his sidearm into the pockets of his pants. He pulled a hard black helmet on and re-strapped his body armor.

"Hey, what are you doing? What's happening?"

"Stay here and keep the door shut. I'll be back when it's safe," David said as he started for the door.

"What?! You're going out there?"

"Yes—"

"Are you *crazy*?"

"Look, we're sitting ducks in here; it's just a matter of time before they reach us. I have to fight in the open, get to cover, and find a way out. I'll be back."

"Well—well—are... Can I get a gun or something?"

He turned to her. She was scared, but he had to give her credit: she had guts. "No, you cannot have a gun."

"Why not?"

"Because you're the only person you're likely to hurt with it. Now close this door behind me." He pulled his goggles down from his helmet, covering his eyes. In one fluid motion, he opened the door and jumped out into the smoke.

Three seconds into his sprint, the bullets began raining down on him. The rifles' report told him what he needed to know: the snipers were on the tops of the buildings to his left.

He darted into an alley across the street, aimed his gun at the roof, and began firing. He hit the closest sniper, saw him go down, and fired two blasts of automatic shots at the other two. Both withdrew behind the brick edifice at the top of the old building.

A bullet whizzed by his head. Another dug into the concrete plaster of the building beside him, spraying shards of brick and concrete into his helmet and body armor. He pivoted to the source: four men on foot, running toward him. Immari Security. Not his men.

He fired three quick blasts at them. They scattered. Two fell.

The second he let off the trigger, he heard the whoosh sound.

He dove to the other side of the alley as the rocket-propelled grenade exploded ten feet from where he had stood a second ago.

He should have killed the snipers first. Or gotten out of their range at least.

Rubble fell around him. Smoke filled the air.

David struggled to fill his lungs again.

The street was quiet. He rolled over.

Footfalls, coming toward him.

He got to his feet and ran into the alley, leaving his rifle behind. He had to get to a defensible position. Bullets ricocheted off the alley walls, and he turned, pulled out his sidearm, and fired a few shots, forcing the two men following him to stop and take refuge in doorways in the alley.

Ahead of him, the alley opened onto an old dusty street that ran along one of Jakarta's thirty-seven rivers. There was a river market, with produce stands, pottery dealers, and vendors of all sorts. They were in full flight, pointing, yelling, gathering the day's take in cash and hurrying away from the shots.

David cleared the alley and more gunfire engulfed him. A shot caught him dead center in the chest, throwing him violently to the ground, knocking the wind out of him.

At his head, more gunshots dug into the ground; the men in the alley were closing fast.

He rolled toward the alley wall, away from the shots. He struggled to breathe.

It was a trap: the men in the alley were herding him.

He took out two grenades. He pulled the pins, waited a full second, threw one behind him, into the alley, and the other around the corner, toward the ambush.

Then he ran flat out for the river, firing at the ambush as he went.

Behind him he heard the muffled sound of the alley explosion, then the louder blast in the open at the ambush.

Just before he reached the banks of the river he heard another explosion, this one much closer, maybe eight feet behind him. The blast threw him off his feet, out over the river.

Inside the armored van, Kate sat again. Then stood again. It sounded like World War III outside: explosions, automatic gunfire, debris hitting the side of the truck.

She walked to the locker with the guns and bulletproof vests. More gunfire. Maybe she should put on some kind of armor? She took out one of the black outfits. It was heavy; so much heavier than she'd thought. She looked down at the rumpled clothes she had slept in at her office. What a weird day.

There was a knock at the door, then, "Dr. Warner?"

She dropped the vest.

It wasn't *his* voice, the one who had gotten her from the police. It wasn't David.

She needed a gun.

"Dr. Warner, we're coming in."

The door opened.

Three men in black armor, like the men who had taken the kids. They approached her.

"We're glad you're safe, Dr. Warner. We're here to rescue you."

"Who are you? Where is he, the man who was here?" She took a step back.

The gunfire had died down. Then two—no, three explosions in the distance.

They inched toward her. She took another step back. She could reach the gun. Could she fire it?

"It's all right, Dr. Warner. Just come on out of there. We're taking you to see Martin. He sent us."

"What? I want to talk to him. I'm not going anywhere until I speak with him."

"It's okay—"

"No, I want you out of here right now," she said.

The man in the back pushed past the other two and said, "I told you Lars, you owe me fifty bucks." Kate knew the voice: the gruff, scratchy voice of the man who had taken her children. It was him. Kate froze, fear running through her.

When the man reached her, he grabbed Kate's arm, hard, and spun her around, sliding his hand down to her wrist. He grabbed her other wrist and held them together with one hand as he zip-tied them with the other.

She tried to pull away, but the thin plastic cut into her, sending sharp pains up her arms.

The man pulled her back by her long blond hair and jerked the black bag over her head, sending Kate into complete darkness.

25

Josh watched the other red dots on the screen wink out. The men at the safe houses; they had moved to the door, then disappeared—dead. A few minutes later, he saw David's convoy stop in the street—then they were gone too, except for David. He watched as David's dot moved around quickly. One last sprint.

Then it went out as well.

Josh exhaled and slumped in the chair. He stared through the glass walls at the outer door. The torch burned up the other side of it now, the burn mark a backwards J. Soon it would be a full U, then an O, then they would be through, and his time would be up. He had two, maybe three minutes.

The letter. He turned, rifled through the stack of folders and found it: David's "open when I'm dead" letter. A few hours ago, Josh had thought he would never need to open it. So many illusions had died today: Clocktower couldn't be compromised, Clocktower couldn't fall, David couldn't be killed, the good guys always won.

He ripped open the letter.

Dear Josh,

Don't feel bad. We were way behind when we started. I can only assume Jakarta Station has fallen or is on its way.

Remember our goal: we must prevent the Immari endgame. Forward whatever you've found to the Director of Clocktower. His name is Howard Keegan. You can trust him.

There's a program on ClockServer1—ClockConnect.exe. It will open a private channel to Central where you can transmit data securely.

One last thing. I've collected a little money over the years, mostly from bad guys we put out of business. There's another program on ClockServer1—distribute.bat. It will disburse the money in my accounts.

I hope they never found this room and that you're reading this letter in safety.

It has been my honor to serve with you.

David

Josh put the letter down.

He typed quickly on the keyboard, first uploading his data to Clocktower Central, then executing the bank transactions. "A little money" had been an understatement. Josh watched five transactions, of five million dollars each, go first to the Red Cross, then UNICEF, and then three other disaster relief organizations. It made sense. But the final transaction didn't. A deposit of five million dollars to a JP Morgan bank account in America—a New York branch. Josh copied the account holders' names and searched. A man, sixty-two, and his wife, fifty-nine. David's parents? There was a news article—a piece in a Long Island newspaper. The couple had lost their only daughter in the 9/11 attacks. She had been an investment analyst at Cantor Fitzgerald at the time of the attacks, had recently graduated from Yale, and was engaged to be married to Andrew Reed, a graduate student at Columbia.

Josh heard it—or rather, didn't hear it. The torch had stopped. The circle was complete, and soon they would begin ramming the door, waiting for the metal to break free.

He gathered the papers, ran to the trash can, and lit them on fire. He moved back to the table and opened the program that would erase the computer. It would take over five minutes. Maybe they wouldn't find it. Or maybe he could buy it some time; he looked at the box with the gun in it.

Something else, on the screen, the location map. Josh thought he'd seen it—a flash, a red dot. But now it was gone. He stared again.

A boom, boom, boom at the door jolted Josh almost out of the chair. The men were beating on the door like a war drum, trying to make the thick metal come free. The pounding matched the throbbing in Josh's chest as his heart beat uncontrollably.

The computer screen displayed the erase progress: twelve percent complete.

The dot lit up again, stayed lit this time: D. Vale. It drifted slowly, in the river. Vitals were faint, but he was alive. His body armor housed the sensors; it must have been damaged.

Josh had to send David what he'd found and a way to contact the source. Options? Normally they would establish an online dead-drop: a public web site where they exchanged coded messages. Clocktower routinely used eBay auctions—the pictures of the products for sale included embedded messages or files that a Clocktower algorithm could decrypt. To the naked eye, the pictures looked normal, but small pixel changes throughout added up to a complex file Clocktower could read.

But he and David hadn't established any system. He couldn't call. Emailing would be a death sentence: Clocktower would monitor any email addresses, and when David checked it, Clocktower would trace the IP of the computer he used. The IP would give them a physical address, or a very close idea. Video surveillance feeds nearby would fill in the rest, and they would have him within minutes. An IP... Josh had an idea. Could it work?

Erasing... 37% complete

He had to work fast, before the computer stopped functioning.

Josh opened a VPN connection to a private server he used mostly as a relay and staging area for online operations—transforming and bouncing encrypted reports around the internet before delivering them to Central. It was just added security to make sure Jakarta Station's downloads to Central weren't intercepted. It was off the grid; no one knew about it. And it already had several security protocols he'd written. It was perfect.

But the server didn't have a web address—it didn't need one—just an IP: 50.31.14.76. Web addresses, like www.google.com or www.apple.com, really translated to IPs. When you type an address in your web browser, a group of servers called domain name servers (DNS) match the address to an IP in their database, and send you to the right place. If you typed the IP into your browser's address bar instead, you'd actually end up in the exact same place without the routing: 74.125.139.100 opens Google.com, 17.149.160.49 opens Apple.com, and so on.

Josh finished uploading the data to the server. The computer was starting to run slowly. Several error messages popped up.

`Erasing... 48% complete`

The drumming had stopped. They were using the torch again. A round bulge of strained metal had formed in the center of the door.

Josh had to send David the IP. He couldn't call or text. All the sources and case officers would be monitored by Clocktower, and besides, he had no idea where David would end up. He needed somewhere David would look. Some way to send the numbers in the IP address. Something only Josh knew about...

David's bank account. It could work.

Josh also maintained a private bank account; he imagined almost everyone in their line of work did.

The cry of bending metal filled the cavernous room like a dying whale. They were close.

Josh opened a web browser and logged in to his bank account. Quickly, he keyed in David's bank routing number and account number. Then he made a series of deposits to David's account:

```
9.11
50.00
31.00
14.00
76.00
9.11
```

It would take a day for the transactions to post, and even after they did, David would only see it if he checked the account. Would he know it was an IP address? Field operatives weren't exactly tech-savvy. It was a long shot.

The door broke. Men were through, soldiers in full battle armor.

Erasing… **65% complete**

Not enough. They would find something.

The box, the capsule. Three to four seconds. Not enough time.

Josh lunged for the box on the table, knocking it off. It crashed to the glass floor and he followed it. His shaking hands reached inside, grabbing the gun. How did it go? Slide, shoot, press here? God. They were at the entrance to the glass room. Three men.

He raised the gun. His arm shook. He steadied it with his other hand, and squeezed the trigger. The bullet ripped through the computer. He had to hit the hard drive. He fired again. The sound was deafening in the room.

Then the sound was all around. Glass was everywhere, tiny pieces. Josh was rushing to the glass wall. Glass fell all around him, on him, cutting into him. He looked down, saw the bullet holes in his chest. He felt blood flow from his mouth and down his chin, joining the growing crimson pool at his chest. He turned his head and watched as the last of the computer lights blinked out.

26

The fishermen paddled the boat down the river, toward the Java Sea. The fishing had been good the last several days, and they had brought extra nets—all they had, in fact. The boat sagged with the weight, riding lower in the water than it normally did. If things went well, they would return as the sun set, dragging the nets behind the boat, full of fish, enough for their small family and enough to sell at the market.

Harto watched his son Eko paddling at the front of the boat, and pride washed over him. Soon, Harto would retire and Eko would do the fishing. Then, in time, Eko would take his son out, just like this, just like Harto's father had taught him to fish.

He hoped it would be so. Lately, Harto had begun to worry that this would not be the way things would come to pass. Every year there were more boats—and less fish. They fished longer each day and yet their nets carried fewer fish. Harto pushed the thought from his mind. Good fortune comes and recedes, just like the seas; it was the way of things. *I must not worry over things I cannot control.*

His son stopped paddling. The boat started to turn.

Harto yelled to him, "Eko, you must paddle, the boat will turn if we don't paddle evenly. Pay attention."

"There's something in the water, Papa."

Harto looked. There was... something black, floating. A man. "Paddle quickly, Eko."

They pulled up beside him, and Harto reached out, grabbed him, and tried to pull him into the narrow boat loaded with nets. He was too heavy. He wore some kind of shell. But the shell floated. Some special material. Harto turned the man over. A helmet and goggles—they had covered his nose, kept him from drowning.

"A diver, Papa?"

"No, he's… a policeman, I think." Harto tried to pull him into the boat again, but it nearly tipped over. "Here, Eko, help me."

Together, father and son dragged the waterlogged man into the boat, but as soon as he cleared the side, the boat began taking on water.

"We're sinking, Papa!" Eko looked about nervously.

Water rushed over the boat's side. What to throw out? The man? The river flowed to the sea; he would surely die there. They couldn't drag him, not far. The water rushed in more quickly now.

Harto eyed the nets, the only other thing with any weight in the boat. But they were Eko's inheritance—the only wealth his family had, their only means of survival, of putting food on their table.

"Throw the nets over, Eko."

The young boy followed his father's orders without question, throwing the nets over one by one, feeding his birthright to the slow-moving river.

When most of the nets were gone, the water stopped, and Harto slumped back into the boat, staring with absent eyes at the man.

"What's wrong, Papa?"

When his father said nothing, Eko scooted closer to him and the man they had rescued. "Is he dead? Did—"

"We must get him home. Help me paddle, son. He may be in some trouble."

They turned the boat and paddled back up the river, against the current, toward Harto's wife and daughter, who would be preparing to clean and store the fish they brought back. There would be no fish today.

27

Associated Press
Wire Release – Breaking News Report
Explosions and Gunfire Rock Indonesian Capital of Jakarta

Jakarta, Indonesia (AP) // The Associated Press has received multiple reports of explosions and gunfire across Jakarta. Although no terrorist groups have claimed responsibility, insiders within the Indonesian Government, speaking on the condition of anonymity, said they believe the attacks were a coordinated strike. It's not clear at this time who the target or targets were.

At about one P.M. local time, three bomb blasts ripped through high-rise buildings in rundown residential neighborhoods across the city. Observers said at least two of the buildings were thought to be abandoned.

Those blasts were followed minutes later by explosions and automatic gunfire on the streets of the market district. Casualty figures are unavailable, and police have declined to comment.

We will update this story as details emerge.

The Jakarta Post
West Jakarta Police Chief Arrested

The Indonesian National Police today confirmed that they have arrested West Jakarta Police Chief Eddi Kusnadi on child pornography charges. The new chief of the station, Paku Kurnia, issued this statement: "This is a sad and shameful day for the Jakarta Metro Police and the West Jakarta Police Station, but our willingness to confront evil within our own ranks will ultimately make us stronger and affirm the public's trust in us."

28

Kate sat in a chair, her hands bound behind her, the dark hood still over her head. The trip had been rough. The soldiers had tossed her about like a rag doll for the past thirty minutes, transferring her from one van to another, marching her down a series of hallways, and finally throwing her into the chair and slamming a door. The sensation of moving in pure darkness had made her nauseated. Her hands ached from the zip ties, and she couldn't see a thing through the thick black hood. The absolute dark and quiet was disorienting, like sensory deprivation. How long had she been there?

Then she heard something coming closer: footfalls in a hallway or large room. They echoed louder with each passing second.

"Take that bag off her head!"

Martin Grey's voice. Martin—the sound of her adoptive father's voice sent waves of relief through Kate's body. The darkness didn't seem so dark, and the pain in her hands near the bindings seemed to ease. She was safe. Martin would help her find her children.

She felt the bag lift off her head. The lights blinded her, and she squinted, grimaced, and turned her head away.

"And unbind her hands! Who did this to her?"

"I did, sir. She was resisting."

She still couldn't see them, but she knew the voice—the man who had taken her from the truck, who had taken the children at the clinic. Ben Adelson's killer.

"You must have been pretty scared of her." Martin's voice was cold and forceful. Kate had never heard him talk to anyone that way. She heard two more men chuckling, then her captor responded, "Complain all you want, Grey. I don't answer to you. And you seemed satisfied with our work earlier."

What did he mean by that?

Martin's voice changed slightly; it was more amused. "You know, it almost sounds like you're resisting, Mr. Tarea. Here, I'll show you what happens when you do."

Kate could see Martin now. His face was hard. He stared at the man, then turned to two other men—soldiers who must have accompanied Martin. "Take him to a holding cell. Shroud him and bind his hands. The tighter the better."

The two men seized the kidnapper, put the bag that had been on Kate's head on him and dragged him out of the room.

Martin bent down to Kate and said, "Are you okay?"

Kate rubbed her hands and leaned forward. "Martin, two children were taken from my lab. That man was one of the kidnappers. We have to find—"

Martin held up a hand. "I know. I'll explain everything. But right now, I need you to tell me what you've done to those children. It's very important, Kate."

Kate opened her mouth to respond, but she didn't know where to start. Questions raced through her head.

Before she could speak, two more men entered the large room and spoke to Martin. "Sir, Director Sloane would like to speak with you."

Martin looked up, annoyed. "I'll call him back, this can't—"

"Sir, he's here."

"In Jakarta?"

"In the building, sir. We've been instructed to escort you to him. I'm sorry, sir."

Martin stood slowly, looking worried. "Take her downstairs, to the observation deck for the excavation. And... guard the door. I'll be along shortly."

Martin's men escorted Kate out, keeping a safe distance but watching her like a hawk. She noticed that the other men treated Martin the same way.

29

Harto watched as the mysterious man pushed up onto his elbows, tore his helmet and goggles off, then looked around, confused. He threw the head gear over the side of the boat, and after lying down for a few minutes more, he struggled with some straps at the side of his suit. Finally, he managed to tear them loose, and he tossed the bulky vest over the side as well. Harto had noticed a large hole in the chest area of the vest. Maybe it was damaged. The man rubbed his chest, breathing heavily.

He was an American, or maybe a European. This surprised Harto. He knew the man was white—he could see part of his face when they brought him aboard the boat—but he assumed the man was Japanese, or maybe Chinese. Why would an armed European be here, in the river? Maybe he wasn't a policeman. Maybe he was a criminal, a terrorist, or a drug cartel soldier. Had helping this man gotten them into something dangerous? He paddled faster. Eko saw the boat starting to turn, and he paddled faster too. The boy was learning so quickly.

When the white man's breathing had leveled off some, he sat up and began speaking English.

Eko looked back. Harto didn't know what to say. The soldier spoke slowly. Harto said the only English he knew. "My wife speak English. She help you."

The man collapsed again to his back. He stared up at the sky and rubbed his chest while Harto and Eko paddled.

David assumed the bullet to the chest had killed the bio-monitor in the body armor. It had sure done a number on him. The tracker in the helmet would still be active, but it was at the bottom of the river.

God bless these Jakartan fisherman. They had saved him, but where were they taking him? Maybe Immari had announced a reward for him—these two had simply caught a lottery ticket. If they were going to turn him in, David needed to get free, but he could barely breathe. He'd cross that bridge when he came to it. He had to rest. He watched the river for a minute, then closed his eyes.

David felt the soft comfort of a bed beneath him. A middle-aged Jakartan woman held a wet rag against his forehead. "Can you hear me?" When she saw his eyes open, she turned away and began yelling in another language.

David grabbed her arm. She looked frightened. "I'm not going to hurt you. Where am I?" he said. He realized that he felt much better. He could breathe again, but the pain was still there in his chest. He sat up and released her arm.

The woman told him their address, but David didn't know it. Before he could ask another question, she backed out of the room, watching him cautiously, her head tilted slightly.

David rubbed the bruise on his chest. *Think.* If they had taken the risk to attack his convoy in the open, they had already taken Jakarta Station HQ.

Josh. Another fallen soldier. *If I don't stop Toba Protocol, there will be many more. And civilians, as there had been before...*

Focus.

The current threat. What does it mean?

They took Warner. They need her. *She's involved somehow.*

But he didn't believe that. Kate Warner had been genuine, sincere. She believed in the research she was doing. She wouldn't be involved in Toba. They needed her *research*; they were going to use it. They would force her to reveal it to them. She would be another innocent victim. He had to focus on getting her back. She was his best lead.

He stood and walked around the home. It was several rooms separated by paper-thin walls covered with homemade art, mostly depicting fishermen. He opened a rickety screen door and walked out onto a terrace. The home was on the third or fourth level of a "building" with many similar homes—all with white plaster walls, dirty screen doors, and terraces stacked like stair steps climbing the banks of the river below. He looked out into the distance. As far as the eye could see, he saw stacks and stacks of these homes, like pasteboard boxes stacked on top of each other. Clothes hung on lines outside each one, and here and there women were beating rugs, sending dust rising into the setting sun like demons fleeing the earth.

David glanced down toward the river. Fishing boats were coming and going. A few had small motors, but most were powered by paddlers. His eyes searched the buildings above. Would they be here already, looking for him?

Then he saw them. Two men, Immari Security, exiting on the second floor below him. David backed into the shadow of the balcony and watched the men go into the next home. How long did he have? Five, maybe ten minutes?

He walked back into the home and found the family huddled together in what passed for a living room, though it had two small beds in it as well. The two parents corralled a boy and a girl behind them, as if David's look could harm them.

At six-foot-three, David was almost two heads taller than the man and woman, and his muscular frame almost filled the narrow doorway, blocking the last rays of the setting sun. He must look like a monster to them, or an alien, a completely different species.

David focused on the woman. "I'm not going to hurt you. Do you speak English?"

"Yes. A little. I sell fish in the market."

"Good. I need help. It is very important. A woman and two children are in danger. Please ask your husband if he will help me."

30

Martin Grey walked into the room cautiously, eyeing Dorian Sloane as if he were an apparition. The director of Immari Security stood on the far side of Martin's corner office on the sixty-sixth floor of the Immari Jakarta Headquarters. Sloane looked out over the Java Sea, watching the boats come and go. Martin thought the younger man hadn't seen him come in, so he was startled when he spoke. "Surprised to see me, Martin?"

Martin realized Sloane had watched him enter in the glass's reflection. He saw Sloane's eyes there now. They were cold, calculating, intense... like a predator watching his prey, waiting to strike. The incomplete reflection hid the rest of his face. His hands were clasped behind his back. His long black trench coat looked so out of place here in Jakarta, where heat and humidity forced even bankers into less formal attire. Only bodyguards, or someone with something to hide, covered up so much.

Martin made an effort to look casual. He strode to his oak desk in the middle of the giant office. "Yes, actually. I'm afraid you've caught me at a bad time—"

"Don't. I know it all, Martin." Sloane turned around slowly and spoke deliberately, never taking his eyes off Martin as he walked toward the older man behind the desk. "I know about your little ice-fishing expedition in Antarctica. Your meddling in Tibet. The kids. The kidnapping."

Martin shifted his feet, angling to get behind the desk, to put something between the two of them, but Sloane altered his vector, approaching from the side. Martin stood his ground. He wouldn't back away, even if the brutal man cut his throat right there in his office.

Martin returned Sloane's stare. Sloane's face was lean, muscular, but rough. Years of hard living had taken its toll. It was a face that knew pain.

Sloane stopped his prowling march three feet from Martin. He smiled slightly, like he knew something Martin didn't; as if some trap had been sprung, and he was simply waiting. "I would have found out sooner, but I've been quite busy with this Clocktower situation. But I think you already know about that."

"I've certainly seen the reports. Unfortunate and untimely, to be sure. And as you mentioned, I've had my hands full as well." Martin's hands started to shake slightly. He stuffed them into his pockets. "I had planned to reveal these recent developments— Antarctica, China—"

"Be careful, Martin. Your next lie could be your last."

Martin swallowed and looked at the floor, thinking.

"I just have one question, old man. Why? I've collected all these threads you've spun, but I still don't see your endgame."

"I haven't betrayed my oath. My goal is *our* goal: to prevent a war we both know we can't win."

"Then we agree. The time has come. Toba Protocol is in effect."

"No. Dorian, there is another way. It's true, I've kept these… developments to myself, but for good reason. It was premature, I didn't know if it would work."

"And it hasn't. I read the reports from China, all the adults died. We're out of time."

"True, the test failed, but because we used the wrong therapy. Kate used something else; we didn't know it at the time, but she will tell me. We could walk into the tombs by this time tomorrow—we could finally learn the truth."

It was a long shot, and Martin was almost surprised when Sloane broke his unblinking glare. His eyes looked away, then down. A moment passed, and finally he turned around, pacing back toward the windows, taking up his original position from when Martin had first entered the room. "We already know the truth. And as for Kate and the new therapy... you took her children. She won't talk."

"She will to me."

"I believe I know her better than you."

Martin felt his blood rising.

"Have you opened the sub yet?" Sloane's voice was quiet.

Martin was surprised by the question. Was Sloane testing him? Or did he think...

"No," Martin said. "We're following a more extensive quarantine protocol, just to be on the safe side. I'm told the site is almost secure."

"I want to be there when they open it."

"It's been sealed for over seventy years, nothing could have—"

"I want to be there."

"Of course. I'll inform the site." Martin reached for the phone. He couldn't believe this break. The hope felt like a breath of fresh air after being underwater for three minutes too long. He dialed quickly.

"You can tell them when we get there."

"I'd like nothing more—"

Sloane turned away from the windows. The bloodthirsty stare had returned. His eyes burned holes in Martin. "I'm not asking. We will open that sub together. I'm not letting you out of my sight, not until this is over."

Martin put the phone down. "Very well, but I must speak with Kate first." Martin inhaled, straightening his back. "And now, *I'm* not asking. You need me, we both know it."

Sloane looked at Martin through the window's reflection, and Martin thought he saw a small smile cross the younger man's lips. "I'll give you ten minutes with her. And *when* you fail, we'll leave for Antarctica, and I'll leave her to people who will make her talk."

31

David watched the Immari Security officers pivot and then run into the five-room plaster home on the corner of the row. He had picked this home specifically because of its layout.

The men swept the rooms, moving in swift, mechanical motions, entering each room with their handguns held in front of them, jerking left, then right.

David listened from his hiding place as the men reported. "Clear. Clear. Clear. Clear. Clear." He heard their pace slow as they walked out of the now "safe" residence.

When the second man passed him, David silently slid behind him, covered the man's mouth with a damp cloth, and waited for the chloroform to fill his mouth and nostrils. The man thrashed about, trying desperately to grab David as he lost control of his limbs with each passing second. David held tightly at his mouth. No sound escaped. The man slumped to the ground, and David was about to turn his attention to the other man when he heard the radio in the next room crackle to life.

"Immari Recon Team Five, be advised, Clocktower reports a field locker in your area has been accessed. Target believed to be in close proximity and could be in possession of weapons and explosives from the locker. Proceed with caution. We're sending backup units."

"Cole? Did you hear that?"

David squatted over the man he had just incapacitated—apparently Cole.

"Cole?" the other man called from the next room. David could hear the dirt grinding beneath the soldier's boots. He was walking slowly now, like a man marching through a minefield, where any step could be his last.

As David rose to his feet, the man burst through the doorway, his gun pointed at David's chest. David lunged for him. They collapsed to the ground and fought for the gun. David slammed the man's hands into the dirty floor, and the gun skidded to the wall.

The man repelled David off of him and began crawling for the gun, but David was on him again before he got far, gripping the man's neck with the crook of his elbow in a tight stranglehold. He placed the heel of his hand on the man's upper back to get more leverage. He could feel his prey's airways close. Not much longer.

The man flopped back and forth and clawed at the arm around his neck. He reached down, trying to grasp... what? His pocket? Then the man had it—a knife from his boot. He stabbed back at David, connecting with his side. David heard his clothes rip and saw the blood on the knife, which was coming at him again. He slid to the side, barely missing the second jab. He moved his hand from the man's back up to his head, and using the cross-grip with his arm around the man's neck, he ripped hard. A loud snap rang out, and the man slumped to the floor.

David rolled off the dead mercenary and stared at the ceiling, watching two flies chase each other.

32

Martin's men had taken Kate deep underground, then led her down a long corridor that opened onto what looked like a large aquarium. The glass window was at least fifteen feet tall and maybe sixty wide.

Kate didn't understand what she saw. The scene beyond the glass was clearly the bottom of the Bay of Jakarta, but it was the creatures moving about that puzzled her. At first she thought they were some sort of illuminated sea creatures, like jellyfish, drifting down to the bottom then floating back to the surface. But the lights were wrong. She walked closer to the glass. Yes—they were robots. Almost like robotic crabs, with lights that swiveled like eyes, and four arms, each with three metallic fingers. They burrowed into the ground, then emerged with items in their mechanical hands. She strained to see. What were the items?

"Our excavation methods have come a long way."

Kate turned to see Martin. The look on his face gave her pause, worried her. He looked tired, dejected, resigned. "Martin, please tell me what's going on. Where are the children who were taken from my lab?"

"In a safe place, for now. We don't have much time, Kate. I need to ask you some questions. It's very important that you tell me what you treated those children with. We know it wasn't ARC-247."

How could he know that? And why did he care what she had treated them with? Kate tried to think. Something was wrong here. What would happen if she told him? Was the soldier, David, right?

For the past four years, Martin had been the only man, the only person, whom Kate could allow herself to fully trust. He had always been distant, buried in his work—a legal guardian more than an adoptive father. But he had been there for her when she needed him. He couldn't possibly be involved in the kidnapping. But... something was wrong here...

"I will tell you about the therapy, but I want the children back first," she said.

Martin walked over, joining her beside the glass wall. "I'm afraid that's not possible, but you have my word: I will protect them. You have to trust me, Kate. Many lives are at stake."

Protect them from what? "I want to know what in the world is going on here, Martin."

Martin turned, walking away from her, seeming to ponder. "What if I told you there was a weapon, somewhere in this world, that was more powerful than anything you can imagine? A weapon capable of wiping out the entire human race. And that what you treated those children with is our only chance at survival, our only means to resist this weapon?"

"I'd say that sounds pretty farfetched."

"Does it? You know enough about evolution to know that it's not. The human race isn't nearly as safe as we think it is." He motioned toward the aquarium wall, toward a robot floating down. "What do you think is going on out there?"

"Digging for treasure? A sunken merchant ship maybe."

"Does this look like a treasure hunt to you?" When Kate said nothing, he continued. "What if I told you there was a lost coastal city out there? And that it was only one of many around the world. Around thirteen thousand years ago, most of Europe was under two miles of ice. New York city was covered by a mile of ice. In the span of a few hundred years, the glaciers melted and sea levels rose almost four hundred feet, wiping out every coastal settlement on the face of the planet.

Even today, almost half the human population lives within a hundred miles of the coast. Imagine how many people lived on the coast then, when fish were the most reliable source of food and the seas were the easiest method of trade. Think of the settlements and early cities that were lost forever, the history we'll never recover. The only surviving record we have of this event is the story of the Great Flood. The people who survived the deluge from the glaciers were keen to warn generations that came after them. The story of the Flood is a historical fact—the geological record proves it—and the story appears in the Bible and all the texts we've recovered before it and after it. Cuneiform tablets from Akkadia, text from Sumer, native American civilizations—they all tell of the Flood, but no one knows what happened before it."

"That's what this is about? Finding lost coastal cities—Atlantis?"

"Atlantis is not what you think it is. My point is that there is so much below the surface, so much of our own history that we don't know. Think about what else was lost at the time of the Flood. You know the genetic history. We know that at least two species of humans survived to the time of the Flood—maybe three. Maybe more. We've recently found Neanderthal bones at Gibraltar that are twenty-three thousand years old. We could find bones that are even younger. We've also found bones that were only about twelve thousand years old—dated to around the time of the Flood—less than a hundred miles from where we now stand, off the main island of Java, on Flores Island. We think these hobbit-like humans walked the earth for almost three hundred thousand years. Then, suddenly, twelve thousand years ago, they die out. The Neanderthals evolved six hundred thousand years ago—they had roamed the earth nearly three times longer than us when they died out. You know the history."

"You know I do, and I don't see what this has to do with kidnapping my children."

"Why do you think the Neanderthals and Hobbits died out? They had been around a long time before humans walked onto the scene."

"We killed them."

"That's right. The human race is the biggest mass murderer of all time. Think about it: we're hard-coded to survive. Even our ancient ancestors were driven by this impulse, driven enough to recognize the Neanderthals and Hobbits as dangerous enemies. They may have slaughtered dozens of human subspecies. And that legacy shamefully lives on. We attack whatever is different, anything we don't understand, anything that might change our world, our environment, reduce our chances of survival. Racism, class warfare, sexism, east versus west, north and south, capitalism and communism, democracy and dictatorships, Islam and Christianity, Israel and Palestine, they're all different faces of the same war: the war for a homogeneous human race, an end to our differences. It's a war we started a long time ago, a war we've been fighting ever since. A war that operates in every human mind below the subconscious level, like a computer program, constantly running in the background, guiding us to some eventuality."

Kate didn't know what to say, couldn't see how it could involve her trial and her children. "You expect me to believe those two children are involved in an ancient cosmic struggle for the human race?"

"Yes. Think about the war between the Neanderthals and humans. The battles between the Hobbits and humans. Why did we win? The Neanderthals had bigger brains than us, and they were certainly larger and stronger. But our brains were wired differently. Our minds were wired to build advanced tools, solve problems, and anticipate the future. Our mental software gave us an advantage, but we still don't know how we got it. We were animals, just like them, fifty thousand years ago. But some Great Leap Forward gave us an advantage we still don't understand. The only thing we know for sure is that it was a change in brain wiring, possibly a change in how we used language and communicated. A sudden change. You know all this. But... what if another change is under way? Those children's brains are wired differently. You know how evolution works. It's never a straight line. It operates on trial and error. Those children's brains could simply be the next version of the operating system for the human mind—like the new version of Windows or Mac OS—a newer, faster version... with advantages over the previous release—us. What if those children, or others like them, are the first members of a new branch emerging in the human genetic tree? A new subspecies. What if, somewhere on this planet, a group already has the new software release? How do you think they would treat us, the old humans? Maybe the same way we treated the last humans that weren't as smart as us—Neanderthals and Hobbits."

"That's absurd; those children are no threat to us." Kate studied Martin. He looked different... the look in his eyes, she couldn't place it. And what he was saying, all the talk of genetics and evolutionary history—telling her things she already knew... but why?

"It may not seem that way, but how can we really know?" Martin continued. "From what we know of the past, every advanced human race has wiped out every race they viewed as a threat. We were the predator last time, but we'll be the prey next time."

"Then we'll cross that bridge when we come to it."

"We've already crossed it, we just don't know it. That's the nature of the Frame Problem—in a complex environment, we simply can't know the consequences of our actions, however good they may seem at the time. Ford thought he was creating a device for mass transportation. He also gave the world the means to destroy the environment."

Kate shook her head. "Listen to yourself, Martin. You sound crazy, delusional."

Martin smiled. "I said the same thing when your father gave me the same speech."

Kate considered Martin's claim. It was a lie; it had to be. At the very least it was a distraction, a play for her trust, an effort to remind her that he had taken her in. She stared him down. "You're telling me you took those children to prevent evolution?"

"Not exactly... I can't explain everything, Kate. I really wish I could. All I can tell you is that those children hold the key to preventing a war that will wipe out the human race. A war that has been coming since the day our ancestors sailed out of Africa sixty to seventy thousand years ago. You *have* to trust me. I need to know what you did."

"What is the Toba Protocol?"

Martin looked confused. Or was he frightened? "Where... did you hear that?"

"The soldier who picked me up from the police station. Are you involved in it—Toba?"

"Toba... is a contingency plan."

"Are you involved?" Her voice was steady, but she dreaded the answer.

"Yes, but... Toba may not be needed—*if* you talk to me, Kate."

Four armed men entered from a side door that Kate hadn't seen before.

Martin turned on them. "I wasn't finished talking to her!"

Two guards took her by the arms, forcing her out of the room and down the long corridor she had traveled down to meet Martin.

In the distance, she heard Martin arguing with the other two men.

"Director Sloane said to tell you your time is up. She won't talk, and she knows too much anyway. He's waiting at the helipad."

33

David slapped Cole again, and he came around. He couldn't have been more than twenty-five. The young man looked up through sleepy eyes that grew wide when they saw David.

He tried to draw away, but David held him. "What's your name?"

The man glanced around, searching for help, or maybe an exit. "William Anders." The man searched his body for weapons but found none.

"Look at me. You see the body armor I'm wearing? You recognize it?" David stood, letting the man take in the head-to-toe Immari battle gear he wore. "Follow me," David said.

The groggy man stumbled into the next room, where his partner's dead body lay, his head turned at an awkward, unnatural angle.

"He lied to me too. I'll only ask one more time, what's your name?"

The man swallowed and steadied himself in the doorway. "Cole. Name's Cole Bryant."

"That's better. Where you from, Cole Bryant?"

"Jakarta Branch, Immari Security Select Forces."

"No, where are you from originally?"

"What?" The young mercenary seemed confused by the question.

"Where did you grow up?"

"Colorado. Fort Collins."

David could see that Cole was coming out of the haze. He would be dangerous soon. He needed to find out if Cole Bryant fit the bill.

"Got a family back there?"

Cole took a few steps away from David. "Nope."

It was a lie. Very promising. Now David needed to make him believe.

"They go trick-or-treating in Fort Collins?"

"What?" Cole edged toward the door.

"Stop moving." David's voice was harder. "That feeling at your back, that tightness. You feel that?"

The man touched his lower back, trying to slide a hand into his armor. Confusion clouded his face.

David walked to a duffel bag in the corner of the room and threw the flap open, revealing several square and rectangular brown blocks that looked like Play-doh wrapped in Saran wrap.

"You know what this is?"

Cole nodded.

"I put a small row of this explosive up your spine. This wireless trigger controls it." David held his left hand out, showing Cole a small cylinder about the size of two AA batteries put end to end. At the top was a round red button that David's thumb held down. "You know what this is?"

Cole froze. "A dead man's trigger."

"Very good, Cole. This *is* a dead man's trigger." David stood and slung the duffel bag strap over his shoulder. "If my thumb slips off this button, those explosives will go off, and it will turn your insides into a gelatinous goo. Keep in mind, there's not enough explosive to hurt me, or even penetrate your body armor. I could be standing right next to you, and if I were shot or came to any harm, the explosion would liquefy your insides, leaving your hard outer shell just like a Cadbury Creme Egg. You like Cadbury Creme Eggs, Cole?" David could see he was really scared now.

Cole shook his head slightly to the side.

"Really? They were my favorite when I was a kid. Loved getting those things at Easter. My mom used to even save some to give me at Halloween after I got through trick-or-treating. Couldn't wait to get home and crack one open. The thick chocolate shell, gooey yellow inside." David looked away, as if remembering how delicious they were. He glanced back at Cole. "But you don't want to be a Cadbury Creme Egg, do you Cole?"

34

Martin stepped out of the elevator onto the helipad. The sun had almost set. The sky was red and the wind at the top of the eighty-story building blew in from the sea, carrying the smell of saltwater. Ahead of him, Dorian Sloane waited with three of his men. When he saw Martin, he turned and motioned for the helicopter pilot to start the takeoff sequence. The engine fired, and the rotor blades started to turn.

"I told you she wouldn't talk," Sloane said.

"She needs time."

"It won't help."

Martin straightened. "I know her far better than you do—"

"That's debatable—"

"Say another word, and I'll make you sorry." Martin stepped toward Sloane, now almost shouting over the roar of the helicopter. "She needs time, Dorian. She will talk. I urge you not to do this."

"You created this situation, Martin. I'm just cleaning it up."

"We have time."

"We both know we don't—you said it yourself. And I was quite amused at the other things you said. I assumed you hated me because you hated my methods and plans."

"I hate you because of what you did to her—"

"Which wasn't a tenth of what she did to my family."

"She had nothing to do with that—"

"Let's agree to disagree, Martin. And let's focus on the task at hand."

Sloane grabbed him by the arm and led him away from the helicopter where it would be easier to talk. And, Martin thought, where Sloane's men couldn't hear him.

"Listen, Martin, I'll make you a deal. I'll delay Toba Protocol until we find out if this can work. You let us work on the girl, we'll get what we need in one, maybe two hours, tops. If we leave now for Antarctica, we'll have the information by the time we land. We could test a true Atlantis Gene retrovirus within eight hours. And yes, I know you're looking for an entrance." Martin began to speak, but Dorian waved his hand dismissively. "Don't bother denying it, Martin. I have a man on the team. Within twenty-four hours, you and I could walk through the gates of the tombs together. No Toba. This is the only play you have. We both know it."

"I want your word that she will not be harmed... permanently harmed."

"Martin. I'm not a monster. We just need what she knows; I would never *permanently* harm her."

"We'll agree to disagree on that point." Martin looked down. "We should leave now. The Antarctica site is rather hard to get to."

As they walked to the helicopter, Sloane pulled one of the men aside. "Get Tarea out of that cell, and tell him to find out what Warner did to those kids."

35

They had driven in silence for almost ten minutes when David said, "Tell me Cole, how does a kid from Fort Collins wind up at Immari Security?"

Cole stared straight ahead, focusing on driving. "You say it like it's a bad thing."

"You have no idea."

"Says the guy who killed my partner and strapped a bomb to my spine."

Cole had a point. But David couldn't explain—that would take away his leverage. Sometimes you had to be a bad guy to save the good guys.

They continued on in silence until they reached the Immari Jakarta Campus—a collection of six buildings surrounded by a high chain-link fence, topped with barbed wire. Guardhouses flanked every entrance. David put the helmet and goggles on and handed Cole the ID of the man he'd killed.

At the gate, the guard stepped out of the booth and sauntered over to the car. "ID?"

Cole handed him two Immari ID Cards. "Bryant and Stevens."

The guard took the IDs. "Thanks, asshole. I've only been reading for forty years now."

Cole held up a hand. "Just trying to be helpful."

The guard leaned in the window. "Take the helmet off," he said to David.

David pulled the helmet off and looked straight forward, then to the side, hoping the side view would pass, that the closer look was just mild professional hazing or the insecure guard pounding his chest.

The guard examined the ID, then scrutinized David. He repeated the motion several times. "Just a minute." He hurried back to the booth.

"That standard?" David asked Cole.

"Never happened before."

The man had the phone at his ear. He was dialing, his eyes glued to the two of them.

David drew his gun and reached across the car in one fluid motion. The guard dropped the phone and reached for his gun. David fired a single shot, hitting the man in the left shoulder, just above where the vest ended. The man collapsed to the ground. He would live, but his attitude probably wouldn't improve.

Cole looked over at David, then gunned the car toward the main Immari Headquarters building.

"Park at the rear entrance, near the boat landing." David reached into the backseat and grabbed a small pack filled with explosives. He pulled the duffel bag with the remaining charges into the floorboard.

In the distance, they heard the wail of sirens erupt across the campus perimeter.

They entered the building through an unguarded loading dock door. David placed a charge on the wall next to the door. He punched a code into the detonator, and it began beeping. It was hard to do one-handed, but he had to keep his thumb on the trigger for Cole's sake.

They moved down the hallway, and David placed additional explosives every twenty feet or so.

David had opted not to tell Cole anything before they arrived—his captive could have found a way to communicate the information to Immari HQ, or they could be intercepted. Either way, there was no upside. Now he had to explain. "Listen, Cole.

They're holding a woman somewhere in this building. Dr. Kate Warner. We need to find her."

Cole hesitated for a moment, then said, "The holding cells and interrogation rooms are in the middle of the building, on the forty-seventh floor... But even if she is there and you get her out of the room, you'll never get out of the building. Security is on its way here now, and there are already dozens of guards in this building alone. Plus field agents who've returned." Cole motioned to the dead man's trigger in David's left hand. "What happens to me if you..."

David thought. "Is there any field ops equipment in this building?"

"Yeah, the main armory on three, but most of the weapons and armor are gone. The entire field regiment was deployed to kill you today."

"It won't matter; they wouldn't have taken what I need. When we have the girl, I'll give you this trigger. You have my word, Cole. Then I'll make my own way out."

Cole nodded once, then said, "There's a service stairwell without cameras."

"One thing before we go." David opened a supply closet and lit a fire. In seconds, the flame licked up the wood racks toward the smoke detector on the ceiling.

Fire alarms called out around them as flickering LED lights punctuated the din, and pandemonium broke out. Doors opened, people ran from rooms left and right, sprinklers sprang to life, and water soaked the fleeing masses.

"Now we can go."

36

In the elevator, Kate had fought at the guards' vice-grip hold on her arms. They pinned her to the wall until the elevator doors opened, then hauled her into a room with what looked like a reclining dentist's chair. They threw her down, strapped her in, and sneered, "The doctor will be right in." They had laughed as they walked out.

Now she waited. Her initial relief at seeing Martin felt like a million years ago. Fear started to grip her. The wide straps cut into her arms, just above where the zip-ties had gouged her wrists. The room's walls were stark white, and except for the chair, the only thing in the room was a steel high-top table with a round bundle on it. She could barely see it from the reclining chair, which forced her gaze up toward the buzzing fluorescent lights.

The door opened, and she craned her head to see. It was him—the man who had taken the kids. The man who took her from the soldier's van. A wide smile spread across his face. It was a mean smile, the kind that said, "I have you now."

He stopped a few feet from her face. "You've gotten me in a lot of trouble today, little girl. But life is about second chances." He walked over to the steel table and unrolled the bundle. Out of the corner of her eye, Kate could barely make out the gleam of steel utensils, long and pointy. He glared back at her over his shoulder. "Oh, who am I kidding? In my experience, life is about payback." He took out one of his tools of torture, a smaller

147

version of a grilling skewer. "You're going to tell me what I need to know, and I hope it takes as long as physically possible."

Another man came in. He wore a white coat and held something Kate couldn't quite see, possibly a syringe. "What are you doing?" he asked the torturer.

"Getting started. What are you doing?"

"That's not the plan. We use the drugs first. Those are the orders."

"Not my orders."

Kate lay there, helpless, as the men stared at each other, the torturer holding the silver prod, the white-coat clutching the syringe.

Finally, syringe-man said, "Whatever. I'm going to give her this, then you can do whatever you want."

"What is it?"

"Something new we're using in Pakistan. Basically turns their brains to mush; they'll tell you anything."

"Is it permanent?" the torturer asked.

"Sometimes. Been lots of different side effects. We're still working on it." He jammed the oversized syringe into Kate's arm and injected slowly. She felt the cold liquid fill her veins. She fought against the straps, but they were too tight.

"How long will it take?"

"Ten, maybe fifteen minutes."

"Will she remember?"

"Probably not."

The torturer set the silver tool down and walked over to Kate. He ran a hand down her chest and legs. "So cute. And feisty. Maybe they'll let me have you when they have their answers."

37

Kate didn't know how long it had been; didn't know if she had been asleep or if she was awake now. Her body didn't hurt. She couldn't feel the straps, couldn't feel anything. She was so thirsty. The lights were blinding. She turned her head to the side, licking her lips. So thirsty.

The ugly man was in her face. He grabbed her chin and jerked her back into the light. She squinted. His face, so mean. Angry. "I'd say we're about ready for our first date, Princess."

He pulled something out of his pocket. A sheet of paper?

"But first, we need to get some paperwork out of the way. Just a couple of questions. Question number one: What did you give those children?" He pointed at the paper. "Ah, and we have a footnote here: 'We know it wasn't A-R-C 2-4-7,' whatever that is. They know it wasn't that, so don't even try it. So, what was it? Final answer, please."

Kate tried to fight the urge to respond. She shook her head side to side, but in her mind's eye, she saw herself in the lab, preparing it, worrying that it wouldn't work, or that it would harm their brains, turn them to... mush... the drug they had given her... She had to...

"What was it? Tell us."

"I gave... my babies..."

He leaned over her. "Speak up, Princess. We can't hear you. Operators are standing by to record your answers."

"I gave... couldn't... gave my babies..."

"Yes, that's it, gave your babies what?"

"Gave my babies..."

He sat up. "Jesus, you guys hearing this? She's fried." He closed the door. "Time for Plan B." He did something in the corner of the room.

She couldn't focus.

Then an alarm—and water, falling from the ceiling. Lights flashing, even brighter than the lights before. Kate squeezed her eyes shut. How much time had passed? A loud sound, more of them. Gunfire. The door exploding.

The ugly man fell, bloody. They unstrapped her, but she couldn't stand. She flowed out of the seat onto the ground like a child going down a waterslide.

She could see him—the soldier from the van. David. He wore a backpack. He handed another man a small device. The other man was scared; he put his thumb on the device. Their voices sounded muffled, like Kate was underwater.

The soldier took her face in his hands. Soft brown eyes met hers. "Gate? Dan view cheer bee? Gate?" His hands were warm. The water was cold. She licked her lips. She should have drunk some. Still so thirsty.

He jumped up, more gun blasts. He left. He was back. "Dan view foot your harms houuround bee?" He held her arms, but she couldn't move them; they fell, lifeless, to the ground. They were made of concrete.

He darted back to the door and threw something.

He picked her up in both his arms, strong arms. He ran. Ahead of them a wall of glass and steel exploded. Shards hit her, but they didn't hurt.

They were flying. No, falling. He held her tight, with only one arm now. He reached back, trying to get something.

Then they were yanked back, caught on something. She flew, fell from his arms, but he held her, by one arm. She dangled as he glided above, suspended by strings from a white cloud. His grip was slipping—she was too wet, her clothes were wet. She was falling.

He trapped her with his feet, digging into her back and ribs.

His hand moved up her arm, and finally he wrapped both legs around her. She faced down now, and she saw them.

Men, gunfire, below—the building and the docks were filling with them. More men ran out of the buildings and began firing. Beeps above. The bottom of the building exploded, throwing shrapnel and pieces of the soldiers into the parking lot.

Ripping sounds above; they fell faster now. The man wiggled, and she felt them flying away, moving farther out over the bay.

More sounds below—motors cranking and more gunfire. They twisted around, and she saw the marina swarming to life. Rapid beeps above. A car in the parking lot winked out of existence, sending a wall of flame and smoke hundreds of feet around it, engulfing everything and everyone. The gunfire stopped.

It was quiet, peaceful now. She saw the last rays of sunlight set over the Java Sea as darkness fell. They hung there for a time. Kate didn't know how long.

Above, she heard another rip, and they were plummeting to the black sea below. Kate felt him struggling, reaching for something. The legs around her slipped; they finally lost their grip, and she was falling faster, by herself. Seconds passed in slow motion. She rolled as she fell, saw the man floating above her, floating away from her.

She heard but didn't feel the loud crack as the water engulfed her, pushing her down, now pulling her down. Water, cold saltwater was in her mouth and her nose, and she couldn't breathe, could only suck in water. It burned. The darkness was almost complete, just a glimmer of light at the surface where the moon kissed the sea.

She drifted now, arms at her side, eyes open, waiting.

Waiting. She fought not to breathe more water. Her mind went blank. No thoughts. Only cold water, all around her and burning in her lungs.

A flare, a burning stick falling down, too far away from her. And something swimming at the surface, like a tiny bug, too far away. Another flare, closer, but still too far. The creature bobbed its head below, swam, then went back up for air. A third flare, and the figure dived down, toward her. It grabbed her and pulled her, kicking violently toward the surface. They would never reach it. She took another gulp of water, had to, needed air. It invaded her, felt like cold concrete being poured down her mouth. And it pulled at her so hard, not letting her rise, and the moon was there and then everything was so dark.

She felt the air now, the wind and the droplets of rain, heard the splashing around. The splashing went on so long, and the arm was around her, keeping her up, her head out of the water.

There was a loud sound, a huge boat, with lights. It would hit them. It was coming straight for them. She saw her rescuer wave his hands and pull her out of its path.

Another man, hands pulling her up, and she was on her back. Her rescuer was over her, pressing on her chest, pinching her nose, and… he kissed her. His breath was so hot; it filled her mouth and pushed into her lungs. She resisted at first, but then she kissed him back. She hadn't done that in so long. She fought to lift her arms, but she couldn't, she tried again, and yes, she reached up, tried to hold him. He pushed her arms away, held them down. She lay there, motionless just before her chest exploded. Water gushed from her mouth and nose as he rolled her over. The water kept coming in coughs and gags. Her stomach spasmed, and she drew air in desperate breaths.

He held her until her breathing slowed. Every breath burned, her lungs still wouldn't fill, every intake was shallow.

He yelled out to the other man, "Tights! Tights!" He drew a hand across his neck in a cutting motion. Nothing happened.

He got up and marched away. A second later, the lights went off and they were moving, fast. The rain whipped at Kate's face, but she just lay there, unable to move.

He picked her up again, just as he had carried her out of the tall tower. He took her below and laid her down on a small bed in a cramped room.

She heard voices. Saw him pointing at a man. "Arto, stop, stop!" He pointed again.

Then he came for her, collecting her in his strong arms, and they were off the boat, on land again. They walked along a beach, toward a wrecked town, like something that had been bombed in World War II. They were inside some kind of cottage, and the lights were on. She was so tired, couldn't stay awake a second longer. He set her down on a bed of flowers—no, a comforter with a floral pattern. She closed her eyes and almost went to sleep, but she felt him at her feet, pulling her wet pants off. She smiled. He reached for her shirt. Panic. He would see it—the scar. His hands gripped the shirt, but she held them, struggling to hold the shirt down.

"Gate, view half dew put dry flows on."

"No." She shook her head and turned over.

"View half..."

She could barely hear him.

He tugged at the shirt.

"Please don't," she mumbled. "Please don't..."

Then he was releasing her, the weight on the bed shifted, and he was gone.

A motor started, a small one. And warm air was around her, on top of her. She twisted, and it warmed her stomach, her hair. Her whole body was warm.

38

Cole lay on his stomach, waiting. He had been waiting for almost an hour as the bomb tech fiddled with his vest. He fought not to squirm, not to lose control of his bladder, not to scream. One thought ran through his head, over and over: *I'll never see my family again.* He should have never taken the job, regardless of the money. They had saved almost enough—$150,000 of the $250,000 they needed to open a Jiffy Lube. With his money from two straight deployments with the Marines, they would have been fine. But he wanted to have "a little extra" saved—just in case business was light those first few years. The Immari recruiter had said, "You're mostly there for show, to make our clients feel safe. As you requested, we'll assign you to a low-security region, definitely not the Middle East, or even South America. Europe requires seniority. Southeast Asia has been very quiet. You'll love the weather in Jakarta." Now some other Immari suit would be knocking on his wife's door. "Ma'am, your husband was killed in an unfortunate Cadbury Creme Egg incident. Our deepest condolences. What? Oh, no ma'am, this never happens. Here are his creme-egg remains." Cole let out a harsh, almost irrational laugh. He was losing it.

"Hang in there, Cole. We're almost in," the bomb tech said from behind a thick curved blast shield. The man wore a bulky helmet and peered through a glass strip at the top of the blast shield. His arms jutted out through two silver accordion-type metal arm sheaths that looked like the arms from the robot on the 60's TV show *Lost in Space*.

The tech carefully cut the straps on Cole's vest. He lifted the vest slightly and bent closer to the glass slit in the blast shield for a better look.

Sweat drops popped up across Cole's already soaked face.

"It's not booby trapped," the tech said. Inch by inch, he peeled the vest back. "Let's see what we've got."

Cole almost jumped when he heard the man throw the vest the rest of the way over. Was there a timer? A backup? He felt the man's hands work quickly at his spine. Then he felt the gloved hands go limp. He heard the screeching of metal on metal as the tech forcefully slid the blast shield out of the way. He worked with his bare hands now.

Cole felt the man lift the bomb off his spine.

"You can get up now, Cole."

Cole turned, holding his breath.

The man looked at him with contempt. "Here's your bomb, Cole. Be careful now, you could be allergic to polyester." He handed Cole a rolled up t-shirt.

Cole couldn't believe it. He was embarrassed, but mostly, he was relieved.

Cole unrolled the t-shirt. It read, in big black magic marker letters: "BOOM!" Below it, in smaller print: "Sorry..."

39

Batavia Marina
Jakarta, Indonesia

Harto put his arm around his wife and gathered his son and daughter at his side. They stood on the wooden dock at the marina where Harto had retrieved the boat the soldier had told him about. The four of them beheld the machine, no one saying a word. It sparkled. It all still seemed like a dream to Harto. The boat was the most beautiful thing he'd seen since his youngest child was born.

"It's ours," he said.

"How, Harto?"

"The soldier man gave it to me."

His wife ran a hand along the boat, maybe to see if it was truly real. "It's almost too nice to fish in."

The boat was a mini-yacht. At sixty feet, it was capable of travel between the small islands off Java. It could hold up to thirty people above deck and sleep as many as eight below deck in the master stateroom, port guest stateroom, and aft guest stateroom. The upper deck and fly bridge would give breathtaking views.

"We're not going to fish with it," Harto said. "We're going to take others fishing. The foreigners living here and the tourists. They pay lots of money for this—to go fishing in the deep sea. And for other things: diving and touring the islands."

His wife looked from Harto to the boat, then back again, as if trying to assess whether it would work, or maybe how much work it would be for her. "You going to finally learn English, Harto?"

"I'll have to. There aren't enough fish in the sea to feed all the Jakartan fishermen. Entertainment is the future."

PART II
A TIBETAN TAPESTRY

40

Kate awoke to the worst headache of her life. It hurt to move. She lay in the bed for a moment, swallowing several times. Opening her eyes hurt. The sunlight hurt. She turned over, away from the window. The window. The bed. Where was she?

She pushed herself up, and with each inch she moved, the pain spread across her. Her body was sore, but it didn't feel like the soreness from exercise—she felt like she'd been beaten all over with wooden spoons. She felt sick, hurt. *What happened to me?*

The room came into focus. A cottage or some kind of vacation home on the beach. The room was small, with one double bed and some rustic wooden furniture. Out the window, she saw a large porch that opened onto a deserted beach. Not the pristine, well-kept kind you saw at resorts, but the type you might find on a real deserted island—a rough, unkempt beach, littered with coconuts, tree bark, tropical plants, and here and there, dead fish that had washed up from last night's violent rain and high tide.

Kate pushed the covers off and moved slowly to get out of bed. A new sensation gripped her: nausea. She waited, hoping it would pass, but it only got worse. She felt the saliva gathering at the back of her throat.

She ran for the bathroom, barely making it in time. She collapsed to her knees and dry heaved into the toilet. Once, then again, and a third time. The convulsions sent shock waves of pain through her already ravaged body. The nausea receded, and she rolled off her knees to sit by the toilet, propping an elbow on the toilet seat and resting her hand on her forehead.

"At least you don't have a walk of shame ahead of you."

She looked up. It was the man from the van, the soldier. David.

"What are you, where are we—"

"We'll catch up later. Drink this."

"No. I'll just throw it up."

He bent down to her and tipped the orange concoction toward her. "Give it a try."

He held the back of her head, and she realized she was drinking it before she could object again. It was sweet and coated her raw throat. She drank it down, and he helped her to her feet.

There was something she had to do. What was it? Something she had to get. Her head still pounded.

He helped her into the bed, but she stopped. "Wait, there's something I have to do."

"We'll get to it. You have to rest."

Without another word, he maneuvered her into the bed. She felt so sleepy, like she had taken a sleeping pill. The sweet orange elixir.

41

Martin Grey leaned toward the plane window and peered out at the giant iceberg below. The Nazi sub jutted out of a mountain of ice near the center of the floating island, which covered almost forty-seven square miles—about the size of Disney World. Where the sub met the ice, workers and heavy machinery were hard at work excavating, searching for the sub's entrance. Cutting into the side was a last resort, but it would come to that if they didn't reach the hatch soon.

The wreckage below the sub was even more mysterious; teams were still working on theories. Martin had one of his own, an idea he would take to his grave if necessary.

"When did you find it?"

Dorian Sloane's voice startled Martin, and he turned to see the younger man standing over him, gazing out another window of the jet.

Martin opened his mouth to respond, but Sloane interrupted him. "No lies, Martin."

Martin slumped in the chair, and continued squinting out the window. "Twelve days ago."

"Is it his?"

"The markings are the same. Carbon dating confirms the age."

"I want to go in first."

Martin turned to him. "I wouldn't advise it. The wreckage is likely unstable. There's no way of knowing what's inside. There could be—"

"And you're coming with me."

"Absolutely not."

"Now Martin, where's that intrepid explorer I knew in my youth?"

"This is a job for robots. They can go into places we can't. They can withstand cold, and it *will* be cold in there, colder than you can imagine. And they're easier to replace."

"Yes, it will be dangerous. Even more dangerous, I think, if I go alone, with, say, you left outside."

"You assume I'm as morally bankrupt as you are."

"I'm not the one kidnapping kids and keeping secrets." Sloane leaned back in a chair across from Martin, readying for a fight.

A steward entered their compartment and said to Sloane, "Sir, there's a call for you. It's urgent."

Dorian picked up the phone from the wall. "Sloane."

He listened, then looked up at Martin, surprised. "How?" A moment passed. "You can't be serious—" He nodded a few times. "No, look, he had to leave by boat. Search the surrounding islands, they couldn't have gone far. Deploy everyone, bring in troops from local Immari Security and secured Clocktower cells if you have to." He listened again. "Fine, whatever, use the media to box them in. Kill him and capture her. Call me back when you have her."

Sloane hung up the phone and scrutinized Martin as he said, "The girl got away. A Clocktower agent helped her."

Martin continued surveying the site below.

Sloane put his elbows on the table and leaned close enough to strike Martin. "Fifty of my men are dead, and three floors of Immari Jakarta have been blown to pieces, not to mention the wharf. You don't seem surprised, Martin."

"I'm looking at an eighty-year-old Nazi sub and what could be an alien spaceship sticking out of an iceberg off the coast of Antarctica. I'm hard to surprise these days, Dorian."

Sloane leaned back. "We both know it's not an alien spaceship."

"Do we?"

"We will soon."

42

Somewhere off the Java Sea

For a while, David leaned against the doorframe in the bedroom, watching Kate sleep, waiting to see if she would wake up again. The Immari thugs had really put her through the wringer, and his rescue of her hadn't exactly been gentle, either.

Seeing her sleeping there while the waves rolled in and the breeze blew through the room somehow put him at peace. He didn't understand it. The fall of Jakarta Station in the face of an imminent terror threat—from the very people he had dedicated his life to stopping—was a nightmare scenario. No—*the* nightmare scenario. But saving Kate had affected David in some way. The world felt less scary now, more manageable. For the first time since he could remember, he was... hopeful. Almost happy. He felt safer. No, that was wrong. Maybe... the people around him were safer, or he felt more confident. Confident that he could protect the people he...

The self-analysis would have to wait. He had work to do.

When it was clear Kate wouldn't wake up again anytime soon, he withdrew from the room and resumed his work in the hidden chamber below the cottage.

He had told the contractors he wanted a bomb shelter. They had said nothing, but the looks they gave each other said it all. *This dude is crazy, but he didn't argue about the price, so get to work.* They had given the room a strong post-apocalyptic, end-of-the-world motif: all concrete walls, a utilitarian built-in metal desk, and just enough room for a small bed and some supplies. It was fitting given his situation.

His next move was crucial. He had deliberated about what to do for most of the morning. His first instinct was to contact Clocktower Central. The director, Howard Keegan, was his mentor and friend. David trusted him. Howard would be doing everything he could to secure Clocktower, and he would definitely need David's help.

The issue was getting in touch. Clocktower didn't have any back-door communication channels, just the official VPN and protocols. Those would no doubt be monitored—connecting would paint a target on his location.

David drummed his fingers on the metal desk, leaned back in the chair, and stared at the lightbulb hanging from the ceiling.

He opened a web browser and scoured all the local and national news. He was procrastinating. There was nothing here that could help him. He did see a wire release about a woman and man sought in connection with a terrorist plot and possible child-trafficking ring. That could slow him down. There were no sketches attached to the article, but they would follow shortly, and every border security agency in Southeast Asia would be on the lookout for both of them.

David had several IDs in the safe house but not much cash.

He opened his bank account. The balance was almost zero. Josh—he had executed the transfers. Was he alive? David had assumed Jakarta Station HQ was attacked when he had been in the streets. There was something else. Several deposits, all small, less than a thousand dollars. All even dollar amounts. It was a code, but what kind? GPS?

9.11
50.00
31.00
14.00
76.00
9.11

9.11—that would be the start and end of the code. The rest: 50.31.14.76. An IP address. Josh had sent him a message.

David opened a web browser and typed in the IP. The page was a letter from Josh.

David,

They're outside the door. It won't hold much longer.

I decoded the messages. Click here to read them. I couldn't figure out what they meant. I'm sorry.

I did find the contact, online at least. He's using the Roswell Craigslist board to pass messages. Click here to go there. I hope he sends another message and that you stop the attack.

I'm really sorry I couldn't help more.

- Josh

PS: I read your letter and executed the transactions (obviously). I thought you were dead—the sensor on your suit showed no vitals. I hope that doesn't mess you up.

David exhaled and looked away from the screen for a long moment. He opened the file with the decoded messages: obituaries from the *New York Times*. In 1947. Josh had done some great work. And he had died thinking he'd failed.

David opened the Roswell Craigslist site, and he saw it immediately: a new message from the contact.

Subject: Running down the clock on a tower of lies
Message:
To my anonymous admirer:

I'm afraid my current relationship has become complicated. I can't meet you or have any contact.

I'm sorry. It's not me. It's you. You're too dangerous
for me.

There are 30 reasons and 88 excuses I've come up with
not to meet you. I've run through 81 lies and 86 stories.

I told myself I would meet you.

I even set a date. 03-12-2013

And a time 10:45:00

But the truth is you're #44 on my list of priorities
at this point. And that's just not enough to pay
attention to. Maybe if you were 33. Or 23. Or even 15.
It's just not enough.

I have to cut the power on this and save my kids.

It's the only responsible thing to do.

David scratched his head. What did it mean? It was clearly a
code of some kind. He could really use Josh's help right now.

David took out a pad and tried to focus. His brain wasn't
built for this sort of thing. Where to start? The first part was
pretty straightforward: the contact was under duress now. He
couldn't meet or send any more messages. Terrific news. The
rest was a series of numbers, and the words around them were
nonsense. They made sense in this missed connection board, but
they had nothing to say and added nothing new to the message.
The numbers. They had to mean something.

David began scribbling on the pad, extracting the numbers
from the message. In order, they were:

30,88. 81,86.
03-12-2013
10:45:00
#44
33-23-15

The first part: *30,88. 81,86.* GPS coordinates. David checked.
Western China, right at the border of Nepal and India. Satellite

images revealed nothing there... except, what was it? An abandoned building. An old train station.

Next: *03-12-2013 and 10:45:00*. A date and time. The contact said he couldn't meet, so what would be at that abandoned train station? A trap? Another clue? If Josh had read the letter—and followed the instructions—he would have sent everything he'd found to Clocktower Central. If Central was compromised, Immari would know all about the obituaries and the Craigslist board. The message could be from Immari. A set of special forces could be there in China, waiting for David to wander into the crosshairs.

David pushed the thought out of his mind and focused on the last set of numbers in the message: *#44* and *33-23-15*. It had to be a locker in the train station. Or maybe the number 44 train or car? David rubbed the bridge of his nose and read the posting again.

The sentences after the numbers... It was a different sort of message. Instructions?

"I have to cut the power on this and save my kids.

It's the only responsible thing to do."

"Have to cut the power." "Save my kids." David turned the phrases over in his mind.

He made the decision: he would go to the coordinates at the specified date and time and see what was really there. He would leave Kate here, where she was safe. She knew something, but he didn't know how it fit in. *She will be safe here*. That was important to him.

Above him, he heard someone walking around the cottage.

43

Al Jazeera Wire Release

Indonesian authorities identify two Americans connected to terror attacks and child-trafficking ring

Jakarta, Indonesia // A string of terror attacks yesterday in Indonesia's capital of Jakarta have sparked a manhunt on land, sea, and air. The Indonesian National Police has deployed half of its twelve-thousand-person-strong marine unit in the Java Sea and called in troops from around the country to search Jakarta and the islands surrounding it. Neighboring governments have also joined the search by putting their border and airport security divisions on alert. Authorities have so far been mum on the reason for the attacks, but they have released brief sketches of the suspects.

The woman, Dr. Katherine Warner, has been identified as a genetics researcher performing unauthorized experiments on impoverished children from rural villages outside Jakarta. "We're still putting the pieces together," said Police Inspector General Nakula Pang. "We know Dr. Warner's clinic was the legal guardian of over 100 Indonesian children who were taken without their parents' consent. We also know Dr. Warner was moving a lot of money via accounts in the Cayman Islands—a common haven for drug smuggling, human trafficking, and other major international crimes. At this time, we believe the clinic was a front for child-trafficking, and from what we can tell, the proceeds may have gone to finance yesterday's attacks."

Those attacks included three separate blasts in residential neighborhoods, a violent firefight in the market district, and a deadly series of explosions in the wharf that claimed the lives of 50 employees of Immari Jakarta. Adam Lynch, a spokesperson for Immari Jakarta, issued this statement: "We mourn yesterday's loss of life, and today we're simply searching for answers. The Indonesian police have confirmed our suspicions that the attack was carried out by David Vale, a former CIA operative who had previous contact with Immari Security—another division of Immari International. We believe these attacks are part of a personal vendetta and that Mr. Vale will continue to attack Immari employees and interests. He's a very dangerous man. He could be suffering from PTSD or another psychological condition. It's a very sad situation for everyone involved. We've offered our help, including assistance from Immari Security, to the Indonesian authorities and neighboring governments. We want to conclude this nightmare. We want to tell our people they're safe as soon as we possibly can."

44

When Kate woke up the second time, she felt much, much better. Her head hurt less, her body barely ached, and—she could think.

She looked around the room. It was almost dark. How long had she slept? Through the windows, the sun was setting over the sea. It was beautiful, and the view held her attention for a brief moment. The breeze was warm and smelled of saltwater. On the porch a ratty rope hammock swayed in the wind, its rusty chains creaking with each gust. The place looked and felt so deserted.

She got up and walked out of the bedroom into a large living room, which opened to the kitchen and a door to the porch. Was she alone? No, there was a man, but—

"Sleeping beauty rises." The man seemed to appear out of nowhere. What was his name? David.

Kate hesitated for a moment, not sure what to say. "You drugged me."

"Yes, but in my defense, I didn't do it to ply you with questions and do terrible things to your kids."

In a flood, it all came back to her. Martin, the drugs, the interrogation. But what had happened after? How did she get here? It didn't matter. "We have to find those children."

"*We* don't have to do anything. You have to rest, and I have to work."

"Look—"

"And before that, you need to eat." He held up something that looked like a prepackaged weight-loss meal, but it was more hardy—like a soldier's ration pack.

Kate leaned closer. Vegetable beef stew with crackers. Or something approximating vegetable beef stew. Kate wanted to turn away, but the sight and smell of the hot food made her stomach rumble—she was starving. She hadn't eaten all day yesterday. She took the meal, sat down, and pulled the plastic off the flimsy carton. A plume of steam rose from it. She took a bite of the beef and almost spit it out. "God, it's terrible."

"Yeah, sorry about that; it's a little past its expiration, and it wasn't that great to begin with. And no, I don't have anything else. Sorry."

Kate took another bite, chewing only briefly before swallowing it down. "Where are we?"

David sat down at the table opposite her. "An abandoned development off the coast of Jakarta. I bought a place here after the developers went bust, figured it would be a good off-the-books safe house in case I ever had to leave Jakarta in a hurry."

"I don't remember much of that." Kate tried the vegetables. The urge to hurl was abating—either it tasted better than the beef or she was getting used to the meal's general repulsiveness. "We have to go to the authorities."

"I wish we could." He slid a printout over to her, an article from Al Jazeera describing a manhunt for them.

Kate choked down some vegetables and half-shouted, "This is absurd. This is—"

He took back the page. "It won't matter soon. Whatever they're planning, it's happening now. They're looking for us, and they have government connections. Our options are pretty limited here. I have a lead, and I need to check it out. You'll be safe here. I need you to tell me—"

"No way I'm staying here." Kate shook her head. "No way."

"I know you don't remember it, but it wasn't that easy extracting you from Immari custody. These are some very bad people. This is not like the movies where the hero and girl go off on a grand adventure for the sake of plot convenience. This is what we're going to do: you're going to tell me everything you know, you have my word that I will do everything I can to save those two children. You will stay here and monitor a website for new messages."

"No deal."

"Look, I'm not offering you a deal, I'm telling you—"

"I'm not doing it. You need me. And I'm not staying here." She finished the last bite of the meal and tossed the plastic spork into the empty carton. "And besides, I think the safest place to be is with you."

"Nice. That's a nice touch, appealing to my ego like that, but unfortunately, I'm just barely, *barely* smart enough not to fall for it."

"You're leaving me here because you think I'll be in your way."

"I'm trying to keep you safe."

"That's not my biggest concern."

The man opened his mouth to respond, then stopped, jerking his head sharply to the side.

"What—"

His hand shot up. "Quiet."

Kate shifted in her seat. Then she saw it—a spotlight, sweeping the beach. The faintest sound of a helicopter. How had he heard that?

He sprang up, grabbed Kate by the arm and half-dragged her to the coat closet near the entrance to the home. He pushed hard on the back wall and it swung inward, revealing a concrete stairway.

Kate looked back at him. "What is this—"

"Get down there. I'm right behind you."

"Where are you going?" Kate asked, but he was gone.

Kate ran back into the home. David was gathering up their things: the meal and his jacket. Kate ran into the bedroom and smoothed the covers, then quickly wiped down the bathroom. The helicopter noise was still in the distance, but it was getting closer. It was dark now, and she could see very little. The faint light barely illuminated the beach.

David popped into the room and looked at Kate. "Good job, now come on."

They raced back to the coat closet, through the passage, and down into a small room that looked like a bomb shelter. There was a desk with a computer, a single light hanging from the ceiling, and a small bed—definitely designed for one.

The soldier forced Kate onto the single bed and held his index finger at his lips. Then he pulled the cord on the bulb, plunging them into total darkness.

Sometime later, Kate heard footsteps on the floor above.

45

Martin Grey watched as the robots twisted the wheel of the submarine's hatch. He could barely move in the suit—an actual astronaut's suit they had purchased hastily from the Chinese Space Agency a week ago. It was the only thing that could withstand the temperature in Antarctica, shield them from the possible radiation, and provide enough oxygen in case their cord got disconnected. Despite the suit's protection, going into the Nazi sub still scared him to death. And the man in the suit beside him—Dorian Sloane—only added to Martin's worries. Sloane had a short fuse, and what they were about to find could definitely set him off. In a sub, even the smallest explosions were fatal.

The hatch groaned loudly, the wail of metal on metal. But it still didn't budge. The robotic arm detached, slid, re-attached, turned again and then—BOOM—the hatch blew straight back like the door on a jack-in-the-box. The robot was instantly crushed against the sub, sending metal and plastic shards scattering across the snow as air hissed out.

Over the radio in his suit, Martin heard Dorian Sloane's disembodied voice. The hollow, mechanical effect of the radio made him sound even more menacing than usual. "After you, Martin."

Martin looked over at the man's cold eyes, then swung back toward the hatch. "Ops, do you have video?"

"Copy, Dr. Grey, we have video for both suits."

"Okay. We're entering now."

Martin lumbered toward the three-foot round entrance at the top of the small ice hill. When he reached the hatch, he turned around, squatted down, and placed a foot on the first step. He took an LED light stick from his side and dropped it into the shaft. It fell about fifteen or twenty feet. A ping of hard plastic on metal echoed through the icy tomb, and light spread out below him, revealing a corridor to the right.

Martin took another step. The metal rungs were coated with ice. Another step and he was holding the ladder with both hands, but he could feel one of his feet slipping. He tried to tighten his grip, but before he could, his feet flew off the ladder. He slammed into the back of the hatch and he was falling—the light engulfed him, then it was dark—and he landed with a puff. The insulation had saved him. But... if the suit had torn, the cold would flood in and freeze him to death in seconds. Martin put his hands on his helmet, feeling around feverishly. Then a light, falling leisurely down the shaft. The glowing lamp landed on Martin's stomach, casting light all around him. He looked at the suit. It looked okay.

Above him, Sloane came into view, blotting out the sunlight. "Looks like you've been riding a desk too long, old man."

"I told you I shouldn't be down here."

"Just move out of the way."

Martin rolled over and crawled out of the opening just as Sloane slid down the ladder, his hands and feet holding it at both sides without ever touching the rungs.

"I've studied the schematic, Martin. The bridge is straight ahead."

They clicked the lights on their helmets on and trudged down the corridor.

The sub, or technically U-boat, was in pristine condition—it had been sealed and frozen. It looked just as it might have eighty years ago when it left port in northern Germany. It could have been a museum piece.

The corridor was tight, especially with the bulk of the suits, and both men had to tug at their air supply cords periodically as they waded deeper into the relic. The corridor opened onto a larger area. Sloane and Martin stopped and rotated their headlamps left and right, revealing the room in flashes, like a lighthouse carving beams of light into the night. The room was clearly the bridge or some sort of command center. Every few seconds, Martin caught a glimpse of horror: a mangled man, lying prostrate over a chair, skin melted from his face; another slumped against the bulkhead, bloodstains all over his clothes; and a group of men, lying face down in a frozen block of blood. These men looked as if they had been put into a giant microwave, then flash-frozen.

Martin heard his radio click on. "This look like Bell radiation?"

"Hard to say, but yes, pretty close," Martin replied.

The two men worked in silence for a few minutes, sweeping the bridge, examining each man.

"We should split up," Martin said.

"I know where his compartment is," Sloane said as he turned and stalked down the rear corridor leading away from the bridge.

Martin trudged after him. He had hoped to distract him, to reach the crew quarters before Sloane.

It was now nearly impossible to move in the suit, and Sloane seemed to manage much better than Martin.

Finally the older man caught up with Sloane as he twisted open the hatch to the room. Sloane tossed a few lamps in, bathing the room in light.

Martin held his breath as he scanned the room. Empty. He exhaled. Would he have been happier to see a body? Maybe.

Sloane moved to the desk and rifled through papers, opening a few spring-loaded drawers. The lights from his suit lit up a black and white photo of a man in a German military uniform. Not a Nazi uniform, something earlier, even before World War I. The man held a woman, his wife, to his right, and two sons to his left. They resembled him strongly. Sloane stared at the photo for a long moment, then slipped it into a pocket on his suit.

At that moment, Martin almost felt sorry for the man. "Dorian, he couldn't have survived—"

"What did you expect to find, Martin?"

"I could ask you the same question."

"I asked you first." Sloane continued searching the desk.

"Maps. And if we're lucky, a tapestry."

"A tapestry?" Sloane twisted the head of his bulky suit around, blinding Martin with his headlamp.

Martin threw a hand up to block the light. "Yes, a large rug with a story—"

"I know what a tapestry is, Martin." He returned his attention to the desk, rummaging through more books. "You know, I may have been wrong about you. You're no threat, you've simply lost it. You've been drinking the Kool-Aid too long. Look at what happened to him—chasing tapestries and superstitious legends." Sloane tossed a bundle of papers and books back onto the frozen desk. "There's nothing here, just some journals."

Journals! It could be *the* journal. Martin fought to act casual. "I can take those. There may be something we could use."

Sloane straightened, made eye contact with Martin, then glanced back at the stack of skinny books. "No, I think I'll take a look first. I'll pass anything... *scientific* along."

Dorian was sick of the suit. He had been in it for six hours: three hours in the sub and three hours in decontamination. Martin and his research eggheads were thorough. Cautious. Fans of overkill. Time wasters.

Now he sat across from Martin in the cleanroom, waiting for the results of the blood test—for the "all clear." What was taking so long?

Every now and then, Martin would glance at the journals. There was obviously something in them, something he wanted to see. Something he didn't want Dorian to see. He pulled the stack of books closer to him.

The sub had been the biggest disappointment of Sloane's life. He was forty-two years old, and since the age of seven, not a day had gone by when he didn't dream of finding that sub. But now that day had come—and he had found nothing. Or almost nothing: six fried bodies and a mint-condition U-boat.

"What now, Martin?" Dorian asked.

"Same thing we always do. We keep digging."

"I want specifics. I know you're excavating under the sub, next to the structure."

"What we think is the other vessel," Martin added quickly.

"Agree to disagree. What have you found?"

"Bones."

"How many?" Dorian leaned back against the wall. A pit developed in his stomach, like the anticipation you get before you go over the drop-off in a roller coaster. He dreaded the answer.

"Enough for about a dozen men so far. But we think there are more," Martin said wearily. The time in the suit had really taken it out of him.

"There's a Bell down there, isn't there?"

"That would be my guess. The area around the sub collapsed when two researchers approached it. One man was incinerated—similar to what we saw on the sub. The other was killed when the ice collapsed. I expect to find the rest of the crew down there."

Dorian was too tired to argue, but the idea scared him to death. The finality of it. "What do you know about the structure?"

"Not much at this point. It's old. At least as old as the ruins in Gibraltar. One hundred thousand years, maybe older."

One thing had bothered Dorian since they had arrived: the lack of progress on the excavation. Even though Martin's people had only found the site twelve days ago, with their resources they should have already had the iceberg carved up like a Thanksgiving turkey. The staff here was almost minimal, like the real action was elsewhere.

"This isn't the main site, is it?"

"We have resources... assigned elsewhere..."

Assigned elsewhere. Dorian turned the idea over in his head. What could be bigger than this? The structure they had spent thousands of years searching for. All the sacrifices. What could be bigger?

Bigger. A larger structure. Or... the main structure.

Dorian leaned forward. "This is just a piece, isn't it? You're looking for a larger structure. This part simply broke off from some primary structure." Dorian still wasn't sure it was true, but if it was...

Martin nodded, slowly, without making eye contact with Dorian.

"My God, Martin." Dorian stood and paced the room. "It could happen at any minute. They could be upon us in days, or even hours. You've put us all at risk. And—you've known about this for twelve days now! Have you lost your mind?"

"We thought it was the primary—"

"Thought, wished, hoped—forget it. Now we need to act! The moment they let us out of this plastic cage, I'm going back to shut down the China operation and start Toba Protocol—don't bother protesting, you know the time has come. I want you to contact me when you find the larger structure. And Martin, I have several detachments of agents on their way here. They'll help you if you have *trouble* operating your sat phone."

Martin put his elbows on his knees and stared at the floor.

The door to the holding room slid open with a hiss as fresh air rushed in ahead of a twenty-something woman carrying a clipboard. She wore an almost skin-tight outfit—she must have selected a suit three sizes too small.

"Gentlemen, you're both cleared for duty." The woman turned to Dorian. "Now, is there anything else I can do for you?" She dropped the clipboard to her side, then clasped her hands behind her, arching her back a little.

"What's your name?" Dorian said.

"Naomi. But you can call me anything you like."

46

Kate couldn't tell if she was awake or asleep. For a moment, she simply floated there in total darkness and dead silence. The only sensation was the soft cloth at her back. She leaned to the side and heard the crackle of the cheap mattress. She must have fallen asleep on the small bed in the bomb shelter. She had lost track of time as she and David had waited while their pursuers marched back and forth above them, searching the cottage for what seemed like hours.

Was it safe to get up?

She felt another sensation now: hunger. How long had she slept?

She swung her legs off the tiny bed and planted them on—

"Awww, Jesus!" David's voice filled the tiny space as he did a sit-up into her legs, then curled up and writhed on the floor.

Kate shifted her weight back to the bed, pawing the floor for a firm foothold—one that wasn't somewhere on David's person. She finally planted her left foot and stood, swatting the air for the string that activated the dangling single-bulb light. Her hand connected with the cord, and she jerked the light on, sending a flash of yellow into the small space. She squinted and waited, standing on one foot. When she could see, she moved to the corner of the room, away from David, who was lying still in a fetal position in the middle of the floor.

She had hit him *there*. God. Why was he on the floor? "We're not in middle school, you know. You could have shared the bed."

David grunted as he finally rolled onto his hands and knees. "Apparently chivalry doesn't pay."

"I didn't—"

"Forget it. We need to get out of here," David said as he sat up.

"Are the men—?"

"No, they left ninety minutes ago, but they may be waiting outside."

"It's not safe here. I'm coming—"

"I know. I know." David held up his hand. He was getting his breath back. "But I have one condition, and it's non-negotiable."

Kate stared at him.

"You do what I say, when I say. No questions, no discussion."

Kate straightened. "I can take orders."

"Yeah, I'll believe it when I see it. When we're out there, seconds could matter. If I tell you to leave me or to run, you have to do it. You could be scared and disoriented, but you will have to focus on what I tell you to do."

"I'm not afraid," she lied.

"Well, that makes one of us." David opened a set of double steel doors built into the concrete. "There's something else."

"I'm listening," Kate said, a little defensively.

David looked her up and down. "You can't wear those clothes. You look almost homeless." He tossed her some clothes. "Might be a little big."

Kate perused her new attire: some old blue jeans and a black V-neck t-shirt.

David threw her a gray sweater. "You'll need this, too. It'll be cold where we're going."

"Which is?"

"I'll explain on the way."

Kate started to pull her shirt off but stopped. "Can you, um."

David smiled. "We're not in middle school."

Kate turned her head, trying to decide what to say.

David seemed to remember something. "Oh, right. The scar."

He spun around, knelt, and began sorting through some boxes in the bottom of the cabinet.

"How did you—?"

David took out a gun and a few boxes of ammo. "The drugs."

Kate flushed. What had she said? Done? For some reason the idea terrified her, and she wished desperately that she could remember. "Did I, or we—?"

"Relax. Apart from the gratuitous violence, it was a very PG evening. Is it safe for kids again?"

Kate pulled the shirt on. "And immature soldiers."

David seemed to ignore the jab. He rose and held a box out to her—another carton meal. Kate read the letters. MRE: Meals Ready to Eat. "Hungry?"

Kate eyed the box: barbecue chicken with black beans and potatoes. "Not that hungry."

"Suit yourself." He peeled the plastic film back, plopped down at the metal desk, and began devouring the cold food with the included spork. He must have heated the meal yesterday just for her sake.

Kate sat on the bed opposite him and pulled on the sneakers he had laid out for her. "Hey, I don't know if I've said it before, but I wanted to... say thank you for..."

David stopped shuffling the papers and forced down the bite he'd been chewing. He didn't glance back at Kate. "Don't mention it. Just doing my job."

Kate tied her shoes. Just doing his job. Why did the answer seem so... unfulfilling?

David shoved the last of the papers in a folder and handed it to her. "This is all I have on the people who took your children. You'll have time to read it on the way."

Kate opened the folder and began reading the papers. There must be fifty pages. "On the way to where?"

David wolfed down a few more bites. "Check out the top page. It's the latest cryptic communication from a source inside

Immari. Someone I've been communicating with for almost two weeks now."

30,88. 81,86.
03-12-2013. 10:45:00
#44. 33-23-15
Cut the power. Save my kids.

Kate put the paper back in the folder. "I don't understand."

"The first part is a set of GPS coordinates; looks like an abandoned train station in western China. The second part is obviously a time, probably a departure time for a train. Not sure about the middle part, but my guess is it's a locker in the station with the combination. I assume the contact has left something in the locker for us—something we need, maybe another message. It's unclear whether the kids will be at this train station or if it's just another clue. Or I could be misreading it. It could be another code or mean something different. I had a partner who decoded all the earlier messages."

"Can you consult him?"

David finished the last bite, tossed the spork in the tray, and gathered up the items he'd pulled from the cabinet. "No, unfortunately I can't."

Kate closed the folder. "Western China? How do we get there?"

"I'm getting to that. One step at a time. First we find out if they left any troops upstairs. Ready?"

Kate nodded, then followed him up the stairs, where he told her to wait while he swept the cottage. "It's clear. Hopefully they moved on. Stay close to me."

They jogged from the cottage, in the thin underbrush along a dirt road that showed no signs of use. The road ended in a cul-de-sac with four large blue warehouses, also clearly abandoned years ago. David led Kate to the second warehouse, where he pulled a piece of the corrugated sheet metal wall out, exposing a triangular hole just big enough for Kate.

"Crawl in."

Kate started to protest, but remembering his one demand, she complied without a word. For reasons she couldn't understand, she tried not to get her knees in the mud, but she couldn't quite fit. David seemed to sense her dilemma, and he strained harder at the metal flange, giving Kate enough space to squeeze through comfortably.

David followed her inside, then unlocked and rolled the building's doors open, revealing the warehouse's hidden "treasure."

It was a plane—but just barely. And an odd one: a sea plane, the type Kate imagined people used to get to remote areas in Alaska... in the 1950s. It probably wasn't *that* old, but it was old. It had four seats inside and two large propellers on each wing. She would probably have to turn one manually, like Amelia Earhart. If it would even turn on—and if he could fly it. She watched as David took the tarp off the tail and kicked the blocks from beneath the wheels.

Back at the cottage, he had said "no questions," but she had to. "You *can* fly this thing, right?" Kate asked.

He stopped, shrugged slowly and looked at her as if he had been caught trying to get away with something. "Ah, well, generally."

"Generally?"

47

Dorian watched Naomi finish the last of her martini, then stretch out on the long couch on the opposite side of the plane. The white terrycloth robe fell to her side, revealing her chest, which rose and receded at a dwindling rate as her breathing slowed, like a contented cat who had just gorged itself on some prey. She licked the last drops of the martini off her fingers and propped herself on her elbow. "Are you ready again?"

She was insatiable. And coming from him, that was saying something. Dorian picked up the phone. "Not just yet."

Naomi made a half pout and flopped back onto the couch.

On the line, Dorian heard the communications officer on the plane say, "Yes sir?"

"Connect me to the China facility."

"Immari Shanghai?"

"No, the new one—in Tibet. I need to speak with Dr. Chase."

Dorian heard mouse clicks in the background.

"Dr. Chang?"

"No, Chase. Nuclear section."

"Stand by."

Dorian watched Naomi scratch at the robe bunched around her on the couch. He wondered how long she could hold out.

The phone clicked. A distracted voice said, "Chase."

"It's Sloane. Where are we with the nukes?"

The man coughed and spoke more slowly. "Mr. Sloane. We have, I think, fifty, or forty-nine operational."

"How many total?"

"That's all we have, sir. We're trying to get more, but the Indians and Pakistanis—neither will sell us anymore."

"Money doesn't matter, whatever it co—"

"We've tried sir, they won't sell them at any price, not without a reason, and we don't have a better story than backups for our nuclear reactor."

"Can you work with Soviet bloc weapons?"

"Yes, but it will take more time. They'll probably be older devices; they'd need to be checked out and converted. And they'll likely be lower yield."

"Fine. I'll see what I can do. Be prepared for a new shipment. And speaking of conversions, I need you to make two bombs portable... something a small person, or... someone... *tired* could carry easily."

"That will take some time."

"How much?" Dorian exhaled. It was never simple with these freaks.

"Depends. What's the weight limit?"

"Weight? I don't know. Maybe thirty or forty pounds. Wait, that's way too much. Maybe... fifteen pounds. Assume fifteen or so, can you do that?"

"It will decrease the yield."

"Can you do it?" Dorian snapped impatiently.

"Yes."

"How long?"

The scientist exhaled. "A day, maybe two."

"I need it in twelve hours—no excuses, Dr. Chase."

A long pause. Then, "Yes, sir."

Dorian hung up the phone.

Naomi had finally broken. She was pouring herself another martini, and she tilted the bottle toward him expectantly.

"Not right now." Dorian never drank when he was working.

He thought for a minute, then picked up the phone again. "Get me the Tibet facility again. Dr. Chang."

"Chase?"

"Chang, rhymes with hang."

The clicks were faster this time.

"Chang here, Mr. Sloane."

"Doctor, I'm en route to your facility, and we need to make some preparations. How many subjects do you have there?"

"I think—" Chang started. Dorian heard papers shuffling, keys clacking, and then the man was back on the line. "382 primates, 119 humans."

"Only 119 humans? I thought the enrollment was much higher. The project plan is for thousands." Dorian looked out the plane window. One hundred nineteen bodies might not be enough.

"Yes it is, but, well, with the lack of results, we've halted human recruitment. We've focused more on rodent and primate trials. Should we start back up? Is there a new therapy—?"

"No. There's a new plan. We'll have to work with what you have. I want you to treat all the humans with the last treatment: Dr. Warner's research."

"Sir, that therapy was ineffective—"

"*Was*, Doctor. I know something you don't. You have to trust me."

"Yes, sir, we'll have them ready. Give us three days—"

"Today, Dr. Chang. Time is one thing we don't have."

"We don't have the staff or facilities—"

"Make it happen." Dorian listened. "Hello?"

"I'm here, Mr. Sloane. We'll make it happen."

"One more thing. Don't incinerate the bodies this time—"

"But the risk—"

"I'm sure you'll find a way to deal with them safely. You have quarantine rooms there, do you not?" Dorian waited, but the scientist didn't say a word. "Good. Oh, I almost forgot. How much weight do you think the two children could support—each?"

Chang seemed surprised by the question, or perhaps distracted or worried about the last order to not destroy the bodies. "Uh, you mean, weight, as in—"

"In a backpack, if they were carrying it."

"I'm not sure—"

Scientists: the bane of Dorian's existence. Risk-averse, scared, time wasters. "*Guess*, Doctor. It doesn't have to be exact."

"I think, about, ten to fifteen pounds maybe. It would depend on how long or far they had to carry it and—"

"Fine, fine. I'll be there shortly. You better be ready." Dorian hung up the phone.

Naomi didn't give him the chance to pick it up again. She downed the last of her martini, sauntered over to him, put her glass on the table, and straddled him, pulling her robe off and letting it drop to the floor. She reached for his zipper, but Dorian grabbed her hands and pinned them to her side, then lifted her off of him and tossed her on the couch beside him. He punched the call button behind him.

Five seconds later, the flight attendant opened the door, and when she saw the scene, began retreating.

"Stop. Stay," Dorian commanded. "Join us."

Comprehension spread over the young woman's face. She gently closed the door as if she were a teenager sneaking out of her bedroom at night.

Naomi heaved herself off the couch and took the woman's face in her hands, kissing her, then pulling her scarf off, and finally fiddling with the buttons on the blue blazer over her white blouse. The woman's top was off before the kiss ended, and Naomi finished the job, pushing her skirt to the floor.

48

Robert Hunt closed the door to his portable living pod and picked up the radio.

"Bounty, this is Snow King. We have reached depth seven-five-zero-zero feet, repeat, our depth is seven-five-zero-zero feet. Status unchanged. We've hit nothing but ice."

"Snow King, Bounty. We read you. Depth is seven thousand five hundred feet. Stand by."

Robert set the radio mic on the foldout table and leaned back in the flimsy chair. He couldn't wait to leave this frozen hellhole. He had drilled for oil in the world's harshest places: northern Canada, Siberia, Alaska, and the North Sea above the Arctic Circle. Nothing compared to Antarctica.

He looked around the pod—his home for the last seven days. It was exactly like the last three pods at the last three drilling sites: a ten by fifteen room with three cots, a large noisy heater, four trunks of equipment and food, and the table with the radio. There was no refrigerator; keeping things cool was the least of their problems.

The radio crackled to life. "Snow King, this is Bounty. Your orders are as follows: extract the drill, cover the hole, and proceed to new location. Please confirm orders when you are ready for new GPS coordinates."

Robert confirmed the orders, took down the new coordinates, and signed off. He sat for a minute, thinking about the job. Three drill sites, all seventy-five hundred feet deep, all the same result: nothing but ice. And the equipment was all snow white and covered by huge white parasail-like canopies. Whatever they were doing, their employer didn't want anyone to see it from the air.

He had assumed they were drilling for oil or some precious metal. Covert drilling wasn't uncommon. You go in, drill, make a strike, cover it up, then get an option on the land. But there were no drilling rights to be had in Antarctica, and there were much easier places—much cheaper places—to find oil and raw materials. The economics didn't make sense. But money didn't seem to be a problem. Each site had about thirty million dollars in equipment—and they didn't seem to care what happened to it. They were paying him two million dollars for what they said would be two months—max—of drilling. He'd signed a non-disclosure agreement. And that was it.

Two million dollars, drill where we say, keep your mouth shut. Robert intended to do just that. Two million dollars would get him out of the trouble he was in and maybe leave him enough to get off the oil rigs for good. He might even fix his own problems, the reason he was in such a bind to begin with. But that was probably wishful thinking, about as likely as striking oil in Antarctica.

49

They had made three passes at landing in the small lake, and Kate couldn't take it anymore. "I thought you said you could fly this thing?"

David continued concentrating on the controls. "Landing is a lot harder than flying."

To Kate, landing was the same thing as flying, but she let it go. She checked her seatbelt buckle for the hundredth time.

David wiped some fog off a few of the ancient dials and tried to line the plane up for another pass.

Kate heard a sputter and felt her side of the plane drop. "Did you do that?"

David tapped the dashboard, first lightly, then harder. "We're out of gas."

"I thought you said—"

"Gauge must be broken." David motioned with his head. "Get in the back."

Kate crawled over him and into the back row of seats, complying, for once, without counterargument or complaint. She buckled herself in. This would be their last landing attempt.

The other engine puffed out its last seconds of life, and the plane leveled off, gliding in the ominous silence.

Kate looked down, surveying the dense green forest surrounding the small blue lake. It was beautiful, like a scene from the Canadian wilderness. She knew it was cold down there; they must be somewhere in northern India or western China.

They had flown most of the way over water, hugging the sea tightly to avoid radar detection. They had gone north most of the way; the sun had hung high in the sky on Kate's right until they crossed the coast, somewhere in the low-lying monsoon areas, probably Bangladesh. Kate hadn't asked any questions—not that she could have over the noise of the now-dead twin engines. Wherever they were, it was remote and untouched. If they were injured—at all—in the landing, it would likely be fatal.

The lake rushed toward them quickly now. David leveled the plane. Or tried—the plane was apparently harder to control without the force of the engines.

Scenarios of doom raced through Kate's mind. What if they went nose first into the lake? There were mountains around them. The lake could be incredibly deep—and cold. The plane would pull them down. They'd never survive the icy abyss. And what if they did level off? How would they stop? They'd hit the trees at full speed. She imagined a series of tree branches stabbing a dozen holes in them, like pins in a voodoo doll. Or the gas, the fumes in the tank would explode at any spark; that would get them fast.

The pontoons skidded unevenly on the water, and the plane rocked from side to side.

One of the pontoons could come off. That would tear the plane—and them—to pieces.

Kate tightened her lap belt. Should she take it off? It could cut her in half.

The pontoons kissed the water again before reeling back into the air, wobbling and wounded.

Kate leaned forward, and for some reason, put her arms around David's neck, holding him tightly to his seat and pressing herself against the back of his seat. She rested her head at the base of his neck. She couldn't watch. She felt the plane plow into the water more violently. The floor shook constantly. The turbulence spread to the thin metal walls, she heard a series of cracks, and she was flung back into her seat, the breath almost knocked out of her. She opened her eyes and sucked in a breath. They had stopped. Branches! In the cockpit. David's head hung lifelessly.

Kate lunged forward but the lap belt nearly tore her in half. She reached for him, disregarding the belt. She felt around his chest. Had a branch gone through him? She couldn't feel anything.

He lifted his head lethargically. "Hey lady, at least buy me a drink first."

Kate slumped back in her chair and shoved his shoulder. She was glad to be alive. And glad he was too, but she said, "I've had better landings."

He glanced back at her. "Over water?"

"As it turns out, this is my first water landing, so, no."

"Yeah, my first water landing too." David unbuckled himself and climbed out the passenger door. He got his footing on the step and released the passenger seat so Kate could get out.

"You're serious, aren't you? You've never landed a plane on water? Are you out of your mind?"

"No, I'm just kidding. I land on water all the time."

"Do you always run out of gas?"

David began unpacking supplies from the plane. "Gas?" He gazed up, as if remembering something. "We didn't run out of gas. I just killed the engines for dramatic effect. You know, just hoping you would do that reach-forward hug-from-behind thing."

"Very funny." Kate began organizing supplies, as if they had been doing this routine for years. She looked over at David. "You're uh, certainly more... *lively* than you were in Jakarta." She had considered not saying anything, but she wondered... "I mean, I'm not complaining—"

"Well, you know, surviving certain death always puts me in a good mood. Speaking of which," he handed her the end of a large green tarp. "Help me spread this over the plane."

Kate ducked under the plane and caught the tarp when he threw it over, then rejoined him at the small pile of supplies. She glanced back at the covered plane. "We're not going to... will we be flying out on..."

David smiled at her. "No, I'd say that was its last flight. And besides, it's out of gas." He held up three MREs, fanning them out like playing cards. "Now, are you continuing your hunger strike or do you wish to partake of one of these fine delicacies?"

Kate pursed her lips and leaned closer as if inspecting the brown packages. "Hmmm. What's on the menu this morning?"

David turned the boxes around. "Let's see, for your culinary enjoyment, we have: meatloaf, beef stroganoff, and chicken noodle soup."

Kate's last meal had been yesterday—late afternoon, before they had retreated into the bomb shelter below the cottage. "Well, I'm not really all *that* hungry, but the chicken noodle soup sounds simply irresistible."

David spun the pack around and ripped. "An excellent choice, ma'am. Please wait several moments while your entree is heated."

Kate stepped toward him. "You don't have to heat it."

"Nonsense, it's no trouble."

Kate considered the tarp covering the plane. "Won't the fire give away our location... put us at risk—?"

David shook his head. "My dear doctor, I admit we're roughing it a bit today, but we're not living in the stone ages, cooking our food on stone hearths like Neanderthals." He plucked what looked like a small penlight from his pack and held it up to her. He twisted the top and a torch-like flame sprang up. He moved the flame back and forth under Kate's meal.

Kate squatted down across from him and watched the "chicken soup" begin to boil. It was no doubt soybeans or some other chicken substitute. "At least no animals will be harmed."

David kept his focus on the flame and the carton as if he were repairing a delicate piece of electronics. "Oh, I think it's real meat. They've come a long way with these things in the last few years. I ate some in Afghanistan that weren't fit for human consumption. Or hominid consumption, I believe you would say."

"Very impressive—yes, we are hominids. Hominins to be exact. The only ones left."

"I've been brushing up on my evolutionary history." David handed her the heated chicken soup, then ripped open another package—meatloaf—and began eating it cold.

Kate stirred the soup with the spork and tentatively took a few bites. Not terrible. Or was she just getting used to how horrid it tasted? It didn't matter. She sipped the soup as they ate in silence. The lake was placid, and the dense green forest that surrounded them swayed in the wind and creaked occasionally as unseen creatures leaped from branch to branch. If not for yesterday's tragic events, they could be campers in an untouched wilderness; and for a moment it felt that way to Kate. She finished the last bite of soup a minute after David, and he took her carton and said, "We should get a move on, we're T minus thirty on the contact's meet time." And just like that, the peace and innocence of the natural setting evaporated. David hoisted a heavy pack and hid the last of their trash under the tarp.

He set a brisk pace as they hiked into the mountainous forest, and Kate fought to keep up, and to hide her heavy breathing. He was in much better shape than she was. He stopped periodically, still breathing through his nose as Kate turned away and sucked in mouthfuls of air.

On the third respite, he leaned against a tree and said, "I know you're not ready to talk about your research, but tell me this: why do you think Immari took those kids?"

"I've actually been thinking about that a lot since Jakarta." Kate leaned over and put her hands on her knees. "Some of the things Martin said to me, when they were questioning me, they make absolutely no sense."

"Such as?"

"He implied there was a weapon, some kind of super-weapon, that could wipe out the human race—"

David pushed off the tree. "Did he say—?"

"No, he didn't say anything else. It was a delusional rant. Part of a tirade about lost cities, and genetics and… what else?" Kate shook her head. "He suggested that children with autism could

196

be a threat, that they were the next step in human evolution."

"Is that possible? The evolution part?"

"I don't know. Maybe. We know the last major breakthrough in evolution was a change in brain wiring. If we look at the genome of humans a hundred thousand years ago and humans fifty thousand years ago, there's very little genetic change, but we know that the genes that did change had a huge impact—mostly on how we thought. Humans began using language and thinking critically, solving problems rather than acting on instinct. Essentially, the brain started acting more like a computer than a processing center for impulses. It's debatable, but there is evidence that another shift in brain wiring is occurring. Autism is essentially a change in brain wiring, and the diagnosis rate for autism spectrum disorders, or ASD, is exploding. In America, it's up five hundred percent in the last twenty years. One in every eighty-eight Americans is somewhere on the spectrum. Some of the increase is due to better diagnosis techniques, but there's no question that ASD is on the rise—in every country around the world. Developed nations seem to be hit the hardest."

"I don't follow. How does ASD connect with evolutionary genetics?"

"We know that almost all of the conditions on the autism spectrum have a strong genetic component. They're all caused by a difference in brain wiring that is controlled by a small group of genes. My research focuses on how those genes affect brain wiring—and more importantly, how a gene therapy might turn on or off genes that would increase their social abilities and improve their quality of life. There are tons of people somewhere on the autism spectrum who live independent, enjoyable lives. For example, individuals diagnosed with Asperger syndrome simply have a lot of difficulties socializing and usually focus intensely on an area of interest—computers, comics, finance, you name it. But it doesn't always have to be limiting. In fact, specializing is the key to success these days. Take a look at the Forbes list—if you tested the individuals who made their fortune in computers, biotech, and finance, I guarantee you the majority would land somewhere on the autism spectrum. But they got lucky—they won the genetic lottery. Their brains operate in a way that allows them to solve complex problems *and* have enough social skills to function in society. That's what I was trying to do, give my kids a fair shot at life." Kate had her breath back, but she kept looking down.

"Don't talk like that. Like it's over. Let's move out. We're T minus fifteen."

They resumed their pace, and Kate kept up this time. Five minutes before the meeting time, the forest waned and an expansive train station came into view.

"It's definitely not abandoned," Kate said.

Before them, the station swarmed with people, all dressed in white coats, security outfits, and other uniforms. David and Kate would stick out among the masses filing into the station.

"Hurry, before they see us walking in from the trees."

50

Immari Corp. Research Complex
Outside Burang, China
Tibet Autonomous Region

Dorian watched the monitors as the researchers led the twenty or so Chinese subjects out of the room. The therapy really did a number on them. Half could barely walk.

The observation room included a large wall with screens monitoring every inch of the research facility and several rows of computer workstations where eggheads typed on computers all day doing God knows what.

Across the room, Naomi leaned against a wall, clearly bored. She looked so strange with clothes on. Dorian motioned for her to come over. She wasn't authorized to hear the scientist's report.

"You want to get out of here?" Naomi said.

"In a bit. Go get acquainted with the facility. I have some work to do. I'll come after you shortly."

"I'll survey the local talent."

"Don't do anything I wouldn't do."

She wandered out of the room without a word.

Dorian turned to the nervous scientist who had been lurking, following, almost stalking him since he had arrived.

"Dr. Chang?"

The man stepped forward. "Yes, sir?"

"What am I looking at here?"

"That's the third cohort. We're working as fast as we can, Mr. Sloane." When Dorian said nothing, Chang continued. "Will, ah, Dr. Grey be joining us?"

"No. You'll communicate with me about this project from here on out. Understood?"

"Ah, yes, sir. Is... there—?"

"Dr. Grey is working on a new project. I'd like you to bring me up to speed."

Chang opened his mouth to speak.

"And be brief." Dorian stared at him impatiently.

"Of course, sir." Chang rubbed his palms together as if he were warming them by a campfire. "Well, as you know, the project dates back to the 1930s, but we've only really made substantial progress in the last few years—and it's all thanks to a few breakthroughs in genetics, in particular rapid genome sequencing."

"I thought they already sequenced the human genome—in the nineties."

"Ah, that's inco—ah, a misnomer, if you will. There is no *one* human genome. The *first* human genome was sequenced in the nineties, and the draft sequence was published in February of 2001—ah, that was the genome of Dr. Craig Venter. But we each have a genome and each is different. That's part of the challenge."

"I don't follow."

"Yes, sorry, I don't often talk about the project." He chuckled nervously. "Ah, for obvious reasons! And especially not to anyone in your position. Yes, where to start? Maybe a little history. Ah, the 1930s—the research then was... radical, but yielded some interesting results, despite the methods." Chang looked around, as if wondering if he had offended Dorian. "Ah, well, we spent decades studying what the Bell actually does to its victims. As you know, it's a form of radiation that we don't fully understand, but the effects are—"

"Don't lecture me about its effects, Doctor. No one on this earth knows more about what it does than I do. Tell me what you know. And be quick."

Chang looked down. He made several fists with his hands and then tried to dry them on his pants. "Of course you know, I only meant to contrast our past research with... Yes, today, genetics, we sequence... We... The... breakthrough has been turning the research on its head—instead of studying the effects of the device, we've focused on finding a way to survive the machine. We've known since the thirties that some subjects fare better than others, but since they all die eventually—" Chang looked up to see Dorian glaring at him. The doctor ducked his head and plowed on. "We, our theory is that if we can isolate the genes that impart immunity to the machine, we can develop a gene therapy to protect us from its effects. We would use a retrovirus to deliver this gene, what we're calling 'The Atlantis Gene.'"

"So why haven't you found it?"

"We thought we were close a few years ago, but no one person seems to have full immunity. Our premise, as you know, was that there was a group of humans that could have withstood the machine at some point and that their DNA has been scattered across the earth—essentially we were on a global genetic egg hunt. But frankly, after as many experiments as we've run, given our sample size, we were beginning to believe that the Atlantis Gene didn't exist—that it never existed in humans."

Dorian held his hand up and the doctor stopped to catch his breath. If what the doctor said was true, it would require a re-examination of everything they believed. And it would vindicate his methods. Or at least come close. But could it be? There were a few problems. "How did the children survive?" Dorian asked.

"Unfortunately we don't know. We aren't even sure what they were treated with—"

"I know that. Tell me what you know."

"We know that the therapy they received was something cutting edge. Possibly something so new we don't have anything to compare it to. But we have some theories. There's been another recent breakthrough in genetics—what we call epigenetics. The idea is that our genome is less like a static blueprint and more like a piano. The piano keys represent the genome. We each get different keys, and the keys don't change throughout our life: we die with the same piano keys, or genome, we're born with. What changes is the sheet music: the epigenetics. That sheet music determines what tune is played—what genes are expressed—and those genes determine our traits—everything from IQ to hair color. The idea is that this complex interaction between our genome and the epigenetics that control gene expression really determines who we become.

"What's interesting is that we have a hand in writing the music, in controlling our own epigenetics. And so do our parents and even our environment. If a certain gene is expressed in your parents and grandparents, it's more likely to activate in you. Essentially, our actions, our parents' actions, and our environment influence what genes could be activated. Our genes might control the possibilities, but epigenetics determines our destiny. It's an incredible breakthrough. We've known something more than pure static genetics was at work for some time. Our twin studies in the thirties and forties told us that. Some twins survived longer in the machine than others, despite having almost exactly the same genome. Epigenetics is the missing link."

"What does this have to do with the kids?"

"My personal theory is that some new kind of therapy inserted new genes into the kids and that those genes had a cascade effect, possibly operating at the epigenetic level as well. We think surviving the Bell is a matter of having the right genes *and* turning this 'Atlantis Gene' on—that's the key. It's strange; the therapy operated almost like a mutation."

"Mutation?"

"Yes, a mutation is simply a random change in the genetic code, a genetic dice roll if you will. Sometimes it pays off big, imparting a new evolutionary advantage and sometimes... you get six fingers or four! But this one provided immunity to the Bell. It's so *fascinating!* I wonder if I could speak with Dr. Warner. It would be incredibly helpful—"

"Forget Dr. Warner." Dorian rubbed his temple. Genetics,

epigenetics, mutations. It all added up to the same thing: failed research, no viable therapy for immunity to the Bell, and no time left on the clock. "How many subjects can your Bell room hold?"

"Ah, we usually limit each trial to fifty subjects, but maybe one hundred, maybe a little more if we pack them in."

Dorian gazed at the monitors. A cadre of white-coat-clad eggheads was corralling a new cohort of subjects into the lounge chairs, then hooking them up to clear plastic bags of death. "How long does it take to run?"

"Not long. Five or ten minutes is about as long as any subject goes."

"Five or ten minutes." His voice was just above a whisper. He leaned back in the chair, turning the idea over in his mind. Then he stood and took a step toward the door. "Start processing all your remaining subjects through the Bell—as quickly as you can." Dr. Chang stepped forward to protest, but Dorian was already halfway out the door. "Oh, and remember, don't destroy the bodies. We need them. I'll be in the nuclear section, Doctor."

51

Kate sat in silence, watching the green countryside fly by at ninety miles an hour. Across from her, David shifted a little on his side of the closed train compartment. *How can he sleep at a time like this? He'll have a crick in his neck from sleeping like that.* Kate leaned forward and nudged his head a little.

Even if her nerves weren't going crazy, Kate's legs hurt too much to sleep. David's brisk pace on their hike from the plane's "landing site" to the train station had taken its toll. And so had the sprint inside, to the bank of lockers and number forty-four, which had been their salvation.

Inside the locker they'd found two outfits—a security outfit for David and a white coat for Kate. There were ID badges, too: Kate was now Dr. Emma West, research associate in "Bell Primary: Genetics Division," whatever that was. David was Conner Anderson. The pictures on the IDs didn't match, but they only had to run them through a swipe machine, like a subway or credit card reader, to get on the 10:45 train—apparently the last train of the morning.

As they had boarded the train, Kate turned to David and asked, "What now?"

David turned her back around and said, "Don't talk, they could be listening. Follow the plan."

"The plan" wasn't much of one. Her goal was to find the children and get back on the train; David would take out the power and join her. It wasn't even half a plan. They would probably be caught before they got off the train. And now he was sleeping.

But... he probably hadn't slept much the night before. Had he stayed up to see if the men searching the cottage would find the entrance to the bomb shelter? How long had he lain on that concrete floor? And then all the hours in that vibrating antique death trap of a plane. Kate wadded up some of the clothes from her bag and put them between his face and the wall.

Another thirty minutes passed, and Kate felt the train slowing. In the corridor, people were making a line.

David grabbed Kate's arm. When had he woken up? Kate looked at him, panic creeping into her face.

"Stay calm," he said. "Remember, you work here. You're taking the kids for a test. Director's orders."

"What director?" Kate hissed.

"If they ask that, say it's above their pay grade and keep walking."

Kate tried to ask another question, but David yanked the compartment door open and shoved Kate into the moving line. By the time she looked back, he was several people behind her and moving the other way, putting distance between them. She was alone. She whipped her head back around and swallowed a few times. She could do this.

She moved with the flow of people, trying to act casual. The workers were mostly Asian, but there were quite a few Europeans, possibly Americans. She was a minority, but she didn't stick out too much.

There were several entrances to the giant facility, each with three lines. She spotted the entrance where most of the white coats were gathering and drifted over to it. She stood in line, waiting to swipe her card, trying to get a glimpse of the badges around her. "Bell Auxiliary: Primate Housing." She looked in the line beside her. "Bell Control: Maintenance and Housekeeping." What was she again? Bell something. It had genetics in it. She had the overwhelming fear that if she glanced down at her fake badge, someone would point at her and scream "Impostor! Get her!", like a playground kid calling you out for peeing in your pants.

Up ahead, white coats were marching forward, scanning their badges like automatons. The line was moving quickly, just as it had at the train station. She now saw something else: six armed guards. Three were spread out, one stationed at each line, scrutinizing every face. The other three loitered behind a chain-link fence, drinking coffee and talking quickly, horsing around with each other like office workers at the water cooler. Each man had an automatic rifle slung over his shoulder as casually as if it were a messenger bag full of memos.

She had to focus. The badge. Kate slipped her card out and sneaked a peek: "Bell Primary: Genetics Division." In the line beside her, she saw a tall blond man, likely in his early forties, holding a card with the same division. He was several people behind her. She would have to wait for him to get through, then follow him.

"Ma'am—"

They were talking to her!

"Ma'am." The guard pointed to the wide post with the magnetic card reader at the top. Beside her people were swiping and hurrying past.

Kate fought to steady her hand as she ripped her card across the slot. A different beep. A red light.

Beside her two more people swiped. Green lights, no beep.

The guard cocked his head and took a step toward her.

Her hands were shaking visibly now. *Act casual.* She got the card in the slot and ran it through, slowly this time. Red light. Bad beep.

The guards behind the fence had stopped talking. They were looking at her. The guard in her line looked back at the other guards.

She tried to line up the card for another try, but someone grabbed her hand. "You're backwards, love."

Kate looked up. The blond man. She couldn't think. What had he said? "I work here," Kate said quickly, looking around. Everyone was looking at them. They were blocking two of the three lines.

"I certainly hope so." The man took her card. "You must be new," he said as he perused the card. "Haven't seen you befo— Hey, this doesn't look like you."

Kate snatched the card. "Don't—don't look at the picture. I'm, uh, new here." She ran a hand through her hair. She was going to get caught, she knew it. The man was still staring at her. Kate tried to think. "They used an old picture. I've lost... some weight."

"And apparently dyed your hair," he said skeptically.

"Yes, well..." Kate sucked in a breath. "Hopefully you'll keep my secret. Blondes have more fun." She tried to smile, but she imagined she looked more scared than confident.

The man nodded and smiled. "Yes, they do."

From the back of the line someone shouted, "Hey, Casanova, work your mojo on your own time." Laughs rang out across the line.

Kate smiled. "How does it go?" She swiped the card again. Red, the beep. She looked up.

The man grasped her hand, flipped the card, and ran it through. Green. Then he turned to his post and swiped his own card. Green. He glided gingerly past the six scowling guards, and Kate chased after him.

"Thank you, Doctor—"

"Prendergast. Barnaby Prendergast." They turned another corner.

"Barnaby Prendergast. I was actually going to guess that."

"Well, you're quite cheeky." He looked over at her. "Quite quick on your feet for someone who couldn't operate the card reader."

Did he know? Kate tried to seem embarrassed; it wasn't a stretch. "Guns make me nervous."

"Then you'll truly hate it here. Seems like everyone without a white coat is 'packin' heat.'" He said the last two words with an American accent. He swiped his card and pushed open a set of wide doors that might have divided sections of a hospital. "Guess they'll be ready if the trees ever attack." He snorted and muttered, "Bloody idiots."

Ahead of them, several overweight men pushed rolling metal cages across their path. Kate stared. The cages were filled with chimps. When they had passed, Kate realized she was alone in the hall. She jogged down the corridor and caught sight of Barnabus, or whatever his name was. She rushed to catch up with him.

He stopped at the swipe terminal to another set of doors. "Where did you say you were going, Dr. West?"

"I… didn't." Kate tried to flutter her eyes at him. She felt like a fool. "Where… are you going?"

"Uh, to my lab in viral. Who are you working with here?" He looked at her, confused. Or was he scrutinizing her?

Kate panicked. It was so much more complicated than she had thought on the train. What did she think, she'd just walk in like it was a day care and say, "I'm here to pick up the two Indonesian kids?" David's advice—*Just tell them it's above their pay grade*—seemed so simplistic, so off-base now. It was obvious now that he had only said it to put her at ease, to get her off the train and in motion. But her mind was blank. "It's above your pay grade," she blurted.

Barnaby was about to swipe his card, but he pulled up short, his card dangling in the air. "Excuse me?" He looked at her, then glanced around as if trying to figure out which direction a sound was coming from.

Kate had the urge to run as fast as she could away from him, but she had no idea which way to go. She needed to figure out where they kept the children. "I'm doing autism research."

Barnaby let his card fall to his side as he turned to face Kate. "Really? I'm not aware of any autism research."

"With Dr. Grey."

"Dr. Grey?" Barnaby's eyes rolled back as he thought. "Haven't heard of him…" His skeptical expression slowly faded as he shuffled toward a white phone on the wall beside the door. He reached back for it. "Maybe I should, ah, get you some help finding your way."

"No!"

Kate's outburst stopped him in his tracks.

"Don't. I'm not lost. I'm working… with two children."

He drew his hand back to his side. "Oh, so it's true. We've heard rumors but everyone is so *hush-hush* about it. So cloak-and-dagger."

He didn't know about the children. What did it mean? Kate needed to buy more time, needed to think. "Uh, yes. I'm sorry I can't say more."

"Well I'm sure it's above my pay grade, as you say." He mumbled something else, maybe "as if you know my bloody pay grade." "Honestly, though, I have to say, what would you be doing with kids in a place like this? We're talking about a zero-percent survival rate. *Zero percent*. Guess your 'pay grade' justifies it. Is that it?"

A new thought gripped Kate, a terror she hadn't considered: zero-percent survival rate. The children could already be dead.

"Did you hear me?"

But Kate couldn't answer. She just stood there, frozen.

He could see it—the fear in her eyes. He cocked his head to the side. "You know, there is something off about you. Something's not right here." He reached. He had the phone.

Kate leaped for him, grabbing the phone from his hand.

His eyes grew wide, a look of *how dare you*.

Kate looked around. David's words—*They could be listening*—echoed in her head. It might already be too late. She hung the phone up and took Barnaby in a hug, whispering in his ear. "Listen to me. Two children are being held here. They're in danger. I'm here to rescue them."

He pushed her away from him. "What? Are you mad?!"

He looked exactly the way Kate had two days ago in that van when David had questioned her.

She leaned in again. "Please. You have to trust me. I need your help. I need to find those children."

He searched her face. His mouth puckered as though he had tasted something awful and couldn't spit it out. "Look, I don't know what you're playing at, some security drill or sick game, but I told you I don't know anything about those children—if there even are any. I've just heard rumors."

"Where would they keep them?"

"I have no idea. I've never even seen the subjects. I just have access to the labs."

"Guess. Please, I need your help."

"I don't know... the residential wings, I assume."

"Take me there."

He waved his card at her, "Hello? I don't have access. I just told you, I can only get into the labs."

Kate looked down at her card. "I bet I can."

The security guard watched as the woman accosted the man, took the phone from him, then grabbed him and whispered in his ear—possibly a threat. The man certainly looked scared. They had just had another seminar on sexual harassment, but it was mostly about men making women have sex with them. So this wasn't that. But it could be something. The guard picked up the phone. "Yeah, this is Post Seven; I think we may have a problem in Bell Primary."

52

David waited in line as they processed the security guards through. The structure was massive—beyond anything he had expected. Three giant vase-shaped cooling towers reached into the sky, billowing white smoke into the clouds. They loomed over the buildings.

The complex must be some kind of combined hospital/medical facility and power plant. Other trains were arriving from other tracks. All the personnel must be shipped in from off-site; there was a very wide quarantine zone around the site, maybe even a hundred miles. Why? The cost would have been staggering. Building something like this in the middle of nowhere and carting supplies and personnel in every day?

"Sir!"

David looked up. His turn. He swiped the card. A red beep. He looked over. He had it backwards. He flipped the card and got a green beep.

He proceeded into the building. Now the hard part: where to go?

Another thought tickled the back of his mind: Kate. She was in way over her head. He had to finish his part and get to her, fast.

He found a map on the wall: the emergency escape route. There was no reactor room on the floor. In fact, based on where the water vapor towers had been, he didn't think it was even in this building.

He moved out of the main corridor, following the flow of mostly men into an open area with rows of lockers. Most of the guards were either conversing with each other or grabbing weapons and radios and heading off.

He heard a few guards talking about the power plant, and he followed them, grabbing a radio and sidearm from the rack before he left. The rear exit to the small security building opened onto a small courtyard, and David got a glimpse of the three buildings beyond: the enormous power plant; a building without many windows, maybe a medical facility; and a smaller building with windows and the Immari Corporate flag flying from the roof—probably the administrative center.

The men ahead of him were lost in conversation.

David reached back to feel the backpack, wondering if he would have enough explosives. Probably not. The place was bigger than he expected.

At the entrance to the power plant, an obese guard sat on a barstool, inspecting IDs and consulting a printed page on the podium in front of him. He extended his sausage fingers to David without a word.

David handed over the ID. In the line outside the train, he had scratched the picture mostly off, just as a precaution.

"What happened to your badge?"

"My dog."

The man half snorted and began searching the list. His face slowly contorted, as if the list had turned into a language he couldn't read. "I don't have you down for today."

"That's what I said when they woke me up this morning. Now if you're saying I can go, I'm out of here." David reached for the ID.

The listmaster threw up a sausage hand. "No, hold on now." He buried his head in the list again and took a pen from behind his ear. He glanced from the ID back to the list every few seconds, scrawling "Conner Anderson" at the bottom of the page in childish block letters. He handed the ID back to David and sausage waved the next guy in line.

The next room was some kind of lobby, with a receptionist at a desk and two guards talking. They eyed him as he walked past, then resumed talking. David found another emergency evacuation route poster and began making his way to the reactor section.

To his relief, his card worked on every door he came to. He was almost to the reactor room.

"Hey, stop."

David turned around. It was one of the guards from the lobby.

"Who are you?"

"Conner Anderson."

The guard looked confused, then drew his gun. "No you're not. Don't move."

53

Barnaby looked as scared as Kate felt. Somehow it made her feel more confident, being the leader of the conspiracy.

Her newfound confidence waned slightly when she saw the skinny Asian guard reading a comic book outside the double doors to the residential wing. When he saw them, he tossed the thin staple of pages on the table and watched them approach the card reader on the wall.

Kate scanned her card. Green.

She pushed the door open and took a step inside. Barnaby followed, close on her heels.

"No! You—you scan too!" The guard pointed at Barnaby, whose eyes grew wide as he stepped back, like he was about to be shot.

"You scan." The man pointed at the scanner.

Barnaby clutched his card to his chest, then swiped it. Red.

The guard rose. "ID." He reached toward Barnaby.

The blond scientist backed into the wall, dropping his ID. "She made me do it. She's crazy!"

Kate stepped between them. "It's okay, Barnaby." She picked up the ID and handed it to him. "I wanted him to walk me to work, but it's okay." She put a hand on the small of his back and pushed him away. "It's okay. See you later, Barnaby." She turned back to the guard, held up her ID and swiped it again. "See—green." She punched through the door and waited for a second.

The doors stayed closed; maybe she was safe. Kate wandered farther into the wing. Every twenty feet or so was a large door, apparently a corridor to some other area. As far as the eye could see, it was the same: doors and symmetrical corridors. And it was quiet, an unnerving kind of quiet.

She swiped her card at the nearest door and ventured inside. It was some sort of barracks or… a college dorm—that was what came to mind. She was standing in a large common room that led to six smaller rooms, each with bunk beds. No, they weren't quite like dorm rooms… they were too sparse, more like cells in a prison. And they were empty. Abandoned, apparently. The cells were disheveled: blankets and clothes littered the floors, personal belongings were strewn across the small sinks beside the bunk beds. It looked as if the occupants had left in a hurry.

Kate retreated from the room and resumed walking in the main corridor for a while. Her tennis shoes made a squeaking sound with every step she took. In the distance, she heard talking. She had to go toward it, but some part of her resisted. It was safe here in the empty rooms, with no people.

She turned at the next "crossroads" and walked toward the talking. She could see it now, something like a nurse's station in a hospital: a high-top bar with files laying on it and two or three women behind it.

There was another sound, from another direction—the loud rhythmic clop of boots echoing in the empty corridor. They were getting close. She inched closer to the nurses. She heard their voices: "They want them all now."—"I know"—"That's what I said"—"Nothing they ever do makes sense"—"They aren't even treating—"

Kate jerked around—the boots, behind her. Six men, guards. They were running toward her, guns drawn. "Stop where you are!"

She could run and maybe make it to the nurses' station. The guards were closing fast now, twenty feet away. She took a step, then another, but they were already there, pointing their guns at her.

Kate held up her hands.

54

David raised his hands.

The guard leveled the gun at him and moved closer. "You're not Conner Anderson."

"No kidding," David said under his breath. "Now put the gun away and shut up; they could be listening."

The guard stopped moving. He looked down, confused. "What?"

"He told me I had to come in for him."

"What?"

"Look, we had a wild night. He said he would get sacked if I didn't come in," David insisted.

"Who are you?"

"His friend. You must be his *really* smart friend at work."

"What?"

"Is that all you can say? Look, put the gun up and act natural."

"Conner isn't scheduled today."

"Yeah, I gathered that, genius. Yet another half-drunk brain fart on his part. I'm going to kill him, if you idiots don't kill me first." David tipped his hands forward and nodded, silently saying, *Well are you or aren't you*? The guard said nothing. "Dude, shoot me, or let me go."

The man reluctantly holstered his gun, still looking thoroughly unsatisfied. "Where are you going?"

David walked toward him. "I'm getting out of here; what's the quickest way?"

The man turned and pointed but didn't get a word out. David knocked him out cold with a sharp blow to the base of his skull.

He had to move fast now. He ran deeper into the facility. There was another problem, one he'd pushed to the back of his mind, given the more pressing survival issues. But now he had to think about *how* to cut the power. His best idea was not to attack the nuclear reactors directly; they would be insulated and well-protected, assuming he could even get close to them. And there were three of them. The power lines were his best guess. If he blew the lines, it would cut the power to the entire facility permanently, including any power they may have stored up from the reactor. But he was out of his element. What if the lines were buried under the facility or otherwise out of reach? Or routed through a heavily guarded building outside the reactor facility? Would he even know them when he saw them? There were a lot of what-ifs...

David found another schematic on the wall and scanned through the areas. Reactor 1, Reactor 2, Reactor 3, Turbine, Control Room, Primary Circuit Room... *Circuit Room*—that could work. It was positioned opposite the reactors, and it looked like lines from every reactor flowed into the room.

He turned from the schematic just as two guards rounded the corner and marched toward him. He nodded and made his way to the circuit room. As he approached it, he could hear the low drone of machines and the buzz of high-voltage power. It seemed to come through the walls and up through the floor. The floor didn't vibrate, but as he scanned his badge and entered the room, his body began to shake from the pulse of the massive machines.

Inside, the room was huge—and cramped. Pipes and metal conduits seemed to snake in every direction, buzzing and popping periodically. He felt like he had been shrunk and beamed inside a circuit board on a computer.

David climbed deeper into the room and placed charges on the larger conduits at the points where they entered the room. There were several metal "closets," for lack of a better word. He placed charges on them as well. He only had a few explosives left. Would they be enough? How much time? He set the detonator for five minutes and hid it at the base of the closet. Where to put the last charges?

He heard another noise over the din of the lines. Or maybe he didn't. He took a charge out and shoved it between two smaller lines. He held it there for a second, withdrawing his hand slowly to make sure it would stay.

Out of the corner of his eye he saw them—three guards, in the room, closing fast. He couldn't talk his way out of this one.

55

The six guards surrounded Kate.

One man said into a radio, "We have her. She was wandering around in Corridor Two."

"What are you doing?" Kate protested.

"Come with us," the man with the radio said.

Two of the guards took her by the arms and began leading her away from the voices at the nurses' station.

"Stop!"

Kate turned to see a woman jogging up behind them. She was young, maybe in her twenties. She was dressed so… wrong, so provocatively, like some sort of Playboy bunny. She looked very out of place.

"I'll take her," she said to the men.

"Who are you?"

"Naomi. I work for Mr. Sloane."

"Never heard of him." The guard who was clearly in charge motioned to another man. "We'll take her in too."

"You'll be sorry if you do," Naomi said. "Call it in. I'll wait. Ask your boss to call Mr. Sloane."

The guards looked at each other.

Naomi grabbed one of their radios. "I'll do it myself." She clicked the button. "This is Naomi, I need to speak with Mr. Sloane."

"Stand by."

"Sloane."

"It's Naomi. I'm bringing a girl to you, but there's a pack of guards harassing us."

"Hold on." Then, Sloane's voice said to someone in the background, "Tell your buffoons to quit harassing my people."

Another voice came on the line. "This is Captain Zhào. Who is this?"

Naomi tried to hand the radio back to the man, but he stepped back, dodging it like a plague blanket. Naomi tossed it to the man who had spoken. "Good luck." She grabbed Kate by the arm and said under her breath, "Be quiet and follow me."

Naomi led Kate away from the guards, who were desperately trying to apologize to the man on the radio.

They took a right, then a left, down another deserted corridor. Naomi asked Kate for her badge at a set of double doors.

"Who are you?" Kate said.

"It's not important. I'm here to help you get the children out."

"Who sent you?"

"The same person who sent you the IDs."

"Thank you," was all Kate could think to say.

The woman nodded. She opened a door, and Kate heard Adi and Surya talking inside. Her heart stopped. The door swung open and there they were, sitting at a table in a white-walled room. Kate ran in, knelt down to hug them, and without a word they ran to her and jumped into her arms, bowling her over. They were alive. She could do it. She could save them. Kate felt a firm hand pull her up.

"I'm sorry, but we don't have time. We have to hurry," Naomi said.

56

The security chief handed the radio back to Dorian. "They won't give your girl any more trouble. I apologize for that, Mr. Sloane. It's all the new faces, we don't do well—"

"Spare me." Dorian turned to the nuclear scientist, Dr. Chase. "Continue."

"The shipments we received from the north—I'm not sure we can use them."

"Why not?"

"The nukes from Belarus have been tampered with. If we had the time, we could probably disassemble them and sort them."

"What does that leave?" Dorian said.

"The Ukrainian and Russian devices look okay, they're just old. And the shipment from China was pristine, very recent builds. How did you—?"

"Never mind that. Numbers?"

"Let's see." He scanned a printout. "One hundred twenty-six total warheads. And most are extremely high-yield. It would be helpful to know the target, outside of that I can't say—"

"What about the portable nukes?"

"Ah, yes, we have them ready." Dr. Chase motioned to an assistant across the room. The young man left the room and returned carrying an oversized silver egg, slightly smaller than a shopping cart. The man could barely get his arms around the slippery egg, so he carried it like a load of firewood, leaning back to make sure it didn't roll out of his cupped arms. When he reached the table, he set the egg down and stepped away, but the egg wobbled awkwardly, then drifted toward the edge. The assistant lurched forward and steadied it with a hand.

Dr. Chase put his hands in his pockets, nodded once to Dorian, and smiled expectantly.

Dorian glared at the egg, then again at Dr. Chase. "What the hell is that?"

The scientist slid his hands from his pockets and took a step toward the egg, pointing at it. "It's the... portable device you requested. It's seven point four kilos, or about sixteen pounds." He shook his head. "We simply couldn't reduce it any more; well, we could with time."

Dorian leaned back in the chair, looking from the egg to the scientist.

The scientist walked closer to the egg, scrutinizing it. "Is there something wrong with it? We have the other one—"

"Portable. I need two portable nukes."

"Oh, and indeed it is. You saw Harvey carrying it. Granted it's a bit bulky, but—"

"Over distance and in a backpack, not some magic egg an ogre could skip across a loch. How long to make it smaller—like something that could actually fit in, key word here Doctor, *a suitcase*?"

"Umm, well... you never said..." The man glanced at the egg.

"How long?" Dorian pressed.

"A couple of days, if—"

"Mr. Sloane, we have an issue in the power plant. You need to see this."

Dorian wheeled his chair over to the tablet the security chief held. Behind him, he heard the scientist pacing and complaining to Harvey. "It's not like in the movies where you just 'clip the green wire' and shove it in a rucksack and take off for a hike up Everest, I mean we have to..." Dorian blocked the scientist out and focused on the video on the tablet: a man moving through some mechanical room.

"Where is this?"

"The main circuit room outside the reactors. There's more." The security chief rewound the video.

Dorian watched the man plant a series of charges. There was something else. Dorian tapped the tablet, paused the video, zoomed in on the face. It couldn't be.

"Do you recognize him, sir?"

Dorian studied the face and thought back to a mountainside village in northern Pakistan, the flames rising from every hut, the women and children running, the men lying in front of the burning homes... and a man shooting back at him. He remembered shooting him, he didn't know how many times. And finishing the job. "Yes, I know him. His name is Andrew Reed. He's a former CIA field operative. You'll need a lot more men to contain him."

"Shoot to kill?"

Dorian glanced away absently. In the background, he heard the radio crackle and the security man barking orders. Reed was here, trying to kill the power. He wouldn't be alone. Where had he been for the last four years—if he wasn't dead? Why the power?

The security chief leaned over. "We have the charges and timer. We're taking them out of the building. We've reviewed the security footage since he entered—they're the only threat. We're surrounding him. Do you want us to—"

"Don't shoot him. Where is he now?" Dorian said.

The chief held up the tablet, pointing to a place on the map.

Dorian tapped another location on the map. "What is this room?"

"One of the reactor halls, just a passageway between Reactors One and Two."

Dorian pointed at two large doors on opposite sides. "These are the only two entrances and exits?"

"Yes. And the room has ten-feet-thick concrete walls on all sides."

"Perfect. Drive him in there and close the door," Dorian said.

What was he missing? He waited while the security chief worked the radio. The children. "What's the status of the children?"

The chief looked confused at the question. "In their holding cell."

"Show me."

The chief jabbed the tablet. Then looked up in surprise.

"Find them," Dorian said.

The chief yelled into his radio. They waited a few moments, the radio squawked a few times, and the chief typed something into the tablet, handing it to Dorian just as another video came to life: Naomi, and with her, Kate Warner and the children. Was it the worst news ever or the best news ever?

The chief was yelling into his radio with the other hand.

Dorian thought. Could it be just the two of them?

"We'll have them momentarily, sir. I don't know how—"

Dorian held a hand up, not looking at the man. "Stop talking."

What to do? Clearly there was still a security breach, a serious one. And there were only a few suspects. Dorian motioned to one of the staffers he'd brought with him. "Logan, send a memo to the Immari Council: 'China facility under attack. We are attempting to secure, but anticipate all research capabilities will be destroyed. As such, proceeding with Toba Protocol with all haste. Will post further updates as events develop.' Include the videos of the man in the power plant and the two girls trying to extract the children. I want to know the minute anyone responds."

The chief rocked back on his heels. "We have them, sir."

"Great work, truly," Dorian said derisively.

The chief swallowed and said with less confidence, "Should we…"

"Take the two girls to the Bell, put them in with all the other subjects that are ready, but make sure they get in. I want them at the front of the line. Then throw the switch as soon as possible— tell Chang no excuses." Dorian paused. Kate Warner, in the Bell room, it was such sweet, sweet justice. And there was nothing Martin could do. Soon, there would be nothing anyone could do.

It was actually working out better than he could have planned. Dorian motioned to Dr. Chase. "Are all the nukes on train cars?"

"Yes, except for the Belarus devices and… the portable—"

"Good." Dorian turned back to the chief. "Put the kids on the train car with the nukes and move it out of here right now." He swiveled on Dr. Chase. "I expect you to be on that train as well, and by the time it reaches the coast, either those eggs will fit in a backpack or you will. You understand?"

Dr. Chase nodded and looked away.

The chief listened, then dropped the radio to his side. "The saboteur is locked in Reactor Hall Two."

"All right. Make sure none of the remaining train cars leave. We need them to move something else." Dorian walked over to Dmitry Kozlov, second-in-command of Dorian's personal Immari Security unit.

"When the Bell is finished, load the bodies on those train cars and move them out," Dorian said. "We need to set up a loading zone, probably northern India, somewhere with access to airports."

"What about the rest of the staff here?"

"I've been thinking about that," Dorian said as he led Dmitry farther away from any of the other staff. "They're a liability. We certainly can't let anyone leave, at least not until Toba is in full swing. We have another problem. There are only one hundred and nineteen human subjects on-site."

The man saw the implication immediately. "Not enough bodies."

"Not even close. I think we can solve both issues, but it won't be easy."

Dmitry nodded and glanced over at the scientists milling around in the lab. "Process the staff through the Bell? I agree. It would require Chang's team to operate the machinery… on their own people. Doable, but it could get ugly. There are at least a hundred security personnel on site. They won't go quietly, even if we segregate them and orchestrate it as a drill."

"What do you need?" Dorian said.

"Fifty, maybe sixty men. Immari Security or Clocktower field agents would be ideal. Immari Security is purging the New Delhi Clocktower station now. We might be able to task the remaining field operatives."

"Make it happen," Dorian said as he stepped away.

"Where will you be?"

"Someone inside Immari has to be working with Reed. I'm going to find out who it is."

57

Kate screamed as the security guards ripped the children from her hands and wrestled her to the ground. She scratched their faces and kicked. She couldn't lose them again. She had to fight.

"No, to the train," one of the guards said. The boys tried to wiggle free.

Kate reached out for them, but a man pinned her arms. Another man rushed to her, and she saw the butt of a rifle coming at her face.

The room was dark and crowded. Kate was being crushed by people from every side. She elbowed people left and right, but no one responded—they were dead on their feet. They would have fallen over if they weren't squeezed in so tight.

Above her, Kate heard a loud boom. A huge metal device was descending from the ceiling. There were lights, flashing from the top now, with synchronized booms. She could feel the booms in her chest and in the bodies of the zombies crowded around her.

Were the children here? She scanned the room. She couldn't see anyone, just blank faces, half-awake. Then—Naomi. The confident woman who had rescued her looked terrified.

The boom-boom-boom above grew deafening, the light blinding. Kate felt the flesh around her heat up. She raised a hand to brush the sweat from her face, but her hand was already so wet, covered in something thick, almost sticky—blood.

58

The concrete doors to the reactor hall slammed shut with a loud boom. The sound was barely audible over the rumble of the massive reactors. David walked deeper into the room, surveying the site of his last stand. Maybe Kate got out.

He slid the clip out of his gun. Two rounds. Should he save the last round? The drugs they used on Kate were serious. Who knew what they could do. He knew valuable intel. That was the selfless reason, but there were others. He pushed the thought from his mind. He'd cross that bridge when he came to it.

He walked around the room—the passageway between the two towering reactors. It resembled a high school gym with a high ceiling dominated by metal scaffolding. It was shaped like an hourglass; the room was almost rectangular save for two round indentations near the center—the thick concrete walls of two reactors. There were two entrances, both of them with concrete slide up-and-down doors—one at the front, the other at the rear of the room. The tall smooth walls surrounding the doors were dotted with metal conduits and tubes that were mostly silver, with a few blue and red mixed in, giving the impression of varicose veins peeking out of a gray forehead over the mouth of the door.

"Hello, Andrew," a voice boomed over the loudspeaker, no doubt intended for evacuation warnings. David knew that voice: someone pre-Clocktower. But he couldn't place it.

David needed to buy time. It was the only thing that could help Kate. "That's not my name anymore." He heard the reactors on each side roar to life. He wondered if the "voice" could hear him over the din.

How long had it been? The bombs should go off soon. Cutting the power would seal his fate but could help Kate.

"We have the girl. And we found your bombs. Not terribly creative. I would have expected more from you."

David looked around. Was the voice lying? Why tell him? What could he do? Shoot the reactors? Bonehead idea—massive concrete walls. Shoot one of the conduits, hope to get lucky? Unlikely. The ceiling? Useless.

The voice wanted something from him; why else question him? Maybe the voice was lying. Kate could be waiting on him at the train. Maybe he didn't have her. "What do you want?" David yelled.

"Who sent you here?" the voice boomed.

"Let her go, and I'll tell you."

The voice laughed. "Sure, it's a deal."

"Sounds good, come on down here, and I'll make a formal statement. Even draw you a picture. I've got his email address too."

"If I have to come in there, I'm going to beat it out of you. I'm on a tight schedule. No time for drugs."

The reactors roared louder. Should it sound like that?

The voice continued, "You don't have any options here, Andrew. We both know it. But you still hang on. That's your problem—your weakness. You're the ultimate sucker for a lost cause. It appeals to your rescue fantasy. Pakistani villagers, Jakartan children, you always go for it. Because you sympathize, you feel like a victim—that's your mentality. You think if you can get even with the people who wronged you, you'll be whole. But you won't. It's over. You know it's true. Listen to my voice. You know who I am. I keep my promises. I'll give the girl a quick death, I promise. That's the best you can do here. Tell me who it was. It's your last play."

Standard interrogation: break down your subject, assert superiority, and convince them that talking is the only option. Actually it *was* pretty convincing at this point. David knew they could simply gas him, toss a grenade in, or storm him with a few guards. He had no options. But now he had figured out who the man behind the microphone was: Dorian Sloane, the Immari field commander in Afghanistan and Pakistan. He should have assumed Sloane would run the entire region for Immari Security at this point. He was ruthless, capable... and vain. Could David use that? His best option was to play for time, on the off chance that something would happen. Or that Sloane was lying and Kate was getting away.

"I gotta tell ya, Sloane, I think you missed your calling. The psychoanalysis... just amazing. You've really got me questioning my whole life here. Can I have a little time to contemplate the deeper issues you touched on? I mean—"

"Stop wasting time, Andrew. It won't matter for you or her. You hear those reactors coming to life? That's the sound of power flowing to a machine that's killing Kate right now. It's just you, now. And Clocktower fell a few hours ago. Now tell me—"

"In that case, you're the one wasting time. I've got nothing to say." David gritted his teeth and tossed his gun on the floor. It slid all the way to the far door. "You want to try to beat it out of me, come on down here and take your best shot. I'm unarmed. You might have half a chance." He stood in the middle of the hourglass-shaped room, looking from door to door, wondering which one would open first... and if he could make it when it did.

The reactor screamed even louder, and David felt heat radiating off of it. Was it malfunctioning? Behind him, a concrete door rumbled to life, lifting up from the two-foot indentation in the floor. The gun lay at the opposite door.

David ran for the opening door. Forty feet away. Thirty feet away. It was his only option: to slide under and fight hand-to-hand, then try to break out of the perimeter they'd set up. Twenty feet.

Sloane ducked under the door and popped up, a gun in his right hand leading the way. He fired three quick shots. The first caught David in his shoulder, cutting him down instantly and sending him sprawling onto the concrete floor. Blood spread out below him as he rolled back and forth, fighting to get to his feet, but Sloane was on him, kicking David's legs out from under him.

"Who told you about this place?"

David could barely hear him over the reactors. His shoulder throbbed. The wound didn't feel like a wound; it felt like a piece of him had been blown off. He couldn't even feel his left arm.

Sloane pointed the gun at David's left leg. "At least die with some dignity, Andrew. Tell me, and I'll end this."

David tried to think. *I need to buy some time.* "I don't have a name."

Sloane moved the gun closer to David's leg.

"But—I do have an IP address. It's how I communicated with him."

Sloane drew back, considering.

David sucked a few more breaths in. "It's in my left pocket; you'll have to get it." He motioned to his arm.

Sloane leaned toward him and pulled the trigger, sending a bullet into David's leg.

David writhed wildly on the ground, screaming in pain. Sloane circled him. "Stop. Lying. To. Me."

When David said nothing, Sloane raised his boot and slammed it into David's forehead, sending his skull into the concrete floor. David saw spots. He was certain he would pass out soon. Above them, the reactors had changed their tone again, a different sound. Sloane looked up. A siren went off just before an explosion rocked the room, throwing shards of concrete and metal debris everywhere. Gas spewed from the pipes and walls, blanketing the room. The other door opened and people were running through.

David rolled over onto his belly and crawled with one arm and one leg, dragging the limp arm and the dead leg. The pain almost overwhelmed him. He had to stop, swallow, and gasp for breath. He clawed a few more feet. He tried not to inhale the dirt and dust coating the floors. He knew it was getting in the holes in his leg and shoulder, but it didn't matter, he had to get away. He saw Sloane swatting the smoke, charging around the room.

Another explosion.

The other reactor?

The smoke was too thick to see anything now.

Talking, in the distance. "Sir, we have to evacuate, there's a problem—"

"Fine. Give me your gun."

Gunshots, everywhere. The walls, the floor. David froze. He held his head dead still against the ground as if listening, waiting for some sign. In the few inches above the floor, he saw bodies dropping here and there, Sloane's own men falling from his last desperate attempt to put one more round in David.

"Sir, we must—"

"All right!"

David heard people running around him. He tried to push up with his good arm, but he couldn't. He was too weak. Too cold. He watched his breath blow the white dust on the ground. Every breath blew a few grains of white powder. All around him, the white was being eaten by the red. It reminded him of something, a thought or memory; what was it? Shaving. It was like the blood from a shaving cut consuming a white tissue. He watched the red crawl over the white dust toward his face as the sirens moaned.

59

Kate thought the masses of people in the room were falling, but she realized in horror that they were melting, or disintegrating, from the ground up. Lights flashed across the room and she caught glimpses of the waves flowing through, like violent tides delivering death, one boom at a time.

But the booming was different now. And the light—the flashing—was getting dimmer, not nearly as blinding. She could see it now—the device suspended from the walls. It was shaped like a bell, or an oversized pawn with windows in the head. She squinted to see something else. It was... dripping. Iron tears fell, draping the unlucky people below it in a molten blanket of death.

More people were dropping, but there were survivors scattered across the room—some looking confused, as if waiting to be picked in an execution lottery; others running, some to the corners; three or four beating on the door.

Kate looked down, seeing her body for the first time since waking up. She was covered in blood, but it wasn't her blood. Aside from the throbbing in her head, she was unharmed. She had to help these people. She knelt down and examined the man at her feet—or what was left of him. It looked like his blood had swollen, bursting his blood vessels from the inside, causing a massive body-wide hemorrhage that tore his skin and erupted from his eyes and nails.

The bell was changing—the light flashed on again, brighter than ever. Kate shielded her eyes with her hand and turned away from the light. Ahead, she saw Naomi, who must have waded through the bodies toward the door. Kate crawled over to her.

The boom was now a constant low-pitched wail, like the knell of a gong that wouldn't end. Iron stretching?

Kate rolled Naomi's head back and pushed the hair out of her face. Dead. Beautiful. The blood hadn't reached her face.

Bodies swarmed around Kate—the living. They crowded the door, beating and screaming. She tried to rise to her feet but couldn't; they were all over her, waving arms in the air and shoving.

The blast deafened Kate and flattened the crowd, pressing a half dozen people into her. She sucked hard for a breath, but none would come. They were crushing her, suffocating her. She punched, twisted, and heaved her head back. It was raining. No—debris was falling. And then water, a huge flood of water into the room, and she was free, floating, drifting with the massive tidal wave that swept over the crumbling walls that had sealed the death room.

Kate inhaled sharply. The breath hurt, but it was a relief. At that moment, she had two thoughts:

I'm alive.

David must have saved me.

60

Dorian Sloane motioned for Dr. Chang to put on one of the helicopter's headsets.

Below them, another explosion rocked the complex, causing the helicopter to shudder, then bank slightly away from it.

The second that Chang's headphones covered his ears, Dorian started in. "What the hell happened?"

"The Bell, some kind of problem."

"Sabotaged?"

"No, or, I don't think so. Everything was normal: power, radiation output. But it... malfunctioned."

"Impossible."

"Look, we still don't completely understand how it works, and it's, you know, old, over one hundred thousand years old, and we've been using it nonstop for about eighty years—"

"This is not a warranty issue, Doctor. You need to figure out what happened—"

Another man broke onto the line. "Sir, there's a call from the facility. The security chief, he says it's urgent."

Dorian tore off his headset and grabbed the sat phone. "What?"

"Mr. Sloane, we have another problem."

"Don't call me and tell me we have a problem. It's quite apparent we have problems. Tell me what the problem is and quit wasting my time."

"Oh course, I'm sorry—"

"What? Tell me!"

"The Bell room. It exploded. We think radiation could have escaped."

Dorian's mind raced. If the bodies—or even radiation—had escaped from the Bell room, he could still salvage Toba Protocol. He just had to sell it to the people on the ground.

"Sir?" the security chief said tentatively. "I'm initiating a quarantine per our SOPs, I just wanted to confirm—"

"No. We're not establishing a quarantine—"

"But my orders—"

"Have changed. As has the situation. We need to rescue our people, Chief. I want you to devote all your resources to getting everyone onto the trains and away from the facilities. And put the bodies on the trains too. Their families deserve the right to bury them."

"But won't there be an outbreak—"

"You worry about getting those people on the trains. I'll take care of the rest. There are factors you're not aware of. Call me when the last train is away. Immari is a family. We don't leave anyone behind. You understand me?"

"Yes, sir, we won't leave a single soul behind—"

Dorian disconnected the line and put his headset back on. He turned to Dmitry Kozlov, the Immari Security officer sitting across from him. "Did Chase get out with the nukes and children?"

"Yes, they're on their way to the coast."

"Good." Dorian thought for a moment. They would still get bodies from the Bell—that was the good news. But the explosions at the facility would draw attention. If the world found out what was at the site... Five thousand years of their work, of well-kept secrets, would all be lost, as would the Immari. "Launch drones from Afghanistan. As soon as the last train leaves, blow the facility."

61

David felt them lift him up and carry him like a rag doll. Around him, he saw a war zone: sirens blared, white dust floated through the air like snow, fires belched black smoke, and voices shouted in Chinese. He watched it all through half-closed eyes as if it were a dream.

Over the loudspeaker, a recording repeated, "Reactor core breach. Evacuate. Evacuer. Evakuieren..." The voice faded, and David felt sunlight on his face. The men tossed him about as they carried him over the rough ground.

"Stop! Let me take a look." A man was in his face. Someone with a white coat. Blond, around forty. British. He grabbed David's face and pulled at his eyelids, then looked him up and down, inspecting the wounds. "No, he won't make it." The man pointed to the ground and drew a hand across his throat. "Put him down. Get someone else." He motioned to the building. The Chinese workers dropped him like a sack of rotten potatoes and ran back toward the building.

From the ground, David watched the man run over to another group holding a body pulled from the rubble. The man perused it briefly. "Yes, she'll make it." He gestured toward the train, and the men carried the woman the remaining twenty feet, tossing her into a car where other workers dragged her in.

The white coat turned to another group. "Supplies? On the train. Hurry."

The train. Twenty feet to freedom. But David couldn't move.

62

Kate arrived just as the passenger train pulled away. She ran after it, her legs burning as she pushed herself until she was lightheaded, and the train was half a football field away.

She stood there, bent over, her hands on her knees, panting as the rhythmic chug-chug-chug of the train faded into the vast green forest.

The children were on that train. She knew it, somewhere, somehow, in a place she couldn't identify. They were out of reach. And she was in over her head. The device, this place. In that moment, she felt utterly defeated.

She looked around. There wasn't another train. The train ride in was almost an hour through nothing but dense forest. She couldn't walk out, and she had another problem: it was getting colder. She needed shelter, but how long could she hide here before some Immari security officer found her?

Another thought broke into her mind: David. Would he be looking for her? His blasts had done a number on the buildings. He was probably on that train, assuming that she was too. Was he searching every car, expecting to find her sitting with the children? What would he do when he couldn't find her? She knew what the Immari would do if they captured her. She glanced back at the burning Immari complex. It was her only option.

Another train horn. Kate spun around, searching. Where had it come from? She twisted again, desperately trying to find the direction. It had to be on the other side of the campus. She set off running, her lungs now burning from both the cold and the impact in the Bell room.

She reached the medical building just as the train horn sounded again. She put her head down and charged through the chaos inside. The rear door of the facility opened onto a small courtyard that led to the power plant, which had clearly taken most of the damage. It was a smoking, crumbling ruin. Two of the huge vase-like smokestacks had toppled completely. The train whistle called again—it was coming from the other side of the building. Kate ran with all the strength she could muster. Another explosion in the power plant filled the air, almost knocking her over. She steadied herself and plowed on.

As she cleared the side of the power building, she saw it—a cargo train. Workers were tossing supplies and bodies through the wide sliding doors as the train rolled slowly by, allowing them to spread the load among the cars.

Seeing the carnage outside the power plant forced another thought into Kate's mind: what if David didn't make it out? He could still be inside. Or on the train. She could see people inside the cargo cars, hovering over bodies. David could be one of them. She would search the train, before it got away, then the power plant. She wouldn't leave without him.

Behind her, Kate heard a voice she knew. The British doctor. Barnaby Prendergast?

She ran to him. "Barnaby, have you seen—" But he was focused on a body. He ignored Kate and yelled at a group of Chinese security guards standing nearby. Kate grabbed him by the lapels of his sodden white coat and turned him around. "Barnaby, I'm looking for a man, a security guard, blond, thirties—"

"You!" Barnaby tried to pull away, but Kate held him tight. When he took in Kate's appearance, her blood-soaked clothes and seeming lack of any wounds, he staggered backward and tried to break her hold. "*You* did this!" He waved to one of the security guards. "Help! This woman is an impostor, a terrorist, she did this, someone help me!"

People stopped what they were doing and looked over. Several security people began walking toward Kate.

Kate released Barnaby and looked around. "He's lying! I didn't—" But the guards kept coming. She had to get out of here. She scanned the platform for an exit, a—

Then she saw David, lying there, not moving, his eyes closed, his body resting awkwardly on the debris-ridden concrete platform. Alone. Dying. Or dead?

Kate sprinted over to him and inspected his wounds. Gunshots. Two: his shoulder and leg. What had happened to him? The wounds were bad, but something bothered Kate even more—they were hardly bleeding. A chill ran through her, and the pit of her stomach seemed to drop.

She had to keep going. She scanned the rest of him. His clothes were in tatters, and a litany of burn marks and shrapnel holes dotted his legs and torso, but nothing as major as the gunshots. She needed—

She felt a hand on her shoulder—a security guard, then another one, three of them were on her. She had blocked everything out when she saw David. They grabbed her by the arms and stood her up. Barnaby was behind them, pointing and egging the mob on, "I tried to stop her!"

Kate struggled to escape the security guard's grip, but he pulled her in tight. Her hand was at his side, on his gun. She ripped at it, but it wouldn't come free. She twisted it again with all her might and she heard a pop; she had it. But they still held her so tight; all three were on her, dragging her to the ground. She pointed toward the air and squeezed the trigger. The gun almost flew out of her hand, but the men scattered, and Barnaby scampered away in full retreat, looking back nervously before putting his head down and charging on.

Kate held the gun out from her, waving it left and right as the men held up their hands and backed away. Her hand shook badly, and she braced it with her other hand. She glanced behind her. The train—it was almost gone now. The last people on the platform had fled into the three remaining cars, which would soon be gone.

"Put him on the train," she commanded the guards. They kept backing away. Kate pointed the gun at David, then the train. "On. Now!" She backed away from David, giving the men space. They picked him up and carried him to the car, placing him right on the edge. Kate kept the gun on them as she shuffled to a clump of medical supplies scattered across the ground, no doubt dropped by the frightened workers. What was the priority? Antibiotics. Something to clean and close the wound. She couldn't save him, but she could try, if only for her own sake.

Another explosion rocked the facility, followed by the sound of an angry Chinese voice shouting over the guards' radios. The guards apparently decided that with everything else going on, they had more urgent priorities than dealing with the crazy woman stealing medical supplies, and Kate found herself suddenly left alone.

Behind her, the train was moving faster, away from the building. Kate started to tuck the gun in her waistband but then paused, eyeing it. Was it still cocked? The hammer was back. She'd probably blow her leg off. She placed it carefully on the ground, gathered as many supplies as she could hold, and ran for the train. A few boxes tumbled off the stack onto the ground, but she kept going. She could barely keep pace with the train. She tossed the supplies on; a few hit the edge of the car and bounced off. She grabbed the handle at the door and jumped, landing on her stomach, her legs dangling off. She pulled herself into the car and watched as first the platform disappeared, then the power plant.

She crawled over to David. "David? Can you hear me? You're going to be okay."

She reached over and began sorting through the paltry pile of supplies.

63

David turned in horror as the building collapsed, engulfing him in concrete, dust, and metallic shards. He felt the rubble press in around him, crushing him, grinding into his wounds. He breathed dust and soot, listening to the screams, some close, some distant. And he waited. For how long, he didn't know. Then they were there, pulling him out.

"We got you. Don't try to move, buddy."

FDNY. They pulled and dug out around him. They called for a stretcher, strapped him to it, and carried him over the uneven ground. Sunlight bathed his face.

A doctor pulled his eyelids back and shone a light over him, then tied something around his leg.

"Can you hear me?" She worked at his leg some more, then returned to his face. "Your leg was crushed, and there's a large laceration in your back, but you're going to be okay. Do you understand?"

Kate tied off the wounds to David's leg and shoulder, but it wouldn't matter—there wasn't much blood flow to stop. He already felt cold.

She told herself it was just the cold wind blowing in through the door to the car. The train was moving fast now, faster than the one coming in. The sun was setting and the temperature was dropping. She stood and struggled with the sliding metal door. She couldn't close it at this speed.

She collapsed back to the floor, took David by the arm, and dragged him to the corner, as far away from the door as she could get. She'd given him a shot of antibiotics and cleaned and closed the wounds as best she could. There was nothing left to do. She leaned back against the wall, pulled him into her lap, and put her legs around his to try to keep him warm. His listless head came to rest on her stomach, and she ran a hand through his short hair. He was getting colder.

64

Beyond the windows of the helicopter, the sun was setting on the Tibetan plateau. Dorian tried to find the facility in the expanse of green forest. It was just a single column of gray and white smoke now, like a campfire in the untouched wilderness.

"The last train is away," Dmitry said.

"Drones?" Dorian didn't look away from the window or the column of smoke.

"Thirty minutes out." When Dorian said nothing, the man continued, "What now?"

"Stop the trains. Catalog everyone, including the dead bodies. Make sure our men are in full quarantine gear."

65

Kate stared out into the black night. A sliver of a moon cast a small twinkle of light over the treetops that rushed by. Or had rushed by. The train was slowing. But there was nothing outside, just forest.

She slid David's head out of her lap and walked to the door. She leaned out and looked toward the front of the train, then to the rear. They were in the last car, and there was nothing on the tracks behind them. Kate turned to go back into the car, and she saw it—through the opposite door, on the track beside them, another train, sitting there as still and dark as the night, almost invisible. And there was something else: dark figures standing on the top of the train. Waiting for what?

The train stopped, and at almost the same instant, she heard the thunder of boots landing on the ceiling. Kate moved back into the shadow of the car just as the soldiers swooped in through the doorway like gymnasts rounding a high bar. They spread out in the room quickly, shining lights in her face and in every corner of the car. They snapped a zip line between the trains and pulled it to test the strength.

A man grabbed Kate, clipped onto the line, and launched out the door toward the second train. Kate looked back. David! But they had him too; another man, right behind her, held David to his chest with one arm like you might carry a sleeping child.

Kate's captor led her into a dining car and shoved her into a booth. "Wait here," he said in Chinese-accented English before turning to leave.

The other man brought David in and plopped him down on

a couch. Kate rushed to him. He didn't look any worse, but that wasn't saying much. He didn't have long.

She raced to the door the soldier was closing. She grabbed it, stopping him. "Hey, we need some help."

He stared at her, then resumed trying to close the door.

"Stop! We need a hospital. Medical supplies. Blood." Did the man understand a word she was saying? "Med kit," she said desperately, looking for anything that might register.

He placed a hand on her chest, shoved her back into the train car and slammed the door.

Kate walked back over to David. The bullets from the gunshots to his shoulder and leg had both gone straight through. Kate had closed the wounds as best she could. She needed to clean the wounds properly, but infection wasn't the biggest risk to his life at the moment. He needed blood—now. Kate could give him blood—she was O negative, the universal donor. If... she could get it inside him.

The train lurched, throwing Kate to the floor. They were moving. She got back to her feet as the train jerked forward in gasps and spurts, picking up speed. Out the window, she couldn't see the other train, the cargo train they had been on. They were taking them in the opposite direction. Who were they? Kate pushed the question out of her mind. Saving David was all that mattered to her right now.

She glanced around. Maybe there was something she could use. The dining car was about forty feet long, most of it dedicated to booths, but at the far end was a small bar with a soft-drink dispenser, glasses, and liquor. Maybe the tube—

The door slid open again and another soldier staggered in, trying to keep his balance as the train accelerated. He set an olive case with a red cross painted on the side down on the floor.

Kate lunged for it.

The soldier had fled the car and closed the door by the time Kate reached the case. She threw it open and ransacked it. Relief spilled over her when she saw the contents.

Fifteen minutes later, the tube ran from Kate's arm to David's. She pumped her fist. The blood flowed. She was so hungry. And sleepy. But she was doing something for him, and that felt very good.

66

Kate awoke to the chime of bells drifting in through a large picture window above the alcove that held her small twin bed. A cool, crisp, clean mountain wind pushed the white linen drapes out over her bed, almost touching her face.

She reached up to touch the cloth but drew back in pain. Inside her elbow, her arm was badly bruised. Pools of dark purple and black extended into her forearm and crawled up her bicep.

David.

She looked out at the room, some sort of classroom maybe. The room was long and wide with a rustic wooden floor, white plaster walls, and wood beams every ten feet.

She barely remembered getting off the train. It had been late in the night. The men had carried her up endless stairs, into a mountain fortress. She remembered it now... a temple or maybe a monastery.

She started to roll off the bed, but something startled her—movement in the room, a figure rising from the floor. He had been sitting so still she hadn't seen him. He walked closer, and Kate could see he was young, a teenager. He looked almost like a teenage Dalai Lama. He wore a thick crimson robe that was clasped at one shoulder and extended to his toes, resting just above his leather sandals. His head was shaved. He smiled at her and said eagerly, "Good morning, Dr. Warner."

She put her feet on the ground. "I'm sorry; you startled me." She felt lightheaded.

He bowed extravagantly, extending one arm out toward the

ground as he bent. "I did not mean to alarm, Madam. I am Milo, at your service." He spoke each word with care.

"Uh, thank you." She rubbed her head, trying to focus. "There was a man with me."

"Ah, yes, Mr. Reed."

Reed?

Milo paced to a table near the bed. "I came to take you to him." He picked up a large ceramic bowl with two hands and walked back to her, extending it toward her face. "But first, breakfast!" He raised his eyebrows as he said it.

Kate reached out to brush the bowl aside, but as she stood, she felt faint. She collapsed back onto the bed, disoriented.

"Breakfast does a Dr. Warner good." Milo smiled and extended the bowl again.

Kate leaned closer, smelled the thick porridge concoction, and reluctantly took the spoon and tried it. Delicious. Or was it that she was so famished, and the ration packs had been so bad? She finished the bowl in seconds and wiped her mouth with the back of her hand. Milo returned the bowl to the table and handed her a thick cloth like a handkerchief. Kate smiled sheepishly and wiped her mouth.

"Now, I'd like to see—"

"Mr. Reed. Of course. Right this way." Milo led her out of the room and down a long breezeway that connected several structures.

The view was breathtaking. A green plateau spread out before them, reaching to the horizon, interrupted only by several snow-capped mountain ranges. Smoke from several villages emerged from the plateau below. In the distance, something dotted the sides of the mountains: other monasteries, built right into the steep snow-capped slopes.

Kate had to fight the urge to stop and take it all in. Milo slowed to let her catch up.

They turned another corner. Below them, a large square wooden deck overlooked the valleys and mountains below. Twenty or thirty men, all with shaved heads and dressed in crimson robes, sat cross-legged, unmoving, staring out into the distance.

Milo turned to Kate. "Morning meditation. Would you like to join?"

"Uh, not today," Kate mumbled as she fought to look away from the scene.

Milo ushered her into another room where she saw David lying in an alcove similar to the one she'd woken up in. Kate ran to him. She knelt at his bedside and examined him quickly. He was awake but listless. Antibiotics—he needed more to fight the infection. Unchecked, it would kill him for sure. She would have to disinfect and close the bullet wounds properly sooner or later.

First things first. She'd left the antibiotics on the train. "Left" when she was abducted. Or rescued? There were so many mysteries at this point.

"Milo, I need some medications, antibiotics—"

The young man motioned her over to a table like the one he'd served her breakfast porridge from. "We assumed as much, Dr. Warner. I have prepared a series of remedies for your use." He waved a hand over several piles of dirt-ridden roots, a pile of orange powder, and a bundle of mushrooms. He smiled and cocked his head, as if to say *Pretty great, huh?*

Kate put her hands on her sides. "Milo, these are, um, very helpful, thank you, but I um... I'm afraid his condition is severe—uh, will require some medi—"

Milo stepped back, grinned like the Cheshire Cat, and pointed at her. "Ahhh, I get you good, Dr. Warner!" He threw open the doors to a floor-to-ceiling wooden cabinet, revealing a bounty of modern medical supplies.

Kate rushed to the cupboard, scanning it row by row. They had a bit of everything: antibiotics, painkillers, anti-fungals, bandages. Where to start? Kate shook her head and smiled warmly at Milo as she sorted through the antibiotics. "Yes, you got me good, Milo." She read a few labels. Definitely made in Europe, possibly Canada. Some were out of date, but she found some she could use. "Your English is excellent. Where did you learn it?"

"Rosetta Stone."

Kate glanced over at him skeptically.

Milo's grin faded as he grew serious. He gazed out the window at the valley below. "They found it in a cave at the base of this mountain. For thirty days and thirty nights, a hundred monks hauled the rocks away, until all that was left was a small passageway. They sent me in—I was the only one who would fit. There, deep in the cave, a yellow light shone down on a stone table, and I found the tablet there. I carried it out that night and earned my robe." He exhaled deeply when his story was finished.

Kate stood there, holding the antibiotics, not sure what to say.

Milo sprang around to face her, pointing. "Ahh, I get you again, Dr. Warner!" He leaned back in a full body laugh.

Kate shook her head as she returned to David's bedside. "Well, you're quite full of yourself, aren't you?" She popped the top off a bottle of antibiotics.

"Milo is full of life, Dr. Warner, and I am happy to entertain guests."

Guests? Clearly Milo saw this as an opportunity to make a new friend. Kate smiled at him. "Call me Kate."

"Yes, of course I will, Dr. Kate."

"So really, how'd you learn English out here?"

"Rosetta Stone—"

Kate eyed him playfully, but the young man just nodded. "It's true. I received it in the mail, from an anonymous benefactor—very, very mysterious. And very fortunate for Milo. We don't get too many visitors. And when they say you speak English, it has to be Milo, no one else speaks English, not as well as Milo. I learned for fun, but look at my luck!"

Kate grabbed a cup of water from the table and helped David wash down a few antibiotic pills. She had selected the broad-spectrum antibiotic, and she hoped it would do the job. IV antibiotics in a hospital setting would be ideal. She fed him a large pain pill as well. When he came out of the delirium, the pain would be real, and she wanted to get ahead of it.

What to do next? A thought occurred to her. Rosetta Stone. "Milo, you have a computer?"

"Of course; that's how we found you." He raised his eyebrows conspiratorially. "Cryptic email."

Kate stood. "Email? Can I use—?"

Milo bowed. "No, I'm sorry, Dr. Kate. Qian wants to see you. He says as soon as you give the medicine to Mr. Reed, I must bring you to him. He is a very serious man, not funny like Milo. He says he has something to give you."

67

Main Auditorium
Indo-Immari Corporate Office
New Delhi, India

The small talk died down as two hundred pairs of eyes in the auditorium focused on him, waiting to learn the reason they had been dragged out of bed at six A.M. Dorian walked to the middle of the stage and surveyed the crowd. Most were Immari Security. There were a few dozen from other Immari subsidiaries: Immari Research, Immari Logistics, Immari Communications, and Immari Capital. They would all play a role in the coming operation. And then there were the Clocktower operatives.

The New Delhi station chief swore he had eliminated anyone who could be a problem. Immari Security had helped with the purge, and there were still a handful of analysts and field operatives in the brig—pending "final assessment." Only the station chief and Dorian's Immari Security unit knew the details of Toba Protocol and what had to be done. Dorian needed to keep it that way, but he also needed help, a lot of it, from all the people in the room. Hence the speech, the convincing—something Dorian wasn't used to. He gave orders, and they were followed. He didn't ask; he told, and his people didn't ask questions. But these people would; they were used to analysis and thinking independently. There wasn't time for that.

"You're all wondering why you're here, at this hour, in a room with so many new faces," Dorian began. "If you're standing in this room, you have been chosen. *Chosen* as a member of a task force, a very special working group, an elite team that

Immari Corporation and all its predecessor organizations are pinning its hopes on. What I'm about to tell you cannot leave this room. You will take what I say here today to your grave. Some of it will be hard to believe. And some of what you'll be asked to do will be even more difficult, in ways you can't yet understand. I must tell you now that I can't give you all the answers. I can't assuage your conscience, at least not right now. After it's over, everything will make sense. You will know the vital role you played in history, and others will know. But you deserve *some* answers, some reasons for the terrible things you're going to be asked to do."

Dorian paused and paced the stage, scanning the faces.

"Here's what I can tell you. Immari Corporation is the descendant, the modern incarnation, of a tribe of people that left this area—we believe somewhere in India, Pakistan, or possibly even Tibet—around twelve thousand years ago, some time shortly after the last ice age, when the flood waters raised sea levels hundreds of feet, destroying the world's coastal communities. This group had one goal: to uncover the true origins and history of the human race. These were people of great faith, and we believe they created religion in their quest for answers. But as time passed and humanity progressed, a new avenue of investigation emerged: science. And science remains the core of our work today. Some of you have seen small parts of this grand operation: archaeological digs, research projects, genetic experiments. It is our great work. But what we found, we never could have imagined.

"I'm reaching the end of what I can tell you, but you must know this: many years ago, we discovered a clear and present danger to the human race. A threat beyond belief. We have known for almost a hundred years that a day would come when we had to battle this enemy. That day has arrived. Each one of you is a soldier in the army that will stop this coming apocalypse. The next two days, and what follows, will be difficult. I'm not talking about a brushfire conflict in a backwater country. This will be a battle for the human race, for our very right to survive. We have one goal: humanity's survival."

Dorian retreated to the center of the stage, letting the audience take the speech in. There were confused looks, but there was also engagement, heads nodding.

"Questions are surfacing in your mind. Why can't we go public? Why not enlist the help of governments around the world? I wish we could, truly. It would ease my conscience about what has to be done. Indeed, your conscience is the other enemy you will fight in the days to come. And going public would also lift the burden, the proverbial weight of the world—knowing we weren't the last line of defense, that help was coming, that there were others battling the enemy, that we could fail. But we cannot fail, just as we cannot reveal the details of the threat. It's the same reason I can't tell you all the details, why I can't sit here and justify every last thing I'm about to ask you to do, though I wish I could. If we went public, the result would be mass panic, hysteria, a meltdown of society at the very instant we must stay intact.

"There are seven billion people on this planet. Imagine if they knew we were facing extinction. Our goal is to save the lives we can. There won't be a lot of them, but if we all do our part, we can ensure that the human race survives. Those are the stakes. And we aren't just facing the great threat. There are other, smaller obstacles: governments, media, intelligence agencies. We can't beat them, but we can hold them at bay long enough for our plan to work. And that's what we must set about doing, right now. The packets my men are passing out are your assignments—subgroups, responsibilities, your marching orders. The actions are drastic, but so is our situation."

Dorian squared his shoulders. "I am a soldier. I was born into this. I've dedicated my life to this cause. My father gave his life for this cause. *Our* cause. But I know you are not a soldier. You've been drafted. But I won't ask you to do what you're not capable of doing. That would be cruel, and I am not a cruel man. Immari is not a cruel organization. If, at any point, you cannot participate in the operation that follows, you can simply inform one of the Immari Security agents in my personal unit. There's no shame in it. We are all links in a chain. If one link breaks, the chain breaks and then disaster happens. And that's what this is all about—preventing disaster, no matter how it may seem. I thank you, and I wish you good luck."

An Immari Security agent greeted Dorian as he exited the stage. "Great speech, boss."

"Don't patronize me. You need to keep a close eye on these people. Any one of them could sink the entire operation. Where are we on the primary task force?"

"They're assembling at the Clocktower Station HQ."

"Good. Give everyone thirty minutes to compile their intel, then convene the group. Where are we on the trains?"

"We should have the roster of live and dead within the hour."

"Speed it up. I want to have it for the meeting."

68

Milo swung the lantern back behind him, illuminating the stone steps. "Not much farther, Dr. Kate."

They had descended the spiral stone staircase for what felt like an hour. Kate thought they must be at the center of the mountain or a mile below the monastery by now. Milo skipped down the stairs, carrying the lantern like a kid carrying a candy bag on Halloween night, never tiring, never stopping to rest. Kate's legs burned. She hadn't yet recovered from yesterday's exertion. She dreaded the return trip up the stairs.

Up ahead, Milo had stopped again, waiting for her, but this time he stood on level ground—a large round opening at the base of the stairs. Finally. He stepped back and held the lantern out, illuminating a wooden tombstone-shaped door with a rounded top.

Kate waited for a moment, wondering if he was waiting on her again.

"Please go in, Dr. Kate. He's waiting for you."

Kate nodded and opened the door, revealing a cramped circular room. The walls were covered in maps and shelves that held glass bottles, figurines, and metal artifacts. The room was... medieval, like an ancient lab in the tower of a castle where someone with a name like Merlin might work. And there was a sorcerer in the room, or at least he looked like one. An old man sat at a shabby wooden desk, reading. He turned his neck slowly as if it pained him. He was Asian, his hair was long since gone, and his face was more wrinkled than any Kate had ever seen. He could easily have been more than one hundred years old.

"Dr. Warner." His voice was a whisper. He stood and ambled toward Kate, leaning heavily on his wooden cane.

"Mister..."

"There are no misters here, Dr. Warner." He paused. Walking and talking were too taxing for him. He stared patiently at the stone floor while he gathered his breath. "Call me Qian. I have something for you. Something I've waited seventy-five years to give you. But first, I have something to show you. Could you help me with the door?" He motioned to a small wooden door Kate hadn't seen before. It was no more than four feet tall. Kate opened the door and was relieved to see that the passage beyond was taller than the doorway. She waited at the door as Qian paced past her, stopping every few feet. How long had it taken him to get down here?

Kate looked into the corridor and was surprised to find that it was illuminated by modern lights. It was short, less than fifteen feet long and seemed to dead-end into a stone wall. It took Qian several minutes to reach the door, where he gestured to a button on the wall.

Kate pressed the button, and the stone wall began to rise up. Kate felt air blow past her feet, rushing into the room. It must have been sealed.

She followed Qian into the room, which was surprisingly big, approximately forty feet by forty feet. It was empty except for a large square rug lying in the center of the floor. The rug must have been at least thirty feet across. Kate glanced to the ceiling and saw a thin linen cloth that covered the entire area of the room. Above the cloth, she could see another identical cloth, and beyond that, another, as far as she could see, like layers of mosquito net reaching to the top of the mountain. A method to wick away moisture? Possibly, but Kate saw something else— tiny pieces of dirt and rock, caught in the cloth.

Qian nodded toward the rug. "This is the treasure we protect here. Our heritage. We have paid a dear price for it." He cleared his throat and continued speaking slowly. "When I was young, men came to my village. They wore military uniforms. I didn't know it at the time, but they were Nazi uniforms. These men sought a group of monks who lived in the mountains beyond my village. No one would talk about these monks. I didn't know any better. The men paid me and some other children to take them there. The monks were not afraid of these men, but they should have been. These men, who had been kind in our village, turned ruthless in the mountains. They searched the monastery, tortured the monks, and finally set fire to the mountain."

Qian paused again, gathering his breath. "My friends were dead, and the soldiers were searching the monastery for me. And then they found me. One of the soldiers took me in his arms and carried me through the monastery into a tunnel. Three monks were waiting there. The man told them that I was the only survivor. He handed me a journal and said that I had to keep it safe until the time was right. The three monks left that night with only me, the clothes on their backs, and this tapestry." Qian settled his gaze on the massive work of art—some sort of biblical story with gods, heroes, monsters, heavens, light, blood, fire, and water.

Kate stood silently. In the back of her mind, she wondered what it had to do with her. She suppressed the urge to say, "Looks great, now can I use your computer?"

"And now you are wondering what this has to do with you."

Kate blushed and tossed her head to the side. "No, I mean, it's beautiful..." And it was. The colors were bold, as vivid as any fresco in a Catholic church, and the threads added depth to the depictions. "But, the man I came here with—he and I are in danger."

"You and Andrew are not the only ones."

Before Kate could speak, Qian continued with an unexpected strength in his voice. "Your enemy is the same group that burned that monastery seventy-five years ago and the same that will unleash an unthinkable evil very soon. That is what the tapestry depicts. Understanding it and the journal are the keys to stopping them. I have clung to life for seventy-five years, waiting, hoping the day would come when I would fulfill my destiny. And yesterday, when I learned what had happened in China, I knew it had come." Qian reached inside his robe, and with a frail hand, offered Kate a small leather-bound book.

He motioned toward the tapestry. "What do you see, my child?"

Kate studied the richly colored images. Angels, gods, fire, water, blood, light, sun. "Some sort of religious depiction?"

"Religion is our desperate attempt to understand our world. And our past. We live in darkness, surrounded by mysteries. Where did we come from? What is our purpose? What will happen to us after we die? Religion also gives us something more: a code of conduct, a blueprint of right and wrong, a guide to human decency. Just like any other tool, it can be misused. But this document was created long before man found solace in his religions."

"How?"

"We believe it was created from oral traditions."

"A legend?"

"Perhaps. But we believe it is a document of both history and prophecy. A depiction of events before man's awakening and tragedies yet to come. We call it the epic of the four floods." Qian pointed to the upper left-hand corner of the tapestry.

Kate followed his finger and studied the image—naked beasts, no humans, in a sparse forest or an African savanna. The people are running, fleeing a darkness descending from the sky—a blanket of ashes that suffocates them and kills the plant life. Just below that, they are alone in a barren, dead wilderness. Then a light emerges, leads them out, and a protector is talking to the savages, giving them a cup with blood in it.

Qian cleared his throat. "The first scene is the Flood of Fire. A flood that almost destroyed the world, almost buried man in ashes, and tore all the food from the world."

"A creation myth." Kate whispered. All major religions had

some form of creation myth, a history of how God created man in his image.

"This is no myth. This is a historical document." Qian's tone was gentle, like a teacher or a parent. "Notice that man already existed before the flood of fire, living as beasts in the forest. The flood would have killed them, but the savior protected them. But he cannot always be there to save them. And so he gives them the greatest gift of all: his blood. A gift that will keep them safe."

In the back of Kate's mind, she thought: the Toba Catastrophe and the Great Leap Forward. Blood. A genetic mutation—a change in brain wiring—that gave humanity a survival advantage, helping them brave the sea of ashes falling from the Toba supervolcano seventy thousand years ago. The Flood of Fire. Could it be?

Kate skipped down the tapestry. The scene was strange. The men from the forest seemed to have transformed into ninjas, or spirits. They wore clothes, and they had begun slaughtering beasts. The scene grew bloody, the horrors growing with every inch of tapestry. Slavery, murder, war.

"This gift made man smart, and strong, and safe from extinction, but he paid a great price. For the first time, he saw the world as it truly was, and he saw dangers all around him—in the beasts of the forest and in his fellow man. As a beast, he had lived in a world of bliss, acting on his instincts, thinking only when he had to, never seeing himself for what he was, never worrying about his mortality, never trying to cheat death. But now his thoughts and fears ruled him. He knew evil for the first time. Your Sigmund Freud came very close to describing these concepts with his id and ego. Man transformed into a Dr. Jekyll and Mr. Hyde. He struggled with his beast-mind, his animal instincts. Passion, rage—no matter how much we evolve, man can't escape these instincts: our heritage as beasts. We can only hope to control the beast inside us. Man also longed to understand his waking mind, with its fears, dreams, and questions of where he came from and what his destiny was. And

261

most of all, he dreamed of cheating death. He built communities on the coast and committed untold atrocities to ensure his own safety and seek immortality, in his deeds or through some magic or alchemy. The coast is the natural place for man; it's how we survived the flood of fire. Sea life was our food source when the land was scorched. But man's reign was short-lived."

Kate surveyed the lower-left quadrant of the tapestry: a great wall of water, just behind a chariot on the sea, which carried the cup-bearing savior from the flood of fire.

"The savior returns and tells his tribes that a great flood is coming, that they must prepare."

"Sounds familiar," Kate said.

"Yes. There is a flood myth in every religion, old and young, around the world. And the flood is a fact. Around twelve thousand years ago, the last ice age ended. Glaciers melted. The planet's axis shifted. Sea levels rose almost four hundred feet over the entire time period, sometimes rising gradually, sometimes in destructive waves and tsunamis."

Kate studied the depiction—of cities falling to the wave of water, of throngs of people drowning, of rulers and the rich standing and smiling at the water, and at the very end, a small band of people, dressed in humble clothes, venturing inland, to the mountains. They carried a chest of some kind.

Qian let her consider the tapestry for a long moment, then continued. "The people ignored the warning of the flood. Man had mastered the world, or so they thought. They were arrogant and decadent. They thumbed their noses at the coming disaster and continued with their wicked ways. Some say God is punishing man for killing his brothers and sisters. One tribe heeds the warning, builds an ark, and retreats from the sea, into the mountains. The flood comes and destroys the cities along the sea, leaving only the primitive villages inland and the scattered nomadic tribes. A rumor spreads that God is dead, that man is now the god of Earth. That the Earth belongs to them for them to do with as they please. But one tribe maintained the faith.

They held to one belief alone: that man is flawed, man is not God, that to embrace humility is to be truly human."

"You were the tribe."

"Yes. We heeded the savior's warning and did as he commanded. We carried the Ark to the highlands."

"And this tapestry was in the Ark?" Kate asked.

"No. Not even I know what was in the Ark. But it must have been real; stories of it survive to this day. And the story is very powerful. It has an incredibly powerful draw for anyone who hears it. It is one of many stories that rise out of the human psyche. We see it as truth, just as we recognize the various versions of the creation myth. These stories have always existed and always will, inside our own minds."

"What happened to the tribe?"

"They dedicated themselves to finding the truth of the tapestry, to understanding the antediluvian—the pre-flood—world, to discovering what happened. One group thought the answers lay in the human mind, in understanding our existence through reflection and self-examination. They became the mountain monks, the Immaru, the Light. I am the last of the Immaru. But some of the monks grew restless. They sought their answers in the world. Like us, they were a group of faith, at least at first. As time passed and they journeyed on, they slowly lost their religion, literally. They turned to a new hope for answers: science. They were tired of myths and allegories. They wanted proof. And they began to find it—but they paid a high price for it. Science lacks something very important that religion provides: a moral code. Survival of the fittest is a scientific fact, but it is a cruel ethic; the way of beasts, not a civilized society. Laws can only take us so far, and they must be based upon something—a shared moral code that rises from something. As that moral foundation recedes, so will society's values."

"I don't think a person has to be religious to be moral. I'm a scientist, and I'm not… terribly religious… but I'm, or I think I'm, a pretty moral person."

"You're also much smarter and more empathetic than the vast majority of people. But they will catch up to you someday, and the world will live in peace, without the need for allegories or moral lessons. I fear that day is further away than anyone believes. I speak of the state of things today, of the masses, not the minority. But I shouldn't be speaking of any of it. I'm preaching about subjects of interest to me, as old men often do, especially lonely ones. You've no doubt guessed the identity of the monks who split from the Immaru so long ago."

"The Immari."

Qian nodded. "We believe that around the time of the Greeks, the separatist monks changed their name to the Immari. Perhaps this was done to sound more Greek, so they might be accepted by the Greek scholars who were making so many breakthroughs in this emerging field of science. The true tragedy and the truth of how that faction changed forever is chronicled in the journal. That's why you must read it."

"What about the rest of the tapestry—the other two floods?"

"Those are events yet to come."

Kate studied the other half of the tapestry. The sea that had consumed the world in the Flood of Water turned from blue to a crimson sea of blood as it flowed into the lower right quadrant of the tapestry. Above the sea of blood, a group of supermen were slaughtering lesser beings. The world was a wasteland; darkness covered the land and blood ran from every man, woman, and child into the crimson pool. The Flood of Blood. Above the battle, a hero fought a monster, killing it and rising into heaven, where he unleashes a Flood of Light, bathing the world and liberating it. Taken in whole, the tapestry moved from the blacks and grays of the Flood of Fire, to the blues and greens of the Flood of Water, to the reds and crimsons of the Flood of Blood, to the whites and yellows of the Flood of Light. It was beautiful. Captivating.

Qian interrupted her concentration. "Now I must rest. And you must do your homework, Dr. Warner."

69

Main Conference Room
Clocktower HQ
New Delhi, India

Dorian held his hand up to stop the analyst. "What is a 'Barnaby Prendergast Report'?"

The thirty-something man looked confused. "It's the report from Barnaby Prendergast."

Dorian glanced around the conference room at the assembled Clocktower and Immari Security personnel. The now-integrated staff were still adjusting to the formal Immari-Clocktower union, and it was slowing the meeting down as roles and jurisdictions were settled. "Can someone please tell me what Barnaby Prendergast is?"

"Oh, that's his name—Barnaby Prendergast," the analyst said.

"Seriously? Did we give him that name—actually, don't tell me, I don't care. He said what? Start over."

The analyst flipped a few stapled pages over. "Prendergast is one of about twenty staffers still on site."

"*Was* on site." Dorian corrected.

The analyst cocked his head. "Well technically he is, or his dead body is, on site."

"Jesus Christ, just give me the report."

The analyst swallowed. "Right, uh, before the drone strike, he—Prendergast—said an unidentified female, his words here, 'accosted him outside his lab and coerced him into aiding her in what she claimed was a rescue of some children.'" The analyst flipped another page. "He goes on to say he 'tried to stop her' and that he 'believed she was using a fake or stolen ID card.' Also, here's the kicker, he says she ran out after the attacks, quote, 'covered in blood but unharmed,' and that she 'attacked him again, stopped him from rescuing workers,' and then she 'took a security guard's gun, tried to shoot him,' Prendergast that is, then got on the cargo train with a dying accomplice, who Prendergast claimed had been shot multiple times."

Dorian leaned back in the chair and stared at the bank of screens. Kate Warner had survived the Bell. How? Reed was likely dead; Dorian had practically turned the fool into a block of Swiss cheese.

The man cleared his throat. "Sir, should we disregard? You think it's bull, maybe the guy was playing for the spotlight?"

"No, I don't." Dorian bit into one of his nails. "It's too elaborate to be made up. Wait—why do you say 'playing for the spotlight'?"

"Prendergast made a call to the BBC right before the strike; that's how we got the report. We were monitoring all the communications in and out of the facility since the... accident. We have him on our list to discredit; his story threatens Immari's earlier industrial accident press release. So—"

"Okay, stop. Stop right there. One thing at a time. Let's focus here." Dorian swiveled his chair to face Dr. Chang, who sat in the corner, staring at the conference room's cheap carpet. "Chang. Pay attention."

Dr. Chang sat up as if the teacher had called on him. The man had been frazzled and absent since the blast in China. "Yes. I'm here."

"For now you are, Doctor, but if you don't figure out how Kate Warner survived the Bell, you won't be."

Chang shrugged his shoulders. "I... can't even begin to—"

"You *will* begin to. How could she have survived?"

Chang brought a closed hand to his face and cleared his throat. "Well, um, let's see, she could have treated herself with whatever she gave the children. Maybe she tested it for safety."

Dorian nodded. "Interesting. Other possibilities?"

"No. Well, there is the obvious—she could have already had immunity—the Atlantis Gene."

Dorian chewed his nail some more. That was very interesting. *Very* interesting. "Okay, that one sounds easy to test—"

Chang shook his head. "My lab was destroyed, and we don't even know where to start—"

"Get a new lab." Dorian turned to one of his staffers. "Find Dr. Chang a new lab." He focused again on Chang. "I'm not a scientist, but I would start by sequencing her genome and checking for any irregularities."

Chang nodded. "Yes of course, that's easy, but with the state of the site, we're not likely to find any DNA—"

Dorian threw his head back. "For God's sake, think outside the box. She has a condo in Jakarta; surely you're clever enough to find a hairbrush or a used tampon, Doctor."

Chang flushed. "Yes, that could work."

A female Clocktower analyst spoke up, "Some women flush their tampons—"

Dorian closed his eyes and held his hands up. "Forget the tampon. There must be tons of Kate Warner's DNA in Jakarta. Go find some. Or better yet, let's find *her*. If she did escape, she's got to be on one of the trains." Dorian turned to Dmitry Kozlov, the Immari Security field commander who had left China with him.

The soldier shook his head. "I just got the list. We checked it against the staff roster. She's not on any of the trains. And neither is Reed. We've got a lot of injured and dead, several people with trauma wounds, but nobody with gunshot wounds."

"You can't be serious. Search the trains again—"

"It will delay Toba—" Dmitry said.

"Do it."

The analyst with the Prendergast report piped up. "She could have jumped."

Dorian rubbed his temples. "She didn't jump."

The analyst shook his head. "How do you know—"

"Because she had Reed with her."

"She could have pushed him off."

"Could have but didn't."

The analyst looked confused. "How do you know?"

"Because she's not as stupid as you apparently are. She's five-eight, a hundred and twenty pounds. Reed is over six feet and at least one-eighty. Warner couldn't hike out of Tibet on her own, much less hauling one-hundred-eighty pounds of dead weight. And trust me, if Reed is alive, he can't walk."

"She could have left him."

"She wouldn't leave him."

"How do you know?"

"Because I know her. Let's wrap this up, come on, move out, people." Dorian stood and waved his arms to usher people out of the crowded room.

"What about the Barnaby Prendergast report?" the analyst said.

"What about it?"

"Should we contradict—"

"Hell no. Confirm it. The media will run with it anyway, it has the word *terrorist* in it. And it's the truth: a terrorist attacked our facility in China. It's the best break we've had. Release the footage of Reed planting the bombs to corroborate it. Tell the press that the attack follows an earlier attack by the same people in Jakarta. Include video of Warner as well." Dorian thought for a moment. This could work out well, maybe buy them some time and provide a cover story. "Let's say we're currently investigating whether Dr. Warner deployed a biological weapon at the facility, and we're asking for a strict quarantine of the site." Dorian waited, staring at the staff. "Okay, tick-tock people, let's go."

He pointed at Dmitry. "You stay."

The tall soldier lumbered over to Dorian as the room cleared. "Someone took them off the train."

"Agree." Dorian paced back to the table. "It has to be them."

"Impossible. We've searched those mountains non-stop since 9/11, they're not there. They were all killed in '38. Or they could be a myth. Maybe the Immaru never existed at all."

"You have a better idea?" Dorian said. When Dmitry didn't respond, Dorian continued, "I want teams searching those mountains."

"I'm sorry sir, we don't have the manpower. The Clocktower purge, plus the end of major hostilities in Afghanistan—our forces in the region were already minimal. Everyone we have local is focused on Toba. If you want teams, they have to be diverted."

"No. Toba is the priority. What about satellite surveillance? Can we track them, figure out where they are?"

Dmitry shook his head. "We've got no eyes in the sky over western China, nobody does. That's one of the reasons Immari Research selected that site—there's nothing there and no reason to look. No cities—in fact there aren't even many villages or roads. We can reposition satellites, but it will take time."

"Do that. And launch the rest of the drones in Afghanistan—"

"How ma—"

"All of them. Have them scour every inch of the plateau—focus on monasteries first. And reassign two men—we can spare them. Toba is important, but so is capturing Warner. She survived the Bell. We have to know why. Have those two men trace the route of every train that left, question villagers, anyone that may have seen anything. Apply pressure. I want her found."

70

David was still asleep when Kate returned to his room. She sat down at his feet, on the twin bed in the alcove and looked out the window for a while. The serenity of this place was like nothing she'd ever experienced. She glanced back at David. He looked almost as peaceful as the green valley and white-top mountains. Kate leaned against the alcove wall and stretched out her legs next to his.

She opened the journal, and a letter fell out. The paper felt old, fragile, like Qian. The letters flowed in thick dark ink, and she could feel the indentations on the back of the page like braille. Kate began reading aloud, hoping David would hear and that the voice would comfort him.

To the Immaru,

I have become a servant to the faction you know as the Immari. I am ashamed of the things I have done, and I fear for the world—for the things I know they are planning. At this moment, in 1938, they seem unstoppable. I pray that I am wrong. In the event I am not, I'm sending you this journal. I hope you can use it to prevent the Immari Armageddon.

Patrick Pierce
11-15-38

April 15, 1917
Allied Hospital
Gibraltar

When they pulled me out of the tunnel on the Western Front and brought me to this field hospital a month ago, I thought I was saved. But this place has grown on me like a cancer, eating me from the inside out, silently at first, without my knowledge, then taking me by surprise, plunging me into a dark sickness I can't escape.

The hospital is almost quiet at this hour, and that's when it's most scary. The priests come every morning and every night, praying, taking confessions, and reading by candlelight. They've all gone now, as have most of the nurses and doctors.

Outside my room, I can hear them, out in the wide open ward with rows of beds. Men scream — most from pain, some from bad dreams; others cry, talk, and play cards in the moonlight and laugh as if half a dozen men won't die before sunrise.

They gave me a private room, put me here. I didn't ask for it. But the door closes and blocks out the cries and the laughs, and I'm glad. I don't like hearing either.

I reach for the bottle of laudanum, drink till it runs down my chin, then drift into the night.

The slap brings me back to life, and I see a jagged set of rotten teeth inside a wicked grin on an unshaven dirty face. "'E's awake!"

The putrid smell of alcohol and disease turns my head and stomach.

Two other men drag me out of bed, and I scream in pain

when my leg hits the ground. I writhe on the floor, fighting not to pass out as they laugh. I want to be awake when they kill me.

The door opens and it's the nurse's voice. "What's going on—"

They grab her and slam the door. "Jus' having a bit of fun wit' da Senata's boy, *Ma'am*, but you's a might bit prettia den 'e is." The man wraps his arm around her and slides behind her. "Mights be we start with you, missy." He rips her dress and undergarments from the left sleeve all the way to her waist. Her breasts fall out, and she raises an arm to cover herself. She fights back desperately with the other arm, but the man catches it and quickly pins it behind her.

The sight of her naked body seems to energize the drunken men.

I struggle to stand, and as soon as I reach my feet, the closest man is on me. He holds a knife to my throat. He stares me straight in the eyes while he blathers on drunkenly. "Big baddy Senata Daddy done sent him off ta war, done sent us all, but he can't save you no more."

The knife bites at my neck as the crazed man glares at me. The other man holds the nurse from behind, craning his head around, trying to kiss her as she turns away. The last man undresses.

Standing on the leg sends waves of pain up through my body—pain so bad it makes me nauseated, lightheaded. I will pass out soon. It's unbearable, even through the laudanum. The laudanum—worth more than gold in a place like this.

I motion to the table, trying to break the man's stare. "There's laudanum, a full bottle on the table."

His concentration breaks for an instant, and I have the knife. I draw it across his neck as I spin him around, then I push him away and lunge knife-out for the naked man, burying the knife to the hilt in his stomach. I land on top of him, jerk the knife out and plant it in his chest. His arms flail, and blood gurgles from his mouth.

The pain from the lunge is overtaking me. I've got nothing left for the last man, the nurse's captor, but his eyes go wide and he turns the nurse loose and runs from the room just as I pass out.

– 2 days later –

I wake up in a different place, like a cottage in the country—that's how it smells and how the sun feels shining in through the open window. It's a bright bedroom, decorated like a woman would, with knick-knacks and small things women like and men never notice except for times like this.

And there she is, reading in the corner, rocking silently, waiting. Through some sixth sense, she seems to instantly know that I'm awake. She sets the book down gently, like it's a piece of fine china, and walks to the bedside. "Hello, Major." She glances down at my left leg, nervous. "They had to operate on your leg again."

I notice the leg now. It's bandaged, thick, almost double the width of my leg. When they brought me in, and for two weeks after, they threatened to take it off. *You'll thank us later. Have to trust us, ol' boy. Seems horrid but it's for the best. You won't be alone at home, I'll guarantee you that, be tons o' youngsters back from war scootin' this way and that on tin legs, just as common as a drink o' water, I tell ya.*

I try to lean forward to get a peek, but the pain meets me as I rise, grabbing me and throwing me flat on my back again.

"It's still there. I insisted they respect your wishes. But they removed a lot of the tissue. They said it was infected and would never heal. The hospital is a bad place for germs, and after..." She swallows. "They said you'll be in bed for two months."

"The men?"

"Deserters, they think. There's to be an inquiry, but... a formality, I presume."

I see it now, the white bottle on the table, just like it was in the hospital. I linger on it. I know she sees me. "You can take that out of here." If I start again, I'll never stop. I know where that road goes.

She steps forward and grabs it quickly, as if it were about to fall off the table.

What's her name? God, the last month is a blur, an opium and alcohol-ridden dream, a nightmare. Barnes? Barrett? Barnett?

"Are you hungry?" She stands there, clutching the bottle to her chest with one hand, holding her dress with the other. Maybe it's the drugs or having gone so long without food, but I have no desire whatsoever to eat.

"Starving," I say.

"It'll just be a minute." She's halfway out the door.

"Nurse... is it..."

She stops and glances back, maybe a little disappointed. "Barton. Helena Barton."

Twenty minutes later, I smell cornbread, pinto beans, and country ham. The smell of it is better than anything I've ever tasted. To my own amazement, I eat three plates that night. I was hungry after all.

71

Dorian read through the list of living and dead from the two trains. "I want to send more bodies to the US. Europe looks okay, I think." He scratched his head. "I think the allotment to Japan should suffice as well. The population density will help." He wished he could consult Chang or one of the scientists, but he needed to limit access to the information.

Dmitry studied the list. "We can still reallocate, but where should we pull them from?"

"Africa and China. I think they'll move slower than we think. China tends to ignore or suppress public health crises, and Africa simply has no infrastructure to deal with an outbreak."

"Or spread it. That's one of the reasons we assigned—"

"Developed nations, they're the real threat. Don't underestimate the CDC. They'll move fast when it hits. And we can always work on Africa after it starts."

•

72

Kate held David's head up as he swallowed the antibiotics with water from the ceramic cup. The last of the water ran from his mouth, and she wiped it away with her shirt. He had drifted in and out of consciousness the entire morning.

She opened the journal again.

I lead my men through the tunnel, holding the candle in front of me. We're almost there, but I stop, holding my hands up as the men stumble into the back of me. Did I hear something? I plant my tuning fork in the ground and watch it, waiting for the verdict. If it vibrates, the Germans are tunneling near us. We've already abandoned two passages for fear of connecting with them. The second one we blew up under them, hopefully stopping their progress.

The fork doesn't move. I stuff it back into my tool belt, and we trudge deeper into the darkness, the candle casting faint shadows on the walls of dirt and stone. Dust and pebbles fall on our heads as we walk.

Then the constant rain of grime stops. I look up and hold my candle closer, trying to discern what's happened.

I turn and shout, "Get back!" as the ceiling collapses and hell pours through. The faint light of the candle winks out as I'm thrown to the ground. The falling rubble crushes my leg, and I almost pass out.

The Germans land on their feet, practically on top of me, and begin firing, killing two of my men instantly. The muzzle flashes of their machine guns and the screams of the dying men are my only guide to the carnage.

I pull my sidearm and fire at them from point-blank range, killing the first two men, who must have either thought I was dead or couldn't see me in the darkness. More men are pouring through, and I shoot them too. Five, six, seven of them dead, but there's an endless line of them, a whole regiment, ready to pour through the tunnel and behind the Allied lines. It will be a massacre. I'm out of rounds. I toss the empty pistol aside and take out a grenade. I pull the pin with my teeth and hurl it with all my might into the German tunnel above, at the feet of the newest wave of soldiers. Two long seconds tick by as the men jump down, firing at me as they come, and then the explosion racks them, collapses their tunnel, and brings both tunnels down around me. I'm pinned. I can't get up and won't ever get out, the debris is suffocating me, but there are suddenly hands on me—

The nurse is there, wiping the sweat from my brow and holding my head.

"They were waiting on us... connected to our tunnel in the night... didn't have a chance..." I say, trying to explain.

"It's all over. It's only a bad dream."

I reach down to the leg, as if touching it will stop the throbbing pain. The nightmare isn't over. Won't ever be over.

The sweating and the pain have gotten worse each night; she must see it. And she does. The white bottle is in her hand and I say, "Just a little bit. I've got to get free of it."

I take a swig, and the beast backs away. And I get some real sleep.

She's there when I wake, knitting in the corner. On the table beside me, three small shot glasses hold the dark brown liquid— the day's ration of the opium-infused concoction that delivers the morphine and codeine I desperately need. Thank God. The sweats are back, and the pain has come with it.

"I'll be home before sundown."

I nod and take the first shot.

Two shot glasses each day.

She reads to me every night, after work and dinner.

I lie there, adding clever comments and witty remarks from time to time. She laughs, and when I've been a little too crude, chastises me playfully.

The pain is almost bearable.

One shot per day. Freedom.

Almost. But the pain persists.

I still can't walk.

I've spent my life in mines, in dark, confined spaces. But I can't take it. Maybe it's the light, or the fresh air, or lying in bed day after day, night after night. A month gone by.

Every day, as three o'clock draws near, I count down the minutes until she gets home. A man, waiting for a woman to get home. It calls into question the premise of the sentence.

I've insisted she stop working in the hospital. Germs. Bombs. Chauvinists. I've tried it all. She won't hear it. I can't win. I don't have a leg to stand on. I simply can't put my foot down. And on top of that, I'm losing it, making lame jokes about myself, to myself.

Out the window, I see her coming down the path. What time is it? Two-thirty. She's early. And—there's a man with her. In the month I've been here, she's never brought a suitor home. The thought's never occurred to me and, now, it strikes me in all the wrong ways. I strain to get a better look out the window, but I can't see them. They're already in the house.

I frantically straighten my bed and push myself up, through the dull pain, so I can sit up in bed and appear stronger than I am. I pick up a book and begin reading it, upside down. I glance up, then flip the book right-side-up just before Helena enters. The mustached, monocle-wearing poser in a three-piece suit is close on her heels like a greedy dog at the hunt.

"Ah, you've gotten into some of the books. What did you choose?" she tips it toward me slightly, reads the title, and cocks her head slightly. "Hmm, *Pride and Prejudice*. One of my favorites."

I close the book and toss it on the table as though she'd just told me it was infected with the plague. "Yes, well, a man's got to stay up on such things. And, appreciate the… classics."

The monocled man looks over at her impatiently. Ready to get on with the visiting—away from the cripple in the spare bedroom.

"Patrick, this is Damien Webster. He's come from America to see you. He won't tell me what about." She raises her eyebrows conspiratorially.

"Pleasure, Mr. Pierce. I knew your father."

He's not courting her. Wait, *knew* my father.

Webster seems to realize my confusion. "We sent a telegraph to the hospital. Have you not received it?"

My father is dead, but he didn't come here about that. What then?

Helena speaks before I can. "Major Pierce has been here for a month. The hospital receives a great many cables each day. What's your business, Mr. Webster?" Her tone has grown serious.

Webster glares at her. He's probably not used to a woman talking to him in such a tone. He could probably do with more of it. "Several matters. The first being your father's estate—"

Outside the window, a bird lands on the fountain. It fidgets, dunks its head, rises and shakes the water off.

"How did he die?" I say, still focused on the bird.

Webster speaks quickly, like it's something to get out of the way, an annoyance. "Automobile accident. He and your mother both perished instantly. Dangerous machines, I say. It was quick. They didn't suffer, I assure you. Now…"

I feel hurt of a different kind, a crushing feeling of loneliness, emptiness, like there's a pit inside me that I can't fill. My mother, gone. Buried by now. I'll never see her again.

"Will that be acceptable, Mr. Pierce?"

"What?"

"The account at First National Bank in Charleston. Your father was a very frugal man. There's almost two hundred thousand dollars in the account."

Frugal to a fault.

Webster is clearly frustrated and plows on hoping for a response. "The account's in your name. There was no will, but as you've no siblings, there's no problem." He waits another moment. "We can transfer the money to a bank here." He glances at Helena. "Or England if you prefer—"

"The West Virginia Children's Home. It's in Elkins. See that they get the balance of the account. And that they know it came from my father."

"Uh, yes, that's… possible. May I ask why?"

A truthful response would be "because he wouldn't want me to have it" or, more exactly, "because he didn't like the man I've become." But I don't say either, maybe because Helena is in the room or maybe because I don't think this shyster deserves an honest response. Instead, I mumble something approximating, "It's what he would have wanted."

He looks at my leg, searching for the right words. "That's all well and good, but the army pensions are… rather sparse, even for a major. I would think you'd be keen to keep a bit of the money, say, one hundred thousand dollars?"

I stare at him full-on now. "Why don't you tell me what you're here about? I doubt it's my father's two-hundred-thousand-dollar estate."

He's taken aback. "Of course, Mr. Pierce. I was only trying to advise… for your best interests. Indeed, that's what I'm here about. I bring a message from Henry Drury Hatfield, governor of the great state of West Virginia. His Excellency wishes you to—well first off, he sends his deepest condolences for your loss, indeed the state's and our great nation's. Additionally, he would like for you to know that he is prepared to appoint you to your father's seat in the US Senate, as this authority has just been vested in him by the state legislature."

I'm beginning to realize how the McCoys could hate these snakes so much. Henry Hatfield is the nephew of Devil Hatfield, the leader of the infamous Hatfield clan. The governor can't run for a second term. He had himself set up for that US Senate seat two years ago, but the states ratified the Seventeenth Amendment the year before, allowing for direct election of US senators, yanking the power away from the corrupt state legislatures and manipulators like Hatfield. My father was in the first class of US senators elected by the people. His death and the talk of the money, now make more sense. But not the appointment.

Webster doesn't let the mystery linger long. He leans against the foot of the bed, speaking like we're old pals now. "Of course your status as a war hero will make you a popular choice. There will be a special election. As you know, senators are now elected by the people," he nods, "as they should be. The governor is ready to appoint you to serve in your father's seat on the condition that you will endorse him in the special election and campaign for him. In return, he is willing to further support your career. Perhaps as a congressional candidate. Congressman Patrick Pierce has a nice ring to it, I think." He pushes off the bed and smiles at me. "So, can I give the governor the good news then?"

I glower at him. I've never wanted to stand so much in my

whole life, to be able to walk this demon to the front door and toss him out.

"I know the circumstances aren't ideal, but we must all rise to the occasion." Webster nods toward the leg. "And with your... limitations, it could be a good fit. You're not likely to find better work—"

"Get out."

"Now, Mr. Pierce, I know—"

"You heard me. And don't come back. You've got the only answer you're ever going to get. Tell that thug Hatfield to do his own dirty work, or maybe one of his cousins. I hear they're good at it."

He steps toward me, but Helena catches him by the arm. "This way, Mr. Webster."

When he's gone, she returns. "I'm very sorry about your parents."

"As am I. My mother was very kind and very loving." I know she can see how sad I am now, but I can't hold it anymore.

"Can I bring you anything?" I can tell she didn't mean to, but her eyes dart to where the bottle would sit beside the bed.

"Yes. A doctor. For my leg."

73

Dorian lingered by the door, surveying the situation room. It looked almost like mission control for a NASA launch. Several rows of analysts were speaking into headsets and working computers that controlled the drones. On the long wall, a patchwork of screens showed telemetry from the drones: scenes of mountains and forests.

Dmitry had been coordinating the search. The burly Russian looked as though he hadn't slept since the explosions in China. He pushed his way through the throngs of analysts and joined Dorian at the back of the room. "We've got nothing so far. There's just too much area to search."

"What about satellite surveillance?"

"Still waiting on it."

"Why? What's taking so long?"

"Repositioning takes time, and there's so much area to cover."

Dorian watched the screens for a moment. "Start shaking the bushes."

"Shaking?"

"Burning," Dorian said as he turned and led Dmitry to the door, out of earshot of the analysts. "See what falls out. My guess is Warner is in one of those monasteries. Where are we on Toba?"

"The bodies are on planes bound for Europe, North America, Australia, and China. The live ones are in local hospitals in India and"—he checked his watch—"Bangladesh within the hour."

"Reports?"

"Nothing so far."

At least there was some good news.

74

Immaru Monastery

Tibet Autonomous Region

The next morning, Milo was waiting on Kate, just as he had the previous morning. *How long does he sit there, waiting for me to wake up?* she wondered.

Kate rose and found another bowl of breakfast in the same place. She and Milo exchanged their morning pleasantries, and he again led her to David's room.

The journal lay on the table beside the bed, but Kate ignored it, moving first to David. She administered the antibiotics and inspected the shoulder and leg wounds. The rings of red had expanded in the night, spreading out to his chest and upper thigh. Kate chewed on the inside of her mouth and gazed absently out the window.

"Milo, I need you to help me with something. It's very important."

"As I said when first we met, Madam," he bowed again, "Milo is at your service."

"Are you squeamish around blood, Milo?"

Several hours later, Kate was securing the last bandage to David's shoulder. A pile of bloody gauze lay in a pool of blood and pus in a bowl on the table. Milo had performed admirably, not as well as an O.R. nurse, but his zen countenance had gone a long way, especially in keeping Kate's nerves in check.

When she finished with the bandages, Kate ran a hand across David's chest and exhaled deeply. Now, all she could do was wait. She leaned back in the alcove and watched his chest rise and fall, the motion almost hard to discern.

After a few moments, she opened the journal and began reading.

———— 📖 ————

June 3rd, 1917

"How about now?" Dr. Carlisle says as he presses the ink pen to my leg.

"Yeah," I say through gritted teeth.

He slides the pen down and jabs again. "And here?"

"Like the dickens."

He straightens and contemplates the results of his prodding.

Before he looked at the leg, he spent some time collecting a "history." It was a welcome departure from the field surgeons who looked at the injury, never at the man, and usually proceeded without a word. I told him I was twenty-six, in otherwise good health, had no "dependencies," and had gotten the wound in a tunnel that collapsed under the Western Front. He nodded and performed a thorough examination, noting that the injury wasn't that different to what he saw in miners and sportsmen in his practice.

I wait for his verdict, wondering if I should say something.

The city doctor scratches his head and takes a seat by the bed. "I have to say, I agree with what the army surgeons told you. It would have been better to have taken it off then, probably just below the knee, or at least that's where I would have started."

"What about now?" I dread the answer.

"Now... I'm not sure. You won't walk on it again or at least not normally. Mostly it will depend on how much pain you have. There's a lot of nerve damage, no doubt. I would recommend you try walking, as best you can manage, for the next month or two. If the pain is unbearable, as I suspect it will be, we'll take it below the knee. Most of the feeling is in the feet; there are more nerves there. That will give you some relief." As if anticipating my distress, he adds, "We're not just fighting the pain here. Vanity is a factor. No man wants to lose half his leg, but it doesn't make him any less of a man. It's best to be practical. You'll be thankful you were. And I suppose the last consideration is what type of work you'll be doing, Captain—no, Major, was it? Never seen a major your age."

"You make rank fast when everyone's dying around you," I say, stalling for time on the other question, one I've refused to face since the tunnel collapsed. Mining is all I know. "I'm not sure what I'll do after... after I'm back on my feet." It's the first expression that comes to mind.

"Desk work would, uh, benefit your disposition, if you can find it." He nods and stands. "Well then, if that's all, ring me or write in a month." He hands me a card with his address in London.

"Thank you, Doctor, truly."

"Well I couldn't very well deny a request from Lord Barton. We go all the way back to our days at Eton, and when he told me you were a war hero and that his little girl was so insistent, that he feared her heart would positively break if I didn't have a look, I was on the train the next day."

There's a racket in the hall, like someone knocking something off a shelf. Dr. Carlisle and I both glance after it, but neither of us says anything. He gathers his black bag and stands. "I'll leave instructions with Helena on how to wrap the leg. Good luck, Major."

August 5th, 1917

Two months have passed, and I've been "walking" for a month

now. Hobbling mostly. On good days, with the use of a cane, limping.

Carlisle came down a week ago to see my gimp performance. He stood beside Helena and cheered like a proud owner at a dog show.

That's unfair. And unkind—to someone who's been nothing but kind to me.

The pills. They dull the pain and everything else, including my thoughts. They make me immune to emotion when I'm on them and ill as a hornet when they're wearing off. Fighting a war in my mind is a strange kind of torture. I think I much preferred shooting the Kaiser's men; at least I knew where I stood and could get a moment's rest when I wasn't on the front. The weeks of walking, popping a pill, and plodding on have left me with another fear: that I'll never rid myself of this beast on my back, constantly goading me to nip the pain. I need the pills, can't do without them, and don't want to. I've traded the devil, the laudanum, for two crutches, one at my side and one in my pocket.

Carlisle says my walking will only improve as I "learn the leg" and find my minimum routine dose with the pain pills. It's so easy to say.

But the pills aren't the thing I've grown most attached to in the months since I left the hospital. She's like no one I've ever met. The idea of moving out, of saying goodbye, terrifies me. I know what I want to do: take her by the hand, board a ship, and sail away from Gibraltar, away from the war, away from the past, and start over new, someplace safe, where our kids can grow up without a care in the world.

It's almost three, and I haven't taken a pill all day. I want my head clear when I talk to her. I don't want to miss a thing, regardless of the pain, in my leg or in my heart.

I will need all my wits. Maybe it's her British upbringing,

with its stoicism and dry humor, or maybe it's the two years of working in the field hospital, where emotions are just as contagious and dangerous as the infections they fight, but the woman is nearly impossible to get a read on. She laughs, she smiles, she is full of life, but she's never out of control, never lets a word slip, never betrays her thoughts. I'd give my other leg to know how she really feels about me.

I've been thinking about my options and making what arrangements I can. The day after that demon Damien Webster came to call, I wrote three letters. The first letter went to the First National Bank in Charleston informing them to disburse the balance of my father's account to the West Virginia Children's Home in Elkins. I sent the second letter to the home notifying them to expect a contribution and that in the event the bequest does not reach them directly, they contact Mr. Damien Webster regarding the matter as he was the last person known to have access to the account. I truly hope they receive the funds.

The final letter I wrote to the City Bank of Charleston, where my own funds are held. I received a reply letter a week and a half later, informing me that my account totaled $5,752.34 and that there would be a fee for sending the sum via cashier's check to Gibraltar. I had fully expected to be nicked on my way out the door, as banks often do, and I replied immediately, thanking them and requesting they send said cashier's check with all possible haste. A courier came round yesterday with it.

I also received the balance of my paltry Army salary, most of which the Army holds for you while you're off fighting. I was honorably discharged last week, so it's the last money that will arrive.

All told, I have $6,382.79—a far cry from what I'll need to support a wife and set myself up. I'll have to find sedentary work, most likely something in banking or investing, possibly in something I know—mining, maybe munitions. But those kinds of jobs are only to be had by a certain type of man, with the right type of connections and the right type of education. If I had my own capital, I could make a go of it, and with a little luck, a strike—coal, gold, diamonds, copper, or silver—money wouldn't be a problem. Twenty-five thousand dollars is the goal I've set. It won't give me much room for error.

I hear Helena open the door, and I walk out into the small anteroom to greet her. Her nurse's uniform is covered in blood, and it strikes a strange contrast with the kind smile that spreads across her face when she sees me. I'd give anything to know if it was a smile of pity or one born of happiness. "You're up. Don't mind the clothes; I'm just going to change," she says as she rushes out of the room.

"Put on something nice," I call to her. "I'm taking you for a walk, then dinner."

She pops her head out from the door to her bedroom. "Really?" The smile has grown, and a hint of surprise has crept into it. "Shall I lay out your uniform?"

"No. Thank you, but I'm done wearing a uniform. Tonight is about the future."

75

Dorian paced the room, waiting to see the telemetry from the drones. The bank of screens sparkled to life one by one, revealing a monastery nestled in a mountainside.

The technician turned to him. "Should we do a few passes to find an optimal target—"

"No, don't bother. Hit it just to the right of the base, doesn't have to be exact. We mostly just want to set it on fire. Have the other drone follow behind and film the aftermath," Dorian said.

A minute later, he watched the rockets fly from the drone into the mountainside. He waited, hoping to see Kate Warner run out of the burning building.

76

Kate set down the journal and strained to see what was happening in the distance. It sounded like explosions. A rock slide? Earthquake? Past the farthest mountain range, smoke rose into the sky, white at first, then black.

Could the Immari be looking for them?

What could she do about it if they were? She gave David his afternoon dose of antibiotics and continued reading the journal to him.

August 5th, 1917

Helena and I walk along the cobblestone wharf, enjoying the warm breeze from the sea and listening to the ships blow their horns as they enter the bay and dock at the harbor. The wooden harbor seems as small as a stack of toothpicks below the towering jagged Rock of Gibraltar. I put my hands in my pockets, and she slips her arm around mine, drifts closer to me, and synchronizes her stride with mine. I count it as a good sign. Gradually, the lights come on along the street as the shopkeepers rouse from their Spanish-style siestas and return to prepare for the rush of dinner and evening shoppers.

Each step twists the knife in my leg, or at least, that's the sensation walking provides. I feel the sweat gathering on my brow from the dull agony, but I don't dare move an arm up to wipe it for fear she'll let go.

Helena stops. She's seen it. "Patrick, are you in pain?"

"No, of course not." I wipe my forehead with my sleeve. "Just not used to the heat. Being indoors under the fans has left me ill-adjusted. And I grew up in West Virginia to boot."

She nods toward the rock. "It's cooler in the caves. And they have monkeys there. Have you seen them?"

I ask her if she's joking and she promises she isn't. I say we have time before dinner and let her lead me over there, mostly because she takes my arm again, and I'd walk anywhere at that point.

The British sergeant gives us a personal tour of the pens they keep the monkeys in, deep inside St. Michael's Cave. Our voices echo as we talk. They call them Barbary macaques, and they are similar to macaques, except without the tail. Apparently the Barbary macaques in Gibraltar are the only free-living primates in all of Europe. Well, besides humans, if the theory of evolution is to be believed, and I'm not certain I do.

As we walk away, toward dinner, I ask her how she knew about the monkeys.

"They treat the sick ones at the British Naval Hospital," she says.

"You're joking."

"It's true."

"Is it safe? Treating monkeys and humans in such proximity?"

"I assume it is. Can't imagine what kind of disease could jump from monkeys to humans."

"Why go to all the trouble?"

"The legend is that as long as the macaques survive on Gibraltar, the British will rule it."

"Yours are a very superstitious people."

"Or maybe we're just keen to take care of anything we care about."

We stroll in silence for a while. I wonder if I'm like a pet to

293

her, or a ward, or someone she owed some kind of debt to for saving her in the hospital.

I'm losing my grip on the pain, and without a word, she stops, and still holding my arm, turns us back to face the Rock as the sun sets across the bay. "There's another legend about the Rock. The Greeks say it is one of the pillars of Hercules and that the caves and tunnels under it extend deep into the earth, leading to the Gates of Hades."

"The Gates of the Underworld."

She raises her eyebrows playfully. "You think it's down there?"

"No, I sort of doubt it. I'm pretty sure hell is a thousand miles from here, in a trench on the Western Front."

Her face grows serious, and she looks down.

She was making a joke, and I was trying to be witty, but I reminded us of the war. It's ruined the mood, and I wish I could go back and do the moment over.

She brightens a bit and tugs at my arm. "Well, I for one am glad you're far away from there... and not going back."

I open my mouth, but she presses on, probably hoping to head me off from saying something dreary. "Are you hungry?"

The wine comes, and I drink two glasses quickly, medicating. She drinks half a glass, probably to be polite. I wish she would drink more—I'd love for that facade to break, if just for a moment, so I could see what she's thinking, how she feels.

But the food arrives, and we're both smelling it and saying how good it looks.

"Helena, I've been meaning to speak with you about something." It comes out way too serious. I had hoped to be casual, to disarm her.

She sets her fork down and chews the small bite she's just taken, barely moving her jaw.

I press on. "It's been very decent of you to put me up. I don't know if I've said thank you, but I do appreciate it."

"It's been no trouble."

"It's been quite a bit of trouble."

"I haven't minded it."

"Nevertheless, I think I should get a place now that I'm out of my... convalescence."

"It might be prudent to wait. Your leg might not be fully healed. Dr. Carlisle said re-injury was a possibility as you walk more." She pushes some of the food around on her plate.

"I'm not worried about my leg. People will talk. An unmarried man and woman, sharing a home."

"People always talk about something."

"I won't have them talking about you. I'll find a place and work as well. I need to begin setting my affairs in order."

"It would seem... reasonable... to wait until you knew where you were to work before making arrangements."

"That's true."

She brightens a bit. "Speaking of, there are some men who want to talk with you about a job. Some friends of my father."

To my dismay, I can't hide the anger in my voice. "You asked him to find me a job."

"No, I promise you. I knew how you'd feel if I did, though I wanted to. He rang me about it a week ago, and they've been keen to see you. I've put it off because I didn't know what your plans were."

"Meeting with them couldn't hurt," I say. It was the worst mistake of my life.

David could hear her reading, or someone reading, as he pushed the door to their studio apartment open. Allison looked up at him, walked over to the stereo, and pressed the pause button.

"You're home early." She smiled and began washing her hands at the kitchen sink.

"Couldn't study." He motioned to the stereo. "Another book on tape?"

"Yeah, makes cooking less boring." She turned the faucet off.

"I can think of something less boring than cooking." He pulled her to him and kissed her on the mouth.

She held her wet hands to her chest and struggled under his embrace. "I can't, hey, come on, they're moving my office tomorrow, I have to be there early."

"Oooh, big investment banker lady getting a window office already?"

"Not a chance. I'm on the 104th floor. It will probably be twenty years before I get a window office up there. Probably a cube next to the bathroom for now."

"Exactly why you should live a little." He picked her up and threw her on the bed. He kissed her again and ran his hands down her body.

She was breathing faster now. "What time do you have class? What's tomorrow? Tuesday, the 11th?"

He pulled his sweater off. "Don't know, don't care."

77

Press Release

Centers for Disease Control and Prevention
1600 Clifton Rd.
Atlanta, GA 30333, USA

For Immediate Release
Contact: Division of News & Electronic Media,
Office of Communication
(404) 639-3286

New flu strain reported in villages in Northern India

A new strain of flu called NII.4 Burang has been reported by India's Ministry of Health & Family Welfare. It is not yet known if the strain is a mutation of an existing flu strain or a completely new virus. The CDC has dispatched a field team to assist Indian health officials in analyzing the new strain.

The outbreak was first reported among villagers outside Dharchula, India.

The severity and mortality rate of the new strain is also unknown at this time.

The CDC has advised the State Department that no travel advisories are called for at this time.

A follow-up press release will be issued when the CDC has more details about NII.4 Burang.

78

Milo wasn't waiting for Kate the next morning, but the bowl of breakfast porridge was there on the table, just as before. It was a little cold but otherwise delicious.

Kate wandered out of the wood-floored room, into the hallway.

"Dr. Kate!" Milo said as he jogged up to meet her. He stopped just short of her, put his hands on his knees and panted until he caught his breath. "I'm sorry, Dr. Kate. I was... I had to work on my special project."

"Special project? Milo, you don't have to meet me every morning."

"I know. I want to," the teenager said as he regained his breath.

They walked together down the open-air, wooden passageways toward David's room.

"What are you working on, Milo?"

He shook his head. "I cannot say, Dr. Kate."

Kate wondered if it was another prank. When they reached David's room, Milo bowed and departed, sprinting in the direction he'd come from.

David's condition had barely changed, although Kate thought maybe his color was returning.

She gave him his morning antibiotics and pain pill and opened the journal again.

I stand to greet the two men as Helena ushers them into the small solarium. Not even the slightest hint of pain crosses my face. I've taken three of the big white pain pills today, preparing, ensuring I seem up to any task.

It's just before noon, and the sun hangs high in the sky, bathing the white wicker furniture and the plants placed around the solarium with light.

The taller man steps forward, outpacing Helena and speaking without waiting for her to make the introduction. "So, you've finally decided to see us." German, a soldier. His eyes are cold, intent.

Before I can speak, the other man pops out from behind the towering man, extending a hand. "Mallory Craig, Mr. Pierce. Pleasure." An Irishman, and a mousey one at that.

The German unbuttons his jacket and sits without asking. "And I'm Konrad Kane."

Craig scurries around the couch and settles in beside Kane, who wrinkles his nose as he looks over, then moves down.

"You're German," I say as if accusing him of murder, which I consider to be fair. I probably could have masked the tone, if not for the drugs, but I'm glad it came out the way it did.

"Mmm. Born in Bonn, but I must say I've lost any interest in politics at this point." Kane responds leisurely, as if I'd asked him if he kept up with the horses, as if his people weren't gassing and murdering allied soldiers by the millions. He cocks his head. "I mean, who could when there are so many more fascinating things in the world?"

Craig nods. "Indeed."

Helena places a tray of coffee and tea between us, and Kane speaks before I can, as if it's his home and *he's* entertaining *me*. "Ah, thank you, Lady Barton."

I motion to the chair and say to her, "Stay," I think just to prove to Kane who's in charge. He looks annoyed, and I feel a little better.

Kane takes a sip of the coffee. "I hear you need work."

"I'm looking for work."

"We have a special kind of job to be done. We need a certain type of man for it. Someone who knows how to keep his mouth shut and think on his feet."

At that moment, I think: intelligence work—for the Germans. I hope it is. I still have my US Army sidearm in the table by my bed. I have a mental image of myself getting it out and returning to the solarium.

"What type of work?" Helena says, breaking the silence.

"Archeology. A dig." Kane stays focused on me, waiting for my reaction. Craig mostly watches Kane. He hasn't made a peep since his "indeed," and I doubt he will.

"I'm looking for local work," I say.

"Then you won't be disappointed. The site's under the Bay of Gibraltar. Quite deep under. We've been excavating it for some time. Forty-five years, in fact." Kane watches me for a reaction, but none comes. He takes a slow sip of coffee, never breaking eye contact. "We've just started to find… make real progress, but the war's put us in a real spot. We keep thinking it will end soon, but we're forced to make other arrangements until then. Ergo, we are here, making this offer to you." Kane finally looks away.

"Is it dangerous?" Helena says.

"No. No more dangerous than, say, the Western Front." Kane waits for her eyebrows to knit up, then reaches over to pat her on the leg. "Oh no, I merely jest, my dear girl." He smiles back at me. "We wouldn't put our little war hero in any danger."

"What happened to your last team?" I ask.

"We had a German mining team, an extremely capable team, but obviously the war and the British control of Gibraltar have complicated matters for us."

I ask the question I should have to begin with. "How many people have you lost?"

"Lost?"

"Dead."

Kane shrugs dismissively. "None." The look on Craig's face tells me it's a lie, and I wonder if Helena knows.

"What are you digging for?" He'll lie, but I'm curious what angle he'll use.

"Historical. Artifacts." Kane spits the words out like spent tobacco.

"I'm sure." My guess: a treasure hunt, probably a sunken pirate ship or merchant ship at the bottom of the bay. It would have to be something substantial to spend forty-five years digging for it, especially underwater. A dangerous assignment. "Compensation?" I ask.

"Fifty Papiermarks per week."

Fifty anything would have been a joke, but Papiermarks is a slap in the face. They may as well pay me in fool's gold. Given how the war is going for Germany, Papiermarks won't be worth burning in a year or two. German families will be carrying them to the baker's shop in wheelbarrows to buy a loaf of bread.

"I'll take my payment in US dollars."

"We have dollars," Kane says casually.

"And a lot more of them. I want five thousand dollars up front—just to look at your tunnels." I look over at Helena. "If they're poorly dug, or the support work is shoddy, I walk away, with the five-thousand-dollar advance."

"They're very well made, Mr. Pierce. They were dug by Germans."

"And I want a thousand a week."

"Absurd. You ask a king's ransom for the work of a peasant."

"Nonsense, I hear kings, kaisers, and czars aren't as valuable as they used to be. But a clear chain of command does have its place. It can keep a man alive, especially in dangerous places like underwater mines. If I take this job, when I'm in the mines, I'm in charge, no exceptions. I won't put my life in the hands of a fool. Those are my terms; take 'em or leave 'em."

Kane snorts and puts his coffee cup down.

I lean back and say, "Of course, you could always wait for the war to end. I agree it won't be long. Then you could get a German team in, assuming there are any Germans left, but... I certainly wouldn't take that bet."

"And I won't take your terms." Kane rises, nods at Helena, and walks out, leaving Craig looking confused. The cagey man stands, hesitates for a moment, whipping his head back and forth between me and his fleeing master, then chases after Kane.

When the door closes, Helena leans back in her chair and runs a hand through her hair. "God, I was scared to death you were going to take that job." She stares at the ceiling for a moment. "They told me they wanted you for some sort of research project. I told them you were quite clever and that it could be a good fit. I never would have let those scoundrels in here if I'd known what they were after."

The next day, when Helena is at work, Mallory Craig calls. He stands on the stoop holding his flat cap in his hand at his chest. "Apologies for that nastiness yesterday, Mr. Pierce. Mr. Kane's under a great deal of pressure, what with... Well, I've, uh, come to say we are quite sorry and to give you this."

He holds out a check. Five thousand US dollars drawn on the account of Immari Gibraltar.

"We'd be honored to have you lead the dig, Mr. Pierce. On your terms of course."

I told him I was uninspired by the conversation yesterday and that I would be in touch, one way or the other.

I spend the rest of the day sitting and thinking, two things I was never good at before I left for war, two things I've had a lot of practice with since. I imagine myself walking back down into that mineshaft, the light of day giving way to candlelight as the air grows cold and damp. I've seen men, just back from a cave-in or other injury, strong men, crack like an egg on the side of a skillet at breakfast as the light disappears. Will I? I try to imagine it, but I won't know until I walk down that tunnel.

I consider what else I could do for work—my options. I can get mining work, at least until the war ends. After that, there will likely be more miners than ever, some newly trained in the war, many more former miners returning from it. But I'll have to leave Gibraltar to find mines that need a man like me—there's no way around it. The other issue, which I don't linger on long, is that it would be something to sail to America or South Africa just to piss myself in a mineshaft and scurry out.

I eye the check. Five thousand dollars would give me a lot of options, and touring their dig could be... revealing... personally.

I'll "just have a look," I decide. I can always walk away, or, depending on my bowel control, run away.

I tell myself that I'll probably rule out the job, and there's no reason to tell Helena. No reason to worry her. Being a nurse at a field hospital is stressful enough.

In the situation room of the Clocktower headquarters in New Delhi, India, Dorian rubbed his temples and glanced at the wall of computer screens.

"We're getting satellite footage, sir," the technician said.

"And?" Dorian replied.

The squirrelly man leaned in, studying his computer screen. "Several targets."

"Send the drones."

The monasteries were like needles in a giant Tibetan haystack, but they finally had eyes on them. It wouldn't be long now.

79

Kate scrutinized the wound and changed David's bandages. It was healing. He would come out of it soon. She hoped. She picked up the journal again.

📖

August 9th, 1917

When Craig called yesterday, he told me Immari Gibraltar was "just a small local concern." He quickly added, "although we're part of a larger organization with other interests here on the continent and overseas." Small local concerns don't own half the wharf, and they don't do it through a half a dozen fronts.

The tour of the dig site is the first indication that Immari isn't what it seems. I arrive at the address on Mallory's card and find a rundown three-story building in the heart of the shipping district. The signs on the buildings all end in some variation of "Import/Export Company" or "Shipping and Sea Freight" or "Shipbuilders and Retrofitters." The long names and liveliness of the buildings contrast sharply with the dimly lit, seemingly abandoned concrete structure with "Immari Gibraltar" scrawled in black block letters just above the door.

Inside, a lithe receptionist pops up and says, "Good morning, Mr. Pierce. Mr. Craig is expecting you."

Either she knew me by the limp, or they don't get many visitors.

The walk through the office reminds me of a battalion HQ, hastily set up in a city that had just fallen in a siege, a place that will be abandoned quickly as soon as more ground is taken or in the event of a sudden retreat. A place that doesn't warrant settling in.

Craig is gracious, telling me how happy he is that I decided to take them up. As I suspected, Kane is nowhere to be seen, but there is another man there, younger, late twenties, about my age, and strikingly similar to Kane—especially the condescending smirk on his face. Craig confirms my suspicions.

"Patrick Pierce, this is Rutger Kane. You've met his father. I asked him to join us on the tour, as you'll be working together."

We shake. His hand is strong, and he squeezes hard, almost grunting. The months in bed have weakened me, and I draw my hand away.

Kane Jr. seems satisfied. "Glad you've finally come, Pierce. I've been after Papa to find me a new miner for months; this damn war's held me up long enough." He sits and crosses his legs. "Gertrude!" He looks over his shoulder as the secretary reaches the door. "Bring coffee. Do you take coffee, Pierce?"

I ignore him, directing my flat statement at Craig. "My conditions were clear. I'm in charge in the mines—*if* I take the job."

Craig holds both his hands up, cutting Rutger off, and speaks quickly, hoping to placate both of us. "Nothing's changed, Mr. Pierce. Rutger has worked on the project going on a decade, practically grew up in those mines! You all probably have a lot in common, I imagine, ah, from what I hear. No, you all will work together. He'll offer invaluable advice, and with his knowledge and your skill in mining, we'll be through, or making smart progress, in no time." He stops the secretary as she creeps in carefully with the tray. "Ah Gertrude, could you put the coffee in a Thermos? We'll take it with us. Uh, and some tea for Mr. Pierce."

The entrance to the mines is almost a mile from the Immari office—inside a warehouse along the harbor, next to the Rock.

Two warehouses to be exact, joined on the interior with two separate facades to make them look like two warehouses from the street. A warehouse this large would stick out and inspire curiosity. Two common-sized warehouse fronts, however, could easily go unnoticed.

Inside the oversized warehouse, four light-skinned black men are waiting for us. Moroccans would be my guess. Upon seeing us, the four men silently set about removing a tarp from a structure in the middle of the warehouse. When it's revealed, I realize it's not a structure at all—it's the opening to the mine. A giant mouth spreading out at each side. I had expected a vertical shaft, but that's the least of the surprises to come.

There's a truck, an electric one. And two large rails leading down into the mine. Clearly they're moving a lot of dirt out.

Craig points to an empty rail car and then toward the harbor and the sea beyond the warehouse door. "We dig by day and unload by night, Mr. Pierce."

"You dump the dirt—"

"In the bay, if we can. If the moon is full, we sail farther out," Craig says.

It makes sense. It's about their only option to get rid of so much dirt.

I walk closer and inspect the mineshaft. It's supported by large timbers, just like our mines in West Virginia, but there's a thick black cord running from timber to timber, stretching as far as I can see. There are two cords, actually, one on each side of the mine shaft. At the far side of the opening to the mine, the left cord attaches to… a telephone. The right-side cord simply runs into a box attached to a post. It has a metal lever, like a switch box. Power? Surely not.

When the Moroccans throw the last of the tarps aside, Rutger strides over and chastises the men in German. I understand a bit, one word in particular: "feuer." Fire. My skin crawls at the sound of it. He points at the truck, then the rails. The men look confused. This is no doubt for my benefit, and I turn away, refusing to watch the show and their humiliation. I hear Rutger retrieving something, and there's clanging on the rails. I turn to see him lighting a wick inside a round paper bag atop a mini railcar, no bigger than a plate. Rutger attaches it to a single rail, and several of the Moroccans help him with a slingshot device that sends the plate and flame whizzing into the dark mine. The paper protects the flame from instantly blowing out.

A minute later we hear the distant poof of an explosion. Firedamp. Probably a methane pocket. Rutger motions for the Moroccans to send another volley, and they rush to the rail with another plate-car carrying a paper bag full of flame. I'm impressed. In West Virginia, I'm sorry to say, our methods aren't nearly as advanced. Hitting a methane pocket is like finding a live grenade—the explosion is instant and total. If the flame doesn't kill you, the cave-in will.

This is a dangerous mine.

We hear the poof of the second volley, deeper this time.

The Moroccans load and launch a third trial.

We wait a bit, and when no sound comes, Rutger throws the switch on the box and gets behind the wheel of the truck. Craig slaps me on the back. "We're ready, Mr. Pierce." Craig takes the passenger seat, and I sit on the bench in the back. Rutger drives recklessly into the mine, almost crashing into the rails at the entrance but swerves at the last minute to straddle them and then straightens up as we plow deeper into the earth like characters out of some Jules Verne novel. Maybe *Journey to the Center of the Earth.*

The tunnel is completely dark except for the truck's dim headlamps, which barely illuminate the area ten feet ahead of us. We drive at high speed for what seems like an hour, and I'm speechless, not that I could say a word over the racket in the tunnel. The scale is staggering, unimaginable. The tunnels are wide and tall, and—much to my chagrin—very, very well made. Not treasure-hunting tunnels; these are subterranean roads made to last.

The first few minutes into the mine is a constant turn. We must be following a spiral tunnel, like a corkscrew boring deep into the earth, deep enough to get under the bay.

The spiral deposits us into a larger staging area, no doubt used to sort and store supplies. I barely get a glimpse of crates and boxes before Rutger floors the truck again, roaring down the straight tunnel with even more speed. We're on a constant decline, and I can almost feel the air growing more damp with each passing second. There are several forks in the tunnel, but nothing slows Rutger down. He drives madly, swerving left and right, barely making the turns. I grip the seat. Craig leans over and touches the youth's arm, but I can't hear his voice over the deafening racket of the truck's engine. Whatever is said, Rutger doesn't care for it. He brushes Craig's arm off and bears down harder than ever. The engine screams, and the tunnel zooms by in flashes.

Rutger's putting on this little thrill ride to prove he knows the tunnels in the dark, that this is his territory, that he has my life in his hands. He wants to intimidate me. It's working.

This mine is the biggest I've ever been in. And there are some giant mines in the mountains of West Virginia.

Finally, the tunnel opens onto a large, roughly shaped area— like a place where the miners had searched for direction and made several false starts. Electric lights hang from the ceiling, illuminating the space, revealing pockmarks and drill holes along the walls, where blasts had started new tunnels but were abandoned. I see a stack of the other black cord, lying in a bundle next to a table that holds another phone, no doubt connected to the surface.

The rail lines end here as well. The three mini rail cars sit in a row at the line's termination point, near the end of the room. The top parts of two of them have been blown away. The third sits quietly at the front of the other two; its flame jumps wildly as it claws for drifting pockets of oxygen in the dank space.

Rutger kills the engine, jumps out, and blows out the candle.

Craig follows him and says to me, "Well, what do you think, Pierce?"

"It's quite a tunnel." I look around, seeing more of the strange room.

Rutger joins us. "Don't play coy, Pierce. You've never seen anything like it."

"I never said I had." I direct my next words at Craig. "You've a methane problem."

"Yes, a rather recent development. We only began hitting pockets in the last year. Obviously we were a bit unprepared. We had assumed that water would be the biggest danger on this dig."

"A safe assumption." Methane is an ever-present danger in many coal mines. I never would have expected it down here, a place with seemingly no coal, oil, or other fuel deposits.

Craig motions above us. "You've no doubt noticed that the mine is on a constant grade—about nine degrees. What you should know is that the sea floor above us slopes at roughly eleven degrees. It's only about eighty yards above us here—we believe."

I realize the implication instantly, and I can't hide my surprise. "You think the methane pockets are from the sea floor?"

"Yes, I'm afraid so."

Rutger smirks like we're two old women gossiping.

I inspect the roof of the room. Craig hands me a helmet and a small backpack. Then he clicks a switch on the side, and the helmet lights up. I stare at it a moment in wonder, then put it on, deciding to deal with the larger mystery at hand.

The rock on the ceiling is dry—a good sign. The unspoken danger is that if a methane pocket exploded, and that pocket was large enough to stretch to the seafloor, you'd get an extremely large explosion, followed by a flood of water that would collapse the entire mine almost instantly. You would either burn, drown, or be crushed to death. Maybe a combination. One spark—from a pickax, from a falling rock, from the friction of the car wheels on the rails—could send the whole place up.

"If the gas is above, between this shaft and the sea, I don't see another option. You'll have to close her off and find another way," I say.

Rutger scoffs. "I told you, Mallory. He's not up to it. We're wasting our time with this gimp American coward."

Craig holds a hand up. "Just a minute, Rutger. We've paid Mr. Pierce to be here; now let's hear what he has to say."

"What would you do, Mr. Pierce?"

"Nothing. I'd abandon the project. The yield can't possibly justify the cost—human or capital."

Rutger rolls his eyes and begins wandering around the room, ignoring Craig and me.

"I'm afraid we can't do that," Craig says.

"You're looking for treasure."

Craig clasps his hands behind his back and walks deeper into the room. "You've seen the size of this dig. You know we're not treasure hunters. In 1861, we sank a ship in the Bay of Gibraltar: the Utopia. A little inside joke. We spent the next five years diving at the wreckage site, which was a cover for what we'd found below it—a structure, nearly a mile off the coast of Gibraltar. But we determined that we couldn't access the structure from the seafloor—it was buried too deep, and our diving technology simply wasn't advanced enough and couldn't be developed quickly enough. And we were frightened of drawing attention. We had already lingered far too long at the site of a sunken merchant ship."

"Structure?"

"Yes. A city or a temple of some sort."

Rutger walks back to us and turns his back to me, facing Craig. "He doesn't need to know this. He'll want more pay if he thinks we're digging for something valuable. Americans are almost as greedy as Jews."

Craig raises his voice. "Be quiet, Rutger."

It's easy to ignore the brat. I'm intrigued. "How did you know where to sink the ship, where to dig?" I ask.

"We... had a general idea."

"From what?"

"Some historical documents."

"How do you know you're under the diving site?"

"We used a compass and calculated the distance, accounting for the pitch of the tunnel. We're right under the site. And we have proof." Craig walked to the wall and grabbed the rock—no, a dingy black cloth, which I thought was rock. He pulls the blanket to the floor, revealing... a passageway, like a bulkhead in a massive ship.

I move closer, shining my headlamp into the strange space. The walls are black, clearly metal, but they shimmer in a different, indescribable way, almost as if they're alive and reacting to my light, like a mirror made of water. And there are lights, twinkling at the top and bottom of the passageway. I peer around the turn and see that the tunnel leads to some sort of door or portal.

"What is this?" I whisper.

Craig leans over my shoulder. "We believe it's Atlantis. The city Plato described. The location is right. Plato said that Atlantis came forth out of the Atlantic Ocean and that it was an island situated in front of the straits of the Pillars of Heracles—"

"Pillars of Heracles—"

"What we call the Pillars of Hercules. The Rock of Gibraltar is one of the Pillars of Hercules. Plato said that Atlantis ruled over all of Europe, Africa, and Asia and that it was the way to other continents. But it fell. In Plato's words: 'There occurred violent earthquakes and floods; and in a single day and night of misfortune all the warlike men in a body sank into the earth, and the island of Atlantis in like manner disappeared in the depths of the sea.'"

Craig paced away from the strange structure. "This is it. We've found it. You see now why we can't stop here, Mr. Pierce. We're very, very close. Will you join us? We need you."

Rutger laughs. "You're wasting your time, Mallory. He's scared to death; I can see it in his eyes."

Craig focuses on me. "Ignore him. I know it's dangerous. We can pay you more than a thousand dollars per week. You tell me what it's worth."

I peer into the tunnel, then inspect the ceiling again. The dry ceiling. "Let me think about it."

80

"What's our depth?" Robert Hunt asked the drilling tech.

"Just passed six thousand feet, sir. Should we stop?"

"No. Keep going. I'll report in. Come get me at sixty-five hundred feet." They had hit nothing but ice for over a mile—the same as the last four drilling sites.

Robert pulled his parka tight and walked from the massive drilling platform toward his field tent. He passed a second man on his way. He wanted to say something, but he couldn't remember the man's name. The two men they had given him were quiet; no one said much about themselves, but they were hard-working and they didn't drink—the best you could hope for in drill operators in extreme conditions. His employer would probably give up soon. Hole number five looked like the four before it: nothing but ice. The whole continent was a giant ice cube. He remembered reading that Antarctica had ninety percent of the world's ice and seventy percent of its freshwater. If you took all the water in the world, in every lake, pond, stream and even water in the clouds, it wouldn't come out to even half of the frozen water in Antarctica. When all that ice melted, the world would be a very different place. The sea would rise two hundred feet, nations would fall—or more accurately, drown— low-lying countries like Indonesia would disappear from the map. New York City, New Orleans, Los Angeles, and most of Florida—also gone.

Ice seemed to be the only thing Antarctica had in abundance. What could they be looking for down here? Oil was the logical answer. Robert was, after all, an oil rig operator. But the equipment was all wrong for oil. The bore diameter was wrong. For oil, you wanted a pipeline. These bits were making holes big enough to drive a truck through. Or lower a truck. What could be down there? Minerals? Something scientific, maybe fossils? Maybe some ploy to stake a claim on the land? Antarctica was massive—seventeen point five million square kilometers. If it were a country, it would be the second largest in the world. Antarctica was just twenty thousand square kilometers smaller than Russia, another hellhole he had drilled—with much more success. Antarctica had once been a lush paradise around two million years ago. It stood to reason that there would be an unimaginable oil reserve under the surface and who knows what else—

Behind him, Robert heard a loud boom.

The pylon sticking out of the ground was spinning wildly—the bit was hitting no resistance. They must have hit a pocket. He had expected this—research teams had recently found large caverns and gaps in the ice, possibly underwater fjords where the ice ran over the mountains below.

"Shut it down!" Robert yelled. The man on the platform couldn't hear him. He ran a hand across his throat, but the man just looked dumbfounded. He grabbed his radio and shouted, "Full stop!"

On the platform, the long pipe sticking out of the ground was starting to wobble, like a top starting to lose its balance.

Robert threw the radio down and ran toward the platform. He pushed the man out of the way and entered commands to stop the bit.

He grabbed the man, and they ran from the platform. They had made it almost to the housing pods when they heard the platform shudder, buckle, and capsize. The drilling column had broken off and spun wildly in the air. Even two hundred feet away, the noise was deafening, like a jet engine roaring at

313

full speed. The platform sank into the snow, and the bit came forward, digging into the ice like a twister on the Kansas plains in Tornado Alley.

Robert and the other man lay face down, enduring the shards of ice and snow raining down until the bit finally came to a stop.

Robert looked up at the scene. His employer wouldn't be pleased. "Don't touch anything," he said to the man.

Inside the living pod, Robert picked up the radio. "Bounty, this is Snow King. I have a status update." Robert wondered what to report. They hadn't hit a pocket. It was something else. The bit would have chewed through any kind of rock or ground, even frozen. Whatever they had hit had taken the bit clean off. It was the only possibility.

"Copy, Snow King. Report status."

Less is more. He wouldn't speculate. "We've hit something," Robert said.

Dr. Martin Grey was staring out the window of the modular headquarters when the Immari technician walked in. Martin didn't look up. Something about the endless expanse of white snow put him at peace.

"Sir, Drill Team Three just reported in. We think they hit the structure."

"An entrance?"

"No, sir."

Martin crossed the room and pointed at the massive screen that displayed a map of Antarctica. "Show me where."

81

When Kate arrived the next morning, David was awake. And angry.

"You have to go. The boy told me we've been here for three days."

"I'm glad you're feeling better," Kate said in a cheerful tone.

She retrieved his antibiotics, pain pills, and a cup of water. He looked even more gaunt than the day before; she would have to get him something to eat as well. She wanted to touch his face, his protruding cheek bones, but he was much more intimidating now—awake.

"Don't ignore me," David said.

"We'll talk once you take your pills." She held out her hand with the two pills.

"What are they?"

Kate pointed. "Antibiotic. Pain pill."

David took the antibiotic and washed it down with water.

Kate moved the hand with the pain pill closer to his face. "You need to—"

"I'm not taking it."

"You were a better patient when you were asleep."

"I've slept enough." David leaned back in the bed. "You've got to get out of here, Kate."

"I'm not going anywhere—"

"Don't. Don't do that. Remember what you promised me?

315

In the cottage by the sea. You said you would follow my orders. That was my only condition. Now I'm telling you to get out of here."

"Well... Well... This is a medical decision, not a... whatever you call it, 'command decision.'"

"Don't play with words. Look at me. You know I can't walk out of here, and I know how long that walk is. I've made it before—"

"About that, who is Andrew Reed?"

David shook his head. "Not important. He's dead."

"But they called y—"

"Killed in the mountains of Pakistan, not far from here, fighting the Immari. They're good at killing people in these mountains. This is not a game, Kate." He took her arm, dragging her down onto the bed. "Listen. You hear that, the low buzzing, like a bee in the distance?"

Kate nodded.

"Those are drones—predator drones. They're looking for us, and when they find us, there's nowhere we can run. You have to go."

"I know. But not today."

"I'm not—"

"I'll go tomorrow, I promise." Kate grabbed his hand and squeezed. "Just give me one day."

"You leave at first light, or I'll go over the side of that mountain—"

"Don't threaten me."

"It's only a threat if you don't intend to do it."

Kate released his hand. "Then I'll be gone tomorrow." She stood and walked out.

Kate returned with two bowls of thick porridge. "I thought you might be hungry."

David simply nodded and began eating, quickly at first, only slowing after he'd eaten a few bites.

"I've been reading to you." She held up the journal. "Do you mind?"

"Reading what?"

"A journal. The old guy... downstairs... he gave it to me."

"Oh, him. Qian." David took two more bites rapid-fire. "What's it about?"

Kate sat down on the bed and spread her legs next to his as she had when he was unconscious. "Mining."

David looked up from the bowl. "Mining?"

"Or war maybe, no, actually, I'm not really sure. It's set in Gibraltar—"

"Gibraltar?"

"Yes. Is that important?"

"Maybe. The code," David searched his pockets like he was looking for his keys or wallet. "Actually, Josh had it..."

"Who's Josh? Had what?"

"He's... I used to work with him. We got a code from the source—the same person who told us about the China facility; I want to talk about that, by the way. Anyway, it was a picture of an iceberg with a sub buried in the middle of it. On the back, it had a code. The code pointed to obituaries in the *New York Times* in 1947. There were three of them." David looked down, trying to remember. "The first was a reference to Gibraltar and the British finding bones near a site."

"The site could be the mine. The Immari are trying to hire an American miner, a former soldier, to excavate a structure several miles under the Bay of Gibraltar. They think it's the lost city of Atlantis."

"Interesting," David said, deep in thought.

Before he could say anything else, Kate cracked the journal open and began reading.

It's late when I arrive home, and Helena is at the small kitchen table. Her elbows are on the table, and she holds her face with both hands, like it will plummet to the ground if she releases her grip. There are no tears, but her eyes are red, as if she's been crying and can't anymore. She looks like the women I used to see leaving the hospital, followed by two men carrying a stretcher covered by a white sheet.

Helena has three brothers, two in the service, one too young to join, or maybe he's just signed up. That's my first thought: I wonder how many brothers she has now?

She jumps up at the sound of the door and stares at me, wild-eyed.

"What's happened?" I say.

She embraces me. "I thought you'd done it, taken that job or gone off and left."

I hug her back, and she buries her face in my chest. When the crying subsides, she peers up at me, her big brown eyes asking a question I can't begin to decipher. I kiss her on the mouth. It's a hungry, reckless kiss, like an animal biting into something he's hunted all day, something he needs to sustain himself, something he can't live without. She feels so delicate in my arms, so small. I reach for her blouse, fingering one of the buttons, but she clasps my hand and takes a step back.

"Patrick, I can't. I'm still... traditional, in many ways."

"I can wait."

"It's not that. It's, well, I'd like you to meet my father. My whole family."

"I'd like that very much, to meet him, all of them."

"Good. I'm off at the hospital for the next week. I'll ring him in the morning. If it suits them, we can leave on the afternoon train."

"Let's... make it the day after. I need... I need to get something."

"Very well."

"And there's something else," I say, searching for the words. I need the job, at least a few weeks of the pay, then I'll be set. "The job, I did, actually, have a look and it, um, might not be so dangerous—"

Her face changes quickly, as if I'd smacked her. The grimace is somewhere between worry and anger. "I can't do it. I won't. Every day, waiting, wondering if you'll come home. I won't live like that."

"This is all I have, Helena. I'm not any good at anything else. I don't know how to do anything else."

"I don't believe that for a second. Men start over all the time."

"And I will, I promise you that. Six weeks, that's all I need, and I'll throw in the towel. The war might be done by that time, and they'll have another team in there, and you'll be shipping out of here, and I'll need to... I'll need money for... making arrangements."

"Arrangements can be made without money. I've got—"

"Out of the question."

"If you get killed in that mine, I'll never get over it. Can you live with that?"

"Mining's a lot less dangerous when people aren't dropping bombs on you."

"How about when you've got the whole ocean on top of you? The whole Bay of Gibraltar over your head. All that water, constantly pressing on those tunnels. How would they ever pull you from that cave-in? It's suicide."

"You can see the sea coming."

"How?"

"The rock sweats," I say.

"I'm sorry, Patrick, I can't." The look in her eyes tells me she means it.

Some decisions are easy. "Then it's settled. I'll tell them no." We kiss again, and I hug her tight.

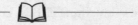

David put a hand on Kate's. "This is what you've been reading? World-War-One-era *Gone With the Wind*?"

She pushed his hand back. "No! I mean, it hasn't been like this so far, but... well, you could probably do with a little romance in your literary diet. Soften that hard soldier heart of yours."

"We'll see. Maybe we can just skip the mushy parts, get right to the point where they say the bombs or secret labs are located here."

"We're not skipping anything. It could be important."

"Well, since you're enjoying it so much, I'll endure it." He clasped his hands on his stomach and stared at the ceiling stoically.

Kate smiled. "Always the martyr."

82

"Sir?"

Dorian looked up at the Immari Security officer lingering nervously in the doorway to his office.

"What?"

"You asked to be kept apprised of the operation—"

"Make your report."

The man swallowed. "The packages are in position in America and Europe."

"Drones?"

"They've acquired another target."

83

Kate thought the buzzing in the distance, the bee searching for them, was getting louder, but she ignored it. David didn't say anything either.

They sat together in the small alcove overlooking the valley, and Kate continued reading, stopping only for an early lunch and to give David his antibiotics.

August 10th, 1917

The pawnbroker watches me like a bird of prey perched in a tree as I browse the glass cases at the front of the store. They're full of rings, all sparkling, all beautiful. I assumed there would be three or four to choose from, that it would be rather simple. What to do...

"A young man seeks an engagement ring, nothing warms my heart more, especially in these dark times." The man stands over the case, smiling a proud, sentimental smile. I didn't even hear him move across the room. The man must move like a thief in the night.

"Yes, I... didn't think there would be this many." I continue skimming the case, waiting for something to jump out at me.

"There are many rings because there are many widows here in Gibraltar. The Kingdom has been at war for almost four years, and the poor women, the war leaves them with no husband and no source of income. They sell their rings so they can buy bread. Bread in your belly is worth more than a stone on your finger or a memory in your heart. We pay them pennies on the dollar." He reaches inside the glass case and pulls out a velvet display rack that holds the largest rings. He places the rack on top of the glass case, just a few inches from me, and spreads his hands over them as if he were about to perform a magic trick. "But their misfortune can be your gain, my friend. Just peek at the prices. You will be surprised."

I take a step back without realizing what I'm doing. I look from the rings to the man, who motions toward them with a greedy grin. "It's all right, you can touch them—"

As if in a dream, I'm out the door and back on the streets of Gibraltar before I realize what's happened. I walk fast, as fast as I can with one and a half working legs. I don't know why, but I walk out of the main business district toward the Rock. Just before I reach it, I cut across Gibraltar, out of the western side, the modern side of the city, which faces the Bay of Gibraltar. I walk into the old village, which lies on the eastern side of the Rock, on Catalin Bay, facing the Mediterranean.

I walk for a while, thinking. My leg hurts like the dickens. I didn't bring any pills. I hadn't expected to walk this much. I did bring five hundred of the nearly eleven thousand dollars I've saved.

I debated at length on how much to spend. I thought of spending more, maybe even a thousand dollars, but two things convinced me not to. The first is that I need capital to start a new life. Eleven thousand dollars probably won't do, but I can find a way. I certainly won't be taking the Immari job, so the capital on hand is all I'm going to have. The second, a more important reason, is that I don't think it's what Helena would want. She would smile and gladly accept the gaudy ring, but she wouldn't want it. She grew up in a world where fine jewelry, silk clothes, and towering homes were as common as a drink of water. I think those things have lost their luster for her. She craves genuine things, real people. We so often seek what we're deprived of in childhood. Sheltered children become reckless. Starving children become ambitious. And some children, like Helena, who grow up in privilege, never wanting for anything, surrounded by people who don't live in the real world, people who drink their brandy every night and gossip about the sons and daughters of this house and that house... sometimes they only want to see the real world, to live in it and make a difference. To have genuine human contact, to see their life *mean* something.

Ahead of me, the street ends as it meets the Rock. I need somewhere to sit down, to get off the leg. I stop and look around. In the shadow of the white rock, rising to the right, there's a simple Catholic church. The arched wooden doors open, and a middle-aged priest steps out into the sweltering Gibraltar sun. Without a word, he extends a hand into the dark opening, and I walk up the stairs and into the small Cathedral.

Light filters in through the stained-glass windows. It's a beautiful church, with dark wood beams and incredible frescoes across the walls.

"Welcome to Our Lady of Sorrow, my son," the priest says as he closes the heavy wood door. "Have you come to make a confession?"

I think about turning back, but the beauty of the church draws me in, and I wander deeper inside. "Uh, no, Father," I say absently.

"What is it you seek?" He walks behind me, his hands clasped in front of him in a stirrup-like pose.

"Seek? Nothing, or, I was in the market to buy a ring and..."

"You were wise to come here. We live in strange times. Our parish has been very fortunate over the years. We've received many bequests from parishioners passing from the world of the living. Farms, art, jewels, and in recent years, many rings." He ushers me out of the worship hall and into a cramped room with a desk and leather-bound volumes crammed into floor-to-ceiling bookcases. "The church holds these items, selling them when we can, using the funds to care for those still among the living."

I nod, not quite sure what to say. "I'm looking… for something special…"

The man frowns and sits down at the desk. "I'm afraid our selection is not what you might find elsewhere."

"It's not selection I want… It's a ring… with a story."

"Every ring tells a story, my son."

"Something with a happy ending then."

The man leans back in the chair. "Happy endings are hard to come by in these dark ages. But… I may know of such a ring. Tell me about the lucky young lady who will receive it."

"She saved my life." I feel awkward answering the question, and it's all I can manage to start.

"You were injured in the war."

"Yes." My limp is hard to miss. "But, not only that, she changed me." It seems like a disgraceful summary of what she's done for me, for the woman who made me want to live again, but the priest simply nods.

"A lovely couple retired here several years ago. She had been an aid worker in South Africa. Have you been to South Africa?"

"No."

"Not surprising. It's only recently of any interest to anyone. Since around 1650, it had only been a watering hole on the trade routes to the East. The Dutch East India Company built Cape Town as a stopover on the Cape Sea Route. Built it with slaves from Indonesia, Madagascar, and India. And that's what it was, a trade stop on the sea, at least until the 1800s, when they found gold and diamonds, and the place became a true hell on earth. The Dutch had massacred the local African population for centuries in a series of frontier wars, but then the British came and brought modern war. The kind that only European countries can fight, but I think you know about that. War with massive casualties, famine, disease, and concentration camps.

"There was a soldier who had fought for the British in the South African War. And as the spoils of war go to the victors, the end of the conflict several years ago left him with quite a bit of money. He used it to invest in the mines. A strike made him rich, but he fell ill. An aid worker, a Spanish woman who had worked in the hospital during the war, nursed him back to health. And softened his heart. She told him she would marry him on one condition: that he leave the mines for good and donate half of his wealth to the hospital.

"He agreed, and they sailed out of South Africa for good. They settled here in Gibraltar, in the old city on the coast of the Mediterranean. But retirement didn't suit the man. He had been a soldier and a miner all his life. Some would say that all he knew was the darkness, pain, struggle; that the light of Gibraltar shone too bright for his heart of darkness, that the easy life left him to reflect on his sins, which haunted him, tormented him, day and night. But whatever the cause, he died a year later. The woman followed him several months after."

I wait, wondering if the story is over. Finally, I say, "Father, we have very different ideas about what constitutes a happy ending."

A smile spreads across the man's face as if he'd just heard a child say something funny. "This story is happier than you think—if you believe what the church teaches. To us, death is only a passage, and a joyous one for the righteous. A beginning, not an end. You see, the man had repented, had chosen to forsake his life of oppression and greed. He had paid for his sins—in all the ways that matter. He was saved, as so many men are, by a good woman. But some lives are harder than others, and some sins haunt us, no matter how much we pay for them or how far we sail from them. Maybe this happened to the man and maybe not. Maybe retirement doesn't suit the industrious. Perhaps there is no solace in rest for a hard-working man.

"And there is another possibility. The man had sought war and riches in South Africa. He craved power, security, a sense of knowing he was safe in a dangerous world. But he forsook it all when he met the woman. It's possible that all he wanted was to be loved and not to be hurt. And when he was, when he finally found love after a life without, he died, happy. And the woman, all she ever wanted was to know that she could change the world, and if she could change the heart of the darkest man, then there was hope for the entire human race."

The priest pauses, takes a breath, studies me. "Or perhaps their only folly was retirement, of living a sedentary life where the past could catch up to them, if only in their dreams at night. Regardless of the causes of their deaths, their destiny was certain: the Kingdom of Heaven is the domain of those who repent, and I believe the man and woman live there to this day."

I consider the priest's tale as he gets to his feet.

"Would you like to see this ring?"

"I don't need to see it." I count out five one-hundred-dollar silver certificates and place them on the table.

The priest's eyes grow wide. "We are happy to accept any donation our patrons see fit, but I should warn you, lest you seek a refund, that five hundred dollars is much more than this ring is worth... in the current... market."

"It's worth every penny to me, Father."

On the walk back to the cottage, I barely notice the pain in my leg. I have a vision of Helena and me sailing the world, never stopping anywhere for more than a few years. In the vision, she works in the hospitals. I invest in the mines, using what I know to find savvy operators and promising sites, mines that pay the workers a fair wage and provide good conditions. It won't be as profitable at first, but we'll attract the best people, and in mining, as in every other business, better people make all the difference. We'll put our competitors out of business, and we'll use the money to make a difference. And we'll never retire, never let the world catch up to us.

Kate closed the journal and leaned forward to inspect the bandages on David's chest. She pulled at the edges of them and then smoothed them out.

"What's wrong?"

"Nothing, but I think you're still bleeding a bit from one of the wounds. I'll change them in a little while."

David sighed theatrically. "I always was a bleeding heart."

Kate smiled. "Don't quit your day job."

84

Helena's childhood home is more grand than I could have imagined, mostly because I've never seen anything like it. It sits just off a massive lake, nestled among thick English forests and rolling hills. It's a masterpiece of stone and wood, like some medieval castle that's been decorated for modern times. The fog is thick in the lane as the loud gas car carries us from the train station, down the tree-lined gravel road to the home.

Her father, mother, and brother are there waiting on us, standing at attention like we're visiting dignitaries. They greet us graciously. Behind us, the house staff unpacks the car and disappears with our bags.

Her father is a tall, burly man, not portly but by no means thin. He shakes my hand and looks in my eyes, squinting like he's inspecting something. My soul, maybe.

The next few hours pass in a haze. The dinner, the small talk in the drawing room, the tour of the home. All I can think about is the moment I ask him for his daughter's hand in marriage. I glance at him every now and then, trying to glean some little bit of information, something that might tell me what he's like and what he might say.

After dinner, Helena lures her mother out of the room with a question about a piece of furniture, and to my relief, her younger brother Edward asks his father's leave.

We are alone at last in the wood-paneled drawing room, and the nerves start to get to me. I've been careful with the pills today, taking only one. The pain has gotten better of late, or

329

maybe I'm just "learning the leg" as Dr. Carlisle said I would. But it's still there, nipping at me through the nervousness. Even so, I stand, waiting for him to sit.

"What do you take, Pierce? Brandy, scotch, bourbon?"

"Bourbon's fine."

He pours a glass almost to the top, doesn't bother with ice, and hands it to me. "I know what you're here to ask, and the answer is no, so let's just get that little bit of unpleasantness out of the way so we can enjoy the evening. Kane tells me you've come around on the Gibraltar dig, says Craig gave you the nickel tour of our little project." He fixes me with a coy smile. "Now I'd like to hear your impression of it—as a professional miner. Will she hold until we can get through?"

I start to speak several times. Wicked thoughts run through my head. *He brushed you aside like a door-to-door salesman. He's Immari, a snake as bad as Kane.* I take a long pull of the drink and speak as evenly as I can. "I'd like to know why."

"Let's not be uncivil, Mr. Pierce."

"She's in love with me."

"I'm sure she is. War is an emotional time. But the war will end, and feelings will fade. The real world will set in, she'll come back to England, and she'll marry someone who can give her the life she truly wants, a life of civility and grace. A life you can't appreciate until you've seen the savagery of the rest of the world. That's what's in store for her. I've already made the arrangements." He crosses his legs and sips at his brandy. "You know, when Helena was a girl, she used to take in every flea-ridden, diseased, wounded, and otherwise half-dead animal that ever wandered onto the estate. She wouldn't relent until they either died or recovered. She has a good heart. But she grew up and lost all interest in rescuing animals. Everyone goes through phases like that, especially girls. Now I'll hear your opinion on our tunnels in Gibraltar."

"I don't give a damn about those tunnels or what's down there. It's a dangerous mine, and I won't work it. What I *will* do is marry your daughter, with or without your permission. I'm not a wounded animal, and she's not a little girl anymore." I set the drink down on the glass table, almost breaking it and sloshing brown liquid all over the place. "Thanks for the drink." I rise to leave, but he sets his own drink down and heads me off at the door.

"Just a minute. You can't be serious. You've seen what's down there. You'd turn away from that?"

"I've found something that interests me a great deal more than lost cities."

"I've told you. I've already made a match for Helena. It's settled. Let's put that aside. As for the dig, we can pay you. That's my role in this, incidentally. I manage the purse—the Immari Treasury. Kane runs the expeditions and a great deal more, as I'm sure you've gathered by now. Mallory's our master of spies. Don't underestimate Craig, he's quite good at it. So what will it take? We can double it. Two thousand dollars per week. In a few months you could set yourself up any way you like."

"I won't work that mine at any price."

"Why not? The safety? You can fix it; I'm sure of it. The army men told us you were quite clever. *The best*, they said."

"I told her I wouldn't work in a mine. I made her a promise. And I won't make her a widow."

"You assume you'll marry her. She won't marry without my permission." Lord Barton inhales and watches for my reaction, satisfied that he's cornered me.

"You underestimate her."

"You *overestimate* her. But if that's your price, you can have it, and the two thousand dollars per week. But you agree, right here and now, that you'll work that dig to the finish. Once you do, I'll give my blessing without delay."

"You'd trade your approval for whatever's buried down there?"

"Easily. I'm a practical man. And a responsible man. Maybe

you will be one day. What's my daughter's future for the fate of the human race?"

I almost laugh, but he fixes me with a stare that's dead serious. I rub my face and try to think. I hadn't expected the man to haggle, least of all over this business under Gibraltar. I know I'm making a mistake, but I don't see what option I have. "I'll have your permission now, not after the dig."

Barton looks away. "How long to get into the structure?"

"I don't know—"

"Weeks, months, years?"

"Months, I think. There's no way to kn—"

"Fine, fine. You have it. We'll announce it tonight, and if you don't keep up your end in Gibraltar, I'll make her a widow."

85

Associated Press—Online Breaking News Bulletin

Clinics throughout US and Western Europe report new flu outbreak

New York City (AP) // Emergency rooms and urgent care clinics across the US and Western Europe have reported a flood of new flu cases, sparking fears that it might be the beginning of an outbreak of a previously unidentified flu strain.

86

Kate leaned her head against the wooden wall of the alcove and stared at the sun, wishing she could stop it right where it was. Out of the corner of her eye, she saw David open his eyes and look up at her. She opened the journal and continued reading before he could say anything.

December 20th, 1917

The Moroccan workers cower as the rock comes down around them. The space fills with smoke, and we retreat back into the shaft. We wait and listen, ready to pile into the truck that straddles the rails, ready to zoom out of the shaft at the first sign of trouble—fire or water in this case.

The first cry of a canary breaks the silence, and one by one, we all exhale and move back into the massive room to see how far the latest roll of the dice has gotten us.

We're close. But not quite there.

"Told you we should have drilled it deeper," Rutger says.

I don't remember him saying anything. In fact, I'm pretty sure he sat indolently, not even inspecting the hole before we packed it with the chemical explosive. He walks to the excavation site for a better look, raking his hand on one of the canary cages as he passes by, sending the bird into a panic.

"Don't touch the cages," I say.

"You'd let them choke to death on methane gas to give yourself a few minutes head start, but I can't even rattle them?"

"Those birds could save every one of our lives. I won't have you torture them for your own enjoyment."

Rutger unloads the rage meant for me on the Moroccan foreman. He shouts at the poor man in French, and the dozen workers begin clearing the rubble from the blast.

It's been almost four months since I first toured the site, since I first set foot in this strange room. In the first few months of digging, it became clear that the part of the structure they had found was an access tunnel at the bottom of the structure. It led to a door that was sealed—with some sort of technology beyond anything we could ever hope to break through. And we tried everything: fire, ice, explosives, chemicals. The Berbers on the work crew even performed some strange tribal ritual, possibly for their own sake. But it soon became clear that we weren't getting through the door. Our theory is that it's some sort of drainage tunnel or emergency evacuation route, sealed for who knows how many thousands of years.

After some debate, the Immari Council—that's Kane, Craig, and Lord Barton, my now father-in-law—decided we should move up the structure, into the area that contains the methane pockets. That's slowed us down, but in the last several weeks, we've uncovered signs that we're reaching some sort of entrance. The smooth surface of the structure, some metal that's harder than steel and makes almost no noise when you strike it, has begun to slope. A week ago, we found steps.

The dust is clearing, and I see more steps. Rutger shouts for the men to work faster, as if this thing is going anywhere.

Beyond the dust behind me, I hear footfalls and see my assistant running. "Mr. Pierce. Your wife is at the office. She's looking for you."

"Rutger!" I yell. He turns. "I'm taking the truck. Don't blast anything until I get back."

"The hell I won't! We're close, Pierce."

I grab the pack of blast caps and run to the truck. "Drive me to the surface," I say to my assistant.

Behind me, Rutger bellows out a tirade about my cowardice.

At the surface, I change quickly and scrub my hands. Before I can leave for the office, the telephone at the warehouse rings, and the manager walks out. "Sorry, Mr. Pierce, she's left."

"What did they tell her?"

"Sorry, sir, I don't know."

"Was she sick? Was she going to the hospital?"

The man shrugs apologetically. "I... I'm sorry, sir, I didn't ask—"

I'm out the door and in the car before he can finish. I rush to the hospital, but she's not there, and they haven't seen her. From the hospital, the switchboard operator connects me to the newly installed phone at our residence. It rings ten times. The operator breaks on. "I'm sorry, sir, there's no answer—"

"Let it ring. I'll wait."

Five more rings. Three more and our butler, Desmond, comes on. "Pierce residence, Desmond speaking."

"Desmond, is Mrs. Pierce there?"

"Yes, sir."

I wait. "Well, put her on then," I say, trying but failing to hide my nervousness.

"Of course, sir!" he says, embarrassed. He's not used to the phone. It's probably why it took him so long to answer.

Three minutes pass, and Desmond comes back on the line. "She's in her room, sir. Shall I have Myrtle go in and see about her—"

"No. I'll be there directly." I hang up, run out of the hospital and hop back in the car.

I order my assistant to drive faster and faster. We zoom recklessly through the streets of Gibraltar, forcing several carriages off the street and scattering shoppers and tourists at each turn.

When we arrive home, I jump out, race up the stairs, throw open the doors, and storm through the foyer. Pain punches at my leg with every step, and I'm sweating profusely, but I plow on, driven by fear. I climb the grand staircase to the second floor, make a beeline for our bedroom, and enter without knocking.

Helena turns over, clearly surprised to see me. And surprised at the sight of me—sweat dripping from my forehead, the panting, the painful grimace. "Patrick?"

"Are you all right?" I say as I sit on the bed with her and brush the thick blankets back. I run my hand over her swollen stomach.

She sits up in the bed. "I could ask you the same thing. Of course I'm all right; why wouldn't I be?"

"I thought you might have come because you, or there was a problem..." I exhale, and the worry flows from my body. I scold her with my eyes. "The doctor said you should stay in bed."

She slumps back into the pillows. "You try staying in bed for months on end—"

I smile at her as she realizes what she's said.

"Sorry, but as I recall, you weren't all that good at it either."

"No, you're right, I wasn't. I'm sorry I missed you; what is it?"

"What?"

"You came by the office?"

"Oh, yes. I wanted to see if you could slip out for lunch, but they told me you were already out."

"Yes. A... problem down at the docks." It's the hundredth time I've lied to Helena. It hasn't gotten any easier, but the alternative is a lot worse.

"The perils of being a shipping magnate." She smiles. "Well, maybe another day."

"Maybe in a few weeks, when it will be three for lunch."

"Three indeed. Or maybe four; I feel that big."

"You don't look it."

"You're a brilliant liar," she says.

Brilliant liar isn't the half of it.

Our revelry is interrupted by the sound of knocking in the next room. I turn my head.

"They're measuring the drawing room and the parlor below," Helena says.

We've already renovated for a nursery and enlarged three bedrooms for the children. I bought us a massive row house with a separate cottage for the house staff, and I can't imagine what else we might need now.

"I thought we could build a dancing room, with a parquet floor, like the one in my parents' house."

Every man has limits. Helena can do whatever she wants to the house; that's not the issue. "If we have a son?" I ask.

"Don't worry." She pats my hand. "I won't subject your strong American son to the dull intricacies of English society dance. But we're having a girl."

I raise my eyebrows. "You know this?"

"I have a feeling."

"Then we'll need a dancing room," I say, smiling.

"Speaking of dancing, an invitation came by messenger today. The Immari Annual Meeting and Christmas Ball, they're having it in Gibraltar this year. There's to be quite a celebration. I rang Mother. She and Father will be there. I'd like to go. I'll take it easy, I assure you."

"Sure. It's a date."

87

Kate squinted, trying to read the journal. The sun was setting over the mountains and dread was building in her stomach. She glanced over at David. His expression was almost blank, unreadable. Maybe somber.

As if reading her mind, Milo entered the large wood-floored room with a gas-burning lantern. Kate liked the smell; it somehow put her at ease.

Milo set the lantern on a table by the bed, where the light would reach the journal, and said, "Good evening, Dr. Kate—" Upon seeing that David was awake, he brightened. "And hello again, Mr. Ree—"

"It's David Vale now. It's nice to see you again, Milo. You've gotten a lot taller."

"And that's not all, Mr. David. Milo has learned the ancient art of communication you know as... English."

David laughed. "And learned it well. I wondered at the time if they would toss it out or actually give it to you—the Rosetta Stone."

"Ah, my mysterious benefactor finally reveals himself!" Milo bowed again. "I thank you for the gift of your language. And now, may I repay the gift, at least partially," he raised his eyebrows mysteriously, "with the evening meal?"

"Please," Kate said, laughing.

David gazed out the window. The last sliver of the sun slipped behind the mountain like a pendulum disappearing in the side of a clock. "You should get your rest, Kate. It's a very long walk."

"I'll rest when we finish. I find reading relaxing." She opened the book again.

December 23rd, 1917

I strain to see as the dust clears. Then I squint, not believing my eyes. We've uncovered more stairs, but there's something else, expanding to the right of the stairs—an opening, like a gash in the metal.

"We're in!" Rutger yells and rushes forward into the darkness and floating dust.

I grab for him, but he breaks my grasp. My leg has gotten some better, to the point where I only take one pain pill, sometimes two, each day, but I'll never catch him.

"You want us go after 'im?" the Moroccan foreman asks.

"No," I say. I wouldn't sacrifice one of them to save Rutger. "Hand me one of the birds." I take the canary cage, switch my headlamp on, and wade into the dark opening.

The jagged portal is clearly the result of a blast or a rip. But we didn't make it. We merely found it—the metal walls are almost five feet thick. As I cross into this structure the Immari have been digging and diving for going on almost sixty years, I'm finally overcome by awe. The first area is a corridor, ten feet wide by thirty feet long. It opens to a circular room with wonders I can't begin to describe. The first thing that catches my eye is an indentation in the wall with four large tubes, like massive oblong capsules or elongated mason jars, standing on their ends, running from the floor to the ceiling. They're empty except for a faint white light and fog that floats at the bottom. Farther over, there are two more tubes. One is damaged, I think. The glass is cracked, and there's no fog. But the tube beside it… there's something in it. Rutger sees it just as I do, and he's at the tube, which seems to sense our presence. The fog clears as we approach, like a curtain rolling back to reveal its secret.

It's a man. No, an ape. Or something in between.

Rutger looks back at me, for the first time with an expression other than arrogance or contempt. He's confused. Maybe scared. I certainly am.

I put my hand on his shoulder and resume scanning the room. "Don't touch anything, Rutger."

88

Helena glows in the dress. The tailor spent a week taking it out and took me for a small fortune, but it was worth the wait and every last shilling I paid him. She's radiant. We dance, both ignoring her promise to take it easy. I can't say no to her. Mostly I stand stationary, but the pain is manageable, and for perhaps once in our lives, we are well-matched on the dance floor. The music slows, she rests her head on my shoulder, and I forget about the ape-man in the tube. The world feels normal again, for the first time since that tunnel exploded on the Western Front.

Then, like the fog in the tube, it all goes away. The music stops, and Lord Barton is speaking, raising a glass. He's toasting me—Immari's new head of shipping, his daughter's husband, and a war hero. Heads nod around the room. There's some joke about a modern day Lazarus man, back from the dead. Laughter. I smile. Helena hugs me closer. Barton's finally finished, and around the room, revelers are downing champagne and nodding at me. I make a silly little bow and escort Helena back to our table.

At that moment, for some reason I can't understand, all I can think about is the last time I saw my father—the day before I shipped off to the war. He got drunk as a sailor that night and lost control—the first, last, and only time I ever saw him lose control. He told me about his childhood that night, and I understood him, or so I thought. How much can you ever really understand any man?

We lived in a modest home in downtown Charleston, West

Virginia, alongside the homes of people who worked for my father. His peers—the other business owners, merchants, and bankers—lived across town, and my father liked it that way.

He paced the living room, spitting as he spoke. I sat there in my pristine tan US Army uniform, the single brass bar of a second lieutenant's rank hanging on my collar.

"You look as foolish as another man I knew who joined the army. He was almost giddy as he ran back to the cabin. He waved the letter in the air like the king himself had written it. He read it to us, but I didn't understand it all then. We were moving down to America—a place called Virginia. The war between the states had broken out about two years earlier. I can't remember exactly when, but it was getting pretty bloody by this point. And both sides needed more men, fresh bodies for the grinder. But if you were rich enough, you didn't have to go. You just had to send a substitute. Some rich southern planter had hired your grandfather as his substitute. A substitute. The idea of hiring another man to die in the war in your place, just because you have the money. When they start the conscriptions this go 'round, I'll see to it in the senate that no man can send a replacement."

"They won't need conscripts. Brave men are joining by the thousands—"

He laughed and poured another drink. "*Brave men by the thousands.* Fools by the train car load—joining because they think there's glory in it, maybe fame and adventure. They don't know the cost of war. The price you pay." He shook his head and took another long pull, almost emptying the glass. "Word will get around soon, and then they'll have to draft, just like the states did during the Civil War. They didn't at first, this was years after the war started, when people got a taste of it, that's when they began the conscriptions and rich men started writing to poor men like my father. But the post runs slow in the Canadian frontier, especially if you're a logger living way out of town. By the time we got down to Virginia, this planter had already hired another substitute, said he hadn't heard from your grandfather, was scared he'd have to *show up himself*, heaven forbid. But we were in Virginia, and he was hell-bent on fighting for a fortune—up to a thousand dollars, that's what the substitutes were paid—and it was a fortune, if you could collect it. Well, he didn't. He found another planter who was up against it, and he wore that wretched gray uniform and died in it. When the South lost, society crumbled, and the huge tract of land promised to your grandfather as payment was bought by some northern carpetbagger on the steps of the county courthouse for pennies on the dollar." He finally sat down, his glass empty.

"But that was the least of the horror of Reconstruction. I watched my only brother die of typhoid while the occupying Union soldiers ate us out of house and home—what home there was, a small run-down shack on the plantation. The new owner kicked us out, but my mother made a deal: she'd work the fields if we could stay. And she did. Worked those fields to death. I was twelve when I walked off the plantation and hitched my way to West Virginia. Work in the mines was hard to get, but they needed boys, the smaller the better—to crawl through the narrow spaces. So that's the cost of war. Now you know. At least you don't have a family. But that's what you have to look forward to: death and misery. If you've ever wondered why I was so hard on you, so frugal, so demanding—there it is. Life is hard—for everyone—but it's hell on earth if you're foolish or weak. You're neither, I've seen to it, and this is how you repay me."

"This is a different war—"

"It's always the same war. Only the names of the dead change. It's always about one thing: which group of rich men get to divvy up the spoils. They call it 'The Great War'—clever marketing. It's a European Civil War, the only question is which kings and queens will divvy up the continent when it's all over. America's got no business over there, that's why I voted against it. The Europeans had the good sense to stay out of *our* civil war, you'd think we might do the same. Whole affair is practically a family feud between the royal families, they're all cousins."

"And they're *our* cousins. Our mother country's back is against the wall. They would come to our aid if we were facing annihilation."

"We don't owe them a thing. America is ours. We've paid for this land with our blood, sweat, and tears—the only currency that's ever mattered."

"They need miners desperately. Tunnel warfare could end the war early. You'd have me stay home? I can save lives."

"You can't save lives." He looked disgusted. "You haven't understood a word I've said, have you? Get out of here. And even if you do make it back from the war, don't come back here. But do me one favor, for all I've given you. When you figure out that you're fighting some other man's war, walk away. And don't start a family until you take that uniform off. Don't be as cruel and greedy as he was. We walked through the devastation of the North to reach that plantation in Virginia. He knew what he was getting into, and he charged on. When you see war, you'll know. Make better choices than the one you made today." He walked out of the room, and I never saw him again.

I'm so lost in the memory I barely notice the throngs of people that file past us, introducing themselves and touching Helena's stomach. We sit there like a royal couple at some state function. There are dozens of scientists, in town no doubt to study the room we recently uncovered. I meet the heads of Immari divisions overseas. The organization is massive. Konrad Kane marches over. His legs and arms are rigid, his back straight and unbending, as if he were being probed with some unseen instrument. He introduces the woman at his side—his wife. Her smile is warm and she speaks kindly, which catches me off guard. I'm a little embarrassed at my harsh demeanor. A young boy runs from behind her and jumps into Helena's lap, crushing her stomach. I grab him by the arm, jerking him off of her and back onto the ground. My face is filled with rage, and the boy looks as though he will cry. Konrad locks eyes with me, but the boy's mother has her arms around him, admonishing, "Be careful, Dieter. Helena is pregnant."

Helena straightens in the chair and reaches for the boy. "It's okay. Give me your hand, Dieter." She takes the boy's arm and pulls him to her, placing the hand on her stomach. "You feel that?" The boy looks up at Helena and nods. Helena smiles at him. "I remember when you were inside your mama's stomach. I remember the day you were born."

Lord Barton steps between Konrad and me. "It's time." He looks at the woman and the child palming Helena's swollen belly. "Excuse us, ladies."

Barton leads us through the hall, to a large conference room.

The other apostles of the apocalypse are here waiting on us: Rutger, Mallory Craig, and a cadre of other men, mostly scientists and researchers. The introductions are hasty. These men are clearly less star-struck with me. There's another quick round of congratulations and hyperbole like we've cured the plague; then they get down to business.

"When will we get through—to the top of the stairwell?" Konrad asks.

I know what I want to say, but curiosity gets the better of me. "What are the devices in the chamber we found?"

One of the scientists speaks. "We're still studying them. Some sort of suspension chamber."

I had assumed as much, but it sounds less crazy when a scientist says it. "The room is some sort of laboratory?"

The scientists nod. "Yes. We believe the building is a science building, possibly one giant lab."

"What if it's not a building?"

The scientist looks confused. "What else could it be?"

"A ship," I say.

Barton lets out a laugh and speaks jovially. "That's rich, Patty. Why don't you focus on the digging and leave the science to these men?" He nods appreciatively at the scientists. "I assure you they're better at it than you are. Now, Rutger has told us you're

346

worried about water and gas above the stairs. What's your plan?"

I press on. "The walls, inside the structure. They look like bulkheads in a ship."

The lead scientist hesitates, then says, "Yes, they do. But they're too thick, almost five feet. No ship would need walls that thick, and it wouldn't float. It's also too large to be a ship. It's a city; we're fairly certain of that. And there are the stairs. Stairs on a ship would be very curious."

Barton holds up his hand. "We'll sort out all these mysteries when we're inside. Can you give us an estimate, Pierce?"

"I can't."

"Why not?"

For a brief moment, my mind drifts back to that night in West Virginia, then I'm back in the room, staring at the Immari Council and the scientists. "Because I'm done digging. Find someone else," I say.

"Now look here, my boy, this isn't some social club, some frivolous thing you join and then quit when the dues become too burdensome. You'll finish the job and make good on your promise," Lord Barton says.

"I said I'd get you through, and I have. This isn't my war to fight. I have a family now."

Barton rises to shout, but Kane catches his arm and speaks for the first time. "War. An interesting choice of words. Tell me, Mr. Pierce, what do you think is in that last tube?"

"I don't know, and I don't care."

"You should," Kane says. "It's not human, and it doesn't match any bones we've ever found." He waits for my reaction. "Let me connect the dots for you, as you seem either unable or remiss to do so. Someone built this structure—the most advanced piece of technology on the planet. And they built it thousands of years ago, maybe hundreds of thousands of years ago. That frozen ape-man has been in there for who-knows-how-many thousands of years. Waiting."

"Waiting for what?"

"We don't know, but I can assure you that when he and the rest of the people who built that structure wake up, the human race is finished on this planet. So you say this isn't your war, but it is. You can't outrun this war, can't simply abstain or move away, because this enemy will chase us to the far corners of the world and exterminate us."

"You assume they're hostile. Because you're hostile, extermination and war and power dominate your thoughts, and you assume the same for them."

"The only thing we know for sure is this: that *thing* is some form of man. My assumptions are valid. And practical. Killing them ensures our survival. Making friends does not."

I consider what he's said, and I'm ashamed to admit I think it makes sense.

Kane seems to sense my wavering. "You know it's true, Pierce. They're smarter than we are, infinitely smarter. If they do let us live, even some of us, we'll be nothing more than pets to them. Maybe they'll breed us to be docile and friendly, feeding us by their proverbial campfire, weeding out the aggressive ones, the same way we molded wild wolves into dogs so many thousands of years ago. They'll make us so civilized we can't imagine fighting back, can't hunt, and can't feed ourselves. Maybe it's already happening, and we don't even know it. Or maybe they won't find us that cute. We could become their slaves. You're familiar with this concept, I believe. A group of brutal yet intelligent humans with advanced technology subjugating a less advanced group. But this time it will be for the rest of eternity; we would never advance or evolve further. Think of it. But we can prevent that fate. It seems harsh, to go in and murder them in their sleep, but think of the alternative. We will be celebrated as heroes when history learns the truth. We are the liberators of the human race, the emancipators—"

"No. Whatever happens from here, happens without me." I can't get the image of Helena's face out of my mind, the thought of holding our child, of growing old by some lake, of teaching our grandchildren to fish in the summers. I can't make a difference in the Immari plan. They'll find another miner. Maybe it will set them back a few months, but whatever is down there will wait.

I stand and stare at Kane and Barton for a long moment. "Gentlemen, you'll have to excuse me. My wife is pregnant, and I should be getting her home." I focus on Barton. "We're expecting our first child. I wish you the best on the project. As you know, I was a soldier. And soldiers can keep secrets. Almost as well as they can fight. But I hope my fighting days are behind me."

David sat up. "I know what they're doing."

"Who?"

"The Immari. Toba Protocol. It makes sense now. They're building an army. I would bet on it. They think humanity is facing an advanced enemy. Toba Protocol, reducing the total population, causing a genetic bottleneck and a second Great Leap Forward—they're doing it to create a race of super-soldiers, advanced humans who can battle whoever built that thing in Gibraltar."

"Maybe. There's something else. In China, there was a device. I think it has something to do with this," Kate said.

She told David about her experience in China, about the bell-shaped object that massacred the subjects before melting and then exploding.

When she finished, David nodded. "I think I know what it is."

"You do?"

"Yeah. Maybe. Keep reading."

89

Jan 18th, 1918

When the butler bursts through the doors to my study, my first thought is Helena: her water's broken... or she's fallen, or—

"Mr. Pierce, your office is on the line. They say it's important, urgent. Regarding the docks, inside the warehouse."

I walk down to the butler's office and pick up the phone. Mallory Craig begins speaking before I say a word. "Patrick. There's been an accident. Rutger wouldn't let them call you, but I thought you should know. He pressed too hard. Went too far too fast. Some of the Moroccan workers are trapped, they say—"

I'm up and out the door before he finishes. I drive myself to the warehouse and hop in the electric truck alongside my former assistant. We drive as recklessly as Rutger did the first day he showed me the tunnel. The fool has done it—he pressed on and caused a cave-in. I dread seeing it, but urge my assistant to drive faster anyway.

As the tunnel opens on the massive stone room I've worked in for the last four months, I notice that the electric lights are off, but the room isn't dark—a dozen beams of light crisscross the room, the headlamps of the miners' helmets. A man, the foreman, grabs me by the arm. "Rutger is on the telly for you, Mr. Pierce."

"On the phone," I say as I traipse across the dark space. I stop. There's water on my forehead. Was it sweat? No, there's another one. A drop of water, from the ceiling—it's sweating.

I grab the phone. "Rutger, they said there's been an accident, where are you?"

"Somewhere safe."

"Don't play games. Where's the accident?"

"Oh, you're in the right place." Rutger's tone is playful and confident. Satisfied.

I glance around the room. The miners are milling about, confused. Why aren't the lights on? I set the phone down and walk over to the electric line. It's connected to a new cable. I shine my light on it, following it around the room. It runs up the wall… to the ceiling and then over to the stairs, to… "Get out!" I yell. I struggle over the uneven ground to the back of the room and try to corral the workers, but they simply stumble over each other in the choppy sea of light and shadows.

Overhead, a blast rings out in the space and rock falls. Dust envelops the room, and it's just like the tunnels at the Western Front. I can't save them. I can't even see them. I stagger back, into the tunnel—the corridor to the lab. The dust follows me, and I hear rock close the entrance off. The screams fade away, just like that, like a door closing, and I'm in total darkness except for the soft glow of the white light and fog in the tubes.

I don't know how much time has passed, but I'm hungry. Very hungry. My headlamp has long since burned out, and I sit in the still darkness, leaning against the wall, thinking. Helena has to be mad with worry. Will she finally find out my secret? Will she forgive me? It all presupposes I'll get out of here.

On the other side of the rock, I hear footsteps. And voices. Both are muffled, but there's just enough space between the rocks to hear them.

"HEEEYYYY!"

I have to choose my words carefully. "Get on the telly and ring Lord Barton. Tell him Patrick Pierce is trapped in the tunnels."

I hear laughter. Rutger. "You're a survivor, Pierce, I'll give you that. And you're a brilliant miner, but when it comes to people, you're about as thick as the walls to the structure."

"Barton will have your head for killing me."

"Barton? Who do you think gave the order? You think I could just knock you off? If so, I would have gotten rid of you a long time ago. No. Barton and Father planned for Helena and me to marry before we were even born. But she wasn't keen on the idea; may have been why she hopped the first train to Gibraltar when the war broke out. But we can't escape fate. The dig brought me here too, and life was about to get back on track until the methane leaks killed my crews and you came along. Barton made a deal, but he promised Papa it could be undone. The pregnancy was about the last straw, but don't worry, I'll take care of it. So many children die right after birth, from all sorts of mysterious diseases. Don't worry, I'll be there to comfort her. We've known each other for ages."

"I'm going to get out of here, Rutger. And when I do, I'm going to kill you. You understand me?"

"Keep quiet, Patty-boy. Men are working here." He moves away from the rock-covered entrance to the corridor. He shouts in German, and I hear footfalls all around the room.

For the next few hours, I don't know how long, I ransack the mysterious lab. There's nothing I can use. All the doors are sealed. This will be my tomb. There has to be some way out. Finally, I sit and stare at the walls, waiting, watching them shimmer like glass, almost reflecting the light from the tubes, but not quite. It's a dull, fuzzy reflection, the kind polished steel makes.

Above me, I occasionally hear drilling and pickaxes striking rocks. They're trying to finish the job. They must be close to the top of the stairs. Suddenly, the noise stops, and I hear yelling. "Wasser! Wasser!" Water—they must have hit— Then loud booms. The unmistakable sound of falling rock.

I run to the entrance and listen. Screams, rushing water. Something else. A drumbeat. Or a pulsing vibration. Getting louder every second. More screams. Men running. The truck cranks and roars away.

I strain, but I can't hear anything else. In the absence of sound, I realize I'm standing in two feet of water. It's seeping in through the loosely stacked rock and quickly.

I slosh back into the corridor. There must be a door to the lab. I bang around on the walls, but nothing works. The water is in the lab now; it will overtake me in minutes.

The tube—it's open, one of the four. What choice do I have? I wade through the water and collapse into it. The fog surrounds me, and the door closes.

90

Snow Camp Alpha
Drill Site #6
East Antarctica

Robert Hunt sat in his housing pod, warming his hands around a fresh cup of burned coffee. After the near-disaster at the last drill site, he was glad they had reached seven thousand feet without so much as a hiccup. No pockets of air, water, or sediment. Maybe the next site would be like the first four sites—nothing but ice. He sipped the coffee and considered what might account for the drilling difference at the last site.

Beyond the pod's door, a high-pitched sound erupted—the unmistakable whirl of a drill under low-to-no tension.

He ran out of the pod, made eye contact with the operator, and jerked his hand across his neck. The man lunged and hit the kill switch. The man was learning, thank God.

Robert jogged to the platform. The technician turned to him and said, "Should we reverse out?"

"No." Robert checked the depth. It read 7,309 feet. "Lower the drill. Let's see how deep the pocket is."

The man lowered the drill, and Robert watched the depth reading climb: 7,400... 7,450... 7,500... 7,550... 7,600. It stopped at 7,624.

Robert's mind raced with possibilities. A cavern a mile and a half below the ice. It could be something on the surface of the ground. But what? The cavern or pocket, whatever it was, was three hundred feet tall. Its ceiling was almost a football field above its floor. The laws of gravity just didn't work that way.

What had the strength to hold up one and a half miles of ice?

The technician turned to Robert and asked, "Start drilling again?"

Robert, still deep in thought, waved a hand over the controls and mumbled, "No. Uh, no, don't do anything. I need to call this in."

Back at his pod, he activated the radio, "Bounty, this is Snow King. I have a status update."

A few seconds passed before the radio crackled, and the reply came, "Go ahead, Snow King."

"We hit a pocket at depth seven-three-zero-nine, repeat seven-three-zero-nine feet. Pocket ends at seven-six-two-four, repeat, seven-six-two-four feet. Request instruction. Over."

"Stand by, Snow King."

Robert began preparing another pot of coffee. His team would probably need some.

"Snow King, what is the status of the drill, over?"

"Bounty, drill is still in the hole at max depth, over."

"Understood, Snow King. Instructions are as follows: extract drill, lock down site, and proceed to location seven. Stand by for GPS coordinates."

As before, he wrote down the coordinates and endured the redundant warning about local contact. He folded the paper with the GPS coordinates and placed it in his pocket, then stood, grabbed the two cups of fresh coffee and headed out of the pod.

They reversed the drill out and prepared the site with ease. The three men worked efficiently, almost mechanically, and silently. From the air, they might have looked like three Eskimo versions of tin soldiers racing around on a track, lifting and stacking crates, opening large white umbrellas to cover small items, and anchoring white metal poles for the massive canopy that covered the drill site. When they finished, the two techs mounted their snowmobiles and waited for Robert to lead them.

He rested his arm on the plastic chest that contained the cameras and looked up at the site. Two million dollars was a lot of money.

The two men glanced back at him. They had started their snowmobiles, but one tech turned his off.

Robert brushed some snow off the chest and opened one latch. The sound of the radio startled him. "Snow King, Bounty. SITREP."

Robert clicked the button on the radio and hesitated for a second. "Bounty, this is Snow King." He glanced at the men. "We're evacuating the site now."

He snapped the latch shut and stood for a moment. The whole thing felt wrong. The radio silence, all the secrecy. But what did he know? He was paid to drill. Maybe they weren't doing anything wrong, maybe they just didn't want the press broadcasting their business to the world. Nothing wrong with that. Getting fired for being curious would be something. He wasn't quite that stupid. He imagined himself telling his son, "I'm sorry, college will have to wait. I just can't afford it right now; yes, I could have, but I couldn't stand the mystery."

Then again... if there was something illegal going on, and he was part of it... "Son, you can't go to college because your dad is an international criminal, and PS: he was too dumb to even know it."

The other man stopped the engine on his snowmobile. Both techs stared at him.

Robert walked over to the excess cover supplies. He picked up a closed, eight-foot-long, white umbrella and tied it to his snowmobile. He cranked the machine and drove toward the next location. The two men followed close behind.

Thirty minutes into their trek, Robert spotted a large rock overhang rising out of the snow. It wasn't deep enough to be a cave, but the indentation cut twenty or thirty feet into the mountain and cast a long shadow. He adjusted their vector to pass close by the overhang, and at the last second, he veered off into the darkness of the shadow. Despite riding close behind him, the two men matched his course quickly and parked their snowmobiles beside his. Robert was still seated. Neither man dismounted.

"I forgot something at the site. I'll be back. Shouldn't take long. Wait here and don't, uh, don't leave the ravine." Neither man said anything. Robert could feel his nervousness growing. He was a terrible liar. He continued, hoping to legitimize his orders, "They've asked us to minimize our visibility from the air." He opened the white umbrella and planted it beside him, anchoring it against the snowmobile, as if he were a medieval knight locking a lance next to him and readying his horse for a charge.

He backed his snowmobile out and returned the way they had come, back to the site.

91

Kate yawned and turned the page. The room was cold, and she and David were wrapped in a thick blanket now.

"Finish it on the walk out," David said through sleepy eyes. "You'll need to stop a lot."

"Okay, I just want to get to a good stopping place," she said.

"You stayed up reading as a kid, didn't you?"

"About every night. You?"

"Video games."

"Figures."

"Sometimes Legos." David yawned again. "How many pages left?"

Kate flipped through the journal. "Not many, actually. Just a few more. I can stay awake if you can."

"Like I said, I've slept enough. And I don't have a hike tomorrow."

I awake to the soft hiss of air flowing into the tube as it opens. At first, the air feels heavy, like water in my lungs, but after a few deep gulps of the damp cold air, my breathing normalizes, and I take stock of my situation. The room is still dark, but there's a faint shaft of light drifting into the lab from the corridor.

I step out of the tube and walk toward the corridor, surveying the room as I go. None of the other tubes are occupied, save for the ape-man, who apparently slept through the flood without incident. I wonder how many he's slept through.

There's still about a foot of water in the corridor. Enough to notice but not enough to slow me down. I slosh toward the jagged opening. The rocks that locked me inside are almost completely gone—washed away, no doubt. A soft amber glow from above drapes the remaining rocks, which I push aside as I step out into the room.

The source of the strange light hangs thirty feet above me, at the top of the stairs. It looks like a bell, or a large pawn, with windows in the top. I eye it, trying to figure out what it is. It seems to stare back at me, the lights pulsing slowly, like a lion's heart beating after it's devoured a victim on the Serengeti.

I stand still, wondering if it will attack me, but nothing happens. My eyes are adjusting, and with every passing second, more of the room comes into focus. The floor is a nightmarish soup of water, ashes, dirt, and blood. At the very bottom, I see the bodies of the Moroccan miners, crushed under the rubble. Above them, Europeans lie prostrate, ripped to shreds, some burned, all mutilated by a weapon I can't imagine. It's not an explosion, or a gun, or a knife. And they didn't die recently. The wounds look old. How long have I been down here?

I search the bodies, hoping to see one in particular. But Rutger isn't here.

I rub my face. I've got to focus. Got to get home. Helena.

The electric truck is gone. I'm weak, tired, and hungry, and at that moment, I'm not sure I will ever see daylight again, but I put one foot in front of the other and start the arduous trek out of the mine. I pump my legs as hard as they'll go and brace for the pain, but it never comes. I'm driven to get out of this place by a strength and fire I didn't know I possessed.

The mine flies by in a flash, and I see the light as I hike out of the last turn of the spiral. They've covered the entrance to the tunnel with a white tent, or a plastic sheet of some type.

I brush the flap aside, and I'm surrounded by soldiers in gas masks and strange plastic suits. They tackle me and hold me to the floor. From the ground, I see a tall soldier stride over. Even through the bulky, plastic suit, I know who it is. Konrad Kane.

One of my captors looks up at him and speaks through the mask in a muffled voice. "He just walked out, sir."

"Bring him," Kane says in a deep, disembodied voice.

The men drag me deeper into the warehouse, to a series of six white tents that remind me of a field hospital. The first tent has row after row of cots, all covered in white sheets. I hear screams in the next tent. Helena.

I struggle against the men at my sides, but I'm too weak—from lack of food, from the walk out, and from whatever the tube did to me. They hold me tight, but I continue to fight.

I can hear her clearly now, at the end of the tent, behind a white curtain. I lunge for her, but the soldiers jerk me back, walking me down the row so I get a good look at the people lying dead on the skinny cots. Horror spreads over me. Lord Barton and Lady Barton are here. Rutger. Kane's wife. All dead. And there are others, people I don't recognize. Scientists. Soldiers. Nurses. We pass a bed with a boy, Kane's son. Dietrich? Dieter?

I can hear the doctors talking to Helena, and as we move past the edge of the curtain, I see them swarming around her, injecting her with something, and holding her down.

The men hold me as I struggle. Kane turns to me. "I want you to see this, Pierce. You can watch her die like I watched Rutger and Marie die."

They drag me closer. "What happened?" I say.

"You unleashed hell, Pierce. You could have helped us. Whatever is down there killed Rutger and half his men. The ones who managed to make it back to the surface were diseased. A plague beyond anything we could imagine. It's devastated Gibraltar and is moving through Spain." He pulls the white curtain back farther, revealing the entire scene: Helena tossing in a bed surrounded by three men and two women working feverishly.

I push the guards off me, and Kane holds a hand up to stop them from chasing me. I run to her, brush her hair back, and kiss her cheek, then her mouth. She's burning up. Feeling her boiling skin terrifies me, and she must see it. She reaches out and caresses my face. "It's okay, Patrick. It's only the flu. Spanish flu. It will pass."

I look up at the doctor. His eyes dart to the ground.

A tear wells in my eye and rolls slowly onto my cheek. Helena brushes it away. "I'm so glad you're safe. They told me you were killed in a mining accident, trying to save the Moroccans who worked for you." She holds my face in her hand. "So brave."

She jerks a hand to her mouth, trying to suppress the cough that shakes her whole body and the rolling hospital bed. She holds her swollen belly with the other hand, trying to keep herself from hitting the rails at the side of the bed. The cough continues for what feels like eternity. It sounds like her lungs are tearing apart.

I hold her shoulders down. "Helena..."

"I forgive you. For not telling me. I know you did it for me."

"Don't forgive me, please don't."

Another round of coughing racks her, and the doctors push me out of the way. They give her oxygen, but it doesn't seem to help.

I watch. And I cry. And Kane watches me. She kicks and fights—and when her body goes limp, I turn to Kane and my voice is flat, lifeless, almost like his voice that comes from the mask. Then and there, in that makeshift Immari hospital, I make a deal with the devil.

The tears rolled down Kate's face. She closed her eyes, and she wasn't in the bed with David in Tibet. She was back in San Francisco, on a cold night five years ago, on a gurney. They were rushing her out of the ambulance and into the hospital. Doctors and nurses shouted around her, and she was yelling at them, but they wouldn't listen to her. She grabbed the doctor's arm. "Save the baby, if it's between me and the baby, save—"

The doctor pulled away from her and shouted at the burly man pushing the gurney. "OR Two. Stat!"

They wheeled her faster, the mask was over her mouth, and she fought to stay awake.

She awoke to a large, empty hospital room. She hurt all over. There were several tubes running from her arm. She reached quickly for her stomach, but she knew before her hands made contact. She pulled the gown back to reveal the long ugly scar. She buried her head in her hands and cried, for how long she didn't know.

"Dr. Warner?"

Kate looked up, startled. Hopeful. A shy nurse stood before her. "My baby?" Kate said, her voice cracking.

The nurse's eyes drifted down, focusing on her feet.

Kate crumbled back in the bed. The tears came in waves now.

"Ma'am, we weren't sure, there's no in-case-of-emergency on file, should—is there anyone we should call? A… father?"

A flash of rage stemmed the tide of tears. The seven-month romance, the dinners, the charm. The internet entrepreneur who seemed to have it all, almost too good to be true. The apparently faulty birth control. His disappearing act. Her decision to keep the baby.

"No, there's no one to call."

David hugged her tight and brushed the tears from her eyes.

"I'm not usually emotional," Kate said, through the sobs. "It's just, I… when I was in…" A dam seemed to be breaking; feelings and thoughts she hadn't let into her mind rushed in.

She felt the words forming, ready to let it spill out—a story she was ready to reveal for the first time, to a man; something unimaginable a few days ago. She felt so safe with him. It was more. She *trusted* him.

"I know." He wiped a new wave of tears from her cheek. "The scar. It's okay." He took the journal from her hand. "That's enough reading for tonight. Let's get some rest." He pulled her down beside him, and they drifted off to sleep.

92

"Sir, we're pretty sure we've found them," the tech said.

"How sure?" Dorian asked.

"The two-man team on the ground, some locals told them a train came through this region." The tech used a laser pointer to circle an area of mountains and forests on the giant screen. "The tracks are supposed to be abandoned, so it couldn't have been cargo. And the drones spotted a monastery not far from there."

"How far out are the drones now?"

The tech punched some keys on the laptop. "A few hours—"

"How? Jesus, we were right on top of them!"

"I'm sorry, sir, they had to refuel. They can be in the air again within the hour. But—it's dark now. The sat image is from earlier. It will be—"

"Do the drones have infrared?"

The tech worked the keyboard. "No. What should—"

"Do *any* of the drones nearby have infrared?" Dorian snapped.

"Stand by." Images from the computer reflected in the technician's glasses. "Yes, a little farther out, but they can reach the target."

"Launch them."

Another tech ran into the command center. "We just got an eyes-only from the Antarctica operation. They've found an entrance."

Dorian leaned back in the chair. "Verified?"

"They're confirming now, but the depth and dimensions are right."

"Are the portable nukes ready?" Dorian asked.

"Yes. Dr. Chase reports they've been retrofitted to slide inside a backpack." The skinny man held up a sheaf of printed pages too thick to be stapled. "Chase actually sent a rather detailed report—"

"Shred it."

The man tucked the report back under his arm. "And Dr. Grey called. He wants to talk with you about precautions at the site."

"I'm sure. Tell him we'll talk when I get there. I'm leaving now." Dorian rose to leave the room.

"There's something else, sir. Infection rates are climbing in Southeast Asia, Australia, and America."

"Is anyone working on it yet?"

"No, we don't think so. They think it's just a new flu strain."

93

Immaru Monastery
Tibet Autonomous Region

Kate opened her sleepy eyes and studied the alcove. It wasn't night, but it wasn't quite morning. The first rays of sunrise peeked through the large window in the alcove, and she turned away from them, putting them off, ignoring the coming of morning. She nestled her head closer to David's and closed her eyes.

"I know you're awake," he said.

"No I'm not." She tucked her head down and lay very still.

He laughed. "You're talking to me."

"I'm talking in my sleep."

David sat up in the small bed. He looked at her for a long moment, then brushed the hair out of her face. She opened her eyes and looked into his eyes. She hoped he would lean closer and—

"Kate, you have to go."

She turned away from him, reeling. She dreaded the argument, but she wouldn't compromise. She wouldn't leave him. But before she could object, Milo appeared, as if out of thin air. He wore his usual cheerful expression, but below it, on his face and in his posture, were the unmistakable signs of exhaustion.

"Good morning, Dr. Kate, Mr. David. You must come with Milo."

David turned to him. "Give us a minute, Milo."

The youth stepped closer to them. "A minute we do not have, Mr. David. Qian says it is time."

"Time for what?" David asked.

Kate sat up.

"Time to go. Time for," Milo raised his eyebrows, "escape plan. Milo's project."

David cocked his head. "Escape plan?"

It was an alternative, or at the very least, a delay of Kate's ongoing argument with David, and she took the opening. She ran to the cupboard and gathered up bottles of antibiotics and pain pills. Milo held a small cloth sack at her side, and she dumped the bottles in it, along with the small journal. She stepped from the cupboard, but returned and grabbed some gauze, bandages, and tape, just in case. "Thank you, Milo."

Behind her, Kate heard David plant his feet on the ground and almost instantly collapse. Kate reached him just in time to break his fall. She dipped her hand into the bag, fished out a pain pill and an antibiotic, and stuffed them in his mouth before he could object. He dry-swallowed the pills as Kate practically dragged him out of the room and into the open-air wooden corridor.

The sun was coming up quickly now, and just beyond the boardwalk floor of the corridor, Kate saw parachutes looming over the mountain. No, they weren't parachutes—they were hot air balloons. There were three of them. She cocked her head and examined the first balloon. Its top was green and brown. A sort of camouflage scene. It was... trees, a forest. So curious.

The sound. The buzzing. It was close. David turned to her. "The drones." He pushed her out from under his arm where she had supported him. "Get to the balloon."

"David," Kate started.

"No. Do it." He took Milo by the arm. "My gun. The one I came here with, the first time. Do you have it?"

Milo nodded. "We have all your things—"

"Bring it, and hurry. I have to get to high ground. Meet me on the observation deck."

Kate thought he might turn to her one last time and... but he was gone, hobbling through the monastery, then struggling up a stone staircase set in the mountainside.

Kate glanced from the balloons to David, but he was already gone. The staircase was empty.

She hurried down the boardwalk, which ended at a spiral staircase made of wood. At the bottom of the stairs, the giant balloons came into view. There were five monks on the lower platform, waiting for her, waving to her.

At the sight of her, two of the monks jumped into the first balloon, released a rope, and pushed away from the platform. The balloon floated away from the mountain as the monks motioned to get her attention. They worked the cords and flame that controlled the balloon, showing her how to operate it. One of the men nodded to her, then pulled a rope that released one of the sacks at the side of the basket, and they rose quickly into the sky, drifting farther away from the mountain. It was beautiful, the serenity of the flight, the colors—red and yellow with patches of blue and green. It sailed out over the plateau, like a giant butterfly taking flight.

The other two monks were in the second butterfly balloon, ready to go, but they didn't cast off. They seemed to be waiting for her. The fifth monk motioned for her to get in the third balloon, the one with the forest scene on top. Kate realized that the bottom side was a cloud scene—blue and white. From below, at the right distance, a drone would see only sky above. If the drone was flying above the balloon, it would only see forest. It was very clever.

She climbed into the cloud-and-forest balloon. The second butterfly balloon cast off ahead of her, and the last monk left standing on the platform, pulled two ropes on her basket, releasing the bags and sending her balloon into the air. The balloon ascended silently, like a surreal dream. Kate turned, and across the plateau she saw dozens—no, hundreds—of balloons, in a panorama of color and beauty, all rising into the sky, the sunrise bathing them in light. Every monastery must have released balloons.

Kate's balloon was rising faster now, leaving the wooden launching platform and the monastery behind.

David.

Kate grabbed the cords that controlled the balloon just as an explosion rocked it. The side of the mountain seemed to disappear in the blink of an eye. The balloon shuddered. Wood and stone flew through the air. Smoke, fire, and ashes floated, filling the space between Kate and the monastery.

She couldn't see anything. But the balloon seemed okay; the drone's missile had hit the mountain below her and on the opposite side of the monastery. She fought at the controls. She was rising fast now. Too fast. Then another sound. A gunshot—from above.

94

The shot missed. The drone had fired one of its two missiles a second before David had pulled the trigger. The loss of weight had propelled the drone slightly faster, past the bullet from David's sniper rifle.

He chambered another round and tried to find the drone again. The smoke rose in thick plumes now. The monastery was almost consumed with flames, and the trees below it had caught fire as well. He stood with a grimace, but his legs responded. The pain pill was working. He had to get to a better vantage point. He turned and was shocked to find Milo sitting in the corner of the wooden observation deck, his legs crossed, his eyes closed. His breathing was shallow and rhythmic.

David grabbed him by the shoulder. "What're you doing?"

"Seeking the stillness within, Mr.—"

David pulled him up and threw him against the mountain. "Seek it at the top of the mountain." David pointed, and when Milo turned back, he spun the youth around and pushed him toward the mountain again. "Climb and keep climbing, Milo, no matter what. Go. I mean it."

Milo reluctantly dug a hand into a jagged opening in the mountain, and David watched for a second as he moved up the wall of rock.

David returned his focus to the observation deck. He walked to the edge of the deck and waited. Then it came—a break in the smoke. He knelt and peered through the scope, and without a single adjustment, he saw the drone—a different drone. This one still had a full complement of two rockets. How many were there? David didn't hesitate. He sucked a breath in and squeezed the trigger slowly. The drone exploded, and a tiny stream of smoke streaked the sky as the drone fell to the ground.

David searched the sky for the other drone, but he couldn't see it. He rose and hobbled across the wooden platform. Through the smoke, a colorful form rose, a scene of sky and trees, parting the black clouds. The balloon. Kate. His eyes met hers just as the mountain exploded below him. Half the platform disappeared in an instant, throwing him off balance. The gun fell from his hands and clanged loudly on the rocks. The monastery was coming down. The first drone had fired its last missile—a death blow.

The balloon had been rocked, but it was still there, five or ten feet below him. The last of the platform was collapsing quickly now.

David got to his feet, ran to the edge of the platform, and jumped. His torso hit the rim of the basket, almost knocking the wind out of him. He tried to grab the side, but his hands slipped off just before he felt Kate's fingers on his forearms, squeezing, holding him as tight as she could. He had stopped falling, but he swung listlessly. He reached for the rim, but the pain from the wound was too much.

He felt the heat below him, creeping up his legs and body, getting closer every second. He was dragging the balloon down into the carnage. Kate had to let go. From this height, it would be a quick death.

"Kate, I can't climb!" Even with the pain pill, the agony from the shoulder wound was overtaking him. "You've got to—"

"I'm not letting go," Kate yelled. She planted her feet into the side of the basket and pulled up in a burst of exertion. David gripped the rim of the basket and held it. She released him, and she was gone.

David waited, his arms tiring, the heat engulfing him. Below, he heard one, then another, and another sandbag fall to the ground. He felt the sweat in his palm coat his grip on the side of the basket. Just as he began to slip and fall into the burning monastery, Kate's hands grasped his forearms again, pulling him over the rim, into the basket with her.

She was drenched in sweat from the exertion, and he was dripping from the heat of the fire. His face was four inches from hers, and he stared into her eyes. He could feel her breath on his face. He pressed into her, moving closer to her mouth.

Just before his lips touched hers, she pushed up, rolling him onto his back.

David closed his eyes. "I'm sorry—"

"No, it's, I felt it. You're bleeding. Your bandages ripped." Kate pulled his shirt back and began working on the wound.

David panted and stared up at the clouds on the balloon. He hoped that somewhere below them, Milo was sitting at the top of the mountain, safe, and that someday, somewhere, he would find the stillness within.

PART III
THE TOMBS OF
ATLANTIS

95

After Kate had finished repairing David's bandages, she crawled to the other side of the balloon's basket and slumped against the wall. For a long time, they simply floated through the air, feeling the breeze on their faces, staring at the snow-capped mountains and green plateau below. Neither said a word. Kate's muscles burned from the exertion of pulling him into the basket.

David finally broke the silence. "Kate."

"I want to finish the journal." She drew the small leather-bound book out of the sack with the medical supplies. "Then we can make plans. Okay?"

David nodded, then leaned his head back against the basket and listened as Kate read the last few pages.

February 4th, 1919
One year after I awoke in the tube...

The world is dying. And we killed it.

I sit at the table with Kane and Craig, listening to the statistics like they were the odds for a horse race. The Spanish flu (that's what we've sold the world on, how we've labeled the pandemic) has moved to every country in the world. Only a few islands have been spared. It's killed countless millions so far. It kills the strong, sparing the weak, unlike any other flu epidemic.

Craig talks at length, using more words than the information deserves. The long and short is that no one has found a vaccine, and of course the Immari don't expect they will. But they think they can still sell it as the flu. That's the "good news," Craig announces.

And there's more of it. Overall the mood and assessment has turned optimistic: the human race will survive, but the losses will be intense. Two to five percent of the total human population, somewhere between thirty-six and ninety million people, are expected to die from the plague we unleashed. Around one billion will be infected. They estimate the current total human population at one point eight billion, so "not a bad shake," in Craig's words. Islands offer good protection, but the reality is that people are scared, and the whole world is holed up, avoiding anyone who might be infected. Estimates from the war are around ten million dead. The plague, or Spanish flu rather, will kill four to ten times more people than the war. Of course hiding it is a problem. The war and outbreak combined, roughly fifty to a hundred million people, gone.

But I only think of one. I wonder why she died and I lived. I am a shell. But I hold on for one reason.

Kane looks at me with cold, wicked eyes, and I stare back. He demands my report, and I speak slowly, in a lifeless, absent tone.

I report that we've excavated the area around the artifact. "Weapon," he corrects. I ignore him. I offer my opinion: once we disconnect it, we can move inside the structure. They ask questions, and I answer mechanically, like an automaton.

There's talk of the war ending, of the press focusing on the pandemic, but of course, there are plans for that.

There's talk of doctors in America studying the virus, talk that they might discover that it's something else. Craig placates, as always. He has the situation well in hand, he assures everyone. He claims that the virus seems to be winding itself down, like a forest fire that has almost run its course. With the pandemic waning, he believes research interest will follow.

The working theory is that this doomsday plague grows

weaker with retransmission. The people in the tunnels were killed instantly. The people who found them got sick and followed shortly after. Anyone infected at this point is likely five or six transmissions away from Gibraltar; hence, the climbing survival rates. There have been two subsequent waves of outbreak. We believe both were caused by early-infection bodies from Gibraltar or Spain reaching high-population areas.

I argue that we should go public, trace anyone who left Gibraltar. Kane disagrees. "Everyone dies, Pierce. Surely I don't have to remind you of that. Their deaths serve a purpose. We learn more every time a wave of infection occurs." We shout at each other until we're both hoarse. I can't even remember what I said. It doesn't matter. Kane controls the organization. And I can't afford to cross him.

Kate closed the journal and looked up. "They were loading bodies onto the trains in China."

David stared out the basket for a moment. "Let's get all the facts first. How many more entries?"

"Just one."

October 12, 1938

Almost twenty years have passed since my last entry. It's a long lapse, but don't think nothing has happened. Try to understand me.

I started this journal as a respite from the dark desperation of being a wounded man in a helpless place. A way to sort through my own despair, an avenue of reflection. Then it became a testament to what I believed to be some conspiracy. But when you watch the thing you love the most in the world die, a victim of something you unknowingly unleashed, the product of a deal you made for her hand, the sum of your whole life reduced to a burning coal in the palm of your hand... it's hard to pick up a pen and write about a life you think no longer matters.

And deeds you're ashamed of. That's what followed that day in that tent.

But things have gone far enough. Too far. This is the end of the road for me. I can't be a party to genocide, but I also can't stop it. I hope you can.

Since my last entry, the following has transpired:

The Device:
We call it the Bell, or for Kane and his German cronies, Die Glocke. Kane is convinced it's a super weapon and that it will either kill the entire human race or cause a rapture, leaving the genetically superior and killing anyone who might be a threat to this chosen race. He's become obsessed with his racial theories, the pursuit of this master race that can survive the coming apocalypse, the machine. Conveniently, he believes he's a member of this supreme race. The research efforts have focused on how to create this master race in a controlled fashion, before the supposed Atlantean attack. Since they extracted the Bell, I've been marginalized, but I still hear things. He has taken the Bell back to Germany to conduct experiments near Dachau. The situation is desperate in his Fatherland, with widespread famine and dangerously high unemployment. The government there is easy to manipulate. He's taken full advantage.

The Immaru:
I've learned more about the history of the Immari and their sister faction, the Immaru. At some point in antiquity, the Immari and the Immaru were one group, presumably as recently as the time of the Sumerians, the first written history we have. In Sumerian mythology, Immaru means "the light." Kane believes

the Immaru have known about the device and the fate of the human race for thousands of years, since before the flood. His theory is that the Immari, his people, were a group of Immaru rebels who believed man could be saved, but they couldn't convince their fellow members of this super race. According to Kane's history, his Immari ancestors forsook their own safety to journey out of the Aryan homeland into Europe, where they believed they would find the ruins of Atlantis that Plato wrote about—and with it, the keys to humanity's salvation.

When he announced this revisionist history, I asked him flatly why this wasn't revealed to the Immari earlier; after all, it seems like helpful historical facts. He lectured me condescendingly, something about "heavy is the head that wears the crown" and "knowing we alone stood between humanity and annihilation would have destroyed us. Our ancestors were wise. They spared us the weight of our actions, so that we could focus on finding the truth and acting to save the world."

It's hard to argue with a maniac who grows more important by the day.

Kane's Expeditions:
Kane has sent expeditions to every region of the Asian highlands: Tibet, Nepal, and northern India. He's convinced the Immaru are there, hiding, sitting on secrets that can deliver us from the coming end of days.

He insists that these Immaru will reside in a cold climate, a highland. He points out that the Nordic peoples of Europe have long dominated the continent because of their connection to the original Immaru bloodline, which flourishes in cold, icy environments. He brushed aside my mention of the advanced Roman and Greek civilizations, in their balmy southern European climate. "Artifacts of genetic gifts bestowed by the Immari as they journeyed to the north, seeking Atlantis and their natural, preferred habitat," he said. He insists that this "Atlantis Gene" which bestowed all humanity's gifts, a genetic heritage most concentrated in the Immari, must be connected to cold weather. From there, he's postulated that the rest of the Atlantean race must be out there somewhere, in the cold, hibernating, waiting to retake the planet.

As such, he's become obsessed with Antarctica. He's sent an expedition there as well, but no word has come yet. He plans to follow up personally, in a super-sub he's building at a shipyard in northern Germany. I've tried desperately to find out its location, hoping I could plant a bomb on it. But I've heard that the sub is nearing completion and that he will soon sail for the Far East to dispense with the Immaru once and for all, before turning south for Antarctica to find the Atlantean capital. It's quite a plan.

I had hoped his absence would provide an opening, that I could take control of Immari in his absence, but he's accounted for that as well. If I'm right, I'll soon be out of the picture, more or less permanently. So, I've made other plans.

I've convinced a soldier in the expedition to carry this journal to you, assuming Kane even finds the Immaru, and that the soldier keeps his promise. If he's caught with it, it's a death sentence for him (and me).

A Chamber of Curiosities:

There's one final thing I wish to tell you. I've found something. A chamber of some kind, deep inside the ruins at Gibraltar. I believe it holds the key to understanding the structure and possibly the Atlanteans. The technology here is advanced—dangerous in the wrong hands. I have gone to great lengths to keep it from Kane. I'm enclosing a map to the chamber, which I've been hiding behind a false wall. Hurry.

Kate unfolded the delicate yellow page with the map, studied it for a few moments, then handed it to David. "It was the same device—the Bell—in China. They used it on me, on hundreds of people. That's what they're doing, trying to find a genetic key that will impart immunity to the device. All my research, all the Immari research into genetics has been about this one end: finding the Atlantis Gene. All Martin's lies, my whole life... they used me."

David handed the map back and gazed out of the basket at the mountains and forest flowing by below. "Well I'm glad they did."

Kate focused on him.

David looked her in the eyes. "It could have been someone else. Someone who wasn't as strong. Or as smart. You can figure this out, and you can still stop them."

"I don't see—"

"Let's just go through what we know. Let's just lay all the pieces of the puzzle out there and see what fits together. Okay?" When Kate nodded, David continued. "Back at the monastery, I said I knew what the Bell was. It's an old World War II legend. Conspiracy theorists still talk about it—Die Glocke or the Bell. They say it was an advanced Nazi weapons project, or possibly a breakthrough energy source. The theories get wilder from there. Everything from anti-gravity to time travel. But if it caused the Spanish flu in 1918, and bodies from China got out—"

"It would be another pandemic, this one much worse than Spanish flu."

"I mean, is that possible?" David said. "Are the Immari statistics even right? How could we not have a vaccine for something that killed two to five percent of the population?"

"We studied Spanish flu in medical school, or the 1918 flu pandemic, as it's now known. Their stats are right or close. We think Spanish flu killed between fifty to one hundred million— so about four percent of the total global population—"

"That would be like... two hundred eighty million dying today—the entire population of the United States. Surely they have a vaccine. And how could the Immari hide this—or sell it as the flu?"

"At first, doctors didn't think it was the flu. It was initially misdiagnosed as dengue, cholera, or typhoid—mostly because the symptoms were very... distinctly un-flu-like. Patients had hemorrhages from mucous membranes, especially from the nose, stomach, and intestines, even bleeding from the skin and ears." Kate thought back to the dark room with the Bell hanging over the cowering crowd, of the bleeding bodies. She had to focus. "Anyway, of all the flu strains in the world, it's still the least understood—and the most deadly. There is no vaccine. Spanish flu essentially caused the body to self-destruct; it killed through a cytokine storm—the body's own immune system ravaged it. Most flu strains are devastating for people with weak immune systems—children and the elderly. That's why we vaccinate: to boost the immune system. Spanish flu was fundamentally different. It killed people with *strong* immune systems. The stronger the person's immune system was, the worse the cytokine storm was. It was deadly for people aged twenty-five to thirty-four."

"It's almost like it killed anyone who could be a threat. No wonder the Immari think it's a weapon," David said. "But why unleash it? The world wouldn't stand a chance. In 1918, at the end of World War I, borders were sealed everywhere, the whole world had ground to a halt. Think about how connected we are today; a similar outbreak would wipe us out in days. If what you say is true, the contagion has already left China and is scouring the world as we speak. Why would they do it?"

"Maybe they don't have a choice."

"There's always a cho—"

"In their minds," Kate said. "Just based on the thinking in the journal, I have a couple of theories. I think they've been looking for the Atlantis Gene so that they can survive the device. That's why they were interested in my research, why they kidnapped the kids. They must be out of time."

"The satellite photo—with the codes on the back. It had a sub in the middle."

"Kane's sub," Kate said.

"I bet so. And there was a structure below it. We know they've been looking for the sub since 1947—the obituary in the *New York Times* decoded to 'Antarctica, U-boat not found, advise if further search authorized.' So they finally found the sub, and under it, another Atlantis—a threat." David shook his head. "But I still don't get it, the science—why unleash another pandemic?"

"I think the bodies from the Bell *are* Toba Protocol. It seems that direct contact with the Bell is the most deadly, but there's only one Bell, or was only one. Maybe they're going to distribute the bodies around the world. The subsequent outbreak would reduce the world's population drastically, to only those that could survive the Bell, to anyone with the Atlantis Gene."

"Yes, but why—aren't there better ways? Couldn't they, I don't know, sequence a bunch of genomes or steal some data and find these people?"

"No, or maybe. You could probably identify people with the Atlantis Gene, but there's a missing piece: epigenetics and gene activation."

"Epi—"

"It's sort of complicated, but the bottom line is that it's not just what genes you have, it's what genes get activated, as well as how those genes interact with each other. The plague conceivably would cause a second Great Leap Forward by activating the Atlantis Gene in anyone who has it. Or maybe it's something else entirely, maybe the plague will reduce the population and force us to mutate or evolve, just like the Toba catastrophe did…" Kate rubbed her temples. There was something else, some other piece, just out of reach. The conversation with Qian flashed through her mind: the tapestry, the flood of fire, the dying band of humans cowering under the blanket of ashes… the savior… offering a cup with his blood, and the beasts of the forest emerging as modern humans. "I think we're missing something."

"You think—"

"What if the first Great Leap Forward wasn't a natural

occurrence? What if it wasn't evolution at all? What if humanity was on the brink of extinction and the Atlanteans came to our rescue? What if the Atlanteans gave that dying band of humans something that would help them survive Toba? A gene, a genetic advantage that made them smart enough to survive. A change in brain wiring. What if they gave us the Atlantis Gene?"

96

David looked around as if deciding what to say. Finally he opened his mouth to speak, but Kate held up her hand.

"I know it sounds crazy, okay, but just hear me out, let me talk through this. It's not like we're going anywhere for a while." She motioned to the basket and the balloon above it.

"Fair enough, but I'm warning you, I'm out of my element here. I'm not sure how much help I can be."

"Just tell me when it starts sounding too crazy."

"Is that retroactive? Because what you just said—"

"Okay, actually, you just listen for a while, then call me out on any craziness. Here are the facts: around seventy thousand years ago, the Mount Toba supervolcano erupts. There's a global volcanic winter that lasts six to ten years, and possibly a one-thousand-year-long cooling episode. Ash blankets southern Asia and Africa. The total human population plummets to somewhere around three thousand to ten thousand, maybe even as low as one thousand viable mating pairs."

"All right, that's true, I can confirm its non-craziness."

"Because I told you about the Toba catastrophe in Jakarta."

David held up his hands. "Hey, just trying to be helpful here."

Kate remembered her own reaction and her words to David in the van days ago, what felt like a lifetime ago. "Very funny. Anyway, the reduction in population caused a genetic bottleneck around that time. We know that every human on the planet is descended from an extremely small population, between one thousand to ten thousand breeding pairs that existed about seventy thousand years ago. Every human outside of Africa is descended from a small tribe that left around fifty thousand years ago with as few as one hundred people. In fact, every human alive today is directly descended from a man who lived in Africa sixty thousand years ago."

"Adam?"

"Actually we call him Y-chromosomal Adam, since we're scientists. There's an Eve too—Mitochondrial Eve—but she lived much earlier, we think about one hundred ninety thousand to two hundred thousand years ago."

"Time travelers? Am I still calling out the crazy—"

"Not time travelers, thank you very much. They're just genetic designations of the people everyone on earth is directly descended from. It's complicated, but the bottom line is that this Adam had a huge advantage—his offspring were far more advanced than any of their peers."

"They had the Atlantis Gene."

"For now, we'll stick to the facts. They had *some* kind of advantage, whatever it was. By around fifty thousand years ago, the human race is beginning to behave differently. There's an explosion in complex behavior: language, tool-making, wall art. It's the greatest advancement in human history—what we call the Great Leap Forward. In looking at the fossils of humans before and after, there's not a ton of difference. There's also not much difference in their genomes. About all we know is that it was a subtle genetic change that caused a difference in the way we thought, possibly a change in our brain wiring."

"The Atlantis Gene."

"Whatever it was, this change in brain wiring, it was the greatest genetic jackpot in the history of time. The human race goes from the brink of extinction—less than ten thousand people, hunting and gathering in the wilderness—to ruling the planet, with over seven billion people, in the span of just fifty thousand years. That's the blink of an eye in evolutionary terms. It's an extraordinary comeback, almost hard to believe for a geneticist. I mean, twelve percent of all the humans who have *ever lived* are *still alive* today. We only evolved around two hundred thousand years ago. We're still riding a mushroom cloud of the effects of the Great Leap Forward, and we have no idea how it happened or where it will lead."

"Yeah, but why us, why did we get so lucky? There were other human species around, right? The Neanderthals, the—I can't remember what you called them; what about them? If the Atlanteans came to our rescue, why not help the others?"

"I have a theory. We know there were at least four subspecies of humans fifty thousand years ago: us or anatomically modern humans, Neanderthals, Denisovans, and Homo floresiensis or Hobbits. There were probably more that we haven't found, but those are the four subspecies—"

"Subspecies?" David said.

"Yes. Technically they're subspecies; they were all humans. We define a species as a group of organisms capable of inter-breeding and producing fertile offspring, and all four of those human groups could interbreed. In fact, we have genetic evidence that they did. When we sequenced the Neanderthal genome a few years ago, we discovered that everyone outside of Africa has somewhere between one to four percent Neanderthal DNA. It was most pronounced in Europe—the Neanderthal homeland. We found the same thing when we sequenced the Denisovan genome. Some people in Melanesia, and especially Papua New Guinea, share up to six percent of their genome with the Denisovans."

"Interesting. So we're all hybrids?"

"Yes, technically."

"So we absorbed the other subspecies into a combined human race?"

"No. Well, a small percentage maybe, but the archaeological evidence suggests the four groups survived as separate subspecies. I think the other subspecies didn't receive the Atlantis Gene because they didn't need it."

"They—"

"Weren't on the brink of extinction," Kate said. "We think Neanderthals existed in Europe as early as six hundred thousand to three hundred fifty thousand years ago. All the other subspecies are also older than we are; they probably had larger populations. And they were out of the blast radius of Toba: the Neanderthals were in Europe, the Denisovans were in present-day Russia, and the Hobbits were in Southeast Asia—farther away from Toba and downwind."

"So they fared better than we did, and we almost die out. Then *we* hit the genetic jackpot, and *they* actually go extinct—at our hands."

"Yes. And they died out quickly. We know Neanderthals were stronger than us, had bigger brains than us, and had lived in Europe for hundreds of thousands of years before we showed up. Then, within ten to twenty thousand years, they're extinct."

"Maybe that's part of the Immari grand plan," David said. "Maybe Toba Protocol is about more than finding the Atlantis Gene. What if the Immari think these advanced humans, these Atlanteans, are hibernating, but if they do come back, they'll eliminate any competing humans, anyone who might be a threat—just as we did in the last fifty thousand years after we received this Atlantis Gene? You read Kane's speech: they thought a war with the Atlanteans was imminent."

Kate considered David's theory, and her mind drifted to her conversation with Martin. His allegations that any advanced race would wipe out any threatening inferior humans; his theory that the human race was like a computer algorithm advancing to one eventuality: a homogeneous human race. That was the last piece of the puzzle. "You're right. Toba is about more than finding the Atlantis Gene. It's about *creating* Atlanteans, transforming the human race by advancing it. They're trying to synchronize humanity with the Atlanteans—to create one race, so that if the Atlanteans do return, they won't see us as a threat. Martin said Toba Protocol was 'a contingency.' They think if the Atlanteans wake up and see seven billion savages, they'll slaughter us. But if they emerge and find a small group of humans, very similar genetically to themselves, they'll allow them to survive—they'll see them as part of their own tribe or race."

"Yes, but I think that's only half the plan," David said. "That's the scientific basis, the genetic angle, the backup plan. The Immari think they're at war. They think like soldiers. I said before that I thought they were creating an army, and I still do. I think they were testing the subjects on the Bell for a specific reason."

"So they could survive it."

"Survive it, yes, but more specifically: to be able to pass under it. In Gibraltar, they had to excavate around it and remove it. I think there could be a Bell at every Atlantis structure—a sort of sentry device that keeps anyone out; but it malfunctioned on us because we're actually human-Atlantean hybrids. If the Immari found a way to activate the Atlantis Gene, they could send an army in and kill the Atlanteans. Toba Protocol would be the ultimate contingency—if they were unsuccessful, the Atlanteans wake up and all that's left are members of their own race."

Kate nodded. "They would be massacring the same people who saved us from extinction, maybe the only people that could help us reverse the plague from the Bell."

Kate sighed. "But it's theory and speculation. We could be wrong."

"Let's stick to what we know. We know bodies were taken from China, and that bodies from the Bell caused a pandemic before."

"We alert health agencies?"

David shook his head. "You read the journal, they know how to hide outbreaks. And they're probably a lot better at it now—they've been preparing for Toba Protocol for a very long time. We need to find out if your theories are correct, and we need some advantage—a way to contact the Atlanteans or stop the Immari."

"Gibraltar."

"It's our best option. The chamber Patrick Pierce found."

Kate glanced at the balloon. They were losing altitude, and they had only a few sandbags left to jettison. "I don't think we'll get that far."

David smiled and looked around the basket, as if searching for something they could use. There was a bundle in the corner. "Did you bring this?"

Kate noticed it for the first time. "No."

David slid over to it and unwrapped it. Inside the layers of rough woven cloth, he found Indian rupees, a change of clothes for each of them, and a paper foldout map of northern India, which they were no doubt flying over now. David unfolded the map, and a small note fell out. He set the map aside, read the note, and handed it to Kate.

> Forgive us our inaction.
> War is not in our nature.
> – Qian.

Kate set the note down and studied the balloon. "I don't think we have much longer up here."

"Agree. I have an idea. It's risky though."

97

1.5 Miles outside Drill Site #6
East Antarctica

Robert Hunt had to drive more slowly; the giant umbrella had almost pulled him off the snowmobile twice. He had finally found a comfortable speed where he could hold on, but even at that speed, the noise of the machine, combined with the umbrella's flapping, was almost deafening. Through the din he heard an unusual noise. He looked back. Had the men followed him? He stopped the snowmobile. It wasn't an engine. It was a voice.

He tore his jacket open and searched for the radio. The signal indicator was lit—they were calling him. He killed the machine, but the signal was gone. He waited. Far in the distance, a wind gust blew snow dust off the top of a rounded peak.

He pressed the radio button and said, "This is Snow King."

He took a deep breath. The abrupt response and the operator's sharp tone startled him. "Snow King—why were you radio silent?"

Robert thought, then pressed the button on the radio and spoke as evenly as he could manage. "We are in transit. The radios are hard to hear."

"Transit? What's your location?"

Robert swallowed. They'd never asked for his location or contacted him between sites before. What could he say... Could they see him from the air?

"Snow King! Do you copy?"

He fidgeted in the seat, then lifted the radio back to his face. "Bounty, this is Snow King. Estimate we are three klicks from location seven." He released the button and lowered it to the snowmobile again. He inhaled. "We have encountered... We have problems with one of the snowmobiles. We are repairing."

"Stand by, Snow King."

The seconds ticked by. It was freezing, but all he could feel was his heart beating in his throat.

"Snow King. Do you require assistance?"

He answered instantly. "Negative, Bounty. We can handle it." He waited for a second and added, "Should we alter our destination?"

"Negative, Snow King. Carry on at best speed and observe standing local blackout protocol."

"Copy that, Bounty."

He dropped the radio to the seat. In that moment, it had felt as heavy as an anvil. His adrenaline slowly receded, and as it did, he realized his right arm was aching. Holding the umbrella had taken its toll. He could barely make a fist, and his shoulder throbbed with every micron he moved. He gritted his teeth and shifted the umbrella to the other side of the snowmobile.

Through his cold and pain, his mind screamed: *Go back now*. He considered why they would have called. There were only two possibilities: A, they were on to him, or B, they wanted to make sure he was clear of the site. If they were on to him, his goose was cooked anyway. If they were doing something at the site they didn't want him to see, that put him in a tough spot.

When he had set out, he had told himself that if they caught him, he'd simply say he left something at the drill site. Nothing wrong with that. The umbrella? *Just observing local blackout protocol*.

But the radio conversation had blown that cover story. If they caught him now, he'd be out of a job at best, and if they were criminals engaged in something illegal... things would get a lot worse for him.

So he made a compromise with himself: he would drive to the top of the closest dune, see what he could see, then head back.

He had tried.

Robert had to drive slowly now. He held the umbrella with his left elbow and braced it against his torso. It took him almost an hour to reach the peak of the dune. He took his binoculars out and scanned the distant horizon for the site.

He couldn't believe his eyes.

The machines towering over the site were on a scale he'd never seen—and he had seen some massive machines. They dwarfed the site, which now looked like a tornado had hit it. The drilling platform lay half-buried in snow, like an overturned microscope lying in a child's sandbox next to construction toys. But this was no sandbox, and the snow tracks on these "toys" must have been at least fifty feet tall. The main vehicle looked like a centipede. It was long, maybe four or five hundred feet, and had a small head, no doubt the "cab" that pulled it. Its body was a series of white, balloon-shaped segments. It curved around the site in a semicircle.

Beside the centipede, a white crane truck, about ten times the size of your standard industrial construction crane, held its crane arm high in the air. Was it pulling something out? Or more likely, lowering something.

Robert zoomed in. Before he could focus on the crane's cable, he caught a glimpse of something, or an outline of something, in front of the centipede. He panned left, but at such high zoom, he lost the site completely. He zoomed out, reacquired the site, and zoomed in again, focusing on the middle of the centipede.

Were they people or robots? Whatever they were, they were wearing what looked like white hazmat suits, except these suits were more bulky. They moved in a labored, slow fashion. They looked almost like the Stay Puft Marshmallow Man from Ghostbusters or the Michelin Man. The height was right for people. Robert followed one with the binoculars as the white figure waddled to the drill site. The crane was rotating toward the centipede. It had pulled something from the hole. Another marshmallow man came into view and helped the other man

393

unhook and lower the crane's bounty to the ground. It looked like a disco ball, but it was black. Behind the men, on the last section of the white centipede, a door opened. It slid from bottom to top, revealing yellow light inside and a bank of computer screens. There was also a large white box, which two suited men inside pushed down a ramp. On the ground, the other two men joined them and began taking the white panels off the side. They came away easily; they must have been flex or some sort of cloth.

Robert focused the binoculars. The box was a cage. It held two monkeys, maybe chimps; they were small enough. They hopped around and clung to each other, avoiding the bars. They must be freezing to death. One of the men quickly dropped to his knees and began punching at what must have been a control panel on the bottom of the cage. At the top of the cage, what had been a faint orange glow became a red ember, and the monkeys settled down a bit.

Another man waved an arm at the crane, and it swung over. They attached it to the top of the cage, then attached the black ball.

The men stood aside as the crane lifted the cage, swung it over to the hole, and lowered it. Two men walked behind the crane and emerged driving crab-like machines. They drove to the drill hole and connected the machines. Joined, the two machines covered the entire hole except for a small slot large enough for the cable to pass through.

All four men hurried into the centipede, and the door slid closed behind them.

Nothing happened for several minutes. Robert's arm began to tire, and he wondered how much longer he should wait. There was no question now—they weren't drilling for oil. But what were they doing? And why did they need marshmallow suits to do it? Why didn't he need one—or the monkeys for that matter?

He might get an answer soon. The marshies were bounding out of the centipede, making for the hole. They backed the cover machines off, and the cage seemed to explode out of the hole. It bounced a few times as the cable snapped back and forth.

Finally it settled to hover a few feet off the ground, the men stabilized it, and jerked the door open.

The monkeys were covered in white or gray... snow, maybe? Both lay lifeless in the cage. When the men pulled them out, the white stuck to them—it wasn't snow. They threw each monkey into a separate white body bag and raced them through the entrance of the second centipede section. As the door opened, Robert got a glimpse of two children, sitting on a bench inside a glass cage, waiting, as if they were next.

98

"Wait here. If I don't come out in fifteen minutes, find a police officer, and tell him a robbery is in progress inside the store," David said.

Kate scanned the street and the exterior of the store: Timepiece Trading Company. The street was busy, filled with older cars and Indians zooming by on bikes. David had told her that the store was one of a series of Clocktower's covert outposts, a sort of back-door communication channel where local sources and agents could send messages to Central. His theory was that it may have been activated if Clocktower was still operational. That was a big *if*. If Clocktower had fallen—fully—then the Immari would be watching, or more likely manning, these outposts, waiting to clean up any rogue agents and loose ends.

Kate nodded, and David was in the street, limping toward the store; in the blink of an eye, he was inside. Kate bit her lip and waited.

The store was crowded. All the clocks seemed to be in glass cases, or at least the ones that weren't standing on the ground. Every item looked so fragile, so intricately made, so breakable. David felt like the proverbial bull in a china shop as he tried to squeeze between two standing glass cases, forcing his wounded leg to cooperate.

It was dark inside the store and bright outside; he could barely see a thing. He brushed against a case full of antique pocket watches, the kind men with monocles and a shiny vest might wear. The case shook, and the timepieces jingled as their edges touched and tiny pieces rattled. David grabbed the case, trying to steady it as he balanced on his good leg. He felt as if one false move could bring the whole place down.

A voice rang out from deep inside the store. "Welcome, sir. How may I be of service today?"

David searched the room once, then again, finally finding the man behind a tall desk toward the rear of the store. He limped over to him while trying to avoid the standing glass mines. "I'm looking for a special piece."

"You've come to the right place, sir. What sort of piece?"

"A Clocktower."

The clerk studied him. "An unusual request. But you're in luck. We've located several Clocktowers for customers over the years. May I know more about what you're looking for? Age, shape, size? Any information is helpful."

David tried to remember the exact words. He never thought he'd have to use them. "A piece that tells more than time. Forged from steel that can't be broken."

"I may know of such a piece. I'll need to make a phone call." His voice changed. "Stay here," he said in a flat tone. Before David could answer, the man disappeared behind a cloth that hung over a doorway.

David strained to see and hear, but nothing emanated from beyond the cloth. He glanced at the clock on the wall. He had been inside for almost ten minutes. Would Kate keep her promise?

The clerk returned. He wore a blank, unreadable expression. "The seller would like to speak with you." He waited.

What David wouldn't have given for a gun at that moment. He simply nodded and stepped behind the desk. The clerk pulled the cloth back and pushed David into the darkness. He could sense the clerk reaching over his back, toward his head, but before David could turn, the clerk's arm was coming down toward his chest, fast.

99

David turned just as the clerk's hand came down.

Light flashed all around him. Above, a single light bulb swayed back and forth. The clerk held the string cord in his hand. "The phone is just there," he said, motioning toward a table in the corner. The phone receiver was made of molded thick plastic, like the ones in phone booths in the eighties. The type that could bludgeon someone to death. The phone was just as old. A rotary dial.

David walked to the table and picked up the handset. He pivoted his body to face the clerk. The man had taken a step toward him.

The line sounded dead. "Central?" David said.

"Identify," a voice said.

"Vale, David Patrick."

"Station?"

"Jakarta," David said. He couldn't quite remember, but he knew it didn't go this way.

"Stand by." The line went dead again. "Access code?"

Access code? There was no access code. This wasn't a Boy Scout's secret hideout. They should have voice-print identified him the second he'd said his name. Unless they were playing for time. Surrounding the building. David tried to get a read on the clerk as he held the phone. How long had he been inside? Almost fifteen minutes by now?

"I... don't have an access code..."

"Hold the line." The voice returned. More nervous? "Given name?"

David considered the request. What did he have to lose? "Reed. Andrew Michael."

The response was quick. "Hold for the director."

Two seconds passed, and then Howard Keegan's grandfatherly voice was on the line. "David, my God, we've been looking everywhere for you. Are you all right? What's your status?"

"Is the line secure?"

"No. But frankly my boy, we've got bigger problems at the moment."

"Clocktower?"

"Fallen. But not broken. I'm organizing a counterstrike. There's another problem. A plague is sweeping the globe. We're racing the clock here."

"I think I have a piece of the puzzle."

"What is it?"

"I'm not sure yet. I need transport."

"Destination?"

"Gibraltar."

"Gibraltar?" Keegan sounded confused.

"Is that a problem?"

"No. It's the best news I've heard. I'm actually in Gibraltar now—the last of the agents and I are planning a counterstrike on the Immari headquarters here. The clerk can arrange transport for you, but before you go, there's... something else I need to tell you, David. Something I want you to know, just in case you don't make it here or... if I'm not here when you arrive. You weren't the only one investigating Immari. Unraveling their conspiracy has been my life's work, but when I ran out of time... I knew you were my best shot at stopping them. I was your source. I used all my contacts within Immari to help you, but it wasn't enough. The tactical mistakes are mine alone—"

"And are in the past. We have new information, possibly something we can use. This is not over. I'll see you in Gibraltar."

100

Dorian had to hand it to Martin Grey: the man was technically competent. The research site in Antarctica was breathtaking. For the last thirty minutes, Martin had walked Dorian through each section of the giant centipede-esque mobile laboratory: the primate lab, with its two dead carcasses, the drill control center, the staff barracks, the conference rooms, and the main control center, where they sat now.

"We're out in the open here, Dorian. We should take precautions. There are several research stations here in Antarctica. Any one of them could stumble across us—"

"And do what?" Dorian said. "Who are they going to call?"

"The nations that fund them, for one—"

"Those nations will soon be consumed with the outbreak. Unauthorized research on some ice cube at the end of the world won't be on their radar, trust me. Let's stop wasting time and get down to business. Tell me what you found at the sub site."

"About what we expected."

"Him?"

"No. General Kane," Martin seemed to wince as he said the word, "wasn't among the bodies we iden—"

"Then he's inside." Dorian's hope betrayed his usually stoic exterior.

"Not necessarily. There are other possibilities."

"Doubtful—"

Martin pressed on. "He could have been killed during the

raid in Tibet. Or en route. It was a long journey. Or—"

"He's inside. I know it."

"If so, it raises several questions. Specifically, why he hasn't exited. And why we haven't heard from him. And there's the reality of the timeline. Kane left for Antarctica in 1938. Seventy-five years ago. If he *is* inside, he would be over one hundred and twenty years old. Long dead."

"Maybe he did try to communicate with us. Roswell. A warning."

Martin thought it over. "Interesting. Even so, your obsession with Kane, with finding him, puts us all in danger. You need a clear head if you're to lead this operation—"

"My head is clear, Martin." Dorian stood. "I admit I'm obsessed with finding Konrad Kane, but you would be too if your father had gone missing."

Robert Hunt left the snowmobile running. He dismounted and walked under the small rock overhang where he'd left the two men. They were gone. But one snowmobile was there. Had they gone on to the next site? Reported him? Had they followed him, backtracking to the last site? That would be as good as reporting him.

He ran out, into the open field of ice, withdrew his binoculars, and scanned the distance in every direction.

Nothing.

He walked back to the cave. It was cold inside. Deathly cold. He tried to turn the stranded snowmobile on, but it was out of gas. How? Had they followed him and barely made it back? No—the tracks were old. They had run it here in the cave. Why? To keep warm? Yes, probably. They had waited as long as they could, until it sputtered out and the warmth receded. Then they had climbed on the last snowmobile and left together. But where had they gone?

101

"I beg you not to do this, Dorian." Martin stepped in front of the door and spread his arms.

"Be reasonable, Martin. You know the time has come."

"We don't know that—"

"What we do know is that a huge chunk of their city has broken off. And that one of their Bells was activated almost seventy-five years ago—we have the bodies from the sub as proof. You want to take the risk? We both know they'll come out of hibernation soon, if they haven't already. We don't have time to research and debate. If they march out of there, the human race is finished."

"You assume—"

"I know it. You know it. We've seen what the Bell can do. And that's just the porch light over the stoop—the doorway to the type of city we won't be capable of building for thousands of years, assuming we're even capable of inventing technology on their scale. Imagine what weapons they have in there. The Bell is simply a bug-zapper to keep the beasts from disturbing their rest. They don't want anyone inside there for a reason. I'm ensuring our survival. This is the only way."

"An act of this magnitude, based upon so much conjecture—"

"Great leaders are forged from the fire of hard decisions," Dorian said. "Now stand aside."

Inside the cell, Dorian knelt down to look the two Indonesian children in the face. They sat on a white bench, just outside the primate lab. Their feet dangled a few inches above the ground.

"I bet you two are glad to be out of those suits, aren't you?"

The boys just stared at him.

"My name is Dorian Sloane. What are your names?"

The boys' eyes were a blank stare that drifted slowly from Dorian to the floor.

"That's okay, we don't need names to play this game. The name game is boring anyway. We're going to play a better game, a very fun game. Have you ever played hide-and-seek? It was my favorite game as a child. I was very good at it." He turned to his assistant. "Get the packs from Dr. Chase."

Dorian fixed the boys with a stare. "We're going to put you inside a maze, a giant maze. Your job is to find a certain room." Dorian held out a picture. "You see this? This is a room with a lot of glass tubes in it. Tubes big enough to hold a man! Can you believe it? If you can find this room and hide in it, you're going to win the prize." Dorian laid the glossy printout on their laps. It was a computer rendering—an extrapolation of what the Immari thought a large tube room might look like.

The boys each studied it. "What prize?" one of them asked.

Dorian spread his hands. "That would be my question too. My, you're clever, so very clever." Dorian looked around. What prize, indeed. He hadn't thought they would ask. He hated kids. Almost as much as their questions. "We actually have several prizes. What... what prize would you like?"

The other boy put the printout on the bench. "Kate."

"You want to see Kate?" Dorian said.

Both boys nodded, matching the rhythmic motion of their dangling legs.

"Well, I tell you what. If you find that room, and hide there, and wait, Kate will come and find you." Dorian nodded when the boys' eyes got bigger. "That's right. I know Kate. We're old friends, actually." Dorian smiled to himself, for the inside joke, but the grin had the desired effect. The boys bounced subtly on the bench, excited.

A lab assistant entered with the packs. "Here they are, sir." He helped Dorian put the packs on the children. "The snap activates the warheads. We've tried our best to make them tamper-resistant. If the snaps are disconnected, the warheads will detonate. As you requested, once they're activated, there's no manual or remote deactivation. We set the countdown for four hours."

"Excellent work." Dorian snapped the chest straps tight. He held the boys by the shoulders. "Now this is a very important part of the game. You can't take these packs off. If you do, the game is over. No prize. No Kate. I know they're kind of heavy. You can stop to rest if you need to, but remember, if you take them off: no Kate. And there's one last thing." Dorian pulled out an envelope and pinned it to the taller boy's chest. It had large script letters that read "Papa."

Dorian put a few more pins in the envelope, ensuring it wouldn't move. "If you see a man inside, an older man in a military uniform, you win the game—if you give him this envelope. So if you see him, you run to him and tell him that Dieter sent you. Can you remember that?"

The boys nodded.

Fifteen minutes later, Dorian watched from the command center as the two boys waddled toward the Bell almost two miles below the lab.

The deadly device didn't so much as flicker. Ahead of them, a giant portal door opened in layers. Like a reptile's eyelid, Dorian thought.

He watched the monitors, which showed the camera feeds from the boys' suits. Each video panned upward as the boys looked up at the Bell several hundred yards above them, hanging there in the massive dome of ice.

Dorian clicked a button. "It's not going to hurt you. Just go on in. Remember the room with the tubes." He released the button and turned to the tech in the command center. "Can you put the computer image of the tubes on their suit display?

Good." He activated the link to the boys' suits again. "There it is. Go in and find the tubes."

Dorian sat back in the chair and watched the boys walk through the portal doors. Their camera feeds turned to static as the portal doors closed. On the other screens in the control room, Dorian could see the outside chamber and the Bell. The domed entryway was still. And dead quiet.

On the wall of screens, a digital readout ticked off the seconds of the countdown: 03:23:57, 03:23:56, 03:23:55.

102

White House Press Briefing regarding the "Flash Flu" Outbreak

Adam Rice (WH Press Secretary): Good morning everyone. I'm going to read a brief statement, then I'll take a few questions. "The President and his administration are taking steps to assess and address the health concern the media is referring to as the 'Flash Flu.' Earlier today, the president ordered the CDC to dedicate all available resources to assessing the threat. Pending the results of that assessment, the White House may take further actions to ensure every American's safety."

[Rice sets the statement down and points at the first reporter.]

Reporter: Has the President set a timetable for closing the borders?

[Rice exhales and looks off-camera.]

Rice: The President has said repeatedly that closing the borders is a last resort. We know what the impact would be on American businesses, both large and small. Look, we understand there's a public health issue here. But there's also an economic risk. Closing the borders poses a very real risk to the American economy. The flu may affect many Americans, but closing the borders would definitely cause an immediate recession that would endanger more Americans than a flu outbreak. We're taking a balanced approach here. The President is not going to put anyone at risk—whether it's at the hands of the flu or a trade recession.

Reporter: What's your official response to the reports from Asia, the Middle East, and Europe?

Rice: We're taking them seriously, but we're also conducting a careful, balanced review of the information. We're still working with incomplete information and, frankly, we don't think all of it is reliable.

Reporter: Are you referring to the eyewitness reports, the videos—

[Rice holds a hand up.]

Rice: As for the videos on the Internet, it's one of those things where you're going to see the worst. No one makes a YouTube video about themselves sitting at home, healthy as can be, eating cereal or doing aerobics. They make these videos when there's something sensational. We've all seen them at this point, and there are going to be more of them. If you live your life based on what you see on YouTube, you're going to make some pretty poor decisions, and that's what we're trying to avoid here. It's not even clear if these videos are real, and if they are, they could be related to any number of acute health issues.

[Rice holds both arms up.]

Rice: Okay, that's it for today, thank you all.

103

The sunset over the Bay of Gibraltar was breathtaking. Soft shades of red, orange, and pink met the deep blue water of the Atlantic in the distance. About a hundred yards away, the harbor ended and the rock rose out of the sea and land. Its gray and black clashed with the burning rays of sunlight sliding down its side.

Kate pulled the glass door back and walked out onto the tile-covered porch four stories above the streets of the harbor. Below her, armed guards patrolled the large house. A warm Mediterranean breeze engulfed her, and Kate leaned against the rail.

Behind her, she heard a wave of laughter erupt around the table. David's eyes met hers. He looked so happy there, sitting among the dozen other Clocktower Station chiefs and agents— the survivors of the fall of Clocktower. Now, "The Resistance." From out here, if she didn't know any better, she'd think it was just a reunion of old college friends, kidding, sharing stories, and planning tomorrow's escapades for tailgating and a big football game. But she knew they were making plans for the assault on Immari Gibraltar's headquarters. The conversation had veered into technical discussions of tactics, debates about the building's layout, and questions about whether the schematics and other intel they had were reliable. Kate had drifted out onto the porch, like a new girlfriend who clearly wasn't part of the core group.

On the plane ride from India, she and David had talked openly, for the first time without any guards or hesitation. She told him about losing her child; how she met a man who disappeared into thin air at almost the moment she'd gotten pregnant. She left San Francisco for Jakarta a week after the miscarriage, and she had thrown herself into her work and autism research in the years that followed.

David had been just as forthcoming. He had told Kate about his fiancée dying in the 9/11 attacks and how he was badly injured, almost paralyzed; then about his recovery and his decision to dedicate himself to finding the people responsible. A week ago, Kate would have brushed off his assertions about the Immari and a global conspiracy, but on the plane, she had just nodded. She didn't know how the pieces fit together, but she believed him.

They had slept after they talked, as if the release had brought the respite. But for Kate, it was a sporadic, restless slumber, mostly because of the plane's noise and partly because it was hard to sleep in the chair. Every time Kate awoke, David was always asleep. She imagined he did the same, watching her until he fell asleep again. She still had so much to say to him. When she woke up the last time, the plane was making its final approach at the Gibraltar airfield. David gazed out the plane window, and when he saw that Kate was awake, he said, "Remember, don't say anything about the journal, Tibet, or the China facility until we know more. I'm still not sure about this."

Clocktower agents swarmed the plane the second they landed, and they were whisked away to the home. She and David had barely said a word since.

Behind her, the door slid open, and Kate turned quickly, smiling, hoping. It was Howard Keegan, the director of Clocktower. Kate's smile faded instantly, and she hoped the man hadn't seen it. He stepped out and closed the door. "May I join you, Dr. Warner?"

"Please. And call me Kate."

Keegan stood beside her at the rail, not leaning and not looking at Kate. He stared out into the darkening bay. He was clearly in his sixties, but he was fit. Robust.

The silence was a bit awkward. "How's the planning going?" Kate asked.

"Well. Though it won't matter." Keegan's voice was flat, emotionless.

A chill ran through Kate. She tried to lighten the mood. "You're that confiden—"

"I am. Tomorrow's outcome has been planned for years now." He motioned to the streets and the guards below. "Those aren't Clocktower agents. They're Immari Security. As are the guards inside. Tomorrow, the last of the non-Immari agents within Clocktower will die, including David."

Kate pushed off the rail and looked back at the table where the men were still laughing and pointing. "I don't un—"

"Don't turn around. I'm here to make you an offer." Keegan's voice was a whisper.

"For what?"

"His life. In exchange for yours. You will leave here tonight, in a few hours, when everyone has knocked off. They'll go to bed early; the raid is at dawn."

"You're lying."

"Am I? I don't want to kill him. I'm genuinely fond of him. We're just on different sides of the coin. Chance. But we want you, badly."

"Why?"

"You survived the Bell. It's the key to everything we've done. We have to understand it. I won't lie: you'll be questioned, then studied, but he will be spared. Look at your options. We can simply kill those agents inside right now. It's messier, here in a residential neighborhood, but acceptable. We've held this operation open too long as it is, waiting, seeing who would come in, hoping he would call. There's more. If you're clever in your negotiations, you may be able to free the children, or perhaps trade yourself for them. They're being held at the same facility." Keegan looked Kate in the eyes. "Now, what's your answer?"

She swallowed and nodded. "Okay."

"There's one more thing. From the recordings on the plane, you and Vale mention a journal. We want it. We've been looking for it for a very long time."

104

Snow Camp Alpha
Drill Site #7
East Antarctica

A surge of relief swept over Robert Hunt when he saw the snowmobile parked outside the small, white-walled barracks at Drill Site Seven. He parked his snowmobile and ran inside. The men were warming themselves beside the wall heater. Both rose when he entered.

"We tried to wait, but we were freezing. We couldn't stay."

"I know. It's okay," Robert said. He surveyed the room. Exactly like the last six. He glanced over at the radio. "Have they called—"

"Three times, on the hour. Asking for you. They're losing patience."

Robert thought about what to say. "What did you tell them?" The answer would tell him where they shook out in all this.

"We didn't answer the first call. The second said they were sending backup. We told them you were working on the drill, and we needed no assistance. What did you see?"

The last question sent Robert's mind racing. *What if they're testing me? What if they talked to the employer and they have orders to kill me? Can I trust them?* "I didn't..."

"Look, I ain't no genius, heck, I didn't even graduate high school, but I've worked an oil rig in the Gulf my whole life, and I know we ain't drilling for oil, so why don't you tell us what you saw?"

Robert sat at the small table with the radio. He suddenly felt so tired. And hungry. He pulled his hood off, then his gloves. "I'm still not sure. There were monkeys. They killed them with something. Then I saw kids, in a glass cage."

105

Clocktower Safe House
Gibraltar

Kate tried to estimate the distance between the balconies. Four feet? Five feet? Could she make it? Below, she heard a guard walking by, and she crept back into her room. She listened. The crunch of fine gravel under the man's feet slowly faded into the distance. She returned to the balcony.

She stepped to the edge and put one leg over, straddling the rail, then cartwheeled the other leg over. She stood on the tiny lip outside the rails, which she held with both hands behind her back. Could she make it?

She reached a leg out, holding the rail with one hand, like a ballet dancer in a lunge during a high note. She extended as far as she could, felt her grip slipping on the rail, and almost fell. She reeled back just in time and slammed back into the rail. She was going to break her neck. The other balcony was just out of reach—less than two feet.

She leaned back against the rail and was about to jump for it when the door on the other balcony slid open and David walked out. He drew back at the first sight of her, but then, after recognizing her, he walked to the rail. He smiled at her. "How romantic." He held out his good arm. "Jump. I'll pull you up. I owe you one."

Kate glanced down. She could feel the sweat on her hands. David held his arm out over the rail. It was a few feet from her. She wanted to leap to him, but could she make it? If she fell, the guards would be on her and Keegan would know instantly. The deal would be off. Could David catch her? Could he get them out of this? She trusted him, believed in him, but...

She jumped, and he caught her and pulled her over the rail and into his arms. Then it all happened so fast, like a dream. He swept her into the room, not bothering to close the door. He tossed her on the bed and climbed on top of her. He pulled his shirt off and ran his hands through her hair. He kissed her on the mouth and pulled her shirt up, only lifting his face from hers long enough to pull the shirt past her face.

She had to tell him. Had to stop it. But she couldn't resist. She wanted this. His touch was like an electric current, lighting up parts of her that had long ago gone dark. He was awakening something, like a supernatural force that overwhelmed her, blotting everything else out. She couldn't think.

Her bra was off, and his pants were coming off.

It felt so good. The release. They could talk after.

Kate watched David's chest rise and fall. It was a deep sleep. She made her decision.

She lay back on the bed, staring at the white plaster ceiling, deliberating, trying to understand what she was feeling. She felt... alive again, whole... safe, even despite Keegan's threat. A part of her wanted to wake David, to tell him they were in danger and that they needed to get out of there. But what could he do? The bullet wounds in his leg and shoulder weren't even half healed. She would only get him killed.

She put her clothes back on and quietly exited his room, slowly closing the door.

"I was clear."

The voice frightened her. She turned—Keegan, standing behind her, wearing an expression of... sadness, disappointment, regret?

"I haven't told him—"

"I doubt that—"

"It's true." Kate cracked the door, revealing David lying on his back, a sheet covering only his lower body. Kate gently eased the door back. "We didn't talk at all." She looked down. "I was saying goodbye."

Thirty minutes later, Kate watched the lights of Northern Africa out of the window as the plane flew south toward Antarctica.

106

"David, wake up."

David opened his eyes. He was still naked, lying in the same place where he'd fallen asleep. He felt the bed beside him. Empty. Cold. Kate had been gone for hours.

"David." Howard Keegan stood over him.

David sat up. "What is it? What time is it?"

His former mentor handed him a note. "It's around two A.M. We found this note in Kate's room. She's gone."

David opened the note.

Dear David,

Don't hate me. I have to try to make a trade for the children. I know you're attacking Immari Headquarters this morning. I hope you're successful. I know what they've taken from you.

Good luck,

~ Kate

David's mind raced. Would Kate do this? Something felt wrong.

"We think she left several hours ago. I thought you should know. I'm sorry, David." Howard walked to the door.

David tried to analyze the tactical situation, tried to be objective. *What am I missing?* His mind kept flashing to Kate; images of her from last night played through his mind like a slide show he couldn't stop. She had been safe, and now she had delivered herself into the hands of his enemy. *Why?* It was his worst nightmare.

Keegan gripped the door handle.

"Wait." David eyed him, thinking. What option did he have? "I know where she went."

Howard turned and looked at David skeptically.

"We were given a journal in Tibet." David dressed as he spoke. "It contained a map of the tunnels below the Rock; there's something down there, something they need."

"What is it?"

"I don't know. But I think she's gone after it—to use it to trade. What's our status?"

"Everyone's suiting up. We're almost ready for the assault."

"I need to speak with them."

Thirty minutes later, David was leading the final twenty-three Clocktower agents in the world through the tunnels under the Rock of Gibraltar. He had told the men that he had to go, that he had to find Kate, and that he might be delayed in joining the assault. His role was largely ceremonial anyway. His wounds, especially the leg wound, disqualified him from playing an active role in the assault. He would be at a desk watching the screens and readouts, coordinating the men during the operation.

His fellow agents had agreed unanimously: they would stay together, investigate the tunnels first, recover Kate, then resume the original plan. The contents of the chamber could offer some tactical advantage in the main operation.

They had anticipated little resistance at the warehouse, and they weren't disappointed. The warehouses weren't even guarded. Or locked, although they had been. The Clocktower team found a common combination lock, the kind used on high-school lockers, laying on the ground, snapped in half. Clearly

Kate's work. Apparently, Immari had abandoned the site a long time ago and regarded it as low value. The lack of security still made David suspicious.

The entrance to the tunnels was just as the journal described it—and in almost the same condition. A black tarp had been thrown off the opening, and the lights leading into the mine were on. Inside the tunnels, there was one change: an electric car system, like a monorail tram with single cars, had been added to provide swift, safe transport through the tunnels. Each car held two passengers, and the team piled into about a dozen cars, with Howard and David riding in the first car. After the dizzying spiral down into the mine, the tunnel straightened out and began forking. David hadn't anticipated this; he had assumed the Immari would have closed any dead ends. The map in the journal was of the inside of the Atlantis structure; he had no idea which way to go at the forks. There was no choice. Howard began dividing their forces and, unfortunately, the rail lines kept forking until David and Howard rode alone, hopefully on the right track.

The plan was to rendezvous at the entrance in one hour. That would still leave time for the pre-dawn raid at Immari Gibraltar.

David stared straight ahead as the tunnel lights flew by in an endless monotony. What was he missing? Howard worked the car's controls, managing their speed. Somewhere, far off in the distance, three faint, rapid-fire pops rang out. David looked over at Howard, and they shared a knowing glance. Howard slowed the car, and they waited for more sounds, hoping to discern the direction.

"We can reverse," Howard said quietly.

They waited. The tunnels were quiet. What to do? The sound was clearly gunfire, but David wasn't in fighting condition, and although Howard was in intelligence, he was a manager, not a soldier. Neither could offer any real resistance. In fact, they would probably be in the way.

"No, we go on," David said.

Five minutes later, they heard another bout of gunfire, but they didn't stop. Five minutes after that, they reached the room that opened onto the Atlantis structure. The steps lay in the center of the room, fully uncovered. To the right was the jagged opening the journal had described. David could also see the rest of the structure, but it was mostly smooth dark metal. Massive steel I-beams reached high overhead, holding the rock and sea at bay.

David looked up, studying the area above the stairs. There was a huge dome and a place where the structure's overhang had been cut away from above.

"What is it?" Howard said.

"This is where they extracted the Bell," David said, almost to himself.

Howard walked to the stairs, put his foot on the first step, and looked back at David.

Without a word, David hobbled forward, moving up the stairs, leaning heavily on his cane. As he grimaced and climbed, an overwhelming sense of déjà vu engulfed him. The tunnel maker, Patrick Pierce, had also been lured down here under the guise of rescuing someone, only to be trapped himself. David crossed the threshold with Howard following closely. He stopped and studied his mentor's eyes. Was he missing something? What could he do about it now?

Inside, the structure was illuminated with LED lights that ran along the floor and ceiling. The corridors were about eight feet tall—not cramped but not exactly spacious. They also weren't square. The bottoms and tops of the corridors curved slightly, giving it an oval shape, except the curves formed in sharper angles. Overall, the halls felt like the corridors of a ship—a *Star Trek* ship.

David led Howard down the corridors, following the mental image he had formed of the map. Memorizing maps and codes was one of the quintessential tools of spycraft, and David was good at it.

The structure was incredible. Many of the doors to the rooms were open, and as they passed by, David saw a series of makeshift labs, like something you might see behind the glass of a museum, where curators carefully studied or restored historical artifacts. Apparently the Immari had dissected every inch of the structure in the past one hundred years.

It was surreal. David had only half-believed the tunnel-maker's tale, had thought that perhaps it was just that—a tale. But here it was.

The false wall to the chamber was coming up—just around the next turn. As it came into view, David felt himself holding his breath. The chamber was... open.

Kate. Was she inside?

"Kate!" David called out. There was nothing to lose. Anyone inside could hear his cane clacking on the metal floor from a mile away, so they didn't exactly have the element of surprise.

No answer.

Howard formed up behind him.

David crept to the edge of the chamber's opening and peered inside. The room looked like some sort of command center. A bridge, with chairs dotted along smooth surfaces—computers? Something more advanced?

David moved into the room as carefully as he could. He pivoted around, leaning on his cane, scanning every inch of the room. "She's not here," he said. "But the journal, the story was true."

Howard stepped inside the room and hit a switch behind him. The door to the room hissed closed, sliding from right to left. "Oh yes, it's quite true."

David studied him. "You've read it?" David wrapped his fingers around the gun tucked in his belt.

Howard's face had changed. His usually mild expression was gone. He looked satisfied. Confident. "I've read it, yes. But just out of curiosity. I knew what it would say, because I was there. I saw it first-hand. *I* hired Patrick Pierce to find this place. I'm Mallory Craig."

107

Kate sat on the small plastic bench and stared at the white walls. She was in some sort of lab or research facility, but she had no idea where. She rubbed her temples. God, she was so groggy. Somewhere over the ocean, a man had walked back into the cabin and offered her a bottle of water. She had declined, and he had proceeded to hold her down and cover her mouth with a white cloth, the type that promptly induced unconsciousness. What had she expected?

She stood and paced the room. There was a small slit in the white door, but the window revealed only the hallway outside and a few more doors like the one to her room.

One of the long walls of the room had a rectangular mirror, recessed a few inches into the wall. This was no doubt an observation room, similar to the ones in her lab in Jakarta, except infinitely more creepy. She stared at the mirror. Was someone in there, watching her right now?

Kate squared her body to the mirror and looked into it as if she could see the mysterious man behind it—her captor. "I did my part. I'm here. I want to see my children."

A voice broke over a loudspeaker. It was muffled and computer-altered. "Tell us what you treated them with."

Kate thought. She would have no leverage after she revealed what she knew. "I want to see them first, then you release them, and I'll tell you."

"You're not in a position to negotiate, Kate."

"I disagree. You need what I know. Now, you show me the children, or we've got nothing to talk about."

Nothing happened for almost a minute, then on one side of the mirror, a video flickered to life. That part of the mirror must have been some sort of computer screen. The video showed the children, walking in a dark hallway. Kate stepped closer to the mirror, holding a hand out. Ahead of the children, a massive portal opened, revealing only darkness inside. The children walked through. The video paused with an image of the portal closing.

"You've read the tunnel-maker's journal. You know about the structure in Gibraltar. There is a similar structure twenty times larger here. It's been here, beneath two miles of ice, for countless thousands of years. The children are inside."

The screen in the mirror switched to a close-up image of the children before they crossed the portal. It zoomed in on packs the children carried. There was a simple LED readout, the type you see on alarm clocks—a series of digital numbers. A countdown.

"The children are carrying nuclear warheads in those packs, Kate. They have less than thirty minutes left. We can deactivate them remotely, but you have to tell us what you did."

Kate stepped back from the mirror. It was insanity. Who would do this to two children? She couldn't trust them. She wouldn't tell them. They would only hurt other children; she was sure of it. She had to think. "I need some time," she mumbled.

The image of the packs disappeared from the mirror.

A few seconds passed, and the door swung open. A man wearing a long black trench coat stepped robotically into the room and...

Kate knew him.

How could it be? Flashes of expensive dinners, her laughing as he charmed her, a candle-filled apartment in San Francisco. And the day she told him she was pregnant—the last day she ever saw him... until now, here.

423

"You—" was all Kate could manage. She stepped back as he marched into the room. Kate felt her back hit the wall.

"Time to talk, Kate. And call me Dorian Sloane. Actually, let's dispense with the aliases. It's Dieter. Dieter Kane."

108

David watched the man pace across the room, the man he had known as Howard Keegan, Clocktower Director, the man who now claimed to be Mallory Craig.

"You're lying. Craig hired Pierce almost a hundred years ago."

"That's true, I did. And we've been looking for his journal almost as long. Pierce was an extremely clever man. We knew he sent the journal to the Immaru in '38, but we weren't sure it made it there. I was curious what he would say, how many secrets he would reveal. When you read it, weren't you curious about the deal he made with us? Why he stayed, working for the Immari for almost twenty years after the Spanish flu killed his wife and unborn child? What did he call it? His 'deal with the devil.'" The man laughed.

David slipped the gun out of his belt. He had to keep him talking, at least a bit longer. "I don't see what that has to do with you."

"Don't you? Why do you think Pierce would have worked with us?"

"You would have killed him."

"Yes, but he didn't fear death. You read the journal's end. He would have welcomed it, would have killed us all in a blaze of glory. We had taken everything from him, everything he loved. But his love for his child was more powerful than his hatred. As I said, Patrick Pierce was very clever. The second he

425

emerged from the tube, he knew what they were. Hibernation tubes, suspension chambers. In that makeshift hospital in the warehouse above us, he made a deal. He would put Helena's dead body in one tube, and Kane would put Dieter, his dying son, in another tube. Both men became obsessed with medical research. They dreamed of the day they could open the tubes and save their loved ones. Of course, Kane's ideas were more radical, more racially charged. He dedicated himself to finding a way to survive the Bell. He took it to Germany, and... you already know about the experiments. We knew Pierce was working against us, planning something. In 1938, on the eve of Kane's expedition, Kane had his storm troopers capture Pierce and place him in a tube."

"Why not just kill him?"

"We would have liked to, but as I said, we knew he had written a journal, and that he was making other plans against us. We assumed the execution of those plans would be triggered upon his death, so we were in a tough position. Killing him was still too risky. Still, I laughed as Pierce fought with all his life until the guards incapacitated him and tossed him in the tube. Then, to my surprise and horror, Kane ordered the storm troopers to put me in another tube. He didn't trust me, even after all my years of loyalty. Kane promised he would bring me back when he returned. He never dreamed he *wouldn't* return, but of course he didn't. We only found his sub a few weeks ago in Antarctica.

"Pierce and I were woken up in 1978, in a different world. Our organization, the Immari, was practically gone—only the shells of our corporations and certain overseas assets remained. The Second World War had decimated us. The Nazis had appropriated many of our assets, including the Bell. The Immari leadership, such as it was then, was desperate—desperate enough to bring back the old guys, the people who had built Immari International in the first place. At least they had that much sense. But of course they didn't know all the history. Patrick

Pierce and I were awoken at the same time, and we picked up almost exactly where we had left off. I set about rebuilding Immari, and Patrick resumed his role of thwarting me. I began by reviving the organization I founded, my division of Immari, the world's first global intelligence organization. You're familiar with it. Clocktower. The Immari intelligence branch."

"You're lying."

"I am not. You know it. You saw the messages we sent in '47, the ones embedded in those *New York Times* obituaries. Why would Immari messages be marked with the words 'clock' and 'tower'? You had to have realized then, when you saw the decoded messages—or perhaps even before. Somewhere in the recesses of your mind, you've known what Clocktower was from the second you heard how many agents were under Immari control. You knew it when the cells fell so quickly. Think about it. Clocktower wasn't compromised by Immari. It was an Immari division, a unit dedicated to gaining the trust of the world's intelligence bureaus, infiltrating them fully, and ensuring that when the day came, when we unleashed the Atlantis Plague, they would be powerless, utterly blind. Clocktower also serves one other purpose: to collect and contain anyone who was on to the Immari master plan—people like you. The entire time you've been at Clocktower, we've been watching you, trying to find out how much you know and who you've told. It's the only solution. People like you don't break under interrogation. And there's another advantage. We've found that, over the years, most agents join us when they learn the full truth. You will too. That's why you're here."

"To get indoctrinated? You think I'll join up if I hear your rationale."

"Things aren't as they seem—"

"I've heard enough." David raised the gun and pulled the trigger.

109

Kate shook her head. How could he be here? She wouldn't cry. All she could manage was, "Why?" Her voice cracked, betraying her.

Dorian's expression changed, as if remembering something frivolous, a needless item he'd forgotten at the grocery store. "Oh, that. Just repaying an old debt. But that's nothing compared to what I'll do to you if you don't tell me what you treated those children with." He moved closer to her, forcing her into the corner of the room.

Kate *wanted* to tell him now, to see the look on his face. "Cord blood."

"What?" Dorian took a step away from her.

"I lost the baby. But a month before I did, I had embryonic stem cells extracted from the umbilical cord, just in case the child ever developed a condition that required stem cells."

"You're lying."

"It's true. I used an experimental stem-cell treatment on the children, using stem cells from the fetus of our dead child. I used them all. There aren't any more."

110

David pulled the trigger again. Another click.

"I removed the firing pin," Craig said. "I knew you'd be able to tell the difference in a loaded and unloaded gun."

"What do you want from me?"

"I've already told you. I'm here to recruit you. By the time we're done talking, you'll know the truth and you'll finally—"

"I won't. You can kill me now."

"I'd rather not. Good men are hard to find. There's another reason: you know more than anyone else. You're in a unique position to—"

"You know why I joined Clocktower, what the Immari took from me. What *you* took from me."

"Not me. Dorian. Dieter Kane. Granted, I used Clocktower to make sure no intelligence agencies got wind of the plot, but *he* planned 9/11. It was his brainchild. He was obsessed with searching those mountains for his father. He desperately needed some kind of closure. It wasn't the only reason. As I said before, our organization was in shambles when I awoke in 1978, and we were still recovering in 2001. We needed money, and a global cover to resume our work."

"Dorian Sloane is Dieter Kane?"

"It's true. When I awoke in 1978, I ordered the staff to open his tube, and he walked right out, as healthy as could be. The tube must also be some sort of healing device, a medical treatment pod. But its powers are limited to treating the living.

429

I watched Patrick Pierce, who had been stoic as a judge for the last twenty years, crumble as they pulled Helena's dead body from the tube. He relived her death all over again. We were, however, able to save the child inside her."

"His child?"

"Daughter. But you know her already. Kate Warner."

111

Kate studied Dorian's face. Confusion? Disbelief? Regret? He stared at the point where the wall met the floor, thinking.

Then he focused on her, grinning an evil, unkind grin. "That was very clever, Kate. Of course you are very smart—when it comes to science. But not when it comes to reading people." He turned away from her and paced toward the door. "You're just like your father in that way. Brilliant but foolish."

What was he talking about? Her father died twenty-eight years ago. Dorian, or Dieter, or whatever his name was... he was a madman. "You're the only fool here," Kate said.

"Am I? All of this is your father's fault. He unleashed all of this. He killed my mother and brother and forced my father to undertake a risky mission to save the world—a mission from which he never returned. There's your *why*, Kate. I've dedicated my whole life to finishing my father's work and to righting the wrongs your father did to my family; and today, you've given me the keys to finally do that."

Before Kate could react, an alarm rang out.

A security guard, or some sort of soldier, burst in the door. "Sir, we're under attack."

112

David's mind raced. He said his thoughts aloud, almost mumbling them. "Kate Warner is Patrick Pierce's daughter? How—"

"I thought new names were in order. If anyone ever connected us to the events during and after World War I, it would have... complicated our lives. Pierce took the name Tom Warner, and Katherine for his newborn daughter. He told her that her mother had died in childbirth, which was actually the truth. Dieter became Dorian Sloane, and he became obsessed with the past and his father's legacy. He was a hateful child. He had seen so much pain, and he was all alone in an age he didn't understand. Imagine, a seven-year-old boy going to sleep in 1918 with the flu, when his parents and brother were alive, and waking up sixty years later, in 1978, healthy and all alone in a strange world. I tried to be a father figure to him, but he was so troubled, so isolated. Like you, he dedicated his life to striking back at the people who had taken the ones he loved, to killing the people who had changed him and ruined his life. For him, that was Tom Warner and the Atlanteans.

"Unfortunately for all of us, Dorian is very capable. And he had support within the Immari organization. To the Immari, he was the heir and savior returned, living proof that the plague and the Bell could be beaten, that the human race could survive. It all went to Dorian's head. He grew into a monster. He's planning to reduce the human race to a select few, the genetically superior, what he believes is his tribe. He's already unleashed the plague.

The apocalypse is happening now, as we speak. But we can stop him. You can kill him, then I alone will run the Immari organization, with you at my side."

Craig watched David, hoping for some indication of how his former apprentice would react to the offer. "I'll take you in as a prisoner. I know him. He'll want to gloat, to debrief and torture you himself. I'll give you a means to kill him when you're left alone with him."

David shook his head. "That's what you want? This whole charade? You want me to kill Sloane—to put you on the throne?"

"Don't you want to? He was responsible for 9/11. He's your enemy. And you can save Kate. She's there with him now. He *will* hurt her. He hurt her before, in San Francisco. The baby? It was his."

"What?"

"It was his revenge. With Tom Warner gone, that left his daughter. Dorian didn't hesitate. He wanted Kate to feel the pain he had, of awakening to realize that your family had been ripped away. He's a monster. Only Martin kept him from killing her, but Martin can't stop Dorian now. *You* can. You can save her. No one else is going to rescue her."

Craig let the words sink in for a long moment, then turned and paced the room. "Think about it, David. You know you can't win. You can't fight us. The gunfire in the tunnels, that was the sound of my Immari Security agents killing the last of the Clocktower loyalists. They're all dead. You're all alone down here. You can't defeat the Immari. No one can. The world is already fighting the plague. You can't prevent catastrophe. But we can change things, from inside Immari. We can shape the world to come."

David considered the offer—his own deal with the devil. Then he looked around the room, for a weapon of some kind. There was something—the wooden handle of a spear, sticking out of the wall. The wood-and-iron spear looked so out of place, here in a room of strange metal and glass and technology David couldn't begin to imagine.

On the other side of the room, a hologram flickered to life, like a 3D video of some sort.

"What is—"

"We don't know for sure," Craig said. He walked closer to the area where the hologram was forming. "Some sort of videos, holograms, on repeat. They play every few minutes. I think they show the past, what happened here. They're the other reason I brought you down here, to this room. They're the secrets this room holds. We think Patrick Pierce hadn't yet uncovered them when he sent the journal in 1938. Or, this is another theory: he had found the room, but nothing worked until he came out of the tube in 1978. We're still sorting it out, but as you'll see, we believe he saw them at some point in the seven years after he resumed his work as Tom Warner. We don't know what they mean yet, but he went to great lengths to keep them from us. We think they're some kind of message."

113

Kate looked up at the sound of the second explosion. She tried the door again. Still locked. She thought she smelled smoke. Her mind raced through Dorian's crazed allegations and the videos of the children walking into that massive structure... with the packs strapped to their backs.

The door swung open, and Martin Grey stepped quickly into the room. He grabbed Kate by the arm and pulled her out into the hall.

"Martin," Kate began, but he cut her off.

"Stay quiet. We have to hurry," Martin said as he led her down the white-walled corridor. They turned a corner, and the corridor ended in what looked like an airlock on a space station. They proceeded through the airlock, and a gust rushed past them as they ventured into the large room beyond—some sort of hangar or warehouse with a high, arched ceiling. Martin squeezed her arm and led her to a stack of hard plastic crates where they knelt and waited in silence. She heard men's voices at the end of the room and the engines of heavy equipment—forklifts, maybe.

"Stay here," Martin said.

"Martin—"

"In a minute," Martin whispered as he got to his feet and began walking quickly.

Kate heard his footfalls stop abruptly as he reached the men. His voice rang with an authority and force Kate had never before heard from her adoptive father. "What are you men doing?"

435

"Unloadin—"

"Sloane has called for all personnel at the North Entrance."

"What? We were told—"

"The station has been breached. If it falls, whatever you're doing here won't matter. He called for you. You can stay here if you like. It's your funeral."

Kate heard more footfalls, moving toward her; then they passed her and moved out another airlock. There was just one set of footfalls now—Martin's. He walked deeper into the hangar and spoke again. "He's called for everyone—"

"Who's going to control the site?"

"Gentlemen, why do you think I'm here?"

More footfalls, running, an airlock opening and closing, and Martin was back. "Come quickly, Kate."

Martin marched her past rows of crates and a makeshift control station of some kind, with a bank of computers and a wall of screens. They showed a long ice corridor and the opening she had seen the children walk through.

"Please Martin, tell me what's going on."

Martin's eyes were soft, sympathetic. "Get into this suit. I'll tell you all I can in the seconds we have left." He motioned to a white, puffy space suit hanging on the wall beside a group of lockers. Kate began slipping into the suit, and Martin looked away from her as he spoke.

"I'm so sorry, Kate. I'm the one that forced you to produce results. And when you did... I had the children kidnapped. I did it because we needed them—"

"The Bell—"

"Yes, to get past the Bell, to get inside the tombs—the structure two miles below the ice here in Antarctica. Since we began studying the Bell, we've known some people can resist it longer than others. They all die, but a few years ago, we identified a set of genes involved in resistance: the Atlantis Gene, we call it. The gene heavily influences brain wiring. We think it's responsible for all sorts of advanced cognitive abilities: problem-solving, advanced reasoning, language, creativity. We, Homo sapiens sapiens that is, have it, and none of the other subspecies of humans have it—not that we've found. It's how we're different. My theory is that the Atlanteans gave it to us around sixty thousand years ago—around the time of the Toba catastrophe. It's what enabled us to survive. But we weren't quite ready for it. We were still very much like our great ape cousins, acting on instinct, living in the wild. The strange thing is, we think it's activated by a sort of neural survival subroutine, the fight-or-flight center of the brain. That mechanism activates the Atlantis Gene—focusing the mind and body. It could be why we're a race of thrill-seekers and why we're so prone to violence. It's fascinating."

Martin shook his head, trying to focus. "Anyway, we're still trying to understand how it works. Everyone has the Atlantis Gene, or at least some of the genetic components for it, but activating the gene is the problem. For some minds—geniuses—activation is more frequent. We think these genius moments, these flashes of insight and clarity, are literally like a light bulb flickering on and off: the Atlantis Gene activates, and for the briefest of moments, we can use the full power of our minds. These people can activate the Atlantis Gene without the fight-or-flight circuit breaker. We began focusing our research on minds that had this sort of sustained activation. We observed activation in some minds on the autism spectrum: savants. That's why we funded your research. It's why the Immari Council forgave Dorian's transgressions with you—he had steered you into an area of Immari interest. And when you succeeded, when the children showed sustained Atlantis Gene activation, I took the kids before he could find out. I created other distractions, with Clocktower, to keep him busy."

"*You* were the source. You sent the information to David."

"Yes. It was a desperate attempt to stop Toba Protocol. I knew David had been investigating the Immari conspiracy. I sent him a message revealing the Immari double agents working as Clocktower analysts, and I was trying to tell him that Clocktower itself *was* the Immari intelligence agency, to warn him about who to trust. I had hoped he could learn the truth in time. I had to be very careful, though—some of the information was only known at the highest level, and I was already under suspicion. At the very least, I hoped the war for Clocktower would consume the Immari, delaying the execution of Toba Protocol—"

"What exactly *is* Toba Protocol?"

"Toba is Sloane's plan: to use the Plague from the Bell to complete the genetic transformation of the human race."

"Why?"

"To synchronize us, genetically, with the Atlanteans. At least, that's the story Sloane and Keegan sell throughout the organization. But that's only half the truth. His real endgame is to create an army for a pre-emptive strike. Sloane and Keegan want to enter the structure below us and kill the Atlanteans."

"That's insane."

"Yes. But in their time, in 1918, the outbreak killed tens of millions worldwide, including Sloane's mother and brother. They believe whoever is inside this structure means us harm, that they will exterminate the human race when they awaken. To them, saving a select few, a genetically superior group, is better than extinction."

Questions raced through Kate's mind. She tried to process Martin's revelations. "Why didn't you tell me? Why not ask for my help?" she asked, almost without thinking.

Martin sighed. "To protect you. And I needed the children quickly. I didn't have time to explain, and doing so would have involved you in the Immari conspiracy. I was trying to fulfill a promise I made a long time ago: to keep you out of this. But I failed. The ops team was supposed to quietly take the children from your lab. You weren't supposed to even be there at that hour. I was horrified when I heard that your assistant had been killed. And I made other mistakes. I underestimated how quickly Dorian would react. I tried to give you clues about what was going on when we met in Jakarta, during my theatrical rant in the observation room. I wasn't sure you could put it all together. Then, Dorian's men had you and... the entire situation spun out of control. After I saw you in Jakarta, I was taken here to Antarctica. Dorian's agents have been watching me. There wasn't much I could do to help you. But I had an agent of my own here—Naomi. I risked sending another coded message to David, telling him about the China facility, and Naomi... found a way to accompany Dorian there. "

"Naomi arranged for the ID badges at the train station."

"Yes. My hope was that between her, you, and David, the three of you could rescue the children and disable the power plant, preventing Toba Protocol. It was a long shot, a desperate move. But given the stakes—literally billions of lives—any chance was better than none."

Kate pulled the last of the bulky suit on. "The boys... You were—"

"Trying to make contact. I'm part of a small faction within the Immari that favors a different path. Our goal has been to find a therapy that activated the Atlantis Gene, allowing us to enter the tombs and greet the Atlanteans as they awaken, not as murderers, but as their children, to ask their help in managing humanity's growing pains. To ask for their help with fixing the Atlantis Gene. We've found some other... interesting aspects of the gene, mysteries we still don't understand. There isn't time to explain, but we need their help. That's what you have to do, Kate. You can cross into the tombs. You've seen what Dorian's plan is—to use the children to annihilate the Atlanteans. You must hurry. Your father gave his life for this cause, and he made so many sacrifices for you. And he tried so desperately to save your mother."

"My mother..." Kate struggled to understand.

Martin shook his head. "Of course. I haven't told you. The journal. It's your father's."

"It can't be..." Kate searched Martin's face. Her mother was Helena Barton? Patrick Pierce was her father? How could it be true?

"It's true. He was a reluctant member of the Immari. He did it to save you. He put you in the tube, inside your mother that day in the field hospital in Gibraltar. He emerged in 1978 and took the name Tom Warner. I was already a staff scientist for the Immari, but I was wavering... the methods, the cruelty. I found in him an ally, someone inside the organization who wanted to stop the madness, someone who favored dialog over genocide. But he never trusted me, not fully." Martin stared at the floor. "I've tried so hard to keep you safe, to honor my promise to him, but I've failed so miserably—"

Behind them another explosion rocked the facility. Martin grabbed the helmet to the suit. "You have to hurry. I'll lower you down. When you get inside, you have to find the children and lead them out first. Whatever you do, make sure they get out. Then find the Atlanteans. There isn't much time left: less than thirty minutes until the bombs the boys are carrying go off." He ushered her to another airlock at the end of the warehouse. "When you get outside, climb into the basket. I can operate it from here. When it reaches the bottom of the ice shaft, run through the portal, just as the children did." He locked the suit helmet in place and pushed her out of the airlock before Kate could say another word.

When the outer airlock opened, Kate saw the steel basket hanging from the crane's thick metal cord. It swayed slightly as the Antarctic winds blew through it, barely catching the metallic mesh on the sides.

She waddled over to it with some effort. The wind almost blew her over as she reached it. The handle was hard to work with her gloved hands, but she managed to get inside. As soon as she closed the door, it began descending into the round hole.

The basket creaked, and above her, the round circle of light shrank with every passing second. It reminded Kate of the end of a cartoon, where the final scene is gradually covered with black as the circle shrinks to the size of a pin and finally winks out into full black. The squeaking basket was an unnerving soundtrack to the darkening descent.

After a few moments, the basket began moving faster, and the last sliver of light above disappeared. The speed and disorienting darkness gave her a sick feeling in her stomach, and she braced herself against the basket. Not much longer, she told herself, but she had no idea. It was two miles deep.

Then there was light—a smattering of faint sparkles below, like stars shining on a clear night. For a moment, Kate gazed down at them, admiring their beauty, not thinking about what they actually were. *Stars*, she thought. Then her scientific mind slowly, subtly began rifling through the possibilities before settling on the most likely candidate: tiny LED lights that had been dropped to illuminate the bottom of the hole. They lay there in a random pattern, glowing in the blackness around them, as if guiding Kate on a cosmic journey to some unknown planet. They were almost... entrancing—

A loud sound—an explosion—echoed down through the shaft, and Kate felt the basket falling faster. And faster still. The thick cable attached at the top of the basket grew slack and gathered in waves above her. She was falling—free falling. The cable had been cut.

114

Craig stepped closer to David as the hologram formed.

David stared at it. The colors were vivid, and the hologram almost filled the room. It felt like he was there. He saw a massive ship rising out of the ocean. The Rock of Gibraltar came into view, and David realized the scale of the machine. The Rock looked like a pebble next to it. There was something else— the location of the Rock was wrong. It was inland, not on the coast, and the land extended beyond the Rock and to the right of it, all the way to Africa. Europe and Africa, joined by a land bridge.

"My God..." David whispered.

Craig paced closer to David. "It's just as Plato described it, a massive island rising out of the sea. We're still trying to nail down the time period, but we think this holomovie was made about twelve thousand to fifteen thousand years ago. It was certainly some point before the last ice age ended. We'll know more as soon as we estimate the sea level. Plato's account says the island sank 12,500 years ago, so that could be about right. And you've noticed the size of the vessel."

"Incredible. You've only found a piece."

"Yes, and a small one at that. We think the structure is over sixty square miles—that is, assuming the Rock is the same size today as it was fifteen thousand years ago. The structure, or piece, as you say, that we stand in now is less than one square mile. The vessel in Antarctica is much larger, about two hundred fifty square miles." Craig nodded to the hologram. "The next movie reveals what this vessel is—we think."

David watched the massive ship move to the shore and stop. The hologram flickered, as if someone were changing the reel in an antique movie projector. The ship was still there, but the water had risen some. Just beyond the ship, on the edge of the coast, there was a city, if you could call it that. Primitive stone monuments, like a series of Stonehenges radiated out from the ship in semicircles. Huts with thatched roofs dotted the landscape. A huge bonfire burned in the middle of the stone structures, and the hologram zoomed in. A band of humans wearing thick furs was dragging another human—no, an ape. Or something in between. The ape was tall. He was naked and fought wildly at the captors at his sides. The humans around him bowed as he neared the fire.

From the ship, two flying objects launched. They looked like chariots or space-age Segways. They floated a few feet above the ground, racing toward the fire. When they reached it, the humans backed away, bowing and facing the ground.

The Atlanteans dismounted their chariots, grabbed the savage, and injected him with something. They wore some sort of body armor with helmets covered almost entirely by mirrored glass, except the rear part. They threw the ape-man across a chariot and rushed back to the ship.

The hologram flickered again, and the scene changed to the inside of the ship. The ape-man lay on the floor. The Atlanteans were still in their suits, and David couldn't tell, but it seemed as if they were saying something to each other... the subtle body language, a few hand gestures.

Craig cleared his throat. "We're still working out what's happening here. Bear in mind we only saw them a few hours ago when we got the map from the journal and accessed the chamber, but we think this is a video of the Atlanteans interrupting a ritual sacrifice. The man is a Neanderthal. We think our ancestors considered it their duty to hunt down every man not made in the image of God and sacrifice him. Some sort of early racial cleansing."

"Is it the same early human that Pierce saw in the tube?"

"Yes, as you'll see."

"What happened to it?"

Craig snorted and shook his head. "Kane thawed him in the early thirties, the second he had the Bell operational. We had a time with the power supply. They ran a series of experiments over a few years. They even tried to recreate the ape-man by breeding humans with chimpanzees: his insane 'humanzee' project. Kane finally lost interest when there was no progress. He fed him to the Bell in '34."

"He didn't survive?"

"No, even after countless thousands of years in the tube. So of course we were shocked when Kate Warner did. We think it has something to do with the tubes, but whatever it does only works on our subspecies. The tubes must somehow activate the Atlantis Gene. Whatever she treated the children with has to be connected to the tubes in some way. Our theory is that every human has the Atlantis Gene, but it's only activated sporadically and by a select few. Clearly the Neanderthal didn't have the genetic precursor."

Craig nodded to the hologram. "Oh, here's the money shot, as they say."

The image moved out of the lab to an outdoor shot again. Behind the ship, a massive tsunami rose in the air. It must have been a hundred feet taller than the ship, which itself could have easily been two hundred feet tall, based on its height relative to the Rock of Gibraltar. The wave washed over the ship and into the primitive city, destroying it in one violent sweep.

The ship was adrift, and the wave carried it into the city, flattening the stone monuments and huts as it went. Then the waters receded, dragging the ship out to sea, more than half of it still underwater. Sparks flew along the bottom as the ship skidded against the seafloor below it. Then the hologram flashed red and white as a massive explosion erupted below the ship, ripping it into two, three, now four pieces.

"We think it was a giant methane pocket on the seabed. It exploded with the force of a dozen nuclear warheads."

The water was rushing back over the broken ship, and the image returned to the lab and the Atlanteans. One of them had been thrown against the bulkhead. The body was limp. Dead? The surviving Atlantean hoisted the Neanderthal like a rag doll and shoved him into a tube. His strength was amazing. David wondered if it was the suit or his natural strength.

The Atlantean turned to his partner and hoisted him up. The image winked out as the man left the room. The hologram followed him as he ran through the ship. He was thrown about—no doubt as the waves rocked the ship and it floated lifelessly to the bottom of the sea. Then he was in the chamber where Craig and David now stood. He worked the panels for a moment. He didn't actually touch the controls, he merely worked his fingers above them as he held his partner on his shoulder.

The computers shut down one by one.

"We think he's activating the Bell here. An anti-intrusion device to keep animals like us out. It makes sense. Then he powers off the computers. We're still scratching our heads at this next part."

On the hologram, the room was almost dark except for the faint glow of emergency lights. The man stepped to the rear of the room and touched something on his forearm. A door slid open before him. David followed it with his eyes—the door was there, but it had the spear in it now. The Atlantean looked around, paused, and walked through. The door shut behind him—with no spear in it.

David looked back to the door.

"Don't bother." Craig shook his head. "We've tried. For hours now."

"What's in the door?" David stepped closer to it.

"Not sure. A couple of scientists think it's the Spear of Destiny, but we're not certain. We think Patrick, or rather Tom

Warner, had it down here, trying to cut a hole in the door or something."

David edged closer. "The Spear of Destiny?" David knew what it was, but he needed to buy some time and distract Craig.

"Yes. You don't know it?"

David shook his head.

"Kane was obsessed with it, and Hitler after him. The legend is that the spear was stabbed into the side of Jesus Christ as he hung on the cross, killing him. The ancients believed that any army that possessed the spear could never be defeated. When Hitler annexed Austria, he took the spear, and he only lost it a few weeks before Germany surrendered. It's one of the many artifacts we collected over the years, hoping it, or anything else from antiquity, would provide clues to the Atlanteans."

"Interesting," David said as he grabbed the end of the spear. He pulled at it, and he felt the door move slightly. He pulled harder, the spear came free, and the door opened. He dropped the cane and lunged through the doorway as Craig pulled his gun out and began firing.

115

"No, don't shoot them!" Dorian yelled into the radio, but it was too late. He watched the second man take two shots to the chest, and the third fall from shots to the shoulder and abdomen. "Stop firing! I will shoot the next idiot who pulls the trigger!"

The gunshots ceased, and Dorian walked out into the open space toward the last man. At the sight of Dorian, he began crawling for his gun, leaving a trail of thick blood as he went.

Dorian jogged to the gun and kicked it to the far wall of the lab. "Stop. I don't want to hurt you. In fact, I'll get you some help. I just want to know who sent you."

"Sent me?" The man coughed, and blood ran down his chin.

"Yes—" Dorian's earpiece crackled, and he looked away from the dying man.

One of the station techs came on. "Sir, we've ID'd the men. They're ours—one of the drill teams."

"A drill team?"

"Yes. They're actually the team that found the entrance."

Dorian turned back to the man. "Who sent you?"

The man looked confused. "Nobody... sent us..."

"I don't believe you."

"I saw..." The man was losing more blood now. The shot in the gut would do him in soon.

"Saw what?" Dorian pressed.

"Children."

"Oh, for God's sake," Dorian said. What was the world

coming to? Even oil-rig operators were bleeding-heart softies these days. He raised the gun and shot the man in the head. He turned and walked back to his Immari Security unit. "Clean this up—"

"Sir, something's happening in portal control." The soldier looked up. "Someone just launched the basket."

Dorian's eyes drifted toward the floor, then darted back and forth. "Martin. Send a team—secure the control station. No one leaves that room." A thought ran through Dorian's mind: the basket was launched. Kate? "How much time?"

"Time?"

"The bombs the children are carrying."

The Immari security agent took out a tablet and tapped at it. "Less than fifteen minutes."

She might still reach them. "Cut the cord on the basket," Dorian said. It was a fitting end. Kate Warner—Patrick Pierce's daughter—would die in a cold dark tunnel, just as Dorian's brother Rutger had.

116

David fell to the floor as the bullets ricocheted off the door closing behind him. He spun around, crouched, and held the spear point-forward over his shoulder, like some prehistoric hunter ready to stick his prey when it emerged from the sliding door.

But the door didn't open. David exhaled and sat down on the floor, giving the wounded leg a rest. He didn't see how Patrick Pierce had done it—all the walking around down here.

When the pain subsided, he got to his feet and took in his surroundings. The room was similar to the one he had just left—the metallic gray walls were the same, and so were the lights at the top and bottom of them. The room seemed to be a lobby of some sort. It had seven doors in all, fanning out in a semicircle, almost like a bank of elevator doors.

Other than the seven oval sliding doors, the room was almost empty, save for a chest-high table opposite the bank of doors. A control station? The surface was covered in dark plastic or glass that matched the controls in the previous chamber.

David stepped up to the desk and leaned the spear against it so he could use his good hand. He held his hand over the surface, like he had seen the Atlantean do in the hologram. Wisps of white and blue fog and light whirled around his hand, giving him tiny electric pops and shocks. He wiggled his fingers, and the light and fog changed radically; the pops and slight electric impulses swirled over his fingers.

David drew his hand back. Talk about being out of your element. He had half-expected, or rather hoped, that some sort of help menu would pop up.

He picked the spear back up. *Stick to what you know: your hunter-gatherer ways*, he told himself. There was another door, set off by itself, next to the control station. An exit? He walked to it, and it slid open, revealing more of the Star-Trek-type corridors that had led to the tunnel-maker's secret chamber. His eyes had now fully adjusted to the faint LED lights that ran along the floor and ceiling.

If the Atlanteans had run to this room when the ship had exploded twelve to fifteen thousand years ago, it stood to reason that this was some kind of escape pod, or maybe a fortified section in the middle of the ship. Another thought popped into David's mind: if they had come here, some of them could still be here. Maybe they had hibernated here, in other tubes.

David looked around. There were certainly no signs of life.

The elevator room opened onto a T intersection. Both directions ended in another oval door. He chose the shorter path and limped along, using the spear as a walking staff. It helped immensely.

At the end of the corridor, the door slid open automatically, and David stepped through.

"Don't move." A man's voice. It was hoarse, as if he hadn't spoken in a while.

David heard a footfall behind him. Based on the echo, the man (or Atlantean) was about his size. David raised his arms, still holding the spear. "I'm not here to hurt you."

"I said don't move." The man was almost upon him.

David turned quickly, catching a glimpse, a flash of the man, or whatever it was, just before he felt the electric prod dig into him. It sent him to the ground and into unconsciousness.

117

2 miles below Immari Research Base Prism
East Antarctica

The steel basket wobbled as it hurtled down the ice shaft. It drifted over and cut into the smooth ice wall, spraying shards of ice all over Kate's suit and visor. She raised her arms to cover her helmet just as the basket lurched back, almost throwing her out. The heavy cable that had bunched above the basket was weighing on it. The basket steadied for a moment, then tipped in one quick motion, the bottom cutting into one side of the ice shaft, the top carving the other. Kate grabbed a bar at the top of the basket and dug her feet into the mesh floor, locking herself in like an astronaut in a zero-g training hoop, preparing in case the basket flipped end over end and side to side. She closed her eyes and pushed against the basket with all the strength she could muster and waited. More ice sprayed around her as the basket bounced against the sides of the tunnel. The impacts were slowing the fall. Then the walls disappeared and two long seconds passed and... crunch. The basket dug into a mound of ice, and Kate was plowed into the ground, knocking the wind out of her.

She fought to suck a breath inside the suit. It was like breathing through a tiny coffee straw. When she had regained her breath, she rolled over and took stock of her situation.

The basket had dug several feet into a mound of ice just below where the drill had punched through the chamber. It must have been the ice shards that had fallen down the shaft as the drill was extracted back to the surface, and the ice spray from her descent. The bed of ice had saved her life.

The mound looked more like a snow globe—bright lights glowed deep within. Kate stared at them for a moment. They looked almost like a flock of fireflies, but they were no doubt the LEDs that had been dropped to illuminate the vast cavern below. They had sunk deep into the chips of ice, and their light refracted out and into the large chamber. They also revealed Kate's situation.

The basket was about half-buried in the loose chips of ice, and the part above the surface of the mound was covered by steel mesh. She was trapped, but there was a small opening—not large enough to crawl out of... but... she could make it larger if she dug under it.

Kate began digging with her hands, like a dog trying to get under a chain-link fence. The cage had broken up the finely shaved ice a bit, but it was still slow going. Finally, she thought the opening was large enough, and she dove head first under it. Her head and arms were through, but the bulky suit caught against the jagged metal mesh. Kate tried to pull back, but the sharp mesh ripped the suit and held her tight. Cold air rushed in through the hole in the suit, assaulting her back as she wiggled to get free. She pressed her belly into the ice as hard as she could and pushed back with her hands, and she was back in the cage.

The cold seemed to be numbing her body, bit by bit, starting with her back and radiating outward. With each passing second, it claimed more of her body. Her hands began to shake. The suit had provided more warmth than she'd realized. It was deathly cold down here. She would freeze to death if she didn't act fast.

She began scooping the ice with both hands, frantically trying to enlarge the hole. She felt her legs grow stiff, and she fought to balance as she heaved another handful of ice into the basket. The hole was almost there.

The cold air burned her lungs now, and her breath was an icy fog against the clear glass helmet. Soon the cold would overtake her lungs. She would suffocate to death before she froze. The fog—it had almost covered the helmet. She wiped it with her hand. Nothing. It was still there. She wiped again. Still there. Why wouldn't it go away? Of course—it was on the inside of the helmet. She knew that. Why did she even try to wipe the outside of the helmet? What was happening to her? The cold. Shutting down her body. She could barely think. What was she doing before the fog? The sheet of ice inside the helmet was complete now—she couldn't see a thing. She turned around, searching for some kind of direction. Like a dog in a cage, on all fours, searching for a sound in the night.

A dog. A cage. The hole. Yes, she was digging to get out. She had to get out. Where was the hole? Kate felt desperately at the ice below her. She scampered around the cage. Nothing but mesh, everywhere. Was there a hole? Then her hands felt something—yes, it was there. But she couldn't dig any more. She couldn't feel her fingers.

She dove into the hole and pushed with her feet. She felt the sharp metal mesh on her back, but she ignored it, pushing even harder with her feet. The mesh was on the backs of her legs now. She was moving. She dug her elbows into the ice and pulled, one elbow over the other, like a soldier crawling under a barbed wire obstacle course. How far had she gone? She kicked a leg up. She was free.

She rolled over and got to her feet. The ice inside her helmet blinded her. Which way was the structure? She started to run, but her legs felt like they were made of lead. The suit, plus her frozen legs—she would never make it. She was getting nowhere. Which direction to walk? It was all the same—ice, and beyond, the faint glow of lights.

She felt the ground rushing up. She was lying on the ground, rolling. The ice touched her back, sending a new wave of cold into her body, shocking her system. She arched her back and her eyes opened wide. She sucked in a breath and bounded onto her knees, breathing heavily.

She had to think. She got to her feet and spun around. Lights. There were more in one direction than the other. The domed chamber was massive. The lights—the snow globe, the fireflies inside... where the drill had come through... the lights would be in the opposite direction from the entrance.

Kate turned and waddled away from the light. She was so cold. Then there was a boom. The drone of metal on metal. It was ahead but slightly to her right. Kate adjusted her vector and kept pressing forward. She fell again but pushed up, putting both hands on one knee and dragging her other leg up. She couldn't feel any part of her body anymore. She was simply swinging her limbs, hoping for a break.

The crunch-crunch-crunch of ice below her feet stopped. Her footsteps had quieted, but it was still cold. She was lightheaded. She took another step, then another. Keep walking.

Behind her, metal on metal. The door closing?

She was still so cold. She fell to her knees and then to the ground, face first.

118

Dorian watched Kate fall, then get up and wander into the giant portal. The Bell hanging above was silent. He glanced over at the countdown clock: 00:01:32.

Less than two minutes. He had been sure the fall would kill her, but a nuclear blast inside the tombs? Just as good. Same end result.

"Release me, Dorian."

Dorian turned and eyed Martin Grey. The gray-haired man struggled against the Immari Security agents who held him at each side. Dorian had been so obsessed with watching Kate die, or so he had hoped, that he had forgotten the old buzzard was still in the control room.

Dorian turned to Martin and smiled. "It was you. The whole charade with Clocktower, then guiding them to the China facility, hoping they could save the children and stop me from executing Toba Protocol." He thought for a moment. "And you helped them escape. It was you, wasn't it? You contacted the Immaru, who rescued them after the Bell exploded. How did you know? How did you find them?"

"You're delusional, Dorian. Release me and stop embarrassing yourself."

"You're very clever, Martin, but you can't talk your way out of this one. You just helped Kate escape."

"I don't deny it. I have never hidden my love for her. Protecting her is my first priority. I would have burned this facility to the ground if I had to."

Dorian smiled. "So you admit it: the drill team that attacked us was acting on your orders."

Martin shook his head dismissively. "Absolutely not. Think about it, Dorian. I don't even have a way to contact them. I've never so much as met them."

"Well, it doesn't matter. I've figured it out, Martin." Dorian studied the older man, waiting for a reaction. "Have you? Yes, I bet you have. The children survived the Bell because they were treated with stem cells from Kate's and my child. Both of us were saved by the tubes: Kate as an unborn fetus in her mother's womb, myself as a child suffering from the Atlantis Plague, or Spanish flu if you like. Which means I can walk through that portal as well. But I'm going to wait a few minutes." He motioned to the giant computer screen with the countdown. The last few seconds ticked off until it read: 00:00:00. The letters flashed in red.

Dorian had expected some tremors on the surface from the explosions, but there was nothing. The structure must have impossibly thick walls, and the two miles of ice provided additional insulation.

Dorian smiled. "Two nuclear warheads just went off down there. Kate didn't make it to the children, I can assure you. She had less than two minutes to reach them, and I think she was in no shape for a footrace. You saw it. She suffered a great deal, Martin. She may have frozen to death inside the suit. Or at the very least, lost most of her fingers and toes—right before she died."

Dorian waited, but Martin said nothing. Dorian nodded to one of his security officers, who moved to the lockers and began readying a space suit. "I'm going to go down there and check on her shortly, as soon as they rig up a harness to lower me. I'll let you know if we find any remains. I doubt it. But before I go, I want to share something else. I've figured out another mystery." Dorian paced in front of him. "Do you care to hear it?"

"It's your freak show, Dorian—"

"Don't insult me. I hold your life in my hands."

"And your own. No council member can kill another—"

"We'll see about that. Mallory Craig forbade me from killing you a few days ago, but he's come around now—he sent Kate to me. He won't veto your execution this time. But, as I was saying: the explosion in China. The children were simply treated with the Atlantis Gene therapy. The Bell radiation didn't harm them, but it acted differently when Kate came into contact with it—the Bell shut down. That's what happened in China. The Bell recognized her as an Atlantean—one of its own—and it shut down, sending a power surge of overwhelming proportions through our grid, destroying the nuclear reactors and every other relay in the entire facility. Do you realize the implications, Martin?"

Martin stared into the distance. "I'm sure you're going to tell me."

"Don't be cheeky. You'll want to hear this. It means our child is the first offspring of two Atlanteans—the first of a new breed of human, the eventuality of human evolution. Its genome holds the clues to understanding how we changed fifty thousand years ago, how we can continue evolving."

"*Could have*, Dorian. Your own—"

"I couldn't do it." Dorian turned away from Martin. "As much as I hated Kate for what her father did to my family, I couldn't bring myself to kill my own child. It's in a lab, in one of the Atlantean tubes, in San Francisco. That's what I wanted to tell you, Martin. All your meddling, it hasn't amounted to anything. I've won. A science team is extracting the fetus now for study. We'll have a viable Atlantis vaccine soon, maybe even in a few weeks or months. And we'll use it selectively—"

A tech interrupted Dorian. "We're ready, sir."

"Gotta go, Martin."

"I wouldn't do that if I were you." Martin stared at him.

"I'm sure you woul—"

"I know why you're going down there."

"You know—"

"The note," Martin said, "that you pinned on those children.

457

I know what was in it. A letter in German, from a hopeful little boy telling his 'Papa' that the children were carrying bombs, and that he needed to get to an entrance as quickly as possible. You're blind, Dorian. Look at the facts. And the carcasses of those primates in lab three. The Bell down there was active when we arrived. And so was the one on the iceberg with the sub several weeks ago. It killed the men on our research team. We found bones below it. Your father never slept in a tube. He was human, very human inde—"

"He was a god. And he's not dead. I've never seen his bones," Dorian said defiantly.

"Not yet. But we wi—"

"He's down there!" Dorian insisted.

"Even if he is, which I doubt, he would be one hundred and twenty-seven years old."

"Then I'll see his bones or whatever I can find, but I'll know. And I'll see some other bones. Female, early thirties. Then I'll finally complete my destiny. I'll remove the Atlantis threat once and for all." Dorian motioned to the security guards. "Make sure he doesn't get out of here. Heavy guard. And if they don't need him for the research on the fetus..." he turned and looked Martin in the eyes. "Then kill him."

Martin's stoic face didn't betray a shred of emotion.

One of the technicians walked over and led Dorian aside. He spoke hesitantly. "Sir, about going down there, it's... we think you should wait."

"Why? The suit will protect me from radiation, you said—"

"Yes, that's true, but there could be other damage from the blasts. Fire. Possibly damage to the structure. The entire thing could collapse for all we know. We're getting some data on the structure in Gibraltar—Director Craig found some sort of archival videos. The structure was actually shattered by methane blasts similar to the nukes we sent, well, actually more powerful, but we know the structures aren't indestructible—"

"What do you suggest?"

458

"Wait a few days—"

"Out of the question. I'll wait a few hours, at most."

The tech nodded.

"There's something else. After I enter the tombs, lower three warheads down this drill shaft. If anyone besides me or my father comes out—human, Atlantean, or otherwise—set them off. Deploy the rest of the nukes down the other drill holes, and rig them all to detonate simultaneously."

"The blasts would melt the ice—"

"The blasts would save the human race. Do it."

119

David opened his eyes and looked around. He was lying on a skinny cot with a gel-like mattress that contoured perfectly to his body. He leaned forward and the gel reacted, helping him up. He smelled something, like garlic mixed with licorice. Actually, it was worse than that. David raised his hand to cover his nose, but the smell only got worse. He realized the stench was coming from him—from a black paste on his shoulder and leg. God it stank, but... his wounds felt better. The paste had eaten through his shirt, but it seemed to be repairing his wounds. He stood, then instantly collapsed back to the gel-cot. Not quite one hundred percent.

"Take it easy." It was the man who had incapacitated him.

David scanned the room for a weapon. The spear was gone.

"Relax, I'm not going to hurt you. At first I assumed they sent you to kill me, but when I saw your wounds... I figured they would have sent someone... in better health."

David scrutinized the man—and he *was* a man, David could see that now. He was in his late forties or maybe early fifties. His face was haggard, as if he hadn't eaten or slept much for some time. But it was more than that... The man's face was hard. A soldier, maybe a mercenary.

"Who are you?" David got another whiff of the black goo on his shoulder and turned his head, trying in vain to get away from it. "And what have you done to me?"

"Frankly, I'm not even sure. It's some kind of medicinal paste. It seems to be able to heal just about anything. I don't know how it works, but it does. I injured myself, was laid up, and thought

I might die. The computer opened a panel with a plate of this stinking stuff, then showed a movie of me putting it on—it was very realistic. So I did, and I got better—quickly. You'll be right as rain soon. Maybe within a few hours."

"Really?" David studied the wounds.

"Perhaps sooner. It's not like you're going anywhere. Now tell me who you are."

"David Vale."

"Organization?"

"Clocktower, Jakarta Station," David said automatically.

The man stepped closer to David and drew a pistol.

David realized what he had said. "No, I was working against the Immari, I just now found out that Clocktower was their organization."

"Don't lie to me. How did you find me?"

"I didn't. I'm not looking for you. Look, I don't even know who you are."

"What are you doing down here? How did you get here?"

"The tunnels under Gibraltar. I found a chamber, with the spear—"

"How?"

"A journal." David shook his head, trying to think. The paste was like having a cold, it was hard to put his thoughts together. "Got it in Tibet, from a monk. You know about it?"

"Of course I do. I wrote it."

120

Kate heard the sound of hissing air all around her. She still couldn't feel her body, but the air was warm, only a little warm at first, but it grew warmer with every passing second. She tried to push up off the floor, but she fell back face first. She was so tired. She let her limp body collapse into the frigid suit.

Gradually, the warmth filled the suit, and the feeling returned to her body. They—whoever they were—were bringing her body temperature up. The fog on the helmet's face mask turned to drops of water that ran down in streaks, and a view of the floor materialized in lines, like a shredded picture being reassembled, one skinny strip at a time. It was a metal grate, except... she couldn't see through it. No, it was a solid metal floor with dimples.

She turned over onto her back and stared at the smooth metallic ceiling. The fog was receding now. It still felt cool, but it was downright balmy compared to the ice cathedral outside. Where was she? Some sort of decontamination chamber?

Kate sat up. She could feel her fingers now, and she began fiddling with the clamps at her wrists. After some effort, the gloves came off, and she worked at the helmet. Ten minutes later, she was free of the suit and standing in the clothes she had left Gibraltar in. She surveyed the room. It was well lit, about forty feet wide, and probably twice as long. Behind her, she saw the enormous door she had entered through—it was much larger than the door at the other end. She walked deeper into the room, and the smaller door opened. She walked through it and lights popped to life at the ceiling and floor. Each light was faint, but taken together, they shed more than enough light on the gray corridor. They reminded her of the running beads of light in the floor of a limo.

She was standing in a giant T intersection. Which way to go? Before she could decide, she heard something moving toward her. Footsteps.

121

David tried to make sense of what the man had said. His head was a haze from the nano-paste that was repairing the wounds in his shoulder and leg and racking his nostrils with its foul odor.

The man claimed to be Patrick Pierce/Tom Warner—Kate's father and the author of the journal. An American soldier who had dug the tunnels for the Immari in exchange for permission to marry the daughter of one of their leaders. But he couldn't be—the timeline was wrong. Although... he *had* spent time in those Atlantean stasis tubes... Did it add up? Could he be telling the truth?

David tried to piece together what he knew.

From 1917 to 1918, Patrick Pierce recovers from WWI wounds and discovers the Atlantis structure under Gibraltar, uncovering the Bell and unleashing a deadly pandemic sold to the world as "Spanish flu." Between fifty and a hundred million people die. Up to a billion are infected on every continent.

In 1918, Pierce puts his wife, Helena, and his unborn child inside a tube.

From 1918 to 1938, Pierce becomes an unwilling member of the Immari Leadership in order to protect his wife and unborn child. He finishes his excavation at Gibraltar, but he, too, is placed in a tube when Konrad Kane embarks on his expedition: first to Tibet to recover artifacts and massacre the Immaru, then to Antarctica to find what he believes is the Atlantis capital city. Kane never returns.

In 1978, after forty years, Mallory Craig, Patrick Pierce, and Dieter Kane are awakened from the tubes. Pierce's wife is still dead, but the child is born. Pierce names her Katherine Warner. The others take new names: Patrick Pierce becomes Tom Warner, Mallory Craig becomes Howard Keegan, and Dieter Kane becomes Dorian Sloane.

In 1985, Tom Warner (Patrick Pierce) goes missing—possibly killed in a research experiment

Could it be true? Could Patrick Pierce/Tom Warner have been down here since 1985?

Assuming Pierce was in his mid twenties during WWI, as the journal said, he would have been in his mid forties in 1938 when he went into the tube... That would make him around fifty-two in 1985 and... eighty today. The man before him was much younger, possibly no more than fifty.

David was already feeling better from the paste. He stood, and the man raised the gun. "Stay where you are. You don't believe me, do you?"

It's hard to argue when you're wounded and your captor has a gun, David thought. He shrugged and looked sheepish. "I believe you."

"Don't be cute. And stop lying to me."

"Look, I'm just trying to put it together, the journal was... 1918 to 1936—"

"I know the journal dates; you'll recall that I wrote it. Now tell me exactly how you got down here."

David sat back on the bed. "I was lured into a trap. By Mallory Craig, Director of Clock—"

"I know what he directs. What was the lure?" The man spoke quickly, trying to corner David, hoping he would make a mistake and reveal himself to be a liar.

"Kate Warner. He told me she had gone into the tombs. I went to find her. They took two children from her lab in Jakarta about a week ago. They were treated with a new autism therapy—"

"What in the world are you talking about?"

"I'm not sure, she won't tell me—"

"Kate Warner is a six-year-old girl. She doesn't have a lab in Jakarta or anywhere else."

David appraised the man. He believed what he was saying. "Kate Warner is a genetics researcher. And she's definitely not six years old."

The man lowered the gun and looked down and away. "Impossible," he mumbled.

"Why?"

"I've only been down here a month."

122

Kate could barely believe her eyes. Adi and Surya ran around the corner, and upon seeing Kate, ran even faster toward her. Kate bent to hug them, but the boys barely stopped.

They tugged at her arms, urging her to follow them. "Come on, Kate, we have to go. They're coming."

Dorian unlatched the orange harness and dropped the remaining three feet to the ice below. The lights on his helmet revealed the mangled basket sticking halfway out of the ice mound like a crab trap on the bottom of the ocean. Beside it, a massive wad of steel cable lay in a sloppy stack. It had fallen on top of and beside Kate, but the basket had shielded her. A shame.

Dorian stood erect and marched to the portal. He stopped right below the Bell that hung far above, at the top of the dome. The lights from his helmet raked over it several times, and he smiled. It sat there silent, still. The wicked device that had killed his brother instantly and his mother with the plague it unleashed on the survivors... now silenced.

The portal opened, as if recognizing that his moment of destiny had arrived. He walked through it.

123

David's mind raced. "Look, I don't know what to say. The year is 2013."

"Impossible." The man held the pistol on David as he walked to a cabinet, reached inside, and withdrew a shiny clump of gold. He threw it to David.

It was a watch. David turned it over and read the date and time: Sept 19th, 1985. "Yeah. Huh. I actually don't have a gold watch with the wrong date, but..." He reached for his pocket.

The man held the pistol up.

David froze. "Relax. I have my own time capsule. A picture in my pocket. Reach in; take a look."

The man stepped forward and drew the glossy photo out of David's pocket. He studied the picture of the iceberg with the sub sticking out.

"I'm guessing the Immari weren't taking satellite photos of icebergs in 1985."

The man shook his head and looked away as if he were still putting the pieces together. "It's Kane's U-boat, isn't it?"

David nodded. "We think they found it a few weeks ago. Listen, I'm just as confused as you are. Let's just talk to each other, try to figure this out. How did you get here?"

"I was working in the hidden chamber. I had figured out how to work their machines."

"You put the videos on repeat?"

"Videos? Oh yes, I did, in case I didn't come back and someone found the chamber." He sat on the cot, looking at his feet, seeming to search his thoughts. "I also put the spear in the door. I was testing different artifacts from the Immari vault, hoping something would bring more of the machines to life.

"I managed to get the door open, but I was stuck; there was nothing else I could discover in the chamber. I assumed there was another control station in the next room, so I went through. I tried to hold the door open with the spear. I wish it had worked. I haven't been able to get back through the door. The machines here are different somehow. Most are turned off. There are a few other mysteries… but I haven't gotten very far in the last month, that is, until just before you showed up. It seems like the entire place is waking up, more machines are working, and doors open that previously wouldn't move. I was exploring when I heard the door open and found you."

"Let's go back to the time difference. I know you're not Patrick Pierce or, what was it, Tom Warner. He would be like eighty. Just tell me who you are—"

"I am Patrick Pierce." The man leaned forward. "Time moves slower here. It must be… A day here to every year outside."

"How?"

"I don't know. But we think it has something to do with the Bell. It could have two functions. It's a sentry device, to keep non-Atlanteans out, but that's just the half of it. When we first began studying the device, we thought it was a time machine. It created a field around it, a sort of time-dilation bubble. Like I said, time moved more slowly near the Bell. We thought it had something to do with gravitational displacement—folding and warping the spacetime around it. We thought it might even be a wormhole generator."

"A what?"

"Forget the jargon. The ideas were based on Einstein's theory of general relativity. I'm sure that's been updated or even thrown out by now. Suffice it to say that in the years after we extracted the Bell in Gibraltar, we noticed that it seemed to slow down time in the space around it. We believed it generated power this way. We were able to essentially reverse the device, by supplying power to it and minimizing its gravitational effects."

"That's interesting, but there's just one problem. The Bell in Gibraltar was removed almost a hundred years ago."

"I know. I removed it. I have another theory. I think when the ship in Gibraltar exploded, the Atlanteans were trapped in the section that broke off. I think the door they went through wasn't a passage to another room in that ship. I think it was a portal to another ship. I don't think we're in Gibraltar."

124

Around the next corner, Kate finally got the boys to stop.

"Tell me what's going on," she pleaded.

"We have to hide, Kate," Adi said.

"From whom?"

"There's no time," Surya said.

Time—the word echoed through Kate's mind, and another fear gripped her. She spun the boys around and searched for the digital readout.

02:51:37. Almost three hours left. Martin had said there was less than thirty minutes before detonation. How? It didn't matter—the clock was still ticking. She had to think.

The boys were pulling at her again, and behind them, a set of double doors opened.

Dorian slipped the last of the suit off and surveyed the room—some kind of decontamination chamber. He walked toward the smaller door. His steps echoed loudly in the tall metal chamber. The door opened as he approached, and he stepped out into a corridor. Just like Gibraltar. It was all true. This was another Atlantean city.

Lights flashed to life at the top and bottom of the corridor. The place looked pristine, untouched. It certainly hadn't endured a nuclear blast. Why not? Had the children made it farther into the tombs? Had the Atlanteans caught them? Disabled the bombs?

Up ahead, Dorian heard footfalls—boots marching, striking the metal floor in unison. He drew his sidearm and moved to the side of the corridor, into the shadow of a support beam.

125

Kate stood and peered into the room.

There were a dozen giant glass tubes, standing on end like the ones Patrick Pierce—her father—had described in the journal. And like those tubes, each of these tubes contained an ape, or a human, or something in between. Kate ventured into the room, marveling at the tubes. It was incredible: a hall of forgotten ancestors. All the missing links in humanity's evolution, neatly collected and cataloged in this oval room, two miles below the ice in Antarctica, like a child might collect butterflies in a mason jar. A few of the specimens were shorter than Kate, no more than four feet tall; most were about her height, and a few were a good bit taller. They were all colors: some black, some brown, others pale white. Scientists could spend lifetimes in this room. Many had already spent lifetimes digging up bones, desperately trying to find mere fragments of the intact humans floating there, suspended in the twelve or so glass tubes.

The boys followed her into the room, and the double doors shut behind them.

Kate scanned the room. Besides the tubes, there wasn't much else, except a chest-high bar with a glass top. Kate walked toward it, but stopped short as the doors to the room began to open again.

126

Patrick Pierce kept his hand on the pistol as he watched the man who called himself David Vale. He had let the younger man lead. His story was plausible, but Patrick still didn't trust him. *Or maybe I just don't want to believe it.*

They walked down one long corridor after another, and Patrick's mind drifted to Helena, to that day seven years ago when the glass tube had hissed open...

The white clouds had parted, and he'd reached out to touch her. He thought his hand would turn to sand, crumble, and blow away like ashes in the wind when he felt her cold skin. He fell to his knees, and the tears ran down his face. Mallory Craig wrapped an arm around him, and Patrick threw the man to the ground, then slugged him twice, three times, four times in the face, before two Immari security guards pulled him off of Craig. Craig—the devil's right hand, the man who had lured him into a trap meant to kill him. A frightened boy—Dieter Kane—cowered in the corner. Craig got to his feet, tried to wipe the blood that kept coming from his face, then collected Dieter and fled from the room.

Patrick had wanted to bury Helena with her family, in England, but Craig wouldn't allow it. "We'll need new names, Pierce. Any connection to the past must be erased." New names. Katherine. Kate, the man—Vale—had called her.

Patrick tried to imagine what it had been like for her. He had been an absentee father, and when he was around, an awkward father at best. From the moment he had held Katherine in his arms, he had dedicated himself to dismantling the Immari threat and unraveling the mysteries of Gibraltar and the Bell—to making the world safe for her. That was the best he could do for her. And he had failed. If what Vale said was true, the Immari were stronger than ever. And Kate... he had missed her whole life. Worse—she had been raised by a stranger. Not only that, she had been drawn into the Immari conspiracy. It was a nightmare. He tried to push the thoughts from his mind, but they seemed to resurface around every corner they turned, seemed to rise out of the floor of every new corridor, like a ghost that wouldn't go away.

Patrick eyed the man hobbling in front of him. Would Vale have answers? Would they even be the truth? Patrick cleared his throat. "What's she like?"

"Who? Oh, Kate?" David looked back and smiled. "She's... amazing. Incredibly smart... and extremely strong willed."

"I have no doubt of that." Hearing the words was so surreal. But it somehow helped Patrick come to terms with the fact that his daughter had grown up without him. He felt like he should say something, but he wasn't sure what. After a moment he said, "It's strange to talk about, Vale. For me, it was just a few weeks ago when I said goodbye to her in West Berlin. It's... awkward to know my own daughter grew up without a father."

"She turned out all right, trust me." David paused for a moment, then continued. "She's like no one I've ever met. She's beautifu—"

"Okay, that's uh, that's enough. Let's uh... let's stay focused, Vale." Patrick picked up the pace. Apparently there was a speed limit to revelations... of a certain type. Patrick moved in front of Vale and began leading the way. He had an arm and a leg on the man—literally—and Vale was unarmed, so he probably wasn't much of a threat. And Vale's last answer had convinced Patrick: the younger man was telling the truth.

David pushed to keep up. "Right," he said.

They plowed down the corridors in silence, and after a while, Patrick stopped to let David catch his breath. "Sorry," he said. "I know the goo takes it out of you." He raised his eyebrows. "Had a few accidents myself exploring in the last month."

"I can keep up," David said between pants.

"Sure you can. Remember who you're talking to. I was hobbling around in these tunnels a hundred years before you. You need to take it easy."

David looked up at him. "Speaking of, you're walking fine now."

"Yes. Though I would trade it to go back. The tube. I walked right out in 1918. A few days in there fixed me right up. I didn't put it in the journal, at the time all I could think about was what was happening around me. Helena... the Spanish flu..." Patrick stared at the wall for a minute. "I think the tubes did something else. When I came out in '78, I could work the machines. I think it's why I could go through the portal in Gibraltar." Patrick eyed David. "But I still don't understand how *you* could. You've never been in a tube."

"True. I admit, I don't understand it."

"Did the Immari treat you with something?"

"No. Or, I don't think so. But, actually, I was treated... I got blood from someone who was in the tubes—Kate. I was wounded in Tibet. I lost a lot of blood, and she... saved my life."

Patrick nodded and paced the corridor. "That's interesting." He glanced over at the goo-covered wounds on David's shoulder and leg. "The wounds were cleaned, but I thought they were gunshot wounds. How did you get them?"

"Dorian Sloane."

"So he's joined the Immari and continued the family legacy. Little devil was growing more evil by the day in 1985. He was fifteen then."

"He hasn't slowed down." David straightened up. "Thanks for the rest. I'm ready."

Patrick led the way again, resuming a brisk but somewhat slower pace. Up ahead, a set of double doors that had never opened for him before cracked and slid aside as they approached.

476

"It's exciting—opening passages that were closed yesterday. Listen to me, I sound like the fools who hired me during the War."

David shook his head. "The War."

"What?"

"It's nothing. It's just strange to hear 'the war' in reference to World War I. These days it means the war in Afghanistan."

Patrick stopped. "The Soviets? We're at war—"

"Oh, no, they've been gone since '89. Actually, the Soviet Union doesn't even exist anymore."

"Who then?"

"Al Qaeda, or actually, now it's the Taliban, a... a radical Islamic tribe of sorts."

"America is at war with an Afghan tribe..."

"Yeah, it's a, uh, long story—"

The lights in the corridor flickered, then went out. Both men froze.

"Has that ever happened before?" David whispered.

"No." Patrick took out an LED bar and snapped a switch. It cast light into the corridor and all around them. He felt like Indiana Jones striking a torch that illuminated some ancient corridor. He started to make a reference, but David probably wouldn't know who Indiana Jones was. *Raiders of the Lost Ark* would be an old movie by now—over thirty years old, and the younger generation probably didn't watch old movies anymore. David raised his good arm to block his eyes and squinted.

Patrick paced ahead, taking each step with care. The lights in the corridor flickered again, almost coming on before winking out. The door at the end of the corridor didn't automatically open as they approached. Patrick extended his hand to the glass panel beside it. Sparse wisps of fog wafted out, and the pops at his hand were less intense. What was happening?

"I think there's a problem with the power or something," Patrick said. He thought he could work the door. He manipulated the controls, and the door slid open slowly.

He held the LED bar up, casting light into the massive space.

The chamber was bigger than any he had ever seen, down here or anywhere else. It looked as though it was miles long and miles wide.

Rows of long glass tubes were stacked to the ceiling, higher than he could see. They stretched into the distance, miles away, far into the darkness.

They were the same type of tubes Patrick had seen in Gibraltar so many years ago, with two exceptions: these tubes were full of bodies... and the white mist inside was changing. Clearing. The dissipating clouds inside the tubes revealed only brief glimpses of the people inside. If they even *were* people. They looked more like humans than the ape-man in Gibraltar. Were these the Atlanteans? If not, who? And what was happening to them? Were they waking up?

Patrick's fascination with the tubes was interrupted by a sound, deep inside the chamber: footsteps.

127

The double doors to the room slid open, and Kate fought to hide her surprise when a tall, middle-aged man wearing a Nazi military uniform strode in. The man came to a halt, and stood still as stone, his back rigid. His eyes moved slowly over Kate and then the children.

Unconsciously, Kate took a step forward, placing herself between the man and her children. His lips curled slightly at the ends, as if her involuntary motion had revealed something, had told him a secret. Maybe the step had betrayed her, but his smile had done the same for him: she knew that cold smile. And she knew who the man was.

"Hello, Herr Kane," Kate said in German. "We have been looking for you for a very long time."

128

Patrick listened as the footsteps somewhere in the darkness stopped. He and David both froze, looking at each other, waiting.

"What is this place?" David whispered.

"I'm not sure."

"You've never been in here?"

"No. But I think, maybe... I have an idea," Patrick said as he gazed at the tubes. The room was dark; the only light came from the tubes that hung in bunches on metal racks, like bananas hanging from a tree. Was it possible? Could the Immari have been right all along? "I think this could be a giant hibernation vessel. The door in Gibraltar—it was a portal to another place. Probably the structure in Antarctica. And that structure is... It's what they thought it was."

"Who?"

"Kane, the Immari. Their theory was that the structure in Gibraltar was a small outpost for the Atlantean homeland, which they assumed was under Antarctica. They believed the Atlanteans were hibernational superhumans, waiting to retake the Earth."

At that moment, the footsteps in the distance resumed.

Patrick glanced at David's cane—the spear. The look on his face exposed his thoughts: if they walked to the footsteps, whoever it was would hear them coming.

"I can wait here," David said. "Or we could call out."

"No," Patrick whispered quickly. "If the Immari have found an entrance in Antarctica... the footsteps could be... might not be friendlies. Or," he glanced at the tubes. "Either way, we wait."

Both men receded behind the closest bunch of tubes and crouched in the shadows as the footsteps coming toward them echoed loudly through the tombs.

129

Dorian watched the Nazi soldiers march past him in the dimly lit corridor. It was true. Some of them were alive. His father could be alive.

He stepped out from behind the shadow, straightened his back, and spoke with force. "Ich heiße Dieter Kane."

The two men spun and pointed their submachine guns at him. "Halt!" one man yelled.

"How dare you!" Dorian spat at him. "I am Konrad Kane's only surviving son. You will lower your weapons and take me to him at once."

Konrad Kane crept closer to Kate, like a big cat studying its prey, calculating whether or when to strike. "Who are you?"

Kate's mind raced. She needed a believable lie. "I am Dr. Carolina Knapp, lead scientist on a special Immari research project sent to find you, sir."

Kane scrutinized her, then the children. "Impossible. I've been here less than three months. Launching another expedition would take far longer."

Kate wondered if he was suspicious of her accent. She hadn't spoken German in so long. A short answer would be better. "You've been here much longer than a few months, sir. But I'm afraid we're out of time. We must go. I need to get these children out of these packs and off—"

Another Nazi soldier rushed in, speaking quickly in German.

"Sir, we've found something and more people." He panted and waited for Kane.

Kane looked from the man to Kate. "I will be back," he appraised her again, "Doctor." He bent down to face the children and to Kate's surprise, spoke English. "Boys, I need your help. Please come with me." He swept them into his arms and left the room before Kate could object.

130

Fifteen minutes of discussion with the oafs had gotten Dorian nowhere. Their heads would roll when he told his father. Holding him at gunpoint like a captured cat burglar. Finally, he had exhaled and stood there, rocking onto his heels and waiting.

Every second felt like an eternity.

Then, slowly, the silence broke. The footfalls rounding the corner echoed with the rhythm of Dorian's heart as the moment he had waited for his entire life arrived. The man he could barely remember, who had tucked his sickly body into a glass coffin, who had saved his life and would save the world, his father, turned the corner and marched up to him.

Dorian wanted so much to run to him, to embrace his father and tell him all the things he'd done, how he had saved him, just as he had saved Dorian almost a hundred years ago. He wanted his father to know that he had grown up to be strong, as strong as his father was, that he was worthy of the sacrifices his father had made. But Dorian kept still. The submachine guns were one reason but not the biggest. His father's eyes were cold, piercing. They seemed to analyze him, as if his eyes were gathering pieces of a puzzle.

"Papa," Dieter whispered.

"Hello, Dieter." His father spoke in German, and the voice was lifeless, business-like.

"There is much I must tell you. I was awakened in 197—"

"1978. Time moves slower here, Dieter. You are forty?"

"Forty-two," Dieter said, amazed that his father had already made the leap.

"2013 outside. Here, seventy-five days. A day for every year. A 360-to-1 time differential."

Dorian's mind raced, trying to catch up. He wanted to say something insightful, to let his father know that he was smart enough to solve the mystery as well, but all he could manage was, "Yes. But why?"

"We've found their hibernation chamber. It is as we suspected," his father said as he turned away and paced the length of the corridor. "Perhaps the Bell also distorts time inside the structure and generates the power they need for the hibernation. Perhaps the hibernation is not perfect. Perhaps they do age, if ever so gradually. Or maybe it is to benefit their machines, which would certainly endure some wear every year. Either way, slowing time would help them leapfrog through the ages. We have also found something else. The Atlanteans are not what we think they are. The truth is more bizarre than we imagined. It will take some time to explain."

Dorian motioned to the packs. "The children are carrying—"

"Explosives. Yes. A clever move. I assume they could pass the Bell?" Konrad said.

"Yes. There was another woman who came through: Kate Warner. She is Patrick Pierce's daughter. I was afraid she would get to them. But it doesn't matter now. We're almost out of time."

Konrad checked the back of the pack. "About two hours left. The woman did find them, but we have her. We'll put them in the tombs. We'll return if we need to finish the job."

"We should leave soon after. It's a thirty-minute walk from here to the portal door." Dorian bent down to the children and spoke in English. "Hello again. I told you Kate would be down here. Did you enjoy the first game?"

The boys simply looked at him. They were as dumb as doornails, Dorian thought. "We're going to play a new game. Would you like that?" Dorian waited, but the boys said nothing. "Okay... I'll take that as a yes. This game is a race. Are you fast runners?"

The boys nodded.

131

David watched the two Nazi soldiers wander deeper into the tombs, gawking at the tubes. They wore thick sweaters and no helmets: they were Kriegsmarine, members of the Nazi navy. They would be very skilled at hand-to-hand combat in close quarters. Surprise was imperative for David and Patrick to take them down. David raised a hand to make signs, but Patrick was already signing to him: wait until they pass.

David tried to squat lower, but his leg burned. That he could squat at all was a miracle. The goo really worked. The goo—would they smell it? Patrick crouched beside him, between two other tubes in the banana cluster closest to the meandering soldiers. Two seconds.

One man stopped. Did he smell it?

Above David and Patrick's hiding position, a burst of white fog spewed from the tubes, drawing the soldiers' attention. They swung their submachine guns off their backs and raised them, but David and Patrick were already up and on them.

The force of David's lunge took his target to the ground, and David slammed the heel of his hand into the man's forehead. The soldier's head hit the metal floor with a crack. A pool of blood spread out around it.

Four feet away, Patrick was struggling with the other soldier. The young soldier was on top of him. The Nazi had a knife and was pressing it into Patrick's chest. David jumped on the man and pulled him off of Patrick. David knocked the knife out of the soldier's hand and pinned him to the ground. Patrick was there, beside him, holding the knife to the man's throat. The

Nazi stopped struggling in a silent surrender, but David still held his arms to the floor.

David didn't speak German, but before he could open his mouth, Patrick began interrogating the man in German. "Wieviele Männer?"

"Vier."

Patrick moved the knife from his neck to the man's left index finger.

"Zwölf!" the man cried.

"Herr Kane?"

The soldier nodded. He was sweating profusely now. "Töten Sie mich schnell," he said.

Patrick questioned him while David pinned him to the floor.

"Schnell," the man pleaded.

Patrick drew the knife across his neck, and the flow of blood and death followed in rapid succession after.

Patrick dropped the knife beside the man and collapsed onto the floor. Blood dripped from his own chest wound.

David crawled over the dead man and gathered the remains of the black goo from his own mostly-healed shoulder and leg wounds. He wiped the paste into Patrick's wound, and the older man grimaced.

"Don't worry, you'll be good as new within a few hours." David grinned. "Maybe sooner."

Patrick sat up. "If we have that long." He motioned to a door in the direction the soldiers had come from. "There's no question now, we're in Antarctica." He drew a few quick breaths.

"How many are there?"

Patrick looked at the dead soldiers. "Twelve. Ten now. Kane is with them. If they get in this chamber, it will be genocide, and after that, maybe... it will be... very bad news for the human race."

David began scavenging the men's bodies, gathering weapons and anything that might be useful. "Did they say anything else?"

Patrick looked at him, confused.

"Have they seen anyone else?" David said hopefully.

Patrick caught his meaning. "No. They haven't seen anyone. They've been here for almost three months, which makes sense if they arrived around 1938. A year per day, a month for every two hours. They said they just found this chamber and a man had gone back to report it."

David handed Patrick one of the machine guns and held his arm out to help Patrick up. "We should hurry, then."

Patrick grabbed David's arm and struggled to his feet. He glanced back at the dead soldier who had overpowered him. "Look, Vale, I haven't been a soldier in twenty-five years—"

"We'll be just fine," David said.

132

Dorian held the children by the shoulders as he marched behind his father.

This was the way of the world: life could turn on a dime. He and his father, reunited, on their way to finish their great work—saving the human race. All his sacrifices, all his decisions... He had been right.

Ahead of them, gunshots rang out.

David dropped the two guards standing at the doors to the tombs before either could get a shot off. To his left, another guard rounded the corner and sprayed bullets into the metal wall beside him, but Patrick caught the soldier full in the chest with three quick shots, sending him quickly to the floor.

David swept the other way in the corridor. Clear. He turned and jogged to catch up with Patrick, who was inching around the corner from which the third soldier had emerged.

"I'll take point," David said. He peeked his head around and—a bullet whizzed past his head.

"I'll cover you," Patrick said, as he extended his handgun around the corner and fired several shots.

David stepped into the corridor and closed on the man who was pressing against the adjacent wall. David hit him with two shots in a tight grouping on his chest. Four down. Five plus Kane left. Still not great odds. And they'd lost the element of surprise. One step at a time.

Patrick was beside him, and both men eyed the double doors the soldier must have come from. They took up positions on either side of the door, and Patrick worked the glass panel until the doors parted, revealing a room with twelve glass tubes holding... ape-men?

David had to focus. Patrick seemed less fazed. He stepped quickly into the room, sweeping his gun from side to side. David followed. The room was empty.

Then, from behind him, David sensed someone closing on them. He spun around and raised the machine gun to fire—

Kate. She had been hiding behind the control station.

He jerked his finger off the trigger and dropped the gun to his side. He moved toward her, ready to sweep her up. Just as he reached her, Kate's eyes met Patrick's. She turned from David. "Dad?"

The old man stood there, a look somewhere between remorse and disbelief on his face. "Katherine..."

A tear dropped from Kate's eye as she walked to him and embraced him. He grunted as he hugged her back. She pushed back. "You're alive." She wrinkled her nose. "And you're hurt, and what, is, that smell—"

"I'm okay, Katherine. I. Oh God, you look so much like her." Tears welled in his eyes. "I was so worried, but I know you... it's... for me, only a few weeks have passed..."

Kate nodded. She seemed to have already put it together. David marveled at her as he stood there, a little awkwardly. She held her arm out, and he walked over and hugged her, pressing his face into the side of her head. She was alive. In that moment, that was all that mattered to him. She had left him in Gibraltar, but she was alive. An emptiness inside of him felt filled once again.

She released them and said, "How did you—"

"Gibraltar," her father said. "A door in the chamber I found—it was a portal to Antarctica, to this larger structure. There are more men. We need to—"

490

"Yes," Kate said. "They have the children. Dorian is making them carry backpacks with nuclear bombs."

David looked around, thinking, and then said, "There's a chamber with tubes; it goes on for miles. I bet that's where they're going." A plan formed in his mind. He wouldn't put her in danger again. "You stay—"

Kate shook her head. "No." She walked to the dead man who had run out of her room and picked up his machine gun. She stared at David. "I'm coming. And I get a gun this time. I'm not asking."

David exhaled.

Patrick looked from Kate to David. "I take it this has been a recurring discussion?"

"Yeah, it's uh, been a weird week." David focused on Kate. "You're not going out there—"

"I can't stay here. You know it."

David resisted, his mind searching for a counter argument.

Patrick looked between them, seeming to understand that something unsaid was going on.

"Unless we stop what's about to happen, I won't be safe anywhere, this room included. You need my help. We need to get those children and get out of this structure. Neither of you know them."

She was right. David knew it. But sending her out there, taking that chance, seemed unbearable to him.

"You have to let me go with you, David. I know what you're afraid of." Kate's eyes scanned him, waiting for a reaction. "We have to do this. The past is the past."

David nodded slowly. The fear was still there, but it was different somehow. Knowing that she accepted the risk, that she believed in him and was going along with him, as his partner; it changed things.

David walked over to Kate and handed her a pistol. "The Luger is less likely to jam. It's loaded and ready to go. Just point and shoot. It holds eight rounds; you'll have plenty. Stay behind us."

133

Dorian held a hand up for the five soldiers behind him to halt. He peeked around the corner. Two dead soldiers, one on each side of the door. Had they come out or gone in? Out, hopefully. He stuck his head out again. Another dead body, at the corner of the hall—he was running toward them. They had come out.

"Clear," he called, and the men and his father spread out in the hall, checking the dead men.

Dorian bent down to the kids. "Oh," he corralled them toward him, away from the dead men. "Don't pay attention to them, they're just playing dead. It's another game. Now it's time for the race. Remember, run as fast as you can. The first to the end of the room gets a huge prize!"

His father worked the glass panel beside the giant double doors. They spread open silently, and Dorian shoved the children through just as the first shots rang out. Two of their five men fell instantly. Dorian lunged and covered his father, but he was too late. The bullet struck Konrad's arm and threw him to the ground.

Dorian pulled his father back behind the door as the remaining three soldiers retreated behind the other side of the doorframe. Dorian tore his father's shirtsleeve and inspected the wound quickly. The older man pushed his hands away. "It's a flesh wound, Dieter. Don't be emotional. Stay focused." He drew his pistol and peered around the doorframe. Shots scraped the metal above his head.

Dorian pressed him to the wall. "Papa, go out the way I came. One of us must get out. I will cover you."

"We must stay—"

Dorian pulled his father to his feet. "I will finish them and then follow you." He shoved him into the hall and fired rapid-fire blasts from the submachine gun until it clicked empty.

His father had cleared the corridor. Dorian had saved him.

He slumped back into the wall. A smile spread across his face.

134

David looked back at Patrick. "We have to go around. We can't get past them—not without superior numbers or explosives."

"This corridor must connect with where we entered the tombs. The kids were running. Maybe we can catch them," Patrick said.

David looked around, as if searching for another way. "Agree. You two go. I'll keep Sloane and his men here."

Kate poked her head between them. "David, no."

"This is what we're doing, Kate," David's voice was flat, cold, final.

She stared him in the eyes for a long moment, then looked away. "What about the bombs?"

David nodded toward Patrick. "Your dad has a plan for that."

Comprehension slowly broke over Patrick's face.

Kate turned to him. "You do?"

"Yes, I do. Now let's move."

Kate followed her father through another entrance to the tombs just as the children crossed the aisle ahead of them.

"Adi! Surya!" Kate screamed.

The boys stopped their sprint, almost falling over. She ran to them and looked at the time on the pack. 00:32:01. 00:32:00. 00:31:59.

"How are you going to disable—?"

"Trust me, Katherine," her father said, tugging at her arm.

From the direction they had come, Kate heard the sound of automatic gunfire. David. Fighting the rest of them—alone. She wanted so much to go back, but the children, the bombs. Her father was tugging at her arm again, and she found herself putting one foot in front of the other, marching quickly away from the gunfire.

135

David heard Kate shout for the children. He chanced a look around the corner. Had the Nazis heard it, too? The soldiers at the door were taking off into the massive chamber. He couldn't let them reach Kate. He stepped toward the doors and fired—empty. He dropped the gun and grabbed the last submachine gun from the fallen Nazi, firing at the two running men, mowing them down. Only one plus Dorian left.

The last soldier peeked around the corner, and David nailed him with a blast of shots that caught him in the head. It had been a trap. The runners were the bait; they had hoped David would panic and run quickly into the tombs after them—giving the sniper an easy shot.

One left—Dorian. David didn't hear any footsteps. Somewhere deep in the tombs, a set of doors slammed shut. Kate, Patrick, and the children were out. He should back away, follow them. He stopped, just before the door. He would have to run to catch up to them. But he stood there. 9/11 was a long time ago. He had Kate. And he had the Immari to fight. The outbreak.

Where would Sloane be? Somewhere deep in the tombs, hiding, waiting, watching the entrance. David could wait him out a bit. Or... He shook his head as if shaking off the thought.

He took a couple of steps back, still holding the submachine gun at the ready, and when no one emerged, he turned from the door and started down the corridor at full speed.

The first shots tore through David's back and exited through his chest, hurling him into the wall and then onto the floor face first. More bullets hit his limp body on the floor, raking over his legs.

Footfalls. A hand, turning him over.

David pulled the trigger of the pistol twice. The bullets ripped through the jeer on Dorian's face, blowing brain and bone out of the back of his head, painting the ceiling red and gray.

A bittersweet smile crossed David's lips as he blew out his last breath.

136

Konrad latched the helmet on the suit and waited for the portal to open. The metal doors parted with a loud boom, revealing a massive ice cathedral very similar to the one he had crossed almost three months ago—or seventy-five years ago. If this one was the same, there would be a Bell hanging just outside, above the entrance. The Bell on the other side of the structure had been turned off when Konrad had crossed—it hadn't so much as flickered as he and his men marched under it. But they had turned that Bell on from inside; he knew that now.

The control systems inside the structure were complex, and he and his men had tried to access a system they thought was hibernation control. It turned out to be the controls for a weather satellite. Kane had actually downed the satellite, somewhere in America, he believed, possibly in New Mexico. Whatever he did triggered some sort of anti-intrusion routine. It locked them out of the systems and activated the Bell, killing the men on his sub.

None of the systems had worked since then. Until today.

He wondered if they had already removed the Bell outside, or if the reactivation of the control systems meant it was disabled. There was also another possibility: maybe the Bell would only attack people trying to enter, not exit.

If it was still on, he would have to move fast to get clear of it.

Kane took a tentative step out of the decontamination chamber. His eyes were adjusting, and he could see a cluster of soft lights, like tiny stars glowing in a mound of snow, just under a mangled metal cage.

There was something else: a metal basket, hanging from a

thick cord. Yes, that was it—his escape route, even if the Bell activated.

Kane took another step, clearing the portal doors. Above him, a loud rumble reverberated through the space and echoed in his suit, maybe even his bones.

There *was* a Bell. And it was thundering to life.

137

Kate tugged at the pack on Adi's back. Finally, it came free. 00:01:53. She turned to Surya. The black goo was eating away at the straps on his backpack as well. They were almost free. Kate's father pulled the boy away from the straps and shoved him toward her. He motioned toward the second of six doors. "Go, Katherine. I'll take care of this."

"No. Tell me. How?" She searched his face, wondering how he could disable the bombs.

He sighed and nodded toward the door. "When the Atlanteans exited the Gibraltar structure, they set the portal up to be a one-way escape hatch to this structure in Antarctica. But the structure here was shut down; that's why I couldn't get back. But if I'm right, the activation of the systems here will allow *Atlanteans* to pass back through it. You have pure Atlantean DNA. You were incubated in the tubes. It will work for you. Now this is important—when you get to the other side, you'll be in Gibraltar, in a control room. Don't touch anything. You must leave the portal open, so that I can follow you through. I need to close the portal... permanently. This bomb can't explode here in Antarctica."

Kate stared at him, trying to comprehend.

"When you get to the other side, you must get to the surface and as far away as you can. You'll have about three hundred and sixty minutes—six hours. A minute here is three hundred and sixty minutes there. Do you understand?" Her father's voice was firm.

A tear fell from Kate's face. She finally understood. She hugged him for three long seconds, but when she tried to pull away, she found that her father was holding her tight. She wrapped her arms around him.

"I made so many mistakes, Katherine. I was trying to protect you and your mother…" His voice broke.

Kate leaned back and looked him in the eyes. "I read the journal, Dad. I know why you did it, all of it. I understand. And I love you."

"I love you too, very much."

138

Konrad felt a bead of sweat form on his forehead as the thump-thump-thump of the Bell above grew louder.

Through the glass of the helmet, an image emerged, as if a miniature version of the person were sitting inside the glass. The gray-haired man was sitting in an office, behind a large wooden desk with an Immari flag behind him. There was a map of the world on the wall, but it was different somehow, all wrong. And the man's face... Konrad knew him.

"Mallory!" Konrad cried out. "Help me—"

"Of course, Konrad. There's a syringe sitting on the basket. Inject yourself."

Konrad bounded forward, desperately trying to reach the basket. He fell twice, then again. He decided that he couldn't run in the suit, so he waddled awkwardly, making the best speed he could as the Bell droned louder each second. "What's in the syringe?"

"Something we're working on. You should hurry, Konrad."

Konrad reached the basket and picked up the large syringe. "Take me up, Mallory. Forget this science experiment."

"We can't take the risk. Inject yourself, Konrad. It's your only chance."

Konrad flipped open the metal case and eyed the syringe for a second as the Bell beat louder. There was something else running down his face. He saw the red reflection in the glass of the helmet. How long did he have? Konrad snatched the syringe, pulled the plastic cover off the needle, and plunged it through his suit into his arm. The case must have been some sort of warming device, but the liquid was still freezing as it flowed into his veins. "I've done it, now lift me up."

"I'm afraid I can't do that, Konrad."

Konrad felt wetness on his arms. It wasn't sweat. The Bell thundered louder. He felt strange, weak inside. "What have you done to me?"

Mallory leaned back in the chair, a satisfied look on his face. "Do you remember giving me that tour of the camp where you were testing the Bell? It was the early thirties, I don't remember exactly when, but I do remember your speech—what you said to the workers to convince them to do those terrible things. I had wondered how you would pull it off. You said, 'This is hideous work, but these people are giving their lives so that we can understand the Bell, so that we can save and purify the human race. Their sacrifice is needed. Their sacrifice will be remembered. The few die so the many can survive.'" Mallory shook his head. "I was so impressed, so enamored with you then. That was before you put me in a tube for forty years, before you took my life. I was loyal. I played second fiddle for so many years, and look at how you repaid me. I won't give you a second chance."

"You can't kill me. I *am* the Immari. They will never stand for it." Konrad fell to his knees. He could feel the Bell beating in his heart, ripping him to shreds from the inside out.

"You aren't the Immari, Konrad. You're a science experiment. You're a sacrifice." Mallory shuffled some papers, then said something to someone off screen. He listened for a moment. "Good news, Konrad. We're getting data from the suit. It should give us everything we need. We have a fetus with sustained Atlantis Gene activation—it's actually the child of Patrick's daughter and Dieter. Talk about irony. Anyway, the trouble is, we needed a genome of the same genetic stock *before* Atlantis Gene activation. A parent, ideally. We also needed to track and test that genome as the Bell attacked it in order to understand exactly which genes and epigenetic factors are involved. As you'll remember, it's a lot of effort to disassemble a Bell, and then there's the whole power issue." Mallory waved his hand in the air nonchalantly. "So, we figured we'd just keep this Bell active, prep a syringe with the gene-tracking therapy, and wait for you to walk out. I was never very good at speeches, not as good as you, but I was good at figuring out what people would do. And you're very predictable, Konrad."

Konrad spit blood as he fell face forward into the ice.

"I guess this is goodbye, old friend. As I said, your sacrifice will be remembered." As Mallory finished, a man ran into the office. Mallory listened and then looked confused. "Gibraltar? When?"

139

Kate held her breath as the portal door slid open. It was just as her father had said: a control room with tons of glass consoles. But there was someone there: a guard, leaning on a stool and reading a magazine.

At the sight of Kate and the two boys, he gawked for a brief moment, then returned the stool to its four legs and scrambled to his feet. A magazine with a nude woman on the cover drifted to the floor as the guard grabbed an automatic rifle that had been leaning against the wall and pointed it at Kate. "Don't move, Dr. Warner." His face was hard. He pulled his shoulder close to his mouth and said, "This is Mills, Chamber Seven. I've got them, Warner and both boys. Request assistance."

Within ten seconds, there were two more guards in the room. They searched all three of them with a brief pat-down. The soldier in charge smiled as he pocketed the pistol from Kate. "Come with us," he said.

140

Mallory Craig paced in his office, waiting for news. He looked up when the Immari agent entered. "We got the biometric data from Kane's suit. Dr. Chang is analyzing it, but he says he needs the body."

"Fine, get him the body. Where are we on Gibraltar?"

"They have Warner and the two children."

"Which Warner?" Mallory snapped.

"The woman."

What was Mallory missing?

"You want us to—"

"Has anyone else come out?"

"No."

Craig sat down at the desk and began scribbling feverishly. When he had finished, he stood, stuffed the letter into an envelope, and scribbled an address on the outside. "I need you to deliver this."

"What about Dr. Warner?"

Mallory looked out the window and thought. Had Vale and her father died in the tombs? "Hold the woman there. We need to interrogate her. And triple the guard on that room. Tell them I'm on my way."

141

Kate held the boys close to her side as they followed the men down a series of corridors. Behind them, a familiar voice called out. "Stop."

Kate and the guards turned to the man, who was accompanied by two guards as well. They wore uniforms with a flag Kate had never seen. Below it were two block letters in a square [II].

"I'll take her from here," Martin Grey said.

"No can do, sir. Chairman Craig's orders." Her lead captor stepped forward, squaring with Martin and his men.

Kate almost gasped as she took in Martin's appearance. His hair was wild and unkempt, he hadn't shaved in... months? He probably hadn't showered in just as long. His long hair and beard, combined with the ragged, worn look in his eyes, was a sharp contrast to the clarity and softness of his voice. "I understand. You have your orders, Captain. I wonder, before you take them, if I could see the children. It's a research request, something we urgently need." Before the man could answer, Martin stepped forward and knelt at the children. He gathered them with his arms and held them close to him, covering their eyes and ears as muzzle flashes and the sound of gunshots filled the cramped corridor.

The three soldiers who had been guarding Kate collapsed to the floor. Martin lifted the children into his arms and marched quickly out of the corridor.

Kate chased after him. "Martin, we have to get out of here quickly."

Martin's guards brought up the rear as they raced through the darkened hallways.

"That's quite the understatement, Kate." Then Martin stopped. "Wait, what are you referring to?"

"A nuclear bomb is coming through, into that room, in less than two hours," Kate said.

Martin glanced at his soldiers. "The submersible."

The soldiers led them through a series of corridors that ended in a round room, made from metal different from that of the Atlantis structure. This section of the structure was new. And manmade. In the middle of the room, a steel ladder hung out of a large round pipe. It reminded Kate of a manhole that led out of a sewer.

"What's going on, Martin? What's happened to you?"

"I've been waiting here, hiding for almost two months, hoping you and your father would come out. We'll talk in the submersible. Get in. Craig is probably on his way by now."

142

Patrick stepped through the portal, into the control room. There were at least a dozen guards in the room, and at the back, behind all of them, a familiar face. For once, Patrick was actually glad to see the man who had given him a tour of the tunnels almost a hundred years ago. A man who had changed his destiny. A man who could have let the Immari die in 1978, when he was awakened, but instead chose to rebuild the monstrous organization.

Mallory Craig's words so many years ago ran through Patrick's head. The call. The lure. The trap. "Patrick. There's been an accident..."

Craig nodded to a man in a white coat who was holding a syringe. "Get the sample."

Patrick raised the pistol and pointed it at the white-coated man, stopping him in his tracks.

A small smile spread across Patrick's face. "Mallory. I guess it's true then. The meek shall inherit the Earth."

Craig's face changed. "I'm not half as meek as you think—"

"Can you withstand a nuclear blast? How about two?"

143

One by one, Kate, Martin, the children, and Martin's men climbed the ladder into the sub. Thirty minutes later, the sub rose through the waters of the Bay of Gibraltar. It was a small vessel with no sub-compartments. When it surfaced, Martin said to the soldiers, "Head out into the Atlantic, and watch your speed, they're patrolling the straits." He motioned for Kate to follow him up another steel ladder that led to the oval lookout deck on top of the sub.

Kate walked to the solid steel half-wall and leaned against the rail, next to Martin. The wind was cooler now, much cooler than yesterday in Gibraltar. How long had she been in the tombs? Something else was different. Gibraltar. It was dark.

"Why aren't there any lights in Gibraltar?" Kate asked.

Martin turned. His unshaven, unkempt appearance still mildly unnerved her. "Evacuated."

"Why?"

"It's a protectorate of the Immari."

"Protectorate?"

"You've been gone for two months, Kate. The world has changed. And not for the better."

Kate continued searching the coastline. Gibraltar was dark, but so was Northern Africa. All the glittering lights she'd seen on the balcony that night, the night when David had caught her...

Kate stood for a while without saying anything. Finally she did see some lights, moving at the coast. "The lights in Northern Africa..."

"There are no lights in Northern Africa."

Kate pointed at the faint twinkling lights. "They're right—"

"A plague barge."

"Plague?"

"The Atlantis Plague," Martin said. He sighed, suddenly looking even more exhausted. "We'll get to all that." He leaned against the rail and gazed toward Gibraltar. "I had hoped to see your father again. But this... this is an end he would have liked." He continued before Kate could speak. "Your father was a very remorseful man. He blamed himself for your mother's death. And for leading the Immari into the city of Atlantis. A death, to save your life, to save the Atlanteans, and to keep the Immari from accessing the portal he found—to keep them out of the structure in Antarctica... it's fitting for him. He would want to die in Gibraltar. Your mother died in Gibraltar."

As if on cue, a geyser of water and light rose into the air, and a sonic boom broke over the sky and echoed in her chest.

Martin put his arm around her. "We need to get below. The wave will be here soon. We have to dive."

Kate took one last look back. Through the light of the blast, she saw the Rock of Gibraltar crumbling—but not all of it. One last shard still held on, rising just above the water line.

144

The lab tech walked into Dr. Chang's office. "Sir, we didn't receive any data from Gibraltar."

"The blast interrupted it?"

"No. The transmission never began. They never got a sample from Pierce. But we've had another break. Craig left a letter. He wouldn't let Pierce bury Helena Barton's body for a reason—Craig actually kept it in case it could be useful some day. It's in a locker in San—"

"Have you gotten a sample?"

The tech nodded. "We're running it through the simulation with the fetus and the data from Kane now. We're not sure if it will work since—"

Chang tossed the tablet on his desk. "How soon will we know?"

"Maybe—" the tech's phone buzzed. "Actually, it's in." He looked up excitedly.

"We've found the Atlantis Gene."

EPILOGUE

David opened his eyes. The view was distorted. A white haze. The curve of glass. He was inside a tube. His eyes were adjusting, as if he were waking up from a deep sleep. He could see his body now. He was naked. His skin was smooth—too smooth. The shoulder and leg wounds were gone. As were the scars on his arms and chest, where the burning pieces of metal and rock from the collapsing buildings had dug into him so long ago.

The white fog was clearing now, and he looked out of the tube. To his left, a light shone into the vast chamber. It was the light from the corridor... the corridor where he had retreated and Dorian had shot him. *Killed* him. David strained to see. There he was. His limp body, lying there in a pool of blood. There was another body lying across him.

David looked away from the scene, trying to comprehend it. To his right, as far as he could see, up and down, right and left, were tubes. They were all asleep.

Except him.

And there was one more.

One more set of eyes scanning the distance beyond. Directly across from him. He wanted to lean closer to see them, but he couldn't move. He waited. A cloud of mist passed, and he saw the eyes and the face in the other tube.

Dorian Sloane.

AUTHOR'S NOTE

Hello, and thank you for reading. *The Atlantis Gene* is my first novel, and I do hope you've enjoyed it. This novel was largely a labor of love and truly a learning experience. It took two years to write, and the journey to get it into your hands would fill another 500-page volume.

For me, the most important take away from the entire process has been how important you, the reader, are. I've benefited immensely from the feedback so many readers before you have given me, and I encourage you to write to me directly with any thoughts you have: ag@agriddle.com. The wisdom, generosity, and kind words I've received from so many of you have absolutely changed the course of my writing career.

As I sit writing this, ten months after I first published *The Atlantis Gene*, the novel has garnered almost six thousand reviews on Amazon. Those reviews put me on the map. I'm a new, unknown author and an independent author at that. Without those reviews, you might have never discovered my work. I'm not asking you to write a review of *The Atlantis Gene*. It likely has enough. My request is this: the next time you read an unknown author's book that doesn't have many reviews, write one if you can. That review could change someone's life.

So what's next for Kate Warner, David Vale, and Dorian Sloane?
The Atlantis Plague—available now!

Find out more at: AtlantisGene.com/Next

Thanks again for reading,

Gerry

PS: The website also contains a "Fact vs. Fiction behind *The Atlantis Gene*" section that explores the science and history in the novel.

ACKNOWLEDGMENTS

Where do I start?

At home, I suppose. To Anna, for everything. Specifically for reading my first draft and making invaluable suggestions. And generally for living with me for the past two years as I wondered whether I was drilling a dry well and why the bottle of Balvenie was always empty (it turns out it did not have a hairline crack). I love you.

I imagine every young man who writes a novel owes a huge thank you to his mother, but for me, it's even more so. I'm very lucky to have parents who always supported me and to have a mother that spent twenty years teaching eighth-grade English (ahem, Language Arts now) at Crest Middle School in Shelby, North Carolina. Thanks Mom, for reading my manuscript, for performing outstanding editing work, and for always believing in your children, inside and outside of the classroom.

From here, the list of people I want to thank gets longer, and I risk leaving someone out. I don't want to take that chance, so to everyone who has had a hand in this, my first novel, and helped me along the way, I say thank you.

THE
ATLANTIS
PLAGUE

A.G. RIDDLE

PROLOGUE

70,000 Years Ago
Near Present-Day Somalia

The scientist opened her eyes and shook her head, trying to clear it. The ship had rushed her awakening sequence. *Why?* The awakening process usually happened more gradually, unless... The thick fog in her tube dissipated a bit, and she saw a flashing red light on the wall—an alarm.

The tube opened, and cold air rushed in around her, biting at her skin and scattering the last wisps of white fog. The scientist stepped out onto the frigid metal floor and stumbled to the control panel. Sparkling waves of green and white light, like a water fountain made of colorful fireflies, sprang up from the panel and engulfed her hand. She wiggled her fingers, and the wall display reacted. Yes—the ten-thousand-year hibernation had ended five hundred years early. She glanced at the two empty tubes behind her, then at the last tube, which held her companion. It was already starting the awakening sequence. She worked her fingers quickly, hoping to stop the process, but it was too late.

His tube hissed opened. "What happened?"

"I'm not sure."

She brought up a map of the world and a series of statistics. "We have a population alert. Maybe an extinction event."

"Source?"

She panned the map to a small island surrounded by a massive plume of black smoke. "A supervolcano near the equator. Global temperatures have plummeted."

"Affected subspecies?" her companion asked as he stepped

518

out of his tube and hobbled over to the control station.

"Just one. 8472. On the central continent."

"That's disappointing," he said. "They were very promising."

"Yes, they were." The scientist pushed up from the console, now able to stand on her own. "I'd like to check it out."

Her companion gave her a questioning look.

"Just to take some samples."

Four hours later, the scientists had moved the massive ship halfway across the small world. In the ship's decontamination chamber, the scientist snapped the last buckles on her suit, secured her helmet, then stood and waited for the door to open.

She activated the speaker in her helmet. "Audio check."

"Audio confirmed," her partner said. "Also receiving video. You're cleared for departure."

The doors parted, revealing a white sandy beach. Twenty feet in, the beach was covered in a thick blanket of ash that stretched to a rocky ridge.

The scientist glanced up at the darkened, ash-filled sky. The remaining ash in the atmosphere would fall eventually, and the sunlight would return, but by then, it would be too late for many of the planet's inhabitants, including subspecies 8472.

The scientist trudged to the top of the ridge and looked back at the massive black ship, beached like an oversized mechanical whale. The world was dark and still, like many of the pre-life planets she had studied.

"Last recorded life signs are just beyond the ridge, bearing two-five degrees."

"Copy," the scientist said as she turned slightly and set out at a brisk pace.

Up ahead, she saw a massive cave, surrounded by a rocky area covered in more ash than the beach. She continued her march to the cave, but the going was slower. Her boots slid against the ash and rock, as if she were walking on glass covered in shredded feathers.

Just before she reached the mouth of the cave, she felt something else under her boot, neither ash nor rock. Flesh and bone. A leg. The scientist stepped back and allowed the display in her helmet to adjust.

"Are you seeing this?" she asked.

"Yes. Enhancing your display."

The scene came into focus. There were dozens of them: bodies, stacked on top of each other all the way to the opening of the cave. The emaciated, black corpses blended seamlessly with the rock below them and the ash that had fallen upon them, forming ridges and lumps that looked more like the aboveground roots of a massive tree.

To the scientist's surprise, the bodies were intact. "Extraordinary. No signs of cannibalism. These survivors knew each other. They could have been members of a tribe with a shared moral code. I think they marched here, to the sea, seeking shelter and food."

Her colleague switched her display to infrared, confirming they were all dead. His unspoken message was clear: get on with it.

She bent and withdrew a small cylinder. "Collecting a sample now." She held the cylinder to the closest body and waited for it to collect the DNA sample. When it finished, she stood and spoke in a formal tone. "*Alpha Lander*, Expedition Science Log, Official Entry: Preliminary observations confirm that subspecies 8472 has experienced an extinction-level event. Suspected cause is a supervolcano and subsequent volcanic winter. Species evolved approximately 130,000 local years before log date. Attempting to collect sample from last known survivor."

She turned and walked into the cave. The lights on each side of her helmet flashed on, revealing the scene inside. Bodies lay clumped together at the walls, but the infrared display showed

PREVIEW

no signs of life. The scientist wandered further into the cave. Several meters in, the bodies stopped. She glanced down. Tracks. Were they recent? She waded deeper into the cave.

On her helmet display, a faint sliver of crimson peeked out from the rock wall. Life signs. She rounded the turn, and the dark red spread into a glow of amber, orange, blues and greens. A survivor.

The scientist tapped quickly at her palm controls, switching to normal view. The survivor was female. Her ribs protruded unnaturally, stretching her black skin as if they could rip through with every shallow breath she drew. Below the ribs, the abdomen wasn't as sunken as the scientist would have expected. She activated the infrared again and confirmed her suspicion. The female was pregnant.

The scientist reached for another sample cylinder but stopped abruptly. Behind her, she heard a sound—footsteps, heavy, like feet dragging on the rock.

She turned her head just in time to see a massive male survivor stumble into the cramped space. He was almost twenty percent taller than the average height of the other male bodies she had seen and more broad-shouldered. The tribe's chief? His ribs protruded grotesquely, worse than the female's. He held a forearm up, shielding his eyes from the lights that shone from the scientist's helmet. He lurched toward the scientist. He had something in his hand. The scientist reached for her stun baton and staggered backward, away from the female, but the massive man kept coming. The scientist activated the baton, but just before the male reached her, he veered away, collapsing against the wall at the female's side. He handed her the item in his hand—a mottled, rotten clump of flesh. She bit into it wildly, and he let his head fall back against the rock wall as his eyes closed.

The scientist fought to control her breathing.

Her partner's voice inside her helmet was crisp, urgent. "Alpha Lander One, I'm reading abnormal vitals. Are you in danger?"

The scientist tapped hastily on her palm control, disabling

the suit's sensors and video feed. "Negative, Lander Two." She paused. "Possible suit malfunction. Proceeding to collect samples from last known survivors of subspecies 8472."

She withdrew a cylinder, knelt beside the large male, and placed the cylinder inside the elbow of his right arm. The second it made contact, the male lifted his other arm toward her. He placed his hand on the scientist's forearm, gripping gently, the only embrace the dying man could manage. Beside him, the female had finished the meal of rotten flesh, likely her last, and looked on through nearly lifeless eyes.

The sample cylinder beeped full once, then again, but the scientist didn't draw it away. She sat there, frozen. Something was happening to her. Then the male's hand slipped off her forearm, and his head rolled back against the wall. Before the scientist knew what was happening, she had hoisted the male up, slung him over her shoulder, and placed the female on her other shoulder. The suit's exoskeleton easily supported the weight, but once she cleared the cave, keeping her balance was more difficult on the ash-covered rocky ridge.

Ten minutes later, she crossed the beach, and the doors of the ship parted. Inside the ship, she placed the bodies on two rolling stretchers, shed her suit, and quickly moved the survivors to an operating room. She looked over her shoulder, then focused on the workstation. She ran several simulations and began adjusting the algorithms.

Behind her, a voice called out, "What are you doing?"

She whipped around, startled. She hadn't heard the door open. Her companion stood in the doorway, surveying the room. Confusion, then alarm spread across his face. "Are you—"

"I'm..." Her mind raced. She said the only thing she could. "I'm conducting an experiment."

PART I
SECRETS

1

Dr. Kate Warner watched the woman convulse and strain against the straps of the makeshift operating table. The seizures grew more violent, and blood flowed from her mouth and ears.

There was nothing Kate could do for the woman, and that bothered her more than anything. Even during medical school and her residency, Kate had never gotten used to seeing a patient die. She hoped she never would.

She stepped forward, gripped the woman's left hand, and stood there until the shaking stopped. The woman blew out her last breath as her head rolled to the side.

The room fell silent except for the pitter-patter of blood falling from the table, splattering on the plastic below. The entire room was wrapped in heavy sheet plastic. The room was the closest thing the resort had to an operating room—a massage room in the spa building. Kate used the table where wealthy tourists had been pampered three months before to conduct experiments she still didn't understand.

Above her, the low whine of an electric motor broke the silence as the tiny video camera panned away from the woman to face Kate, prompting her, saying: file your report.

Kate jerked her mask down and gently placed the woman's hand on her abdomen. "Atlantis Plague Trial Alpha-493: Result Negative. Subject Marbella-2918." Kate eyed the woman, trying to think of a name. They refused to name the subjects, but Kate made up a name for every one of them. It wasn't like they could

525

punish her for it. Maybe they thought withholding the names would make her job easier. It didn't. No one deserved to be a number or to die without a name.

Kate cleared her throat. "Subject's name is Marie Romero. Time of death: 15:14 local time. Suspected cause of death... Cause of death is the same as the last thirty people on this table."

Kate pulled her rubber gloves off with a loud crack and tossed them on the plastic-covered floor next to the growing pool of blood. She turned and reached for the door.

The speakers in the ceiling crackled to life.

"You need to do an autopsy."

Kate glared at the camera. "Do it yourself."

"Please, Kate."

They had kept Kate almost completely in the dark, but she knew one thing: they needed her. She was immune to the Atlantis Plague, the perfect person to carry out their trials. She had gone along for weeks now, since Martin Grey, her adoptive father, had brought her here. Gradually, she had begun demanding answers. There were always promises, but the revelations never came.

She cleared her throat and spoke with more force. "I'm done for the day." She pulled the door open.

"Stop. I know you want answers. Just take the sample, and we'll talk."

Kate inspected the metal cart that waited outside the room, just as it had thirty times before. A single thought ran through her mind: leverage. She took the blood draw kit, returned to Marie, and inserted the needle into the crook of her arm. It always took longer after the heart had stopped.

When the tube was full, she withdrew the needle, walked back to the cart, and placed the tube in the centrifuge. A few minutes passed while the tube spun. Behind her, the speakers called out an order. She knew what it was. She eyed the centrifuge as it came to a stop. She grabbed the tube, tucked it in her pocket, and walked down the hall.

She usually looked in on the boys after she finished work, but today she needed to do something else first. She entered her tiny room and plopped down on the "bed." The room was almost like a jail cell: no windows, nothing on the walls, and a steel-frame cot with a mattress from the Middle Ages. She assumed it had previously housed a member of the cleaning staff. Kate considered it to be barely humane.

She bent over and began feeling around in the darkness under the cot. Finally, she grasped the bottle of vodka and brought it out. She grabbed a paper cup from the bedside table, blew out the dust, poured a sailor-sized gulp, and turned the bottom up.

She set the bottle down and stretched out on the bed. She extended her arm past her head and punched the button to turn the old radio on. It was her only source of information on the outside world, but what she heard she hardly believed.

The radio reports described a world that had been saved from the Atlantis Plague by a miracle drug: Orchid. In the wake of the global outbreak, industrialized nations had closed their borders and declared martial law. She had never heard how many had died from the pandemic. The surviving population, however many there were, had been herded into Orchid Districts—massive camps where the people clung to life and took their daily dose of Orchid, a drug that kept the plague at bay but never fully cured it.

Kate had spent the last ten years doing clinical research, most recently focused on finding a cure for autism. Drugs weren't developed overnight, no matter how much money was spent or how urgent the need. Orchid had to be a lie. And if it was, what was the world outside really like?

She had only seen glimpses. Three weeks ago, Martin had saved her and two of the boys in her autism trial from certain death in a massive structure buried under the Bay of Gibraltar. Kate and the boys had escaped to the Gibraltar structure—what she now believed to be the lost city of Atlantis—from a similar complex two miles below the surface of Antarctica.

Her biological father, Patrick Pierce, had covered their retreat in Gibraltar by exploding two nuclear bombs, destroying the ancient ruin and spewing debris into the straits, almost closing them. Martin had spirited them away in a short-range submersible just minutes before the blasts. The sub barely had enough power to navigate the debris field and reach Marbella, Spain—a resort town roughly fifty miles up the coast from Gibraltar. They had abandoned the sub in the marina and entered Marbella under the cover of night. Martin had said it would only be temporary, and Kate hadn't taken any notice of her surroundings. She knew they had entered a guarded complex, and she and the two boys had been confined to the spa building since.

Martin had told Kate that she could contribute to the research being done here—trying to find a cure for the Atlantis Plague. But since her arrival, she had rarely seen him or anyone else, save for the handlers who brought food and instructions for her work.

She turned the tube around in her hand, wondering why it was so important to them and when they would come for it. And who would come for it.

She looked over at the clock. The afternoon update would come on soon. She never missed it. She told herself she wanted to know what was happening out there, but the truth was more simple. What she really wanted to hear was news of one person: David Vale. But that report never came, and it probably wouldn't. There were two ways out of the tombs in Antarctica—through the ice entrance there in Antarctica or via the portal to Gibraltar. Her father had closed the Gibraltar exit permanently, and the Immari army was waiting in Antarctica. They would never let David live. Kate tried to push the thought away as the radio announcer came on.

You're listening to the BBC, the voice of human triumph on this, the 78th day of the Atlantis Plague. In this hour, we bring you three special reports. First, a group of four offshore oil rig operators who survived three days at sea without food to reach safety and salvation in the Orchid District of Corpus Christi,

528

Texas. Second, a special report from Hugo Gordon, who visited the massive Orchid production facility outside Dresden, Germany and dispels vicious rumors that production of the plague-fighting drug is slowing. We end the hour with a roundtable discussion featuring four distinguished members of the royal society who predict a cure could come in weeks, not months.

But first, reports of courage and perseverance from Southern Brazil, where freedom fighters won a decisive victory yesterday against guerrilla forces from Immari-controlled Argentina...

2

Dr. Paul Brenner rubbed his eyelids as he sat down at his computer. He hadn't slept in twenty hours. His brain was fried, and it was affecting his work. Intellectually, he knew he needed rest, but he couldn't bring himself to stop. The computer screen flashed to life, and he decided he would check his messages, then allow himself a one-hour nap—tops.

1 NEW MESSAGE

He grabbed his mouse and clicked it, feeling a new surge of energy...

FROM: Marbella (OD-108)

SUBJECT: Alpha-493 Results (Subject MB-2918)

The message contained no text, only a video that instantly began playing. Dr. Kate Warner filled his screen, and Paul fidgeted in his chair. She was gorgeous. For some reason, just seeing her made him nervous.

Atlantis Plague, Trial Alpha-493... result negative.

When the video ended, Paul picked up the phone. "Set up a conference—All of them—Yes, now."

Fifteen minutes later, he sat at the end of a conference table, staring at the twelve screens in front of him, each filled with the face of a different researcher at a different site around the world.

Paul stood. "I just received the results of Trial Alpha-493. Negative. I—"

The scientists erupted with questions and incriminations. Eleven weeks ago, in the wake of the outbreak, this group had been clinical, civil... focused.

Now the prevailing feeling was fear. And it was warranted.

3

It was the same dream, and that pleased Kate to no end. She almost felt as though she could control it now, like a video she could rewind and relive at will. It was the only thing that brought her joy anymore.

She lay in a bed in Gibraltar, on the second floor of a villa just steps from the shore. A cool breeze blew through the open doors to the veranda, pushing the thin, white linen curtains into the room, then letting them fall back to the wall. The breeze seemed to drift in and retreat in sync with the waves below and with her long, slow breaths there in the bed. It was a perfect moment, all things in harmony, as if the entire world were a single heart, beating as one.

She lay on her back, staring at the ceiling, not daring to close her eyes. David was asleep beside her, on his stomach. His muscular arm rested haphazardly across her stomach, covering most of the large scar there. She wanted to touch his arm, but she wouldn't risk it—or any act that could end the dream.

She felt the arm move slightly. The subtle motion seemed to shatter the scene, like an earthquake shaking, then bringing down the walls and ceiling. The room shuddered one last time and faded to black, to the dark, cramped "cell" she occupied in Marbella. The soft comfort of the queen bed was gone, and she lay again on the harsh mattress of the narrow cot. But... the arm was still there. Not David's. A different arm. It was moving, reaching across her stomach. Kate froze. The hand wrapped around her, patted her pocket, then fumbled for her closed hand, trying to get the tube. She grabbed the thief's wrist and twisted it as hard as she could.

A man screamed in pain as Kate stood, jerked the chain on the light above, and stared down at...

Martin.

"So they sent you."

Her adoptive father struggled to get back to his feet. He was well past sixty, and the last few months had taken a toll on him physically. He looked haggard, but his voice was still soft, grandfatherly. "You know, you can be overly dramatic some-times, Kate."

"I'm not the one breaking into people's rooms and patting them down in the dark." She held the tube up. "Why do you need this? What's going on here?"

Martin rubbed his wrist and squinted at her, as if the single light bulb swinging in the room were blinding him. He turned, grabbed a sack off the small table in the corner, and handed it to her. "Put this on."

Kate turned it over. It wasn't a sack at all—it was a floppy white sun hat. Martin must have taken it from the remains of one of the Marbellan vacationers. "Why?" Kate asked.

"Can't you just trust me?"

"Apparently I can't." She motioned to the bed.

Martin's voice was flat, cold, and matter of fact. "It's to hide your face. There are guards outside this building, and if they see you, they'll take you into custody or worse, shoot you on sight." He walked out of the room.

Kate hesitated a moment, then followed him, clutching the hat at her side. "Wait. Why would they shoot *me*? Where are you taking me?"

"You want some answers?"

"Yes." She hesitated. "But I want to check on the boys before we go."

Martin eyed her, then nodded.

Kate cracked the door to the boys' small room and found them doing what they spent ninety-nine percent of their time doing: writing on the walls. For most seven- and eight-year-old boys, the scribblings would have been dinosaurs and soldiers, but Adi and Surya had created an almost wall-to-wall tapestry of equations and math symbols.

The two Indonesian children still displayed so many of the hallmark characteristics of autism. They were completely consumed with their work; neither noticed Kate enter the room. Adi was balancing on a chair he had placed on one of the desks, reaching up, writing on one of the last empty places on the wall.

Kate rushed to him and pulled him off the chair. He waved the pencil in the air and protested in words Kate couldn't make out. She moved the chair back to its rightful place: in front of the desk, not on top of it.

She squatted down and held Adi by the shoulders. "Adi, I've told you: do not stack furniture and stand on it."

"We're out of room."

She turned to Martin. "Get them something to write on."

He looked at her incredulously.

"I'm serious."

He left, and Kate again focused on the boys. "Are you hungry?"

"They brought sandwiches earlier."

"What are you working on?"

"Can't tell you, Kate."

Kate nodded seriously. "Right. Top secret."

Martin returned and handed her two yellow legal pads.

Kate reached over and took Surya by the arm to make sure she had his attention. She held up the pads. "From now on, you write on these, understand?"

Both boys nodded and took the pads. They flipped through them, inspecting each page for marks. When they were satisfied, they wandered back to their desks, climbed in the chairs, and resumed working quietly.

Kate and Martin retreated from the room without another word. Martin led Kate down the hall. "Do you think it's wise to let them go on like that?" Martin asked.

"They don't show it, but they're scared. And confused. They enjoy math, and it takes their minds off things."

"Yes, but is it healthy to let them obsess like that? Doesn't it make them worse off?"

Kate stopped walking. "Worse off than what?"

"Now, Kate—"

"The world's most successful people are simply obsessed with something—something the world needs. The boys have found something productive that they love. That's good for them."

"I only meant... that it would be disruptive for them if we had to move them."

"Are we moving them?"

Martin sighed and looked away. "Put your hat on." He led her down another hallway and swiped a key card at the door at the end. He swung it open, and the rays of sunlight almost blinded Kate. She threw her arm up and tried to keep up with Martin.

Slowly, the scene came into focus. They had exited a one-story building right on the coast, at the edge of the resort compound. To her right, three whitewashed resort towers rose high above the lush tropical trees and previously well-maintained grounds. The glitzy hotel towers struck a harsh contrast to the twenty-foot tall chain-link fence topped with barbed wire that lined the development. In the light of day, this place looked like a resort that had been made into a prison. Were the fences to keep people in—or out? Or both?

With each passing step, the strong odor that hung in the air seemed to grow more pungent. What was it? Sickness? Death? Maybe but there was something else. Kate scanned the grounds near the bases of the towers, searching for the source. A series of long white tents covered tables where people worked with knives, processing something. Fish. That was the smell but only part of it.

"Where are we?"

"The Marbella Orchid Ghetto."

"An Orchid District?"

"The people inside call it a ghetto but yes."

Kate jogged to catch up. She held her hat in place. Seeing this place and the fences had instantly made her take Martin's words more seriously.

She glanced back at the spa building they had exited. Its walls and roof were covered in a dull, gray sheeting. Lead was Kate's first thought, but it looked so odd—the small, gray, lead-encased building by the coast, sitting in the shadow of the gleaming white towers.

As they moved along the path, Kate caught more glimpses of the camp. In every building, on every floor, there were a few people standing, looking out the sliding glass doors, but there wasn't a single person on a balcony. Then she saw why: a jagged silver scar ran the length of the metal frame of every door. They had been welded shut.

"Where are you taking me?"

Martin motioned to the single-story building ahead. "To the hospital." The "hospital" had clearly been a large beachside restaurant on the resort grounds.

At the other end of the camp, beyond the white towers, a convoy of loud diesel trucks roared to the gate and stopped. Kate paused to watch them. The trucks were old, and they hid their cargo behind flopping green canvases pulled over the ridges of their spines. The lead driver shouted to the guards, and the chain-link gate parted to let the trucks pass.

Kate noticed blue flags hanging from the guard towers on each side of the gate. At first she thought it was the UN flag—it was light blue with a white design in the middle. But the white design in the center wasn't a white globe surrounded by olive branches. It was an orchid. The white petals were symmetrical, but the red pattern that spread out from the center was uneven, like rays of sunlight peeking out from behind a darkened moon during a solar eclipse.

The trucks pulled to a stop just beyond the gate and soldiers began dragging people out—men, women, and even a few children. Each person's hands were bound, and many struggled with the guards, shouting in Spanish.

"They're rounding up survivors," Martin whispered, as if they could hear him from this distance. "It's illegal to be caught outside."

"Why?" Another thought struck Kate. "There are survivors—who aren't taking Orchid?"

"Yes. But… they aren't what we expected. You'll see." He led her the rest of the way to the restaurant, and after a few words with the guard, they passed inside—into a plastic-lined decontamination chamber. Sprinkler nozzles at the top and sides opened and sprayed them down with a mist that stung slightly. For the second time, Kate was glad to have the hat. In the corner of the plastic chamber, the red miniature traffic light changed from red to green, and Martin pushed through the flaps. He paused just outside the threshold. "You won't need the hat. Everyone here knows who you are."

As Kate pulled the hat from her head, she got her first full view of the large room—what had been the dining room. She could barely believe the scene that spread out before her. "What is this?"

Martin spoke softly. "The world isn't what they describe on the radio. This is the true shape of the Atlantis Plague."

A letter from the publisher

We hope you enjoyed this book. We are an independent
publisher dedicated to discovering brilliant books,
new authors and great storytelling. Please join us at
www.headofzeus.com and become part of our
community of book-lovers.

We will keep you up to date with our latest books, author
blogs, special previews, tempting offers, chances to win
signed editions and much more.

If you have any questions, feedback or just want to say hi,
please drop us a line on hello@headofzeus.com

 @HoZ_Books

 HeadofZeusBooks

www.headofzeus.com

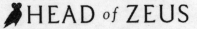

The story starts here